THE VICTORY OF
GERALDINE GULL

THE VICTORY OF GERALDINE GULL

Joan Clark

Macmillan of Canada
A Division of Canada Publishing Corporation
Toronto, Ontario, Canada

Canadian Cataloguing in Publication Data
  Clark, Joan, date.
    The victory of Geraldine Gull

  ISBN 0-7715-9281-7

  1. Title.

PS8555.L353V52 1988	C813'.54	C88-093178-7
PR9199.3.C35V52 1988		

Design: David Montle

Macmillan of Canada
A Division of Canada Publishing Corporation

Printed in Canada

For Jack
and
For the people of Winisk

ACKNOWLEDGEMENTS

In addition to the encouragement of my writer friends during the writing of this novel, I am particularly grateful for the assistance of David Pentland, Doug Sayers, Frank Hunter, Father Gaston Grenon, Luke Gull, Gail Crawford, Hugh Dempsey, Maeve Spain, Eric Mac Alary, Joyce Day, Victoria Maxwell, Anne Holloway and Nancy Colbert as well as the Wawatay Communications Society, the Glenbow Museum and the Thunder Bay Exhibition Centre.

Death is swallowed up in victory.
O death, where is thy sting?

1 Corinthians 15:54–55

PROLOGUE

Winter, 1947. Geraldine Bear was in the bush waiting for her father to come home. Before he went away, Elias Bear was a big man in Osnaburgh. He was Chief. He was a good hunter, and people did what he said. That was when her mother was alive and her brothers were here. Then her mother died of the coughing sickness and her brothers went away. One day the priest came and took Elias Bear to the hospital because he was spitting blood. The priest wanted to take Geraldine back to residential school, but Geraldine ran into the bush and hid until the priest went away.

Every day after the darkness left, Geraldine got up from the bed in the house her grandfather had made, the first log house in Osnaburgh, which Moses Bear built with an axe and a handsaw. Every day she got up, strapped on snowshoes and walked through the woods. When she reached the lake, she stopped and looked across the ice, across the white that went on and on, farther than anyone could see. She stood on the edge of the whiteness and waited for a mark to appear, a small speck far out on the ice, a black spot that would grow large as it came near.

Day after day Geraldine stood in the cold and waited. Sometimes she waited so long her legs became red and her hair turned white. She saw crows, black and cawing. They cawed and flew from tree to tree. They did not fly out over the ice, whirling in a large black circle as they sometimes did. Geraldine waited. She waited until her blood thickened and slowed, but no speck appeared. Finally she turned away, back the way she had come. Tied to her leg was a deerskin sheath her oldest brother had made for her knife. Inside the pocket of her parka was a noose. She snowshoed through the woods, looking for sharptail grouse. It had to be grouse, something she could pick off a tree.

But there were no grouse. Or rabbits or squirrels. Even the smallest animals had disappeared when her father went away. The noose stayed inside Geraldine's pocket, the knife inside its sheath.

After she reached the log house, Geraldine made a fire in the stove. She ate a handful of flour and drank a cup of melted snow. Then she lay down on the bed beneath the fur blanket.

When she opened her eyes again, it was becoming dark. Thomas Skunk was standing beside her. Small Thomas Skunk with his narrow mouth and big nose, a man half the size of Elias Bear. Thomas Skunk was opening and shutting his mouth. Words were coming out. Words saying her father was dead. Puny Thomas Skunk dared to speak. Dared to say that Elias Bear had frozen to death. Dared to say that he was found asleep in a snowbank outside the hospital. Naked as a baby except for this. Thomas Skunk put out his hand. In it was the red beret Elias Bear had won off a white man in a fight. Thomas Skunk put the beret on the table. Stupid Thomas Skunk who never had been a good hunter, who never had been Chief. Geraldine wanted to slap his mouth where the words came out. Knock out his teeth. Jam the words back down his throat. Come stay with us, the puny voice said, you help my wife. She's having a baby soon.

Geraldine sat on the bed and opened her mouth wide. She roared so loud that puny Thomas Skunk turned tail and ran. He ran away, that's how scared he was. When he had gone, Geraldine lay down on the bed and laughed. She laughed and laughed.

The next day, she got up from the bed, stiff and sore from lying so long beneath the fur blanket. After she had eaten, she put the rest of the flour in a sack and carried it outside. She put on the red beret and went to the leather pouch that hung beside the door. She took out a wad of paper, dirty and torn from so much unfolding and refolding. There were words on the paper, words she could read. Below the words was a picture of the sacred medicine bear, suns and moons inside his belly. Geraldine put the paper deep into her sheath below the knife tip. She put her snare inside her pocket with the noose. Then she set fire to the house and walked out of the bush.

ONE

1: Stab this country in the heart and your knife enters Hudson Bay. Slit the bottom of the bay, peel back the tundra, and brown water spews forth from an open wound, a mouth lined with rows of jagged teeth. Behind the mouth is a long, sinuous river that winds northward past thousands of lakes. With sharpened tip, make a small nick beside the river where it empties into the bay. Inside this nick, this scratch, some would say scar, lives a handful of Swampy Crees. The Crows, the Birds, the Gulls, the Loons, the Eagles, the Hunters. Within memory, their people followed the caribou north after the invasion, wandering until the land ran out. Here on the edge of tundra they pitched their teepees. North of the tree-line, south of the icebergs, they huddled together like sled dogs in a storm, their master an unholy trinity of church, government, store. Lying across the village, horizontally like a muddy plank of Christ's cross, is a rickety wooden boardwalk. The priest lives at one end of this plank near the small school, the store manager at the other. Scattered randomly between are shacks, cabins, houses, one or two teepees.

2: *June 25, 1978.* Father Aulneau steps carefully across the boardwalk, avoiding broken slats. He goes to the bell mounted on a platform beside the church. He turns the handle round and round as if drawing water. The bell chimes, announcing afternoon catechism class. The sound of the bell drifts over the shacks and houses, the circles of sound widening, spreading over the river, rising over the bush until they are swallowed by the vastness of water and tundra.

Nearby in the gully, a stray that once belonged to Gerald Gull lifts its head and howls. It's a thin, plaintive wail, chilling, primeval. The wail is picked up by other strays, passed to the Crows' dogs, then to the Birds', then the Loons', the sound travelling up the boardwalk to the Hunters' dogs until there's a sad ululation, a mournful dissonance, a dirge to accompany a village into its grave.

In the name of the Father and the Son and the Holy Spirit.

Children run up the boardwalk, skipping nimbly over broken slats. They move with thin-armed, agile grace, smiles flashing in dark-eyed faces. It will be boring and stuffy inside the church, but they enter cheerfully because they know that later, after they have sat fidgeting on the wooden chairs, reciting answers for the priest, each will be given a candy to tuck inside her cheek.

Geraldine Gull emerges from the bush beside the church. She stops, listens to the priest's staccato voice inside, the children's droned replies.

"Do you like to see the sunshine?"

Yes, we like to see the sunshine.

"Do you like to hear the running water?"

Yes, we like to hear the running water.

Geraldine snorts. Waste of time, kids in church today. Should be outside in sunshine instead of making words about it, even if the priest gives them candy for answers. Not his candy anyway. Nazarene Rose, who keeps the mission house, says the candy comes from white churchwomen at Christmas and Easter, comes in bags, one for every kid. Priest empties the bags into the drawer in his office where he keeps those crummy Jesus calendars he gives out to the people. Some of the candy he eats himself. The rest he gives to kids for sitting in church on a sunny day. First time in weeks that it's sunny. All spring it's been rain, rain, rain. And wind. Lots of wind. Niska's a windy place. Especially inside the church. Because the priest's full of air.

"Do you like to look at birds and animals?"

Yes, we like to look at birds and animals.

"Do you like to play with pets?"

Yes, we like to play with pets.

Should get a whole handful of candy for that one. No pets

here. Nothing but dogs that are bags of bones with fur on them, most of them half-wolves that have forgotten how to hunt and hang around for garbage instead.

"Now we will pray. Our Father who art in heaven. Hallowed be thy name. Thy kingdom come. Thy will be done. . . ."

Geraldine turns away in digust. She wouldn't do His will if she got a whole boxful of O'Henrys. A boatload wouldn't do it. Because she knows. Geraldine Gull's been around. She knows people got it a lot better other places. The priest knows this also, but still he tells the people to pray, to love God, to come to church and things will get better. What a joke. Priest's nothing but one big windy fart.

Geraldine crouches inside the bushes, waits until she hears children skipping along the boardwalk, hears the priest, tap-tap of pointed shoes inside, back and forth against the wooden floor, hears him close the door and cross the boardwalk. Nazarene Rose says she tells him if he doesn't come when supper is ready, she lets the food get cold. Geraldine comes out of the bushes, scoots down the side of the church and tries the front door. Sucker. He left it unlocked for evening mass. She finds the catechism books stacked neatly on a table inside the door. Geraldine looks around for something to carry the books in, but there's nothing. The inside of the church is bare except for statues, crosses, candles, books. It smells musty, damp, airless. The windows have been painted shut.

Geraldine carries an armload of books outside, around to the back of the church where she throws them into the bushes. When she leaves the church with the second load, she closes the door behind her. She doesn't want anyone to see an open door, to discover the books are missing, until she's finished this job. She carries the books through the low bush to the edge of the tundra, where she tosses them onto the damp grass. She tries to force the books to stay open, but the covers shut tight as soon as she lets go of them. She squats down and holds each book open until its pages burn. She grows impatient with this so that the last books aren't burned through, the pages merely scorched at the edges. Geraldine hears boys whooping in the bushes behind her. They've had supper and will be outside until dark. Geraldine heads down a path leading toward the gully where the poorest shacks are.

She hears the ring of Gerald's hammer. This means he's eaten his supper and is working before coming to church. Stupid man. The only man in Niska who goes to mass every day. The only man who takes all the wood he can find and builds a stupid raft. All these years he's been too lazy to build them a house or a table or a shithouse. Ever since the Holy Rollers got him in Severn, Gerald's been working on that stupid raft. Where's the raft going to go? Out in the bay with the ice and polar bears, that's where. Wapusk will cross the ice and eat up stupid Gerald Gull. Geraldine takes her time walking through the bushes, avoiding the boardwalk which stinks of garbage and pee. She's in no hurry to get back to the old lady, Gerald's mother, who sits in front of the tent all day, cackling and laughing. Won't work, won't talk. Won't eat unless Gerald feeds her. There's nothing to eat anyway, except cold porridge. This is what they eat until the government cheques come in. Stupid Gerald spends his cheque on nails, so after her government money is used up, they eat porridge. Raft's so full of nails it'll sink to the bottom of the bay for sure. Geraldine pulls out her last O'Henry bar, rips off the wrapper and throws it into the bush. Bites off half the bar. She's careful to chew on the good side so the bad tooth won't ache. The nuts crunch like pine cones, the gooey chocolate coats her tongue, muddies her spit. Tomorrow, when she's in the store, she'll lift another handful of bars off George.

The O'Henry doesn't satisfy. Her stomach feels hollow. She expected to feel better about burning the books. Instead she feels restless, uneasy. Her skin prickles as if it's being stuck with porcupine quills. Her mouth waters. What she needs is a drink. She finished her last bottle two weeks ago. Only person in Niska besides George who has a bottle is Morris Mack. He got half a case of rum last month. Geraldine saw him hand over his cheque to the pilot at the airstrip, saw him carry the box to his canoe. Geraldine knows Morris has a bottle because he always hides the last one like a dog with a bone. That is how he lost his fingers. Tried to dig up the bottle before he remembered to spring the trap. Over the years, Geraldine has found a bottle inside Morris's shithouse, under his woodpile and beneath his front step. Once this year she had to beat Patrick Eagle to finding it first, but now that Patrick's quit drinking so much, she's got a clear field. Geraldine rubs her belly and thinks about the different places Morris might have hidden his last bottle. He might have taken it to one of the islands, but his canoe motor broke a while back, so that isn't likely or he would've fixed the motor by now. Maybe he buried it inside the river bank. He hasn't hid one there for a long time.

Geraldine gets up and walks along the top of the gully toward the river. A grey bitch with a slack udder comes up behind her, fawning against her legs. Geraldine gives the dog a kick. It rolls whimpering into the bushes.

The river is swollen from the heavy rains. All but two of the steps Gerald built down the embankment have disappeared. Morris Mack's steps are one over from Gerald's. Geraldine saunters past Morris's shack and peers in the window. Empty. Elizabeth has gone outside to have the baby, and Morris is over at Henry Sutherland's, where he always goes for a smoke after supper. Geraldine kneels down and gropes along the sides of the embankment, searching for something hard. The mud is so soft it slides into the water. Morris wouldn't hide a bottle here. It would end up on the river bottom for sure. Geraldine goes back to the shack, sits on the wooden step, feels under both sides of it. Nothing. Then she gets down on all fours, squeezes into the crawl-space beneath the shack and pokes her fingers into the openings in the woodpile. No bottle there. Not much wood, either. She lies on her back and stares up at the beams. Except for George's house and the mission, none of the homes in Niska have foundations but sit on posts and beams scrounged from the air force base after it closed twelve years ago. Same with windows and aluminum siding. Geraldine reaches up and gropes along each beam between the floor joists where there is an opening large enough to hide a bottle. Geraldine is exploring the second beam when she strikes pay dirt. She pulls out the bottle. Lamb's Navy Rum. Full. Large size. Wooeee. This is her day. She hugs the bottle to her chest and wriggles out from beneath the shack. Once she's on her feet, she hides the bottle under her jacket and scoots through the bush, avoiding the path. She continues through the bush, circling round shacks and kids playing in the mud. She keeps going until the bush opens up and islands of spruce dot the tundra. Geraldine walks until she comes to one of the larger islands. She wades through a clump of lowbush cranberry and crawls beneath the largest spruce. The spruce is stunted, but it covers her head. When she sits, she feels the wet moss beneath her haunches. She takes her knife out of its sheath and hacks off the lower branches to make a spruce bed. She sits on the boughs, unscrews the cap, tips up the bottle and takes a swallow. The rum slides down her throat, burning as it enters her stomach. Starved for alcohol, her body shudders. Shivers of pleasure and satisfaction ripple down her arms and legs.

She sure showed that priest who's the boss around here. He wouldn't let her put Alexander in the graveyard. He said the Church would not allow it, not after what Alexander did to himself. The priest is stupid. He doesn't know nothing about Alexander. He doesn't know nothing about Geraldine Gull. All year she'd been on his trail, scaring him when he's picking flowers for his crummy pictures, bellowing outside the church during mass, throwing rocks at his bedroom window. After today, he'll know what she thinks of his Church. Geraldine takes another swallow of rum. She doesn't care about the graveyard. She doesn't want Alexander here no more. This place stinks. The graveyard, the village, the people stink. The people here are toads. They are sleepy Crees stuck in a swamp. She's only staying here until she figures out what to do with the pictures. She's got plans for those pictures. Big plans. Plans these sleepy toads don't know about. As Geraldine drinks, the rum numbs her throat, becomes a liquid furnace inside her stomach, warming the blood flowing through her veins. Gradually its numbing warmth spreads upward to her brain. Geraldine forgets the priest, the pictures, Alexander. She lies spread-eagled on the spruce boughs and closes her eyes. The bottle, half empty, slides from her hand.

Geraldine doesn't hear the circles of sound widening over her head as the priest rings the bells for evening mass. She doesn't hear the mournful chorus of dogs, the priest's mournful chant as he leads the people through the service.

> *Lamb of the living God,*
> *You who take upon the sins of the World,*
> *Have mercy upon us,*
> *Grant us peace, O Lord.*

Geraldine snores through the cacophony of voices that bursts through the bush afterwards: the clangorous shouts of boys as they show Father Aulneau the half-burnt books, the priest's high womanish voice as he shows the books to the Chief, the angry buzz of women who gather to accuse and condemn.

Niska has two band constables: Luke Hunter and Francis Crow. Neither wears a uniform or a badge. Having constables is something new in Niska. The band council has voted to try it out on an informal basis before they decide on uniforms and an Ontario Provincial Police training course. They want to see how it works first.

The two young men who are crossing the tundra toward Geraldine are dressed in plaid shirts and jeans. Luke is carrying a gun; Francis, the handcuffs donated by the OPP. For men who have tracked rabbits and deer, it's easy to follow Geraldine's trail, especially since she has done nothing to cover it up. It's easy to figure out who burned the catechism books. Geraldine Gull is the only one in Niska who makes trouble like this. She is the main reason for the band police. Except for her, there is nothing much for the constables to do. Unless the band council votes for a dry reserve, they can't stop people from bringing liquor in on planes. The council figures if they stop the liquor coming in, people will sniff gasoline and Lysol instead.

The constables feel foolish coming out here after Geraldine. Unless the priest lays charges, they are wasting their time locking her up. They are doing it because the Chief, Luke's father, says they got to show Geraldine she can't walk over everybody and do what she wants. They got to show her the band won't take it lying down. As Luke and Francis approach the spruce island, they break their stride and walk softly. Geraldine is dangerous. She is cunning as a fox, unpredictable as a bear, savage as a wolverine. Everyone knows how she sliced her husband's forehead open with a broken bottle. Everyone knows she carries a knife strapped to her leg. This is not a job either one of them would do alone.

When they reach the lowbush cranberry, they hear Geraldine snore. Luke grins and raises his gun.

Geraldine wakens to a gun barrel pointed between her eyes. Ignoring the gun, she rolls on her side and vomits onto the boughs. She should've eaten something besides an O'Henry before starting on the rum. She reaches for the botttle, but Luke has already picked it up. He gestures with the bottle, and Francis snaps the handcuff on Geraldine's wrist.

Geraldine lurches to her feet and stumbles through the spruce trees after Francis, Luke following with the bottle and the gun. Nobody says anything. Geraldine knows they are taking her to the schoolhouse. She has been taken there before. This is where they put you until the OPP come and take you outside to Cochrane, where the judge sends you to jail. But the OPP won't come this time. The priest won't call the police. He will make a big fuss, jumping up and down as if a mouse were inside his pants. Then he'll pray, using those stupid books. The priest is a sissy. That is all he will do. Geraldine is going along with these constables because the school house is warm and dry; the spruce boughs are damp and her bones ache from sleeping on them. If these boys were real policemen, she might give them a hard time, but Luke and Francis are only pretending. It is all a joke on the priest. Geraldine doesn't laugh. She doesn't feel so good. She bends over and retches onto the grass.

When they reach the edge of the bush, five boys come out to meet the policemen. They had intended to yell out bad words at the crazy Ojibwa woman, knowing their mothers would never punish them for this, but when they see Geraldine, huge and scowling, they lower their eyes and file silently behind, hitting their sticks against the willow bushes. A small knot of women stands in front of the church. Lucy and Mary Bird, Denise Wabano, Josephine Loon and Betsy Bluecoat talk in angry, scolding voices. When they see Geraldine being led up the steps of the schoolhouse, which is next to the church, they avert their eyes and turn their backs.

Inside the schoolhouse, Francis removes the handcuff from his wrist and snaps it onto the back of the teacher's chair, because the desk leg is too thick for the handcuff to go around. Geraldine turns the chair sideways and, crooking her free arm on the desk, puts her head down and goes to sleep.

Luke takes the first shift. He sits near the back of the room on top of a desk. Because it's the end of June, the desks are empty, the books and notebooks put away. The teacher, Patrick Eagle, has taken the maps and pictures off the walls and put them in the cupboard at the back, so there is nothing to look at. Luke stares out the window at the rising moon. It grows dark. Geraldine snores. She awakens once to throw up in the waste basket, then asks for water. There is no running water in the school, so Luke goes home and brings back a mug of water from their bucket. Geraldine drinks the water and goes back to sleep.

Around midnight, Francis takes Luke's place. He sits on the desk, lighting one cigarette after another to keep himself awake. After two hours of this, he goes home to bed. There's no point sitting here. Geraldine can't go anywhere. They will probably let her go free tomorrow anyway. Francis slides noiselessly off the desk and goes to the door. The only sound he makes is the click of the lock as he turns the key.

Geraldine hears the click. She lifts her head and looks around. With moonlight streaming into the room, she can make out the desks and windows. Geraldine picks up the chair and carries it to a back window. Using her free hand, she opens the window and, holding the chair in front of her, she puts first one leg, then the other over the sill. Holding the chair as high as she can, Geraldine falls forward onto the grass. The back of the chair comes up and hits her on the chin. Geraldine curses, picks up the chair, goes into the bush behind the school and follows the path to the gully. No one is out at this time of night, but the boardwalk creaks, so she sticks to the path. When she comes to the gully, Geraldine crosses the planks Gerald has put over the gap and steps onto the wooden deck. She lifts the canvas tarp on the deck and paws through the jumble of tools until she finds a saw. It is one of the tools she stole off George. Geraldine sits on a pile of decking and saws off one end of the chair slat. Old Martha will wake up for sure because she sleeps outside in the tent, but she will think it is Gerald. It does not take Geraldine long to finish the job. The handcuff slides from the chair. Geraldine stands up. She will pick the lock in the morning. It's too dark to do it now. Geraldine goes down the ladder to the room Gerald built below deck and crawls onto the mattress beside her husband. She grins into the dark. If the constables start looking for her, they won't come here. Last place they'd look for her is in bed with Gerald Gull.

3: *June 26.* Flying into Niska aboard a ten-seater, you no longer see the village as a small nick on an aerial photograph taken from two thousand feet. The Otter flies low. You look down and see that a wide incision has been made on the lip of the river bank, then clumsily stitched up again. Stuck at either end of the scar like white-tipped pins are the store and the church. In between are brown and grey patches, the cabins and shacks where the Swampy Crees live. Some of the people are coming out of these homes to stare at the plane as the pilot buzzes the village.

There are 102 Indians in Niska, 103 if you count the passenger aboard the Otter with Willa Coyle. Officially, the band has 223 registered as living here, but over half of them live elsewhere. Some have married into other bands and live on other reserves. Some have married white men and live in towns and cities in the south: these women have lost their status and aren't allowed back to the reserve except to visit. Some live on city streets. Perhaps you've seen Gabriel Hunter on Seventh Avenue in Calgary, trying to sell his Stetson for a bottle of cheap wine. Or maybe you've seen Marie Crow huddled against the outside of the McLaren bar in Winnipeg at four in the morning. You may not notice the lawyers, teachers and social workers in these cities, Indians who, when they wear suits and polished shoes, can walk past a doorman. There are 107 dogs in Niska, outnumbering the people by four. Many of these strays are left over from the days when dogs were used to pull sleds to winter traplines. Now people use skidoos. Chief Xavier Hunter is the only one in the village who still uses a dog team.

Niska is a small dot on government maps, a blank space on tourist maps, a forgotten backwater, a mistake. Less than one hundred years ago, at the turn of the century, a small band of nomadic hunters pitched their teepees here, close to the caribou and winter traplines. Theirs was a communal life, a cluster of families who often did not need a Chief. They were exceptional hunters, a fact not lost on the Hudson's Bay Company. A small outpost was built where flour, whisky, cloth, steel traps and guns were traded for furs. A missionary priest arrived soon after, beating the Anglicans to the draw. The caribou left. The trap-lines thinned. There were fewer furs to trade. People starved, sickened with TB. Nailed to the cross, they asked to sign Treaty Number 9. From time to time, letters and petitions written by the priest or the post manager or an RCMP officer on behalf of the Chief were sent to the various district commissioners.

From Chief Albert Stoney of Big Trout Lake:

Hunting is getting less now and that is all we can live on. We are afraid of starving winter and summer. We have been waiting patiently to hear from the government. There has been no official from the government to see us for years, no one to hear our petition.

David Moonias of Sandy Lake dictated this letter when he was hospitalized in West Selkirk, Manitoba:

There are about 200 in our band, amongst them a good many hard-up widows which need help as soon as possible. Hunting is all that we can live on. We help each other but it is not enough. Many people die. Our babies do not live. People have been waiting for the government to decide and cannot wait much longer.

From Isaiah Bighead, Weagamow:

My father, I salute you, the Secretary, the Department of Indian Affairs, with a good heart in misery. I am writing to ask a favour of you as we are miserably in need. We are not as strong as the white people. We have always sickness among us. Please, Father, hear our prayer in giving us what we ask.

In 1912, after visiting the territory north of the Albany River, the district commissioner, Mr. Archibald MacKay, wrote a memorandum to the lieutenant governor of Ontario, Sir John Morison Gibson, that said in part:

As far as I am aware, the building of a railway through this district is not contemplated. I do not think that there is any appreciable settlement, nor have extensive mining operations been pushed further north than the Albany River. For these reasons, I do not think there will be any ingress of settlers to that district in the near future, and therefore, I see no reason why any immediate steps should be taken to extend treaty to the Indians inhabiting these parts of the country.

Eventually the government agreed to sign Treaty Number 9 with the bands north of the Albany River. In exchange for their land, the Indians were to receive bolts of cloth, tea, and sacks of sugar and flour. The year the Swampy Crees of Niska took treaty, 1929, the government paid the band $1,325.13 in relief supplies.

When Treaty Number 9 was signed in Attawapiskat, a young man with wild eyes and wearing deerskin breeches ran in from the bush. After his name, Charles Wabinoo, had been found on the pay list, he was given four one-dollar bills. As he took the crisp new notes from the district commissioner, he lifted the crucifux from his breast, kissed it and said, "From the bottom of my heart, I thank you."

Willa Coyle has the front seat behind the pilot. The other passenger, a broad-shouldered, bulky woman, sleeps in the seat by the door where there are no windows. Willa hasn't slept since the plane left Timmins, though she was up at five this morning to catch the early flight from Ottawa. Pressed to the window, she has followed the plane's journey as it traced the great river northward. The river was wide, spreading over the tundra in deep, reptilian curves that shone bright as fish scales in the sun.

It looked like a giant snake whose yawning mouth emptied into Hudson Bay.

The pilot buzzes the village once more and heads for the airstrip at the mouth of the bay. Willa looks across the cold blue strip of water, at the dirty ice pans, blunt-edged and solid, floating on the bay. Willa's surprised by the ice. She knew it was here, but not this much. She thought more ice would have melted by the end of June.

The plane flies low over the river. Close up, the water is dark, blackish in the middle, tea-coloured at the edges. Rocks stick up from the bottom, rows of jagged teeth. The river looks different from the pictures Willa has seen. Dick Simpson's photographs showed a flat, grey river with an impassive surface, the kind of surface that covers a muddy bottom, a harmless, indistinguishable bottom where suckers and catfish scavenge. Willa didn't expect to see a river bottom lined with sharp teeth, a bottom that seemed to be waiting for this flimsy plane to drop out of the sky into its monstrous open jaws. Willa's never flown in a two-engine propeller plane before. The plane has the latest comforts, reading lights and tweed-covered seats. Still, she feels vulnerable, as if the plane might suddenly plunge into the dark water below. She can hear the stone teeth breaking off the wings, the engines dropping, thud, thud, into the subterranean stomach.

Looking down, Willa sees that pieces of ice have broken loose and floated into the river mouth like flakes of white paint. The river mouth is wide, maybe a mile or two across. It's difficult to judge from up here. Islands, dozens of them, choke the river mouth. They are multi-sized, variations of grey rock and green willow. Willa has also seen photographs of these islands. Dick Simpson took dozens of photographs up here — not just of the islands, but of the village and of the goose camp, the hunters holding the geese by their necks. Willa's job had been to sort through the photographs, choose ten that would fit the glowing descriptions Dick had written about the camp in an effort to promote it as a goose hunter's paradise. In addition to designing the brochure, Willa rewrote most of Dick's heavy-handed and awkward prose. Willa hasn't seen the finished product. Dick said he would pick up the brochures from the printer and send in a few dozen so people in Niska could have them for Treaty Day.

The plane banks sharply toward the airstrip. Willa grips the arms of the seat as the plane bumps onto the runway and coasts to a stop. The co-pilot, a brisk young man about Willa's age — in his mid-twenties — comes down the aisle and opens the laddered door.

"Time to get off, Elizabeth," he says to the other passenger.

The woman wakes up and smiles at him.

Coming down the aisle, Willa gets a look at her face. The features are slightly Mongoloid. She picks up her tote bag and portfolio and follows the woman down the ladder. When she reaches the tarmac, the co-pilot hands her the backpack, carton and suitcase. The suitcase slips from Willa's hand and lands on her booted foot. Willa's wearing hiking boots, jeans and a red squall jacket.

Once she's cleared the wings with her gear, Willa looks around, and the isolation of the place hits her. Except for the old barracks, the tarmac, the plane, the other woman and herself, the landscape is empty. The pilot doesn't even get off the plane. The co-pilot lugs the cargo off the plane by himself, six cartons which he sets on the edge of the tarmac.

"I wish he'd hurry," he says to Willa. "We're supposed to pick up a kid in Severn. He has a ruptured appendix and we have to get him out of there this afternoon."

"Are you waiting for Patrick Eagle?" Willa asks. Patrick Eagle is the person who hired her to work up here. Dick Simpson, who arranged this contract, said Mr. Eagle would probably meet the plane.

"No," the co-pilot says. "I'm waiting for Ralph. He works for the Bay." He gestures at the cartons. "He's the one who comes for the supplies and mail. Usually he's here waiting for us, but we're a few minutes early today." The co-pilot looks at Willa and says, "Are you a nurse?"

Willa laughs. "No. Why?"

The co-pilot shrugs. "Nurses are the only white women we bring up here. Once or twice we've brought in a woman dentist."

"I'm an artist," Willa says. "I've been hired to give the kids in Niska art classes for the next six weeks."

The co-pilot whistles. "That a fact? Things must be looking up over there." He glances toward the plane. "Just a minute."

He goes inside the plane and returns moments later with a small plastic bag. "Listen, Ralph will be arriving soon. He'll have heard us buzzing the village. Can you give him the mail?"

Willa nods at the woman named Elizabeth, who is walking along the edge of the tarmac.

"I can't give it to her," the co-pilot says. "She's not all there."

"Okay, I'll take it," Willa says. She puts the mail into her tote bag.

The co-pilot goes back up the ladder, pulls the door shut and the plane taxis down the runway.

Once the plane has taken off, Willa hears the sound of a motor boat in the distance. While she waits for it to arrive, she walks over to the barracks and looks in the windows. She sees two big kitchen stoves, cupboards, a central table with a chopping-block top. Four windows over, she sees long trestle tables covered with oilcloth. Tucked beneath these are folding metal chairs. This is the dining room. Some paradise. She walks around to the other side of the building where the generator is housed and looks in the windows. This looks more like one of Dick's photographs. She sees stuffed leather chairs, chesterfields, coffee tables, a bar. The hunters' lounge, the old mess. She recognizes it from the photograph. The photograph showed hunters sitting around in Icelandic sweaters and wool socks, holding half-full glasses, big smiles on their faces.

Willa goes back to the tarmac and sees a blond man dressed

in rubber boots and a windbreaker pushing a rusty forklift over the rough tarmac. As he comes closer, Willa realizes that he's hardly more than a boy, probably still in his teens. His cheeks are smooth, unshaven.

"You must be Ralph." Willa says.

"Are you the art teacher?" he asks.

"Yes." Willa hands him the mail. "The co-pilot asked me to give you this."

Ralph takes the package and puts it inside his windbreaker and zips up.

"Patrick Eagle told me to bring you over," he says.

He lifts the cartons on top of the forklift, puts her luggage on top, and they set off down the cracked and bumpy tarmac.

"Have you been up here long?" Willa asks conversationally.

"Eight months."

"How do you like it?"

"It's a job." After a few minutes, Ralph adds, "There's not much to do up here. No TV or anything. In winter there's ski-dooing."

The Hudson's Bay boat is green with yellow trim. The largest boat in Niska, it's used for carrying provisions from the airstrip to the store. The Indians use canoes equipped with outboard motors to go upriver to hunt and fish and bring back firewood.

Elizabeth is already sitting in the prow, legs spread wide, hands loose against her cotton skirt. She has straight hair, cut short like a Japanese doll's. Her lower lip juts out in a way that suggests recalcitrance, maybe defiance.

Ralph loads the cartons and luggage into the middle of the boat.

Willa sits on the seat in front of Elizabeth, facing Ralph. She watches him pull the starting cord, manoeuvre the boat backward, then across the river mouth. The river mouth is much wider than it seemed from the plane. Down here, it's lake-sized, swelling like the sea. On its bluish surface are whirling eddies of foam. The water surges, restless, greedy, moving quickly to close the white cut made by the boat's passage. On either side of the river are islands with low willows seeming to grow out of rock. As the boat pushes upstream against the current, the islands gradually close in like hedges. Willa sees the rocks spiking up from the bottom. The water is darker here, almost black. They are travelling a channel. The channel snakes between spikes, and Ralph must weave a zigzag course while keeping the motor revved up to counteract the strong pull of the current. The deeper they travel into this labyrinth of islands, the more Willa feels she is entering a maze. It occurs to her that this boat trip is more dangerous than the plane ride. One of these spikes could rip a hole in the bottom of the boat and down they'd go. She pokes an exploratory finger into the water: ice-cold. They wouldn't last long in that.

They come out of the channel, and the river broadens. Ralph opens the motor wide. The boat bounces across the water, spray splashing against the sides. Willa looks over her shoulder, and there on the lip of muskeg are the buildings she saw from the plane.

Ralph cuts back the throttle. Willa sees a row of people looking down at the boat. The people are clumped into three groups: men on one side of wooden steps built up the embankment, women on the other, a group of children between. The men are wearing faded green pants and plaid jackets that hang loosely on their frames. The women are heavier, though stork-legged. They are wearing flowered skirts, cardigans and brightly coloured kerchiefs. The children are in jeans, T-shirts, runners. There must be thirty people up there. They stare at her wide-eyed and solemn.

"Do people usually meet the boat?" Willa asks Ralph.

"There's always half a dozen or so," he says. "Some are here to welcome Elizabeth back. Most of them are here to see you." He stands up and throws a rope to one of the men. Then he adds, "They don't see many white people, especially a woman with red hair."

Willa has carroty hair, so kinky and thick it must be tamed on either side with clips. Her freckled complexion is as transparent as onionskin. She shrugs on her backpack, picks up her tote bag and portfolio.

"You go first," Ralph says, "I'll bring up your suitcase."

Elizabeth has already gone ashore and is being thumped on the back by a big, heavy-set woman wearing a red beret.

As Willa climbs out of the boat, her backpack slips and she loses her balance. With no railing to hold on to, she nearly falls into the water. A woman giggles. Willa steadies herself and steps onto the embankment. She stands up and looks at the group of men, expecting one of them to come forward and announce he's Patrick Eagle. But the men stare at her impassively. None of them move.

The woman wearing the red beret breaks away from Elizabeth and comes toward Willa. She's taller than Willa and has a broad face, a crooked nose and long braids. Willa assumes the woman is going to say something friendly to greet her, perhaps *wachiyi*, which Dick told her means hello and good-bye. But the woman isn't smiling. She's scowling. Her eyes flash angrily. Too late Willa sees the anger. She cannot back up without falling into the river. The woman closes in on Willa. She lifts her hand and swings it sideways against Willa's cheek. *Slap.* Hard. Willa's glasses fly off her nose and onto the grass. The portfolio slides to the ground.

"Go back," the woman says. "Go back where you come from. We don't want you here." She shoves her ugly face close to Willa's, so close Willa can smell her sour breath. "Got it?" The woman turns on her booted heel and, steering Elizabeth by the arm, leads her away.

Ralph drops Willa's suitcase onto the grass and runs after the woman.

"Why, you bitch!" he yells, his shyness gone. "You can't get away with that!" He chases after the red-bereted woman. She laughs and breaks into a run.

Willa stands on the river bank, holding her cheek, watching Ralph disappear into the bushes. The children run after him, shouting and waving their sticks.

The women giggle nervously, the men shift feet. Wordlessly, they turn and walk away.

This is the art teacher's welcome; so much for *wachiyi*.

In the aftershock of Geraldine's attack, Willa rubs the area where she's been slapped. It burns as if a large W has been branded on her cheek. Her eyes smart, tears of rage, confusion, fear. Willa's like a soldier who's been parachuted behind enemy lines with no idea where she's come down. She has no idea who of these people is on her side and who isn't. Perhaps they're all against her. No, that can't be. If they're all against her, she wouldn't have been asked here to teach, would she? Where is Patrick Eagle? If he'd been here like Dick said he would, this wouldn't have happened. Since he isn't, she feels like marching right out of here. Of course that's impossible. The next plane isn't due for three days.

Willa picks up her glasses. One arm has broken off. Isn't that dandy. She's been here ten minutes and her glasses are broken. She squints at the blurred shacks along the boardwalk. Well, there's no place to repair them here, that's for sure. She'll have to fix them with tape. She puts her glasses in her squall jacket pocket, picks up her suitcase and folder — she'll come back for the art supplies later — and crosses the swampy grass to the boardwalk. Willa's not an RC, but with no other salvation in sight she does what refugees, outcasts and pilgrims have done for centuries: she heads for the sanctuary of the Roman Catholic Church — and enters the fragile embrace of Father Aulneau.

4: Father Aulneau looks out his study window, which has a view of the river on one side and the boardwalk on the other. He's feeling good. It's three o'clock in the afternoon, and he has just finished translating Deuteronomy, the Fifth Book of Moses, into Swampy Cree. He's been struggling with the books of Moses for a year now, and he's finally finished. Tomorrow he can begin Joshua, which is more interesting, like Genesis. He is not exactly translating or translating exactly. It is more like a précis. Many of the words in the Old Testament do not mean much to a Roman Catholic, but there is something in them for the people to learn. He's not one for throwing the baby out with the bath water.

Father Aulneau hasn't been asked to do this work. He's undertaken these translations because it's his opinion that the job hasn't yet been properly done and because he gains satisfaction from it. He hopes it's God's will that he's doing this. Someday he will make a gift of the finished work to Bishop Bonhomme. He will do this out of the blue, as they say. Often he imagines what the bishop's face will look like when he makes the presentation, what words he will say. Making the presentation is the closest Father Aulneau expects to come to sainthood.

When he was a postulant in Rougemont, Father Aulneau yearned for sainthood. Even as a child dressed in vestments his sister Agnes had made from lace curtains, he prayed at a small chapel in his bedroom for the Virgin Mary to make him a saint. Alas, since he has been in the North working among the Indians, he knows true sainthood will be denied him. The problems are too big, and God did not grant him enough gifts. His gift is translation. He has made small stories for the people from Genesis, stories about Adam and Eve, Cain and Abel, Noah and the ark, Jonah and the whale, which he had told them on Sundays. The stories are well suited to the people. They are not as intellectual as the Gospel of St. John, where Father Aulneau finds his personal inspiration. He has not been able to find many stories in Deuteronomy, only rules and more rules. He's found it difficult to translate because of this, not wanting to repeat himself and not wanting to omit anything, either. But now he's finished. He can take a deserved rest, some refreshment. Maybe Nazarene Rose has baked tea biscuits today. He asked her this morning if she would, thinking he might finish chapter 33 today, but she only grunted as usual and went on doing the breakfast dishes. First he will sharpen his pencil and put it beside the notebook to be ready for tomorrow. Then he will ask Nazarene Rose to make tea. He must ask her the same thing every day. Two and a half years he's been in Niska. Two and a half years he has had tea every day at three o'clock. Still, every day he must say to Nazarene Rose, "Could I have tea now, please?" She knows. Still, he must ask. Such strange people. Such hardness of heart. Father Aulneau immediately regrets this thought. He must pray to God to help him understand his flock, understand and accept. All the years he has spent at Weagamow, Fort Albany, Fort Rupert, and still he must pray to God to help him accept.

As he turns from the window, Father Aulneau catches sight of a red-haired woman carrying a suitcase, a backpack and a folder, plodding across the grass toward his door, three dogs following her. Mon Dieu, the art teacher. The person Patrick Eagle has hired to teach the children. The person who will be staying in the mission cabin. Did Patrick tell me she was coming today or didn't he? It is not as if I get so many visitors here I can forget. When the translation is going well, I am not even on this earth. With those miserable dogs after her like wolves and that red jacket, the woman looks like Red Riding Hood coming to grandmaman's house. The joke pleases Father Aulneau. He hears a knock at the side door, but he will wait until Nazarene Rose opens it before going into the kitchen to greet his visitor.

The mission is a square white building with a back door painted a battleship grey. Willa waits in front of this door. She hears a shuffling inside before the door is opened by a Cree of indeterminate age. The woman fills the doorway. She's tall, though not as heavy as the woman who slapped Willa. She's lean, rangy and is wearing a blue cotton housedress and a pair of plaid slippers.

"Is the priest in?" Willa says.

The woman jerks her thumb toward the kitchen. Wrestling

her gear through the doorway, Willa steps inside. She puts her suitcase and folder on the entryway floor and slips off her backpack. The entryway is a room that's been built onto the back of the mission. One wall of this room is stacked with kindling, the other is hung with brooms, mops and pails. The floor planking is painted grey like the door. The woman lopes into the kitchen, leaving Willa standing on the doormat.

Father Aulneau chooses this moment to make his entrance. Sweeping into the kitchen with outstretched arms, he comes straight to Willa and takes her hands.

"Bonjour, mademoiselle. C'est une surprise," he says. "Asseyez-vous."

One thing Father Aulneau has noticed is that when he talks to a white woman up here — the public health nurse, for example — he uses French. He doesn't know why this is. Maybe it's because he doesn't see many white women. He ushers Willa to a kitchen chair. He notices an ugly red mark on her left cheek, but he says nothing. Perhaps it's a birthmark. He once saw a woman with one that size. It grew on her neck and had hair on it.

'C'est un grand plaisir," he says. "'Would you like some tea?"

"Please."

Father Aulneau looks toward Nazarene Rose, who is poking the fire in the huge wood stove.

"Nazarene Rose, could we have tea please?"

Nazarene Rose grunts.

"Did you make tea biscuits today, Nazarene Rose?"

Another grunt.

Father Aulneau claps his hands. "C'est bon. We will have a jar of blueberry jam. It will make a ver-ee good feast." He sits down, facing Willa. "The jam is home-made. My sister's jam. From Bathurst, New Brunswick."

Father Aulneau is in his late fifties, a small man, much smaller than Nazarene Rose, with a pale, sharp-featured face. It is the face of an aesthete: long of nose, narrow of brow. Wire-rimmed glasses do nothing to widen the colourless eyes.

"I grew up in New Brunswick," his guest says.

"Vraiment? Où? A quelle place?"

"Sussex."

"Ah! Une petite ville mais belle."

"Très belle."

"Vous parlez français?"

"Un peu." She holds two fingers together. "Très peu."

"Vous parlez plus que ça. Comment vous appelez-vous?" Father Aulneau asks. He cannot remember if Patrick told him her name.

"Willa Coyle."

"Ah," the priest says. He thinks Willa is a strange name for a woman, ver-ee strange. It is a name for a horse. This woman does not look like a horse. People often remind Father Aulneau of animals. With her hair over her forehead and her deep-set eyes, she looks like a monkey. But of course she is much too pretty for a monkey, pas une beauté, non, mais belle. And she speaks French. Patrick said she is une artiste, which is something. She may dress in those detestable cowboy pants and workboots, but if she is une artiste, she must have une bonne sensibilité.

Nazarene Rose brings two cups of tea with milk added. She slams them onto the table so hard that tea slops into the saucers. She brings biscuits smeared with butter and a bottle of purple jam with a spoon stuck upright in it. Nazarene Rose never fails to show her dislike of extra work.

"Two knives and plates," the priest snaps.

He imposes a miffed silence while knives and plates are brought and placed unceremoniously on the table. Then he passes the biscuits and jam to Willa. As his guest, she can have the first spoonful, though this is the first jar of blueberry jam he's opened since he returned from his spring furlough in Bathurst.

"What art do you do?" he asks cautiously, reminding himself that artists do many strange things nowadays. They carry bricks, soup cans, hubcaps into galleries, put them against the walls and call it art when it is nothing but a sham.

"I draw and paint," Willa says. She takes a bite of biscuit and says, "These are delicious, Nazarene Rose."

Nazarene Rose says nothing. Keeping her back to the table, she picks up the poker and stabs the fire in the stove.

"When I have time," Willa goes on. "Unfortunately, that hasn't been nearly enough for the past few years. Since I got my fine arts degree, I've had to take other jobs to support myself."

"Where did you study?" Father Aulneau asks.

"Mount Allison," she says. "In Sackville."

Then she is Protestant.

"What do you draw?" he asks.

"I prefer doing portraits, but I do landscapes, too."

"C'est bon, ça," Father Aulneau says. "Je suis un artiste aussi."

"Do you draw or paint?" Willa asks.

"I paint wildflowers," he says, sipping daintily from his cup. "The Arctic has many flowers. I collect the specimens and preserve them with glycerine. That way, I keep them to sketch all winter. The season here is too short: two months summer, two months fall, the rest is winter. And my health will not permit me to go outside in ill weather. I will show you."

Father Aulneau goes into his office and comes back with a heavy coiled notebook designed to hold photographs. Behind each cellophane panel is a sketch of a wildflower. Each flower has been rendered in great detail, then given a delicate colour wash. Father Aulneau has included the Latin name for each flower. Bog wintergreen, *Pyrola asarifolia*. Arctic raspberry, *Rubus arcticus*. Purple butterwort, *Pinquincula vulgaris*. Arctic avens, *Geum strictum*. Water plantain, *Alisma trivale*. Sticky asphodel, *Tufieldia glutinosa*.

"These are lovely," Willa says. "You have a fine hand."

"Merci," Father Aulneau says humbly, looking into his tea-cup. He's overcome. It's not often someone appreciates his flower sketches. He takes them home to show Agnes, but it is not the same as showing them to another artist. "I must give some credit to my encyclopaedia," he says, though he does not want to give it too much credit, because many of his flowers are not in the book and he must guess. "It is like detective work, n'est-ce pas?"

"It sounds like it might be."

"It is the same with translation work. You must hunt for the correct word. Sometimes the correct word is difficult to find, ver-ee difficult."

"Do you go out sketching often?"

"This year, no. It is not a good summer for flowers. A wet spring. So much water," Father Aulneau says sadly. He sees his guest shift uncomfortably in her chair. Perhaps she has need of a toilet. There was the long plane ride to get here. Then the journey in the boat. There is a chemical toilet beside his office, but he would be embarrassed to suggest she use it.

"Do you wish to see your quarters?" he asks diplomatically.

"I don't know where I'm staying," Willa says.

"Pas un problème. You are staying here. In the mission cabin, just across the grass." The priest gestures toward the door. "Here, I will show you."

Father Aulneau waits while Willa shoulders her backpack, picks up her suitcase and portfolio, and bumps through the doorway and down the step. He turns away so he does not see her struggling with this load. He cannot help her. There is the arthritis in his elbows and knees, which is bad now because of the dampness. And it is his opinion, and Agnes's, too — they were talking about this in March — that if women today insist on dressing like men, they must expect to be treated like men.

Once they are inside the cabin, Father Aulneau shows his guest the wood stove with its cavernous oven. He opens the cupboards to reveal four chipped plates, a battered coffeepot, two dented pots, three glasses, two mugs, and a salt shaker in the shape of a squirrel. He shows her the two oil lamps and the sink with a pipe that empties onto the grass beneath the cabin. He shows her the small sitting-room, which has a sofa, a chair and a bookshelf, and the bedroom containing a metal bed and a rod with a shelf on top, which passes for a closet. He ignores the cubicle containing the chemical toilet; she will find it herself. He points to the buckets on the back porch.

"There is no shortage of water with the river so close," he says. "Unfortunately, we do not have so much firewood. The wood must be hauled from twenty-five miles away. There is wood beneath the cabin, but it will not be enough."

"How can I get wood?"

"Ah. C'est un problème. Wood is scarce here, ver-ee scarce. Chief Hunter will get you wood, but you will have to pay much money for it, ver-ee much money." Father Aulneau opens the porch door. "I will go now." Before he leaves, he coughs delicately and says, "It would give me much pleasure if you would join me for supper. I eat at six. Mass is at seven."

"Merci," she says.

"C'est bon, ça. A bientôt."

As he returns to the mission house, Father Aulneau's step is light on the grass. It will be ver-ee good to have someone here who is une artiste and who speaks French. And she is a woman, which means she will know how to make rice pudding. For two and a half years, he has been asking Nazarene Rose to make rice pudding, but she has refused. Tonight, at supper, he will ask his guest to show Nazarene Rose how it is done.

5: The Hudson's Bay store in Niska is a white box with a green banner over the door. The yellow lettering on the banner reads: Hudson's Bay Co. Incorporated, May 1690. Across the front are windows with venetian blinds. Except for the back-door window, these are the only windows in the building, which is low and narrow, built like a warehouse. Inside, the walls on either side are lined with shelves. Fluorescent lights hang over the middle aisle, the electricity supplied by a gasoline generator. On one side of the aisle is a counter. Behind it are shelves of tinned and packaged food. On the other side of the aisle are islands of parkas, men's work pants, shirts, boots, sweaters, women's blouses, children's clothing, caps, scarves, mittens made in Taiwan. There's a bin for sleeping bags and tents, another for disposable diapers and baby blankets. The shelves against the side wall are crammed with bowls, pots, pans, kettles, dishes, washbasins, infant seats, kerosene lamps, oil cans, ammunition, rope, flashlights, transistor radios, blankets and bolts of cloth. At the back are kegs of nails and a pegged board full of carpenter's tools.

Xavier Hunter is standing just inside the door rolling a cigarette and keeping an eye on the white woman at the counter. He knows who she is. She's the one Patrick asked inside to teach the kids how to draw and paint. Only he didn't stick around to meet her, but got Ralph to bring her over instead. Patrick is still at the ridge, where he went as soon as school was out. Xavier watches what this teacher buys: kerosene, a door hook, yellow cloth with red flowers on it, thread, dish cloths, two cans of tuna, a can of beans, apple juice, peanut butter, a tin of ham (but she tells George to put that back when she sees how much it costs), salt, baking powder, flour, oatmeal, lard, tea, coffee, corn flakes, a tin of milk, two cans of tomato soup, a box of crackers, raisins, and a loaf of bread that came in on today's plane. He notices the way she shakes her head when she sees the prices George has marked on everything. She is finding out pretty quick what it costs to live up here. When she asks for fresh milk, George tells her there is none. Easier to get liquor up here than fresh milk. The government sees to that.

When his daughter Nina came inside last time, she brought a whole case of ham with her. The cans were half the Bay price.

Same with everything she brings from Calgary. Xavier has never been to Calgary. He was outside once when he had TB. That was enough. Spent three years in a TB san, which was where he learned to speak English. After that, he worked six months in Winnipeg at a sheet metal plant. He wanted to come back with money for Bernice and the kids, but he couldn't stick it out longer than six months, so he quit. He couldn't stand to see what was happening to his people, so many of them falling down drunk. Girls as young as Nina selling themselves to anyone who would pay them, even old men. It made him feel bad to look at it. He came back to Niska and stayed put. He flies to meetings sometimes, places like Sandy Lake and Big Trout, but he doesn't go to big places outside. He's too old to be going here and there.

His three oldest kids are gone: Nina, Gabriel and Ruth. All started in school and went away. Nina left for residential school while he was sick. It was hard for Bernice, looking after those kids by herself. She got help from some people. Before he died, Joseph Eagle gave her meat and geese. His brother Toby helped. The baby, Maria, died the first winter he was away, but after he came back, Luke was born, then Josh and Rachel. Luke hasn't decided if he'll leave. Used to be people thought it was better for kids to leave. There was more for them to do outside and they got a chance at education. But that's changing. Indians like Patrick Eagle are teaching school inside so kids can stay home longer where parents can keep a lookout for them. People found out their kids were getting into trouble outside, drinking and fighting and going to jail. But Niska has troubles also. As long as it's a wet reserve, some kids will get drunk and hurt themselves. That's how Tom Sutherland got himself killed three years ago when a skidoo rolled over on him. He was seventeen.

Xavier told his kids that if they get into trouble outside to come back here. He told Gabriel this before he went to work on the oil rigs. He said the same thing to Ruth, but he's got no worries there. Ruth liked residential school so much she's study-ing to be a nun. He told Nina to come back also. He told her this even though sometimes she forgets who she is. She walked away from Patrick Eagle, married a white man and threw away her status. She's got no rights on the reserve now. He doesn't like her doing that. But she's his daughter, so he tells her: you get into trouble and you come back inside. Some people, like Dave Wabano, think different. Dave told Lucille not to come back. He says since Lucille married a white man, she isn't Indian any more.

Xavier figures if his kids can go out and be with white people, then it's okay for this white woman to come inside. Depends. As long as white people come here one or two at a time, they got no worries. But too many come at once and things change too fast. Like when the base was over at the airstrip. Lots of people from here worked over there, which was okay. But they started drinking over there. Women also. The women took up with the white men. Some half-Indian babies came out of it. People didn't know who they were.

Sometimes whites have trouble this way also. Like the white teacher who was here before Patrick Eagle came. He wore moccasins, a deerskin jacket, stuck a feather in his hair and asked too many questions. He was trying to be an Indian so he could write a book about it. After his first winter here, he gave up and left. Maybe he wrote a book about Niska anyway. If he did, Xavier won't read it. Only people who can write about Indians are Indians. This is why he's keeping a notebook, writing down the old stories, what he thinks about this and that. Maybe Rachel will make a book out of it someday. She is the best one for books. She's only ten years old, but already she's good at putting words on paper. She will have a big job ahead of her. Like telling how it used to be up here before the air base, before the Bay and the church got here, back when the people were like a herd of caribou wintering in a secret valley. Back when Kitche Manitou gave the sun to men and the moon to women. The earth also. Rachel will have to bring it all the way up to now, when there's no secret valley left, when planes make white trails across the sky, when satellites crawl through the night like animals with red and green eyes.

These satellites are how they keep in touch now. That's how they got their telephones. Xavier's in no hurry to get TV inside, but he likes the telephone. Saves him from going over to the band office at the goose camp all the time. And it's a way for Indians to stick together and talk things out. It's a way for them to keep themselves from being wiped out like that woolly elephant he heard they dug out of the ice a long time ago. Even had fur on it after all that time.

The art teacher has red hair. That is the first thing Xavier noticed when she walked through the door. Second thing he noticed was that she was wearing men's pants. Women don't wear men's pants. Some of the young girls here wear men's pants. Xavier doesn't like it. Nina wears men's pants. She says lots of women wear them nowadays. She says he's old-fashioned. He tells her sometimes he's old-fashioned, sometimes he isn't. Depends. When it comes to women, he is. Nina says women have the same rights as men. She told Bernice that also. Maybe Nina's been outside so long she forgets how he and Bernice give to each other so it works out okay. Equal rights don't touch the matter.

Xavier looks at the teacher's hands. No wedding ring. A white woman coming alone might make trouble inside. He told Patrick that at the band council meeting, but Patrick said it would be okay, most of the single men would be going outside to work on construction jobs for the summer. This is true. Aglace and Frances's three boys have gone, Henry and Agnes's son also. Eli Crow's gone. Only Luke and Francis are left, and Patrick. Patrick had better get back here quick and tell this teacher what to do. As for himself, he'll pay her a visit later on today. Tell her about firewood and where to empty the white toilet she's got. He's Chief, that's his job. The district manager keeps calling him "band administrator," but all that means is more white pages to fill out on the fancy typing machine that's over at the band office, a machine he can't use and is too old to learn how.

6: *June 26*

Dear Karen,

Well, here I am in Niska. It's evening, well past nine but still light outside. I'm not at all sleepy, so I'll fill you in on what's happened to me since I left Ottawa this morning. (Was it only this morning?) I want to get the details down while they're still fresh in my mind.

Such as: flying north over endless terrain (what I think our geography texts used to call the "boreal forest region") with its myriad lakes winking at me like those pocket mirrors we used as kids to catch the sunlight.

Such as: watching a cow moose and her calf, top-heavy, knobby-kneed, rangy beasts loping across the tundra. They were surprisingly graceful.

Such as: me feeling unexpectedly, unabashedly patriotic. I felt like bursting forth with "O Canada, my home and native land." *The monumental size of the landscape overwhelmed me. I thought of those stories we read in grade school — you know, all that mythology stuff about giants tramping through muskeg, making lakes with their footprints. There's a sculptural quality to the North which, when you think of the Eskimo carvings, is hardly surprising. I never realized until today what paradoxes those carvings are, that small polished miniatures could suggest such hugeness. (I'm thinking of the earlier sculptures, not those gross chunks of soapstone you see in gift shops nowadays.)*

The plane landed on this tiny airstrip on Hudson Bay. No airport, of course, nothing but run-down air force barracks. Two of us got off — we were the only passengers. As soon as the plane left, abandoned us (that's how it felt), the barrenness and the space seized me and I felt I was shrinking. After a while a young man named Ralph, who works for the Bay, picked us up in a boat and took us six miles through a dangerous, winding channel with sharp rocks sticking up from the bottom. I felt I was passing through a no man's land, that the river was one way, that I wouldn't be able to find my way back. Now that I'm here, I feel I've been swallowed up, that I've disappeared inside the map. It must be the isolation working on me, being suddenly cut off with no roads, railways, no phone to connect me with the familiar.

What happened next made me feel even more disconnected. As soon as I got out of the boat at the village and stepped onto the river bank, a big, ugly brute of a woman with a red beret suddenly came up and slapped my face! She slapped me so hard my glasses flew off my nose. She said, "Go back where you came from. We don't want you here." Then she walked away. I think I lost six inches with that slap. To make matters worse, the person who is supposed to be looking after the art classes, Patrick Eagle, didn't show up, though a lot of other people did. Apparently they line up to see who gets off the plane. Not one of them said a word to me. They simply walked away. And Ralph had taken off after the woman who slapped me, which meant I was left standing there alone, wondering what to do next. I felt like I had walked into an enemy camp, that someone had made a mistake asking me up here. I figured the most sensible thing I could do was head for the church, so I picked up my stuff and started walking down the boardwalk.

I had tea with the priest, a scholarly, frail-looking man, French, high-strung, not the sort of priest I would have expected to find in a place like this. He seemed glad to have company, which made me feel a bit better. He has this tall, silent house-keeper, Nazarene Rose, who looks as if she might be hostile. Anyway, the priest showed me the mission cabin where I'm staying. It's a tiny, three-room affair with a big wood stove in the kitchen. He asked me to supper. That was when I found out that the woman who slapped me was someone named Geraldine Gull. Apparently, she burned the church's catechism books yesterday afternoon, was locked in the schoolhouse, but escaped last night. (I put a hook on the porch door in case she comes prowling around here.) The priest said this Geraldine character is crazy, that people in the village are afraid of her. It was a relief to find out that I'm not the only one she's picked on.

Before I left the mission house, the priest, whose name is Father Aulneau, asked me if I would show his housekeeper how to make rice pudding. Apparently it's his favourite dessert, and even though he's asked Nazarene Rose to make it many times, she refuses to do it. He says that if I show her, she might make it. Help! I haven't made rice pudding since home ec in grade 8, and there's not a recipe book in sight. I said I'd try. I couldn't very well refuse. He was feeding me supper and I'm getting this cabin rent-free.

You'll be curious to know what this place looks like. It won't take long to tell you. There's the boardwalk I referred to. At one end of it — about a quarter mile from here — is the Hudson's Bay store. At this end is the mission, which is the church, the priest's house, this cabin and the schoolhouse. In between are the cabins and shacks where the Indians live. There can't be more than thirty of these homes, their backs to the bushes — willow bushes. There aren't any tall trees here. This place is slightly above the tree-line. It's really a swamp. When I went to the store, I felt the boardwalk squish — that is the only word for it — beneath my feet. That's how wet it is. And it stinks — a heavy, acrid pee smell. I could see greasy pockets of water where people have thrown dishwater and garbage.

There's no TV or radio up here (no electricity except for a few generators), but there are phones, though none in this cabin. I should have brought up the transistor radio you offered to lend me. I saw one like it in the store for $149. The prices here are sky-high. I don't know how people manage to eat. Not much fresh food, either. I did buy some cheap cotton to cover the cabin windows. I have to have curtains. The Indians here stare and stare. I feel as if every move I've made since I got here this afternoon has been watched. And I planned to do the watching. It's dark now, so I've lit a kerosene lamp and hung a towel over the kitchen window in case someone (I hope not that Gull woman) is going by. Before I sign off and go to bed, I want to tell you a couple more things.

The faces. The Indian faces are wonderful. After I get to know the people here better, I may ask if I can draw some of them. I saw two old people in the store earlier, a man sitting on a pile of flour sacks and a woman with grey film over her eyes. She's blind. Both of them had wrinkled, weathered, time-worn skin. Their expressions were such a mixture of forbearance, I guess you could say, wisdom — and knowledge, not book knowledge. You don't get faces like that from reading books. The Chief is another face I'd like to draw. Xavier Hunter. The priest told me his name. I didn't even know he was the Chief when he came to see me, but I wasn't surprised to learn afterwards that he was. The wisdom again, the knowing, the stoicism. It was funny to hear such a dignified man tell me where to empty my chemical toilet. "That toilet you got," he said (I'm quoting him exactly), "you empty it behind the church, past the graveyard. You put it in a big hole that has a board over it to keep out the dogs. That's where Nazarene Rose puts the Little Father's." He also told me they would supply me with free wood because I was the art teacher. He said Patrick Eagle, the man in charge of the classes, isn't here. He's gone upriver and will be back tomorrow or the next day. So, I guess I can do what I want until then. Tomorrow I start sketching.

I just heard a howl which reminds me to tell you one last thing before I go to bed. It's the dogs. They're everywhere here. You should have heard them when the church bell rang for mass tonight. There was a chorus of them howling. Spooky. Like wolves. Some of them look like wolves, others like huskies.

*They're big, scruffy, mean-looking creatures, many with bare
patches of skin. A pack of them followed me back from the
store, growling and snapping at one another. One of them, a
black and white dog with a rope around its neck, kept pushing
against the back of my legs. I had to carry the box of groceries
on top of my head. I was terrified. I thought if I tripped on a
broken slat, they'd pounce on me and tear me to shreds. That's
the last time I go anywhere without a stick. What have I got
myself in for? I feel just by getting here, I've earned half my
salary.*

*Well, Sis, I've rambled on long enough. Must get to bed. The
next plane out isn't for three more days, so I'll leave the envelope open in case I want to add more later.*

Love,
Willa

7: Geraldine sits on the pile of planking, her skirt hitched
up so the morning sun can warm her legs. They're good legs, the
one part of her that isn't fat. They're strong, straight, not bad for
a woman who had six kids in her belly different times, not
counting the ones that never got born. No more babies grow
inside. Not like Elizabeth Mack. Three times Elizabeth has gone
outside to have a baby. Three times the nuns take away the baby
and give it to someone else. They don't fix her so she can't have
more. A goose hunter gave her the last baby when she and
Geraldine were poking around the goose camp last fall looking
for something to eat. Geraldine didn't go with any of the men.
She won't go with a white man unless she gets paid. But the
goose hunters don't ask her no more. They like a young woman
like Elizabeth.

Geraldine takes her knife out of its sheath and sharpens it
with the whetstone she stole from the Bay store. She holds up
the blade, testing it with her tongue. The edge glints in the

sunlight. When it's sharp enough to suit her, she puts the knife back in the sheath, then watches Gerald trying to straighten a bent nail with the claw of his old hammer.

"You do that with every nail?" she asks. She rubs the skin beneath the handcuff.

Gerald grunts.

"Going to take you forever to get the deck done," Geraldine mocks him. "You be dead before this raft floats."

Gerald says nothing. As usual. Worst man to talk to. All he does is work on this stupid raft. Look at the size of it. Bigger than the Bay store. Eight shacks would fit on it. It'll sink for sure. Too much wood in it. There's Brother Charlie's wood from the saw-mill, wood from people's houses that never got built, new shithouses that never got built either, people shitting through the same dirty holes or using the bush. Gerald says the Lord told him to take the wood. That's the way he talks now, always going on about the Lord. Gets himself lathered up, yelling and shout-ing about the Holy Ghost and all that crapshit. Lost his head over it. Won't drink with her no more. Won't fight with her no more. She's got to admit he looks better now with a flat belly. Geraldine hikes her skirt higher and says, "What happened to the ham-mer?" Least he can do is treat it good after she stole it for him.

"The handle broke."

"You need another one," Geraldine says. She rubs her belly. "What'll you give me if I get you another one?" She sees Gerald look at her brown legs, what's between. He looks away, then back again.

"A piece of tail," he says.

Next to the Lord, tail is Gerald's answer for everything. You feel bad? Have some tail. Hungry? Try tail. Sick? You need tail. It's why Geraldine has stuck with him so long. She can't think of another reason. Even the Holy Rollers don't take that away from Gerald.

"I need an electric saw also."

"You got no place to plug it in," Geraldine says.

"Dave Wabano's lending me his generator. Without an electric saw, I can't finish on time. I need an electric cord, one that will reach Wabano's."

"For an electric saw and a cord and a hammer, you got to go a long time. Twice. You don't fall asleep on me."

"I won't."

"And you got to pick the lock on my handcuff."

"I will. You go down first."

Geraldine's too smart to fall for that one. She'd be down there on the mattress asleep before Gerald would quit work.

"I stay here until you go down," she says.

Gerald wrestles another bent nail out of the plank.

"We got a deal or not? I can go over to Morris Mack," Geraldine taunts. "He's good for a piece of tail."

Gerald puts down the hammer and follows Geraldine down the ladder.

After they have done it once, Gerald lies in the lazy gloom below deck and says, "The priest told me there's an artist woman living in his cabin. A white teacher."

Geraldine thinks about Alexander's pictures. Gerald is the only one who knows about the pictures. Telling Gerald something is like tying a rock around it and dropping it into the bay.

"What artist woman?" Geraldine says carelessly, though she has already dealt with the woman who was on the plane with Elizabeth yesterday. Geraldine keeps track of everyone who comes to the village. One of them could be a cop. Sometimes they wear ordinary clothes to fool you.

"Why is a white artist coming inside, not an Indian artist?" Geraldine says belligerently.

"Patrick Eagle wanted someone to teach the kids drawing and painting," Gerald says. "Maybe he couldn't get an Indian artist." Then he adds, "A white artist is better than no artist."

Geraldine squirms. She knows this is true, that Gerald is telling her the white artist might help with Alexander's pictures, but she doesn't want to think about that now. She rolls sideways on the mattress and puts her hand on Gerald's crotch. She rubs until his cock grows hard.

After they have done it again and returned to the deck, Gerald picks the lock on the handcuffs, throws them into the gully and goes back to work. Geraldine heads for the store.

On her way down the boardwalk, she stops at the mission cabin and opens the porch door. She clomps across the plywood floor in her rubber boots and looks in the kitchen. No one there. She goes into the sitting-room, the bedroom. No one there, either. The artist woman has gone. Geraldine walks to the closet and fingers the blouses and sweaters. Snorts at the white nightgown which has lace on the collar. Who does she think she is wearing that up here, the Queen of England? Geraldine goes into the sitting-room. She sees pads, pencils, paint brushes, tins of powdered paint on the shelves. She picks up a tin and sniffs. Alexander never used this kind of stuff. He used tubes like toothpaste comes in.

Geraldine hears a tapping noise on the back door, a voice. It's the priest.

"Mademoiselle," he is saying, the nosy bugger. "Mademoiselle!" He taps on the door again.

Walking softly, Geraldine enters the toilet cubicle, where there are no windows. She lifts her skirt and sits on the cool white seat. She'll take a piss in here where it's warm and dry, where no bushes scratch her ass. If the priest comes snooping inside and opens the toilet door, she'll tell him she had to go bad, that her husband is too busy going to church to build her a shithouse.

But he only calls "Mademoiselle!" once more, and then he goes away.

Through the thin plywood walls, Geraldine hears the scrape of his black pointed shoes on the step as he goes back to his house. Geraldine waits until she hears the back door of the mission house slam shut, then she spreads her legs wide and lets the yellow fluid gush out, enjoying the sound of it hitting the metal can. Geraldine likes the idea of pissing in the church's toilet. When she's finished, she gets up, pulls down her skirt and goes outside. In the distance, she hears the sound of Gerald's hammer. He has stopped pulling out nails and gone back to work.

Geraldine starts down the boardwalk, then stops, steps off into the swamp and walks toward the river. She'll walk along the river bank to get to Morris Mack's. This is a big job, bigger than usual. George will be watching her close. She'll need Elizabeth Mack for cover. Her pockets also. Stupid Gerald Gull thinks she is doing this for the Lord, but he is wrong. She is doing it to screw the Bay.

8: To understand what follows, you have to accept the fact that in the North, isolation does strange things to people. People who would be considered eccentrics in larger centres to the south are taken for granted, could even be said to flourish in the North. Because of the isolation, people are driven to seek strange alliances. For example, in Severn, where seven denominations struggle for the souls of 220 people, the wife of Reverend Arthur Bidwell, the Anglican minister, went over to Pastor Tracey's Pentecostal church; the Reverend Roland Innis, the Lutheran minister, went over to Reverend Bidwell's church, so that a replacement, Reverend Wilford Tucker, fresh out of the Lutheran Bible College in Camrose, Alberta, had to be brought in. The Roman Catholic brother left the church to marry a teacher, Sister Helen Fernandez. (This was Brother Philip, not Brother Charlie. Brother Philip's departure was two years before the Roman Catholic church burned down and Brother Charlie was sent in to build a new one.) It's interesting to note that although the Roman Catholic church had by far the largest congregation in Severn, it was the one that burned down, while other, much smaller churches such as the Fire Baptized Holiness church, which had only a handful of worshippers, was spared. *God moves in a mysterious way, His wonders to perform.*

The way Gerald Gull has it figured, it was Geraldine who brought him back to the Lord. That's the way he looks at it. If it weren't for her cutting him up, he never would've gone to Severn, never would've met Pastor Tracey, never would've been saved. He would've kept on with his bad ways, drinking and fighting, same as Geraldine is doing. There's the devil and the Lord inside Geraldine same as there is in everyone else. Only Geraldine gives the devil more room inside than most people.

This was how Gerald remembers Geraldine dragging him to the Lord:

She'd been off somewhere, same as usual, he didn't know where. She was always taking off on him. Claimed she was looking for a son named Alexander that was stole from her before they got married. She never told him about this son when they first met in the hospital in Sioux Lookout, where they were both getting their appendixes out. She never told him any of this until after they got married and came back to Niska and started having kids: five girls, the twins dead in the first year from weak chests. After they died, Geraldine started taking off outside. Looking for this son wasn't the only thing she was doing out there. She was stealing, fornicating, beating up on people. He knew this because the cops used to come looking for her after she'd done something wrong, used to think he was hiding her somewhere. Sometimes she landed in jail. She was in the clink for swearing at the judge, claimed she did it on purpose so she could spend the winter in jail, where it was warm and there was enough to eat.

The last time Gerald drank, before he was saved, Geraldine showed up with two bottles of booze. Whisky. He and Geraldine left the old lady by herself and went into the bush and started drinking. They went through the first bottle, and he got to roughing up Geraldine for taking off on him and treating him so bad. He messed her up pretty good. He made her so mad she broke the bottle and cut his forehead. It was only when the blood was running down his face and he couldn't see out of his eye that he knew she'd cut him bad. Geraldine dragged him out of the bush to Xavier's cabin and told Xavier to get a doctor quick.

Xavier took them to Severn in his canoe. The canoe had a motor on it, so they got there before dark. The doctor stitched up the cut, bandaged half of Gerald's head and told him he was lucky to still have his eye. He gave him some pills and told him to get some rest. When Gerald went outside again, Xavier was gone. There was no sign of Geraldine, either. Gerald had no place to sleep, so he went into the first building he came to, which happened to be the Fire Baptized Holiness church. He shoved four chairs together, lay down on them and went to sleep.

Mrs. Tracey found him the next afternoon when she came in to sweep out the church before evening service. Gerald heard something moving across the wood floor. He opened his good eye and saw a large white woman with huge tits, wire glasses and frizzy grey hair, holding a broom. She was wearing a dress with orange flowers on it and an apron on top.

"Good day, brother," she said. "Did you have a restful sleep? Looks like you had an accident."

Gerald got up and separated the chairs. He smelled the stink of sour whisky on himself. The woman passed close by, but she never said a word about how he stank. He went behind her while she swept, straightening the chairs in rows the way he figured they should go.

"Why, thank you," she said and smiled. There was a lot of shiny metal on her teeth. "I'm Thelma Tracey. What would your name be?"

"Gerald Gull."

"I've been here six months, Mr. Gull, but I've never seen you before."

"I live in Niska."

"Where's that?"

"Down the coast a ways. Came here for a doctor."

"Have you got a place to stay, Mr. Gull?"

"No." Gerald liked being called Mr. Gull.

"Come on over to our house and I'll fix you a good supper. Pastor Tracey would *love* to meet you." Mrs. Tracey spoke her words like they were furry animals and she was stroking their backs.

Gerald had never been inside a white man's house before, but he was starving.

Their house had four rooms: a kitchen, two bedrooms and a room for sitting only. Pastor Tracey was in the kitchen with his pants on a board, pressing them flat with a chunk of hot metal. When Mrs. Tracey walked in with Gerald, Pastor Tracey never blinked an eye. He acted as if his legs, white as two peeled sticks, weren't bare. Pastor Tracey was skinny and small, smaller than his wife. He, too, had grey hair, wire glasses and a smile as big as hers.

"Why, hello there," he said. He picked Gerald's hand up and shook it.

"Lester, this here is Mr. Gerald Gull from Niska."

"Welcome to our home, I'm sure," Pastor Tracey said. He took his pants off the board and pulled them on.

"Mr. Gull's agreed to stay for supper," Mrs. Tracey said. "Lester, why don't you and him go into the front room while I get supper fixed? It won't take long."

Gerald shuffled into the front room and sat down on the sofa. The pastor came into the room, took a wooden box off a shelf and showed Gerald his collection of home-made lures.

"This is the one I caught our supper on," he said. He handed the lure to Gerald. "Carved it when I was a boy in Arkansas."

The lure looked like a yellow banana with red spots.

"I didn't know it would be any good up here, but I've done good with it so far," Pastor Tracey said. He showed Gerald the other lures he'd carved, telling him where he'd used them, what he'd caught.

For supper they had fried whitefish, boiled potatoes, tinned peas, bread and butter. Mrs. Tracey opened a can of white stuff with frog's eggs in it that she called tapioca pudding. It was the best meal Gerald had eaten since he left the hospital where he'd met Geraldine.

When they were done, Mrs. Tracey said, "Why don't you two go over to the church while I clean up here? The books need laying out, and I never dusted the chairs."

So Pastor Tracey and Gerald went back to the church, laid out the books and wiped the chairs. Then Mrs. Tracey showed up in the same dress but without the apron. She was carrying an accordion. Gerald knew what it was because he'd seen one like it in the Bay store.

Some people came in, mostly women, six altogether, and one old man who had a limp and carried a stick. Pastor Tracey said hello to each one and shook their hands before they sat down. Gerald took a chair at the back beside the stove. The service began with them singing something about being washed in the blood of the Lamb. Mrs. Tracey pumped the accordion, smiling and singing. While she sang, she stamped her foot, the others clapped their hands. People sang so loud it sounded like the church was full instead of half empty. When the singing was done, the old man with the limp shouted, "Praise the Lord!"

"Amen, brother!" Pastor Tracey shouted back. Then he started telling a story about a bunch of men getting together to talk about the Lord Jesus Christ who was up in heaven. The men wanted to tell the good news about Jesus, but they couldn't do it, because they couldn't speak the different languages. While they were sitting around wondering what to do about it, a big wind came up and opened a hole in the clouds. Tongues of fire came through this hole and sat on people's heads. The people caught fire, or maybe their tongues did, Gerald wasn't sure which. Pastor Tracey said people got up afterwards and spoke in strange languages. They couldn't understand each other, but that was good because now they could go to places where people understood what they were saying and teach about the Lord Jesus Christ.

"They'd been baptized by the Holy Spirit!" Pastor Tracey shouted. "They were ready to do God's work!"

The old man screamed out strange words. He stood up, threw down the stick and flung himself on the floor between the rows of chairs. His eyes rolled and his body jerked and bobbed. Gerald saw his tongue between his teeth. He got up off his chair and tried to prevent the old man from choking himself.

"No! No!" Mrs. Tracey screamed at him. "Leave him lay where Jesus flang him!"

Gerald backed off. After a while, the old man stopped jerking and bobbing, and his tongue started working again.

"Praise the Lord!" he shouted. He stood up, shook both legs and walked around without his stick, as easily as a young man.

After that there was more singing about the Lamb of God dying for me. Gerald kept his eye on Mrs. Tracey, who was smiling and nodding at him, and on her big tits jiggling up and down. When they had finished singing, Pastor Tracey said, "Brothers and sisters, all of us here have got our struggles. We have problems. There's things we'd like to change."

"True, oh, how true," Mrs. Tracey said, and she rolled her eyes up to the ceiling.

Gerald felt himself nodding.

"We get thinking our misery will go on forever. Sickness, hunger, too much drink, there's all kinds of problems. Sometimes we got so many problems, we end up hating ourselves. Now, the Lord doesn't want us to do that. No, siree. The Lord God loves us. So He made a way out of all this trouble." Pastor Tracey smiled at Gerald. "All we got to do is repent of our wrongdoings and the Holy Spirit will come down on us and make us good as new."

Until now, Gerald Gull thought there was only one person inside him. He never guessed there was a better one in there, waiting to come out. This other one jumped to his feet and shouted, "I got drunk! I beat up on my wife!" He wasn't thinking only of the last time he'd done it, but all the other times he'd tried to knock Geraldine around. Oh, he'd been a bad man, a wicked, wicked man.

"You've been saved!" Pastor Tracey shouted back. "The Lord's taken away your sins. Praise Him. Praise Him!"

Mrs. Tracey kept on smiling.

Gerald sat down. He felt lighter, freer. The part of him, the old Gerald Gull, the part the devil liked, had flown clean away.

Gerald slept the next week in the church. Mrs. Tracey brought him blankets and a pillow. She fed him big meals. He had never had it so good. He didn't want to leave. The more he talked to Mrs. Tracey as she worked around the place with him helping her, the better his English got. Gerald figured that this was what gift of tongues meant.

The day after he'd been saved, Gerald was walking back from the Traceys' when who should he see but Geraldine. She was sitting on the rail fence that marked off the graveyard behind the RC church, glowering at him. One eye was swole up and both cheeks were greenish-yellow.

"I never should've done that to you," he told her. "I won't do it no more."

He figured she might say something about cutting him up, but she took the knife out of its sheath and held it up.

"Better not," she said, "or I'll finish you off."

"I been baptized by fire," Gerald said. "I'm safe in the arms of Jesus."

"Ha! I been baptized by fire also," Geraldine said scornfully, "but I ain't in the arms of no Jesus." She spit at him.

That night the RC church in Severn burnt to the ground, and Geraldine disappeared again for over a year. Two weeks after the fire, Pastor Tracey told Gerald they were going to paint the inside of the Fire Baptized Holiness church, so he wouldn't be able to sleep there any more. Gerald said he'd help, but Pastor Tracey said no, he should be moving on.

Gerald had only been back in Niska a few months when he started getting restless to be back with the Traceys. It was hard being strong when there was no one to pray with. And the way Gerald had it figured, the Lord had saved him *for* something. Trouble was, he didn't know what that something was. He figured if he got himself inside a church, any church, that maybe the Lord would tell him. So he started going to the RC church. The new priest wasn't like Pastor Tracey. Father Aulneau didn't smile, but went around stiff and straight like he had a poker shoved up his ass. There was no one like Mrs. Tracey with her accordion and jiggling tits. Brother Charlie had gone. There was only the priest. But Gerald kept going to mass. He always sat at the back near the window away from the women, across the aisle from Saul Crow. The only thing he liked about the RC church was the stories the priest told in Swampy Cree.

One story was about a man named Adam who had a wife like Geraldine who made a lot of trouble for everybody. Another was about a man named Noah who built himself a big boat — an ark, the priest called it. This boat, which was big enough to hold everyone in the village, was to save the people from a big flood the Lord sent. The day this story was told, Gerald kept looking out the window while the priest spoke.

He saw a bunch of clouds stirring themselves up outside, like a big wind was inside them. The clouds took on the shape of a face, a giant face with hollow eyes and a long nose and beard. There was a hole in the clouds like a mouth opening and shutting. It crossed Gerald's mind that this might be the Lord's way of talking to him.

Gerald Gull, the cloud-hole said, *I will build you an ark.* Did he really say that? Gerald waited and stared, but the hole filled in and the face disappeared.

Gerald left the church feeling better than he'd felt since he was in Severn. He went back to the gully and sat with Old Martha, waiting for the ark to appear, the same kind of ark the priest told them about. He kept walking to the river — that was where the Lord would put it — but there was never anything to see except the islands that had been there since Wesakaychuk put them there after the big flood a long time ago. Gerald went to mass regularly and took the seat by the window beside Saul Crow, but nothing more happened. A month went by. He figured maybe the cloud-hole hadn't spoken after all. Still, he kept watching the sky.

One day, when he was standing on the river bank beside the mission, he looked up and saw grey storm clouds approaching, riding fast on the wind. One of the clouds looked like a huge white stallion, the kind Pastor Tracey said would come on Judgment Day. Riding the stallion was the cloud shape of a bearded man carrying a spear which flashed lightning. Gerald waited, wondering if this was going to amount to something or whether it would disappoint him like the last time.

The cloud rider sailed right over Gerald's head. There was a clap of thunder that sounded as if someone was roaring at him: "Gerald Gull, why haven't you built my ark?"

If this was the Lord, he sure was mad.

"*Me*, Lord? I thought *you* was building it. I've been waiting since you told me you was doing it."

"You've done too much waiting already. That's why you're stuck in this swamp," the Lord rumbled. "You get busy and do the building. *I'll* do the providing."

"I need lumber," Gerald said.

"There's some coming. Meantime, use *that*." The spear flashed toward Brother Charlie's shed, the shed that had saws inside it and a huge pile of wood outside it, beneath a canvas tarp.

"That's RC wood," Gerald said.

"IT'S ALL MY WOOD!" the Lord thundered. "TAKE IT. BROTHER CHARLIE WON'T NEED IT. I SENT HIM TO SEVERN TO REBUILD THE CHURCH THAT BURNED DOWN!"

"Tools. I'll need tools." Brother Charlie had taken his tools with him.

The spear flashed again. "You'll get your tools."

"Nails. I'll need nails."

"You'll get them. What else?"

"That's all I can think of now," he said, then quickly added, "I'll need more things later on."

"Build the biggest ark you can," the Lord continued, "enough to hold everyone in the village. When you're done, I'll see to it you get enough water to take you to the Promised Land."

"Do I do all this by myself?" Gerald whined.

"NOAH DID IT, DIDN'T HE?" the Lord roared. The stallion reared up on its hind legs. "IF YOU RUN OUT OF ANYTHING, LET ME KNOW." The words blew down on the gust of wind. The clouds shifted and the Lord vanished.

After this there was no more waiting. The next day, enough wood for six cabins arrived from the government, but only John Bird and Henry Sutherland wanted their wood. The others told Gerald he could help himself to their wood, saying it wasn't worth building anything new in a swamp that flooded. Gerald started using Brother Charlie's wood also. He never told Father Aulneau about taking the wood. The little priest wasn't interested in carpentering and never noticed that the tarp was held up by empty frames. Gerald bought what tools he could with his government cheque. He used his mother's also, but it wasn't enough. He was always running out of nails, having to use bent saw blades. Then Geraldine showed up again, and Gerald started getting whatever tools he wanted, like the Lord had said he would.

9: "I think you fellas better get up here as soon as you can," George Kostiuk, the Bay manager, shouts into the office phone. It's a bad connection, and George wants the people in the store to hear what he's saying to the cops. One thing Indians are good at is listening. Soon, some of them will go away and tell others, who will tell others, and within an hour everyone in the village will know what he's saying on the phone, including Geraldine. He wants Geraldine to know she won't get away with it this time. He's just finished explaining to Sergeant Forbes how Geraldine walked off with a saw worth three hundred dollars and a cord worth seventy-five, then pulled a knife on him when he tried to stop her.

"Why can't you send in someone today?" he says. "What? . . . First thing tomorrow? . . . I'll count on that. There's something else you fellas should know. Geraldine assaulted the art teacher who came up here yesterday." George knows the teacher is in the store now, and he wants her to hear this so she knows somebody around here is making sure Geraldine will be put behind bars.

"You can bet your bottom dollar I'll press charges. All you fellas have to do is catch her." George knows you don't go around telling the OPP how to run their business, but he does tell them to bring their dogs. "She'll head for the bush. You'll never catch her without them. By the way, she may have a woman with her — Elizabeth Mack — but she's harmless, she wouldn't hurt a fly. . . . What? . . . Yeah, there's two of them here, but — " George doesn't want to come right out and say the band constables are as useless as ice cubes in winter, that they're no match for a hardened criminal like Geraldine Gull. He doesn't want to get on the bad side of people in the store. They're his customers. "The band constables don't have the proper equipment," he says to the sergeant. "You need the chopper and trained dogs." He and the sergeant talk for a while longer before George rings off.

He sits down at the desk. He feels bad about calling the cops. Most of the people in the village are quiet and law-abiding. They wouldn't steal so much as a package of matches. They're as lazy as sin, the men especially, from being on the dole for most of their lives, but they're good people. Geraldine Gull's the bad apple in the barrel. George knows the other Indians here don't like Geraldine. No one's told him this. Indians don't give out this kind of information to whites. But George notices that whenever Geraldine is around the store, people steer clear of her, except for Nazarene Rose and that half-wit, Elizabeth Mack.

He could kick himself for not noticing Geraldine and Elizabeth come in. They must have come in when he was in here getting the money out of the safe for Bernice Hunter. Her daughter Nina had sent her a cheque, and Bernice was cashing it. Geraldine and Elizabeth must have ducked down when he went up front. Funny that Ralph didn't see them go past. He'll have to ask him about that. Maybe Nazarene Rose had him rooting under the counter for something. She's got this trick of sending you off on a wild-goose chase every once in a while.

George Kostiuk has been in Niska six years. Before that he was in Sandy Lake, Moose Factory and Sachigo. Moose Factory was his longest stretch, nine years. During his first five years in Niska, Geraldine wasn't here much. It's only been the last year that she's stuck around. Before that she showed up every few months, stayed a while, then went away again. Since she's been back, George figures she has cost the store over a thousand dollars in stolen merchandise: jackets, sleeping bags, plastic sheeting, food and tools. The tools are for that evangelist husband of hers, who is building some kind of boat because he says the Lord told him to. George has never seen a boat like it, bits of this and bits of that. It certainly doesn't look as if it'll ever float. George was poking around it one day a few weeks back, searching for stolen tools. All he brought back was a level and a crowbar. Everything else was either too rusty or worn to bother taking back. There's no point going after the cord and the electric saw until after the cops get here. Geraldine will have them stashed away somewhere. Gerald must've wanted that saw real bad, because Geraldine usually waits until George has gone over to the house, leaving Ralph to tend the store, before she makes a move. Maybe she didn't do that today because Ralph chased her yesterday. George gave him a hard time about that. He told Ralph he thought he was too shy to look at a woman, let alone one as ugly as Geraldine. He teased Ralph about trying to impress the teacher until Ralph's ears went red.

George fills in his order list — which he forgot to do last night — and goes back to the store. There's only four people left. The others have gone, including the teacher. Jeremiah Crow's still here, sitting where he always sits, on top of the flour sacks, smoking even though there's a No Smoking sign tacked to the wall over his head. Most of the men hang around this area, behind the front door where they can see people coming and going. Most of them smoke. George has warned them about the sign, but they ignore it and toe their butts into the floor for Ralph to sweep up after closing time.

Jeremiah's granddaughter, Evangeline, is here also with her two boys, buying chips and pop. Evangeline's about twenty-five. She's one of those girls who went outside before finishing residential school, married a white man, had kids, and when it didn't work out, came back to live with her parents, Saul and Martha Crow. Because she has no status, she says she's just visiting, but she's been inside six months now and shows no sign of leaving. She's in here a lot with those kids. There's not much for them to do in the village, and the Crows only have a one-room shack. Evangeline's running to fat as most of these women do after they've had a couple of kids, but she has a pretty face. Keeps herself looking good: clean hair, plucked eyebrows, pierced ears. George has tried being friendly with her, but she's standoffish with him. Maybe she's had enough of white men.

George lived with an Indian woman for two years when he was posted in Sachigo. Her name was Marian Tait. She started off as his housekeeper, and pretty soon one thing led to another. What he liked about Marian was that she was easygoing and quiet. Merle, his ex-wife, nagged and complained so much she nearly drove him crazy. Never shut up from dawn to dusk, which was one of the reasons he came north twenty-five years ago. He wanted to get away from her and earn enough money so their boy could go to college.

George never finished high school himself. Bobby has already finished college and is an accountant in Edmonton. Now George is putting his money away for retirement. In another three years he'll be able to return to civilization and start a new life. He'll be fifty-five by then, young enough to start up a small business. He was thinking of buying himself a motel or cabins somewhere in B.C. where there's mountains, not flat like here. He might even get hitched again, if he found the right woman.

He never thought of hitching up with Marian. He's seen too much of Indians to get mixed up with them that way. Marry one and before you know it you've got the whole tribe camped on your doorstep. And it's bad for business. You need to keep your distance or you'll find yourself giving some people more credit than others and making unprofitable trades. George's supervisor has told him to use his own judgement when it comes to making trades. George sometimes takes caribou and moose steaks instead of cash. Moccasins. But you can only eat so many steaks, and he's already given moccasins and mitts to all his relatives.

The trade George would like to make is the polar bear skin the Chief has outside his cabin. A beauty, it is. The women did a good job cleaning and stretching it. A month ago the polar bear walked into the village and down the boardwalk. It was the first time George had seen a polar bear in the village. Usually the bears stay out on the ice. This one must've drifted ashore on a big pan. Xavier Hunter bagged it. Brought it down in one shot. Xavier's well up in his fifties and he's still the best marksman in the village. Best hunter, too. He's one of the few people here who isn't living on credit, so George isn't likely to get the polar bear skin. Whenever he mentions it to Xavier, Xavier doesn't answer. Pretends he doesn't hear.

George returns to the office and sits down at the desk. He hasn't touched the ledger in a week. He doesn't like it to get behind. Some people are way overdrawn on their next government cheque, and his supervisor said not to authorize expenditures over five hundred dollars or you can expect to write them off. George hates keeping track of these accounts. Some of the people here are in bad shape. He hates telling them they can't charge more until their cheque comes in, because he knows they won't eat much until it does. George opens the ledger and takes the invoices out of the top drawer. Better get the job over with. One good thing: there's only three more days before the end of the month and the cheques come in.

10: *June 27*

Dear Karen,

Back again. The big news is that the woman who slapped my face, Geraldine Gull, was shoplifting in the Bay this morning when I was there buying a pair of scissors. There were fourteen or fifteen people in the store: some men behind the door, Nazarene Rose and another woman in front of the counter. Ralph and the post manager, whose name I think is George, were behind the counter waiting on these women. There was a young woman with two boys and the blind woman and the old man whose faces I mentioned earlier. Geraldine was at the back of the store with Elizabeth, the retarded woman who was on the plane with me. I was at the back, too, in the hardware section, if you can call it that, looking for scissors. This Geraldine came right up behind me, reached over my shoulder and lifted a hammer off the tackboard. She did it so fast that by the time I turned around she had the hammer in her hand. For a second, I thought she was going to hit me with it. I ducked. Then I heard her laugh. I looked up and there she was, grinning at me, if you can believe it, with her brown and broken teeth. She put the hammer in a pocket. She had on a parka with deep pockets. The pockets were absolutely bulging. So were Elizabeth's. Then Geraldine picked up a hundred-foot coil of electrical cord, ripped off the plastic covering and slipped it up her arm to her shoulder. After that, she picked up an electric saw, a Black & Decker — it was the only one there — and walked up the centre aisle, Elizabeth following.

I'm not sure what happened next. I wasn't even aware that I was following her, but I must have because I saw Geraldine open the door and shove Elizabeth outside. The post manager came out from behind the counter and tried to stop Geraldine. She reached beneath her skirt and pulled out a knife. None of the men standing behind the door made any attempt to stop her. They just watched. Geraldine was crouched, legs astride, her shoulders slightly forward as if she was ready to spring, the saw in one hand, the knife in the other. She was so fierce, she looked like she would slit the post manager right up the middle. He backed up, cursed and told her he was calling the OPP. Geraldine bolted out the door and the manager went back to his office and phoned the police. The place was so quiet, you could have heard a pin drop. I paid for my scissors and got out of there.

I came back here and spent the rest of the morning making curtains. After lunch I took my sketchbook and a big stick I found under the cabin and went to the graveyard to draw the markers, plain wooden crosses, an easy subject, a good way to get my hand back. I'll never let myself get this rusty again. By the way, most of the names on the markers were French or biblical: Antoine, Jeannine, Joseph, Leah. A few were Scottish, left by fur traders, I guess. I saw people watching me as they went past on the boardwalk, but I pretended not to notice. One advantage of sketching is I can observe people without them minding. A camera wouldn't work up here; the people seem so shy that faced with a lens they would probably avoid me completely.

I was only in the graveyard a couple of hours when Father Aulneau came to get me. He said Nazarene Rose had bought the ingredients for the rice pudding and could I come and make it now. I nearly asked him how she would know what to buy if she couldn't make it, but I didn't; he seems easily offended.

I decided to go to the mission and get it over with. Sure enough, when I got there, I saw rice, tinned milk, salt, sugar, raisins, etc. lined up on the table. She even had a Pyrex dish set out. She sat beside the table and watched me while I mixed all this stuff up, speaking to her in that stupid, exaggerated way you do when you think someone's deaf or doesn't understand what you're saying. She understood all right. After I put the casserole in the oven (you bake it, right?), I turned around and saw Nazarene Rose laughing. She had a hand over her mouth and her shoulders were shaking. She stopped when I looked at her, even though I was grinning. I got the feeling she let me go through the motions to show me who had the upper hand.

Don't forget to send this letter on to Mum & Dad and ask them to send it to Bev. Be sure and write me back — soon. I'm bound to be lonely.

Love,
Willa

11: Geraldine's ready to leave the village. She has the food she and Elizabeth took from the store in a plastic bag, and a flashlight also. She found the flashlight behind the Sutherlands' shack. One of the kids left it out there in the bush. It's an Eveready and works good. She's not taking Elizabeth with her to the ridge. She took her to the hide-out once before and it worked out okay, but this time she's got to go alone. Tomorrow the cops will be after her with the chopper and the dogs. She's got to move fast. Elizabeth is like a little kid and doesn't always do what you tell her. She might do something stupid and then the cops will catch them. The cops aren't going to get Geraldine Gull. This time she's staying out of jail. It's summer, and she's got big plans. She's been making these plans since she came back inside. Since Alexander died, she's been lying low, waiting. Now is her big chance to move. She will ask the artist woman about it now, before she takes off.

Geraldine avoids the boardwalk and walks through the bush in case the band constables come looking for her again. She doesn't think they will come. They are leaving her for the OPP. Geraldine comes out of the bush behind the church, crosses the boardwalk, scoots across the grass to the mission cabin and tries the porch door. It won't open. She jerks harder, but the door remains shut. The artist woman has put something on it, a hook maybe. Geraldine didn't notice that when she was inside yesterday. She walks around the outside of the cabin and looks at the windows. Curtains — she has put yellow curtains on the windows. The curtains are closed. But there is a light behind one curtain. Geraldine bangs on the door.

"Who's there?" the artist woman says. She's come out into the porch.

"Geraldine Gull. Open the door."

"What do you want?"

"Open the door. I'm coming in."

There's a long wait while the woman's making up her mind. Geraldine hears the door being unhooked. She pulls it open, stomps inside and hooks the door after her. The artist woman looks scared. Geraldine brushes past her into the kitchen. There's a fire in the stove, an oil lamp and a drawing book on the table. Geraldine sits on the chair beside the stove, puts the green plastic bag on the floor and picks up the book. She looks at the pictures. The artist woman has drawn the crosses in the grave-yard. That is a stupid thing to draw. Alexander would not draw anything so stupid. Geraldine throws the book onto the table.

"What do you want?" the woman asks. She's standing in the porch doorway like she's ready to run away.

"I come to talk," Geraldine says, "before I leave the village tonight." She grins to show she's being friendly.

The woman comes over, sits on the other side of the table, on top of the woodbox.

"To talk about what?" she says.

"Alexander Bear," Geraldine says, and waits. This woman won't be much of an artist if she doesn't know about Peetanaquot.

"What about him?" the woman says.

"Have you seen his work?" Geraldine says.

"Yes."

"Where?" Geraldine shoots back.

"The Purcell Art Gallery in Ottawa. Risser's Gallery in Toronto. A couple of group shows on native artists. Why do you ask?"

Geraldine grins. This woman is somebody. Not a big artist like Peetanaquot, but somebody. She can be part of Geraldine's plan.

"How much money are his pictures worth now?" Geraldine asks. She knows people paid hundreds of dollars for a picture before Alexander died. But Alexander said the price would go higher because he was famous.

"It's been several years since I saw the show in Ottawa. I think his prints were going for about four or five hundred dollars then. But now, that figure has probably doubled." The woman adds, "Now that he's dead."

Geraldine stares at the kerosene lamp. There is a black spot on the glass where the flame has smoked. Sometimes Geraldine thinks Alexander did that to himself because he knew his pictures would be worth more money if he weren't here. She stares at the black spot so hard her eyes hurt. Then she says, "So, how much money?"

"I'd guess seven or eight hundred dollars for each piece. Those are original prints I'm talking about. I didn't see any of the paintings he was supposed to have done before he died, the larger acrylics. Those would probably be worth quite a bit more. Thousands maybe."

Geraldine tips back the chair, balancing her weight on the tips of her rubber boots, and grins.

"Why do you want to know about Alexander Bear?" the artist woman asks. Her elbows are on the table so she can hold up her head with her hands. She wants to know about Alexander so bad she forgets to be afraid.

Geraldine's never seen a face with so many brown spots over it. It looks as if someone shook a paint brush at her. And her hair sticks out like wings. Geraldine ignores the question. Instead she says, "Those places you saw Alexander Bear's work — what were they?"

"You mean the Purcell Gallery?" the woman says. "Risser's Gallery?"

"Gallery," Geraldine says. She was inside one of those places in Thunder Bay with Alexander. His pictures were on the walls. There was a big party, and everybody made a big fuss over Alexander. "How much is a gallery?" Geraldine asks.

"To buy one, you mean?"

"To make one," Geraldine says.

"I don't know," the woman says. "In a big city it would cost a lot, but in a small place, like a town or a village, not so much."

"That's what I think," Geraldine says.

"But you'd need electricity for lighting and to keep the gallery dry. Artwork has to be maintained at a certain temperature and kept dry to stay in good condition or it won't last."

Geraldine squirms uncomfortably on the chair. That is not so easy, keeping Alexander's work in good condition. That is why she's got to make her big move soon. The pictures can't stay where they are.

Geraldine stands up, picks up the plastic bag, goes through the porch and unhooks the door. She grins at the woman, who has followed her into the porch. Geraldine steps outside. As she crosses the grass, she hears the porch door close, being shut tight. The woman is hooking the door.

Geraldine goes to the river and walks along the edge of the embankment where she won't step on sleeping dogs. She is on her way to John Bird's. She doesn't like John Bird: he is brown on the outside, white on the inside. When government men come around, he sucks up to them. When John Bird's inside the store with Geraldine, he watches what she takes and tells George. When Gerald asks to use John Bird's ladder, he says no. She will take John Bird's canoe.

There's enough moonlight for Geraldine to find his canoe. Because it's yellow, she doesn't need a flashlight to pick it out from the other canoes that are turned upside-down on the embankment. Geraldine turns John Bird's canoe over and slides it into the water. She hears a dog bark from somewhere close to John Bird's cabin. Next to George, John has the biggest house in Niska — five rooms. The house is dark: he and Mary are in bed. The dog barks again, but no lights come on.

Geraldine takes hold of the rope and tows the canoe through the water. She intends to walk the canoe upriver until she is far enough away that she can start the motor without anyone hearing. When people sleep in Niska, the river noise is the loudest sound they hear. Geraldine tows the canoe nearly half a mile. All she hears is the river's voice and the *sssssst* sound the canoe makes as she pulls it upstream. There is no wind, no other voice but the river's.

Geraldine does not like the river's voice. It calls you. Over and over it says in its cold, sliding voice, *Come . . . Come . . .* She does not trust the river, which slides through the night like a black snake with white scales. There's snakes in the river, giant snakes that can twist around you, swallow you whole. The Mishipashoo are in the river also. Hundreds of Mishipashoo with lynx heads and serpent tails. Listen to the river, and snakes will pull you down. They will reach up and drag you underwater, holding you down so you can't breathe.

Geraldine stops walking. She gets into the canoe and pulls the starting cord. The roaring motor drowns out the sliding river noise. Geraldine sits in the boat and grins at the moon. She enjoys the rollicking bounce of the canoe as it skips over the water. The roar scares away the snakes and opens up the water behind her, showing a deep, empty V.

12: Willa lies awake, listening to the river. At the other end of the village, she hears a dog bark twice, then there's nothing except the sound of the rushing, sucking water. Moonlight penetrates the thin cotton curtains, illuminates the metal bed frame, the closet shelf, the wooden crucifix, Jesus hanging on the wall like a limp, bedraggled sparrow. For the third time since Geraldine's visit, Willa goes over their conversation. Why was Geraldine asking all those questions about Alexander Bear? Willa can see no connection between them. Bear's work has been described as sophisticated, elegant, polished — words that could never be used to describe Geraldine Gull. "As a stylist," Graham Ursell wrote in the *Ottawa Citizen*, "Alexander Bear uses lyrical lines to express emotion. His animal and bird designs are never static but always in motion. They flow on the paper like water or wind." Or words to that effect. This clipping is on file in Dick Simpson's office in Hull. Bear's file is one of a dozen Willa put together on native and Métis artists. Dick, who works in the publications section of the Communications Department in Indian Affairs, hired Willa on a six-month contract to assemble and design a desk calendar featuring the work of these artists. A short biographical note was included with each one.

Dick intended to sell the calendar to civil servants and politicians. If the first printing went well, he planned to seek commercial outlets, add cards and posters to the project. The profit, he said, would be used to build a scholarship fund for native and Métis art students. Unfortunately, the project bogged down from lack of funds. Dick had filled in the application without consulting any design or layout artists. The colour reproductions came in at twice the budget estimates. An application for more funds was turned down.

In the project file, there's a biographical note about Alexander Bear that Willa wrote. Willa can't remember reading anything that would connect Bear with Geraldine Gull. She remembers he lived in Toronto and Thunder Bay, that he lived in a series of foster homes as a child, that he was a self-taught artist who never finished school. This information was gleaned from the two interviews Bear gave. Willa recalls that it was difficult to dig up facts about Alexander Bear.

And this talk about a gallery. Surely Geraldine Gull wasn't thinking about opening a gallery in this backwater. Who would patronize it? It's not as if people would jet into the narrow little airstrip at the goose camp and take a boat six miles upriver to look at pictures. The idea is ridiculous. Geraldine Gull must have had something else in mind. Willa goes over this terrain again and again, circling, recircling. Finally, she gives up and abandons herself to the river's rushing sound. It picks her up and carries her, carries her far away. She drifts on top of the water like a cork or twig, while beneath the surface, questions about Geraldine coil and uncoil in the liquid dark.

13: Because she doesn't have to worry about Geraldine breaking in, Willa sleeps ten hours straight. She's awakened mid-morning by loud clattering in the distance. She sits up and lifts the curtain. The cloud cover is too low for her to see the plane. Willa slides out of bed and dresses quickly. She doesn't bother lighting the stove, but eats a peanut butter sandwich, drinks a cup of water, shrugs on her squall jacket and goes outside. Now she can see the helicopter. It's black and white, the OPP. The chopper follows a zigzag course over the tundra. People run out of shacks and cabins and look up at the chopper: men, women, children, two mothers with babies in cradleboards. By the time the helicopter is hovering over the grassy area in front of the store, everyone is outside, standing well back to watch and wait.

Willa stands close to the row of women, a little to one side. She notices the priest is absent, though his housekeeper towers over the other women. The Chief is in a second row with the men. A gust of wind from the helicopter blades sweeps past, but no one moves. The faces remain vigilant, impassive. The helicopter door opens, and two uniformed men jump out. Ducking low to avoid the blade, they run across the grass and shake hands with the Bay manager, who's waiting for them in front of the store. They go inside. The blade circles, recircles, stops. The watchers do not move.

14: Xavier takes out his paper and tobacco, rolls himself three cigarettes, puts one behind each ear, and the third he puts between his lips and lights. He looks through the smoke and sees two dogs inside the helicopter. That means one thing: the police will have to ask him for the bottle Geraldine Gull stole off Morris Mack. It has her smell on it. The dogs might need that to pick up her scent. Xavier knows how things work. He wasn't born yesterday. The police won't get anything out of Gerald. Though his wife cut up Gerald so bad Xavier had to take him to the doctor in Severn, Gerald won't help the police. He will pretend he's stupid and doesn't know a thing. The police will ask for Geraldine's smell. It will be Xavier. Xavier will do this because Geraldine is bad for the village. She causes trouble for the people here. Gives the village people a bad name. Anyone goes by Geraldine, he gets the wrong opinion of Indians. He gets the idea they are all the time drinking and fighting. Most Indians up here are not like that. Geraldine is not from this village. She only comes back because Gerald is here.

Xavier turns away from the watchers, walks to his house and sits on the back step to wait for the police to come. He will not go to them. George did not tell him he was bringing the police. George acts like *he's* Chief around here, not Xavier Hunter. George is okay sometimes, but he's got no respect for the people, no respect for the band police. How are Luke and Francis going to learn their job if they don't get a chance? George told the OPP to bring in dogs. They don't need dogs. Xavier can track better than dogs. Hell of a lot smarter also. He could find Geraldine quicker than those dogs. But he won't do it. The police bring in dogs, they can use dogs.

Xavier smokes all three cigarettes and rolls three more. He is rolling the sixth when the police come to ask him for the bottle. Luke or Francis must have told them about it. George didn't know about the bottle. George likes to find out what goes on around here, but no one tells him much, not even Lucy Bird, who works for him. Lots of things about the people George doesn't know. Xavier watches the policeman come toward him, a young man who looks like the boy George has working in the store instead of an Indian like they got working in Bay stores on some other reserves. Only difference is, this man lets a thin line of hair grow beneath his nose. Xavier puts his head down and rolls another cigarette, watching his fingers work the paper back and forth though he could do it blind. He doesn't look up until the policeman speaks.

"Are you Chief Hunter?"

"That's me." Xavier doesn't ask him to sit down.

"One of your people told me you have a bottle the Gull woman had in her possession recently," the policeman says.

"Yup."

"I wonder if I could have it? We need something she's touched to help the dogs pick up her scent."

"Yup."

Xavier takes his time lighting the cigarette. When he gets it going good, he stands up and says, "Wait here."

He goes inside the cabin, crosses to the bed where he and Bernice sleep, leans down and pulls a box from beneath the bed. This is what he calls his office box, where he keeps papers, letters from the band office. He lifts the bottle gingerly by its top and carries it outside and gives it to the policeman.

"Thanks," the constable says. "You'll get it back."

"Not mine," Xavier says. "I don't drink." Because he doesn't want the police or George or any kids to get their hands on it, he adds, "But you give it back afterwards."

Now that this has been done, Xavier walks alongside the policeman to the front of the store where the other policeman waits with the dogs. Most of the people are still here except the white teacher and the women who have gone home to feed their babies.

15: The dogs are Doberman pinschers. Soldier is an eight-year veteran, Constable Kulyk's pride and joy. Holmes is younger and more excitable. Twice within the last year, he has broken training and mauled his quarry. Both dogs stand obediently, sleek and well fed. Their ears and nostrils quiver as they look toward the bush.

At the far end of the village, a dog howls. This is answered by another dog at this end, in the bush. There are more howls and yips, not the mournful dirge of the church chorus but sporadic outbursts like gunshots. The two dog packs are signalling each other. There are two large dog packs in Niska on the outskirts of either end of the village. The remaining dogs occupy the ground between, roaming in small groups, shifting alliances. They are cringing, wary pariahs, easily spooked. When one of the large packs kills a dog for food, it is usually a dog from this uncertain territory. Unless driven by hunger, the dog packs avoid the middle of the village where Xavier's sled dogs are staked. Some of them have gone after Xavier's well-fed dogs and been shot. One of the leaders of these packs is a grey and white husky who used to lead Henry Sutherland's team before Henry got a skidoo and let his dogs go. The leader of the second pack is a grey, wolfish dog who was born in the bush. This dog howls, a long, drawn-out call, followed by three yips, a warning to the other pack that the new dogs are in his territory. The pack, nine of them, stands in the bush close to the river, all eyes on the Doberman pinschers.

When Constable Kulyk and Xavier Hunter come close, Constable Hicks points to the pack. He and Constable Kulyk have done this sort of work on other northern reserves and know what is required. Constable Kulyk takes his pistol from his holster and fires two shots at the pack, deliberately missing. The dogs yelp and disperse, run deeper into the bush. Constable Kulyk holds the rum bottle in front of Soldier and Holmes. The dogs sniff the bottle and then the grass. Constable Hicks unfastens each leash, and the dogs move eagerly across the grass, noses to the ground. Soon they are on the path above the river, the constables walking fast to keep up with them. Constable Kulyk keeps his pistol out of its holster in case they should come across the Gull woman.

Most of the people drift back home except for a group of young boys: Josh Hunter, his cousins, Marcel and Edward, Jake and Danny Gull, Richard Bluecoat, Eustace Bird. It is Eustace who notices his father's canoe is missing. He yells to the other boys, who huddle together near the remaining canoes. Josh, the oldest boy, yells to the police that the canoe is gone, but the police pay no attention. They follow Soldier and Holmes along the river bank to the point where the scent runs out.

* * *

16: Patrick Eagle sits in his canoe, hand on the throttle, eyes scanning the land on either side of the river. He has never seen the river so high at this time of the year. The marsh where the geese feed is so far underwater only the tops of the bulrushes show, like cigar tips bobbing up and down. Patrick's only seen it this high once or twice before in spring, after break-up, never this late in June. If this weather system keeps dumping rain on them, the village will flood for sure.

Patrick is two miles from the village, going as slow as he can with the current, which is so strong he only needs the motor to steer. Except for being hungry and curious about why the OPP helicopter was heading toward the village, he's reluctant to return to Niska. He likes it better upriver. He's built a small log cabin there, in the woods below the ridge. As soon as school was out, he headed for the cabin to unwind. Now he has to get back and see if the art teacher showed up. If she did, he'll get the classes going before the kids have time to get bored.

He spent all of last summer at the ridge, building his cabin. While he was there, Esther Crow and Rita Marie Wabano got into gas sniffing. Esther damaged her brain so bad she died from it. He still feels sad about that. This year he decided to get something organized to help keep the kids out of trouble. He applied for a government grant to pay an art teacher and buy art supplies. There's never been art lessons in Niska, so that fact alone should interest the kids. Patrick's often noticed Rita Marie and Rosena Sutherland drawing in their notebooks when he's been trying to teach them math. Marcel Hunter also.

Niska's a dead-end place, not much for kids to do here except get into trouble. Patrick's been saying this over and over since he came back two years ago to teach school. He's trying to get the people serious about moving to the ridge, where they can build better houses and facilities like a gym and sports centre. No point building anything like that in Niska. That is why nobody used the wood the government sent in for new houses which Gerald Gull got his hands on instead. No point building new houses or getting in electricity when it'll be swept away. There've been two major floods in Niska since Patrick was born: one in '55 when he was a baby, the other in '66 when he was away in residential school. His mother told him how she got out of bed one morning and stepped into water up to her knees. Twenty-seven houses got carried into the bush. People towed them back, set them on posts and staked the corners. Nothing to stop something like this happening again.

Three miles from the village there are two large rocks on the west side of the river. The larger of the two breaks the current, so that between it and the smaller rock there is a quiet pool where they sometimes catch whitefish. The pool is finger-shaped, narrowest where the rocks are close together. Patrick spots a yellow canoe wedged upside-down between these rocks. It's John Bird's canoe. Only yellow one in Niska. The others are brown, red or green. The canoe has a big hole on the bottom. Patrick can see that from here. He cuts back the throttle and steers his canoe toward the rocks so he can get a better look at the canoe. The hole is bigger than his hand when it's spread. There is something about the hole that makes him doubt it was busted by a rock spike. It looks like it was busted from the inside out. He could be wrong. Maybe from the inside it looks different. More likely a large rock smashed the bottom somewhere along the way. Though Patrick didn't see any rocks high enough to do that, it could've happened farther upstream. Maybe John Bird was fishing past the ridge and went overboard. If that happened, he's a goner for sure. People here can't swim. No place to learn. River's too cold for swimming. Patrick doesn't like John Bird, but he reaches into the icy water for the rope so he can tow the canoe. Could be Eustace Bird was using the canoe with one of the other boys.

As the river surges toward the river mouth, the canoe moves more swiftly. Patrick revs up the motor and steers a wide arc around the bend in the river bank, turning east toward the village. Ahead, on the path beside the water, he sees two cops, the OPP — he recognizes their uniforms. They have dogs with them, Dobermans. Who in hell are they tracking? Has this something to do with the smashed canoe? If so, why look for whoever was in it this far downstream? It doesn't make sense.

As he nears the store end of the village, Patrick sees a chopper in front of the Bay, a knot of people beside it. Beside the river is a bunch of boys. Patrick picks out Eustace, so he's okay. He sees Josh Hunter and his cousins, the Bluecoat boys. Then he sees John Bird. John wears a peaked cap, yellow like his canoe. The Dobermans come into the grassy area where the chopper is and start going in circles, noses to the ground. Eustace yells to the cops and points to the yellow canoe. He's so excited when he sees Patrick pulling the canoe that he's jumping up and down. By the time Patrick is cutting back the throttle and coming alongside, the boys are nearly in the water, each one wanting to be thrown the rope. Patrick throws the rope to Richard Bluecoat, who is quiet and never gets to be a leader. Richard holds the rope importantly while Patrick leaps ashore. Soon the boys are all over the canoes, hauling them onto the embankment.

The cops are waiting for him. The one with the mustache says, "Where did you get that yellow canoe?"

Patrick tells him. "You can see it's got a big hole in it."

"You see anyone along the shore?"

"Nope," Patrick says. "Who are you looking for?"

"Geraldine Gull."

"Didn't see her." Patrick shrugs. He should have guessed she'd be the one the cops were after. Goes without saying. Patrick's relieved it was her and not some kid who was in the canoe. Still, he probably wouldn't have told the cops even if he'd seen her. Wild as she is, he's got a soft spot for Geraldine. He figures it comes from being on the bottle himself. That was before he came back inside — he doesn't count the once or twice he's slipped since he's been back. One of the reasons he came back was to lick it, and he's licked it. It was hard to do, but he got off.

The cops ask Patrick a few more questions, then leave him alone. He picks up the sack with the trout inside and carries it to his cabin. He ran out of Nattie's bannock yesterday and his belly is growling for more. As he walks along the boardwalk, he starts thinking about John Bird's canoe. He'd feel bad if Geraldine drowned. Not many people in Niska would feel bad. Most of them want her to go away. The thing is, Patrick doesn't feel bad — more like uneasy, like there's something that doesn't add up. Maybe it's just that Geraldine's so loud and obnoxious, he thinks it would take more than a hole in a canoe to wipe her out.

17:   Nattie Eagle sits in front of the window and keeps her sightless eyes trained on the door. She heard Patrick's canoe motor coming toward the village, heard two boys shouting by the river, Eustace Bird and Joshua Hunter. She cannot see, but she can hear better than most. Now there are many voices together; she picks out Patrick's. Soon he will be coming in the door. She has the bannock waiting and soup she made from the rabbit Xavier gave her last week. Maybe Patrick will bring more rabbits today.

After he has eaten, she will tell Patrick about Geraldine Gull stealing from George. Nattie was there talking to Lucy Bird when it happened. She felt Geraldine go by on her way to the front of the store, heard the store manager shout, felt the air move when Geraldine opened the door and pushed Elizabeth Mack outside. She will tell him about the plane the police came in, the plane Lucy says looks like a big dragonfly. Patrick will see it because it is still here. She will tell him about the artist woman. Lucy says she has red hair and an ugly spotted face, like she has brown measles. Lucy has a bad tongue in her head. Lucy once said Patrick looked like a heron, with his long skinny legs. Now she cannot say enough good about him because she wants him for Bernadette, who is outside studying to be a nurse. Bernadette is a good worker. Not like some girls who smear their faces with paint and complain because there is no TV in the village. Bernadette is better for Patrick than Nina, who thought only of what clothes to put on her back and married a white man.

Nattie does not like the white artist woman being here. She told Patrick she did not like it when he spoke of bringing her inside, but he said it will be good for the kids. Said he tried to get an Indian teacher, but she backed out, so he was stuck with this one. This is the first time a white woman has lived in the village. This is the first time Wapusk walks down the boardwalk in summer. This is the first time the river is so high this time of year. The omens are strange enough without a white woman getting herself mixed up with the people.

18: Constables Kulyk and Hicks leave in the early afternoon. They swing out over the bay, then head upriver, flying low over the water, looking for signs of the Gull woman. The chopper puts down twenty-five miles upriver at a place called the ridge. John Bird advised this. He said his people often camped at the ridge. Once he saw the Gull woman down here. Constable Hicks doesn't expect to find the Gull woman here. He thinks she's drowned. Constable Kulyk isn't so sure. He things the hole in the canoe might have been a put-up job. He also thinks that if the Gull woman gave them the slip, they won't find her. Even with the dogs, they won't. Indians up here know how to disappear in this wilderness. Nevertheless, it won't hurt to give the place a quick once-over. At the very least, he can file this lead in his report.

19: Willa didn't wait around after the police left with the dogs, hot on Geraldine's trail. She figured it would take hours for them to track down Geraldine. She went back to the cabin and addressed an envelope, thinking she'd ask the police to mail her letter to Karen. Then she changed her mind, deciding instead to send the letter on Thursday's plane.

Since George mentioned the word "assault" on the phone, the police may want to question her, and Willa's decided to play down Geraldine's attack. She won't press charges. It was only a slap. Nothing was broken except her glasses. She doesn't know how people up here feel about the incident. Though they're afraid of Geraldine, they might resent a white visitor making a fuss. After coming all the way up here, she doesn't want to risk losing her job. She needs the money. Willa knows that her not wanting to press charges has to do with the fact that Geraldine's an Indian, that if she were at home in Ottawa and a white stranger hit her, she would report it to the police at once. She suspects this discrepancy is the collective guilt many whites feel toward Indians. It annoys her that she should feel this, that she should think Indians need special treatment, that she would react to them differently than she would someone white. After all, she doesn't have anything to do with their problems, she didn't create them. She's simply an artist who came here to do a job for the summer. Period. She has no intention of becoming involved with their problems.

Willa has always thought her attitude toward Indians was open-minded. Not for her the stereotype of Indians as silent, sly, shiftless, uncommunicative and unreliable. This open-mindedness wasn't difficult to sustain. Before working on the art calendar, Willa never had much to do with Indians. She never thought about them one way or another. Having lived in small New Brunswick towns where there were no Indians, she'd never even seen one until she moved to Ottawa. Even there, those she saw on the street looked no different from the political crowd. When she looked closely at native-Canadian art, there was no stereotype. The sophistication and elegance in Bear's stylized prints, the confidence and energy in Morrisseau's bold paintings, the eloquence and vision in Hunt's Haida designs cancelled old myths and made new ones. It's the new ones that have brought her up here. She's looking forward to seeing the images the kids come up with.

Willa's sitting outside the cabin on the chopping block, sketching. She hears the helicopter motor, hears the clattering blades. She looks up and sees the chopper rise over the village and zoom out over the water. She tries to see if Geraldine is aboard, but the helicopter is too far away for her to see anyone but the pilot and one of the policemen. She returns to her sketch, which is of a dog who seems to have adopted her. When she first saw the dog huddled against the door yesterday, she thought it was a pup. Except for the short fur, it looks like a husky. It's grey and white with a neck ruff, pointed ears and snout. As she sketches the dog, studying the mature genitalia and the coarseness of its fur, she realizes it's a runt, a dwarf. The dog is a good model. He sits against the porch door, motionless except for his ears. Willa finishes the sketch, a quick study in charcoal. Then she goes inside for a pencil so she can make a more detailed drawing. She comes back outside and sits on the chopping block, not far from the dog, and hunches over her sketchbook.

For the past five minutes, someone has been standing six feet behind Willa, watching her. He's a tall, thin man in faded jeans and a T-shirt, wearing horn-rimmed glasses and long black braids. The centre part makes his face appear more egg-shaped than it is. Acne has pocked and cratered his skin. This gives him a ravaged, wounded look.

He stands there, sizing up the new teacher before she notices him. From her back, he sees that she's a medium-sized woman about his age, wide across the beam and narrow across the shoulders. She has wild red hair, the colour of a golden retriever. There's no ring on her finger, no jewellery, nothing like that.

When she turns sideways to look at Agnes Sutherland walking down the boardwalk, he sees she wears glasses, same as him. He shoves his hands in his jeans and saunters toward her.

She looks up, startled. "Oh," she says, and the sketchbook slides to the ground, "I didn't hear you." She picks it up.

"You're Willa Coyle," he says. "The new art teacher."

"Yes, and you must be Patrick Eagle."

"Right. I see you got here, no problems."

"Well, I wouldn't say that." She stands up and hugs the sketch-book close to her chest. "The main thing is that I got here," she says. "When do classes start?"

"Any time. Tomorrow, the next day, whenever you want." Patrick looks at the sketchbook, then at the runt, but she quickly closes the book.

"Would you like a cup of coffee?" she asks.

"Sure."

Patrick watches while she nudges the runt aside and opens the door. Then she tips the dog into the porch and goes inside. It's a mistake bringing this dog inside, but Patrick doesn't say anything. White people make a big fuss over dogs wherever they are.

He follows her inside, straddles a kitchen chair and watches as she pokes the fire and adds more wood, knowing the watching makes her nervous. She drops the stove cover on the floor, then tries to pick it up with a bent coat hanger that she uses for a poker. The lid falls off the hanger, so she picks it up with her hands, which get smeared with soot. She wipes the soot on her jeans. Patrick likes that. He told Dick not to send in one of those ivory-white types. She fills the tin kettle with water, puts it over the opening, then sits on the other chair.

"How many kids will I be teaching?" she asks.

"I have twenty-six in my class," Patrick says, "but you won't have that many. All of them won't come."

"Your class," she says. "Are you a teacher?" The surprise is written all over her face.

Patrick notices her glasses are taped on one side. They keep falling down her nose. Twice already, she's pushed them up.

"Did you think these kids were being taught by nuns?" he says.

"I didn't know."

"Yeah, well, there's more and more of us teaching our own people," Patrick says, "which is the way it should be."

"Of course," she says, very polite.

"But I'm lousy in art. I have my hands full with the basics," Patrick says. "I think the kids need something different during the summer."

"Have they had any drawing lessons?"

"Nope, but some of them draw on their own."

"How often do you want these classes?"

"Every day except Sunday. Mornings only."

"Good. Then I'll do my own work in the afternoons."

"I think we should divide the kids into two groups," Patrick goes on. "The older kids fom age ten and up. There's about seven of them. There'll be about twelve in the younger group. You'd rotate each class every second morning. How's that sound?"

"Fine."

Patrick watches her jump up to check the kettle and sit down again. Her boots clomp heavily on the plywood floor.

"How do you want to be paid?" he says. "At the end of the month, or every two weeks?"

"Two weeks."

"If you give me your ticket and any other travel expenses, I'll reimburse you now," Patrick says. "By the way, did you get the paint and the extra paper? I told Dick to ask you to bring more stuff inside. We don't have much."

"I brought a carton full of supplies."

"Better give me the receipt for that while you're at it."

Willa goes into the bedroom. When she comes back with the receipts, Patrick takes out his cheque book and writes her a cheque. Willa puts a mug of instant coffee in front of him, sugar and tinned milk.

"I assume we'll be using the school," she says.

"Right. I'll take you over afterwards and show you the set-up." Patrick moves to the top of the woodbox so he can put his feet on the chair. "So, how's Dick?" he says.

"You know him?"

"Sure. He's been inside several times visiting. Last time he was here, he took pictures of the goose camp for a brochure."

"I worked on that brochure," she says. "It's all ready for the printers. It should be finished in a couple of weeks."

Patrick doesn't say anything. He's not sure the brochure is such a hot idea. The goose camp has been full every year without them doing any advertising. If they get more hunters, they'll have to turn them away. Dick's not so bad, but like so many others in Indian Affairs he's got his own ideas of how to spend government money.

"Did the dogs track down Geraldine Gull?" Willa asks.

"Nope."

"When I left the Bay, the police had picked up her trail."

"Yeah, but they lost it again. She took off in a canoe."

"So now they'll look for her on the water."

"Nope. I found the canoe she took off in. It was empty. There was a hole in the bottom. The cops figure she drowned."

"Drowned!" she says, as if she can't believe it. "Are you sure?"

Patrick shrugs. What's it to her? "The cops are," he says.

"I'm sorry to hear that," she says, "in spite of the way she greeted me when I arrived. Did anyone tell you what she did?" She tells Patrick about Geraldine Gull on the embankment. She shoves her glasses back up her nose. "That's how these broke."

She stops talking and waits. Does she expect him to pat her on the back and give her a medal? There's hardly a person up here Geraldine hasn't roughed up one way or another. "They look okay to me," Patrick says.

"She came to see me last night," Willa goes on. "She was just the opposite, very friendly. She asked me how much it would cost to start a gallery. Then she asked me about Alexander Bear."

"Who's he?" Patrick says.

"Don't you know? Alexander Bear was a well-known Indian artist."

"That's what I'm paying you to know," Patrick says. He hates it when someone expects him to know something he doesn't, especially when that someone is white and a woman. He's got a good education, better than most, but there are big gaps in it that make him feel stupid sometimes. He puts the mug on the table. "I'll have more coffee."

This time she only puts hot water in his mug. She pushes the jar of instant toward him. He notices that her tits are small and pointed.

"Help yourself." She sits down and says, "Alexander Bear was Ojibwa. He died a little over a year ago."

"Geraldine's Ojibwa," Patrick says. "She's not from here. Originally she came from a reserve farther south. Until last year, she wasn't here much." He spoons coffee into his mug, adds milk and says, "Of course, neither was I. I left here when I was ten to go to residential school. After that I was in Thunder Bay, Toronto and Calgary." Patrick wants this teacher to know she's talking to someone who's been around.

"Doing what?"

"Taking courses. Teaching."

"Geraldine asked me how much Alexander Bear's pictures were worth," Willa says. "I got the impression she had some of them in her possession, though she didn't say that. I could be mistaken."

A few months ago, Patrick had heard Geraldine bragging to Xavier about having a son who was a famous artist. Xavier ignored her. He doesn't like Geraldine. He calls her *kesquakan*, crazy person. Geraldine claimed her father and grandfather had both been Chiefs. She said her grandfather had spoken out against the treaty and refused to sign. Geraldine was usually on the bottle when she was bragging like this, so Patrick didn't believe her, either. Maybe there was some truth in what she said after all.

"So this Alexander Bear made a name for himself," he says.

"That's right. He wasn't as big a name as Norval Morrisseau, but he might have become one if he'd lived. If Geraldine has drowned, we'll never know why she was asking about him."

Patrick thinks about the hole in the canoe. He wouldn't put it past Geraldine to bust John Bird's canoe with a rock and set it adrift to throw the cops off her trail. If she did that, he knows where she is.

"Maybe she hasn't drowned," he says.

"You think she's still alive?"

"Could be," Patrick says evasively. He doesn't want to tell this white woman too much, but that conversation she had with Geraldine intrigues him. Who knows? It might lead to something.

Willa smiles.

Patrick notices her teeth are small, even, perfect as a baby's teeth. He avoids smiling himself. His teeth are too large and too white. He's only had dentures for two years, and he's not used to them yet. Most everybody inside wears dentures except for the little kids, who are checked by the dentist who flies in twice a year to paint their teeth and warn them about the dangers of too much candy and pop.

"Where would she be?"

"You wouldn't know even if I told you," Patrick says. He takes his feet off the chair and stands up. "Come on. I'll show you the school."

Outside the cabin, he says, "Hey, don't say anything about this Alexander Bear or the fact that Geraldine may be alive. Don't tell the priest, for instance. You wouldn't believe how fast the grapevine works up here. Faster than smoke signals."

"Why not?"

Patrick shrugs and opens the schoolhouse door.

"I've got a key to this door. So has the Chief. But we never use them. You can get in here any time. You won't need a key. We never lock doors up here."

20: *P.S. Patrick Eagle showed up today. He's about my age, attractive in a bruised sort of way. A teacher. Well-spoken. Been south a long time. Came back recently, I gather. Very intelligent. I think I'm going to like him. By the way, Geraldine Gull took off in someone's canoe. The police are after her for stealing the saw and the cord. Patrick Eagle found the canoe. It had a big hole in it and no Geraldine. He said the police think Geraldine drowned, but he seems to think otherwise. Classes start tomorrow morning. I have afternoons free.*

P.P.S. Did I tell you the arm on the glasses broke when I was slapped? I thought of asking you to send me a new one, but I Scotch-taped this arm back on and it's holding up fine.

Love,
Willa

21:   Geraldine's hide-out is in the woods at the top of the ridge where she can see the field and the river below. Behind her are solid woods, trees that go all the way to the lake. She built this hide-out last year so she'd have a place to put the pictures that was away from everybody. And she wanted a place to come also. Sometimes she's got to get away from that dump called Niska with its sleepy Crees and stink of piss. Here the air smells clean.

The teepee is made from poles Patrick Eagle left when he was cutting logs for his cabin last summer. She dragged them here and built this teepee, tying the poles at the top with rope. She uses a roll of plastic she stole off George to make an inside cover to keep out rain. She wrapped the suitcases containing the pictures in plastic to keep them dry also. She put spruce boughs over the outside of the teepee so it looks like it's part of the woods. The woods are so thick an army could hide up here and no one would see it.

Geraldine hears the chopper coming upriver. She goes outside and walks along the ridge to a place where trees have been cut down and she can get a clear view below. She stands behind a clump of waist-high bushes and keeps her eyes on the river. Soon she sees the chopper come into view. It's on the other side of the trees that grow on top of the river bank. As the chopper clears the trees, Geraldine takes off her red beret and ducks into the bushes. The chopper moves over the trees and comes down in the clearing. The door opens and two cops get out with two black dogs. If someone has told them about her hide-out, she'll have to go through the woods to the lake. At the end of the lake there's a cave above the water where the dogs can't go. If she makes a run for it, she won't take the pictures with her. The suitcases would slow her down and the branches would scratch and tear the plastic covering.

She watches to see what the dogs do. They are sniffing the grass. Round and round they go, but they don't get her scent. Geraldine Gull's too smart to leave her scent down there. After she set the canoe free downstream, she walked east, then came through the woods above the ridge to make sure there is nothing of Geraldine Gull close to the water. Down there where they are looking is John Bird's trapline. Up here is Patrick Eagle's trapline. His cabin is below her at the bottom of the ridge. She doesn't think John Bird knows about her hide-out. Only person who knows is Patrick Eagle. If he told John Bird about it, she is a goner for sure.

The cops come toward Patrick's cabin. The dogs also. Geraldine braces herself in case she has to run quick. But the cops walk once around the cabin, look in the window, and then they go back to the chopper. Geraldine grins. Patrick didn't tell. Maybe John Bird told the cops to come here because once he saw her by the river getting a bucket of water. Geraldine watches the cops walk along the enbankment above the river. Back and forth they go, then they get into the chopper. Geraldine waits until she sees the door close. Then she backs out of the bushes and crawls fast between tree stumps and low bushes until she reaches the cover of the woods. She ducks into her teepee and stands there, heart pounding fast, listening for the sound of the chopper.

The chopper doesn't fly over the ridge. It rises in the clearing, flattening the grass with its wind. It swings sideways, over the trees, then clatters noisily upriver. Inside the teepee, Geraldine listens as the sound gradually disappears. The plane is going outside, flying to Sioux Lookout, the place where Alexander was born.

TWO

1: *June, 1947.* The precise spot where Geraldine left the bush was a road construction camp three miles outside of town. By the time Geraldine had reached the rocky slope overlooking this camp, she was as thin as a willow tree, her long hair matted and coarse. Her eyes burned huge and dark above the hollows of her cheeks. This gave her a wild, hungry look. Her sack of flour had run out months before. She'd been surviving on the occasional snared rabbit and some dried venison she took from a white trapper when he was away from his cabin. Farther on she met up with a small band of her people, but they were sick and starving because there was so little food. After spring break-up, when the snow melted and leaves came on the trees, she left them and moved on. She kept moving until she came to the slope.

Geraldine looked down at the clearing where people were camped in long white boxes. The camp was empty: there weren't even dogs in this camp. Remembering the trapper chasing her with a gun, Geraldine was careful. She collected fir branches, made herself a sleeping cave beneath an overhanging rock. Then she sat down and waited.

Just before dark, she heard a rattling sound. She saw men driving into the camp in big machines. They got out of the machines and went into the white boxes. Lights went on inside. After a while they came outside and put food in big shiny tins they kept behind the boxes. Geraldine was hungry, but she didn't go down the hill that night. She waited until morning, until after the men had driven the machines away and the camp was empty. Geraldine crept down the slope toward one of the shiny tins. She looked around, waited, then lifted off the top. Inside the tin were chicken bones, egg shells, coffee grounds, orange peels. Geraldine ate the food quickly. She didn't know what some of it was, but it filled the empty place inside her. Later, when she was back in the woods, she gagged and spat it on the ground. The next day she did better. She found bones with meat on them and one potato.

The third day, after waiting until after the men had gone, Geraldine went down the hill. She was bolder this time, knowing she had all day before the men came back. She was careless lifting a top from its tin. The lid slid from her hands and clattered noisily to the ground. Geraldine heard another sound. Before she could run, a man came out of the smallest box in his bare feet and waved a gun at her. He told her to go inside. The woods were too far away for her to make a run for it, and there was the gun, so she did what she was told.

Once they were inside the box, he told her to sit down. Geraldine sat on a chair beside a table. She rubbed her arms to stop herself shivering. It wasn't cold inside, but she was shivering. The man gave her a cup of coffee he heated on a small stove. Before he gave it to her, he poured whisky into the cup. The whisky burned her throat, but it made her stomach warm. She stopped shivering. She took another swallow and made a face. The man laughed at her and drank some whisky from the bottle. Geraldine took another swallow and pulled the red beret over her face. After she'd drained the cup, the man filled it again. Then he gave her bread and eggs. Geraldine saw he wasn't so bad, that he wasn't going to use the gun on her. She moved out of the woods and into the box.

Vince had lots of food. He fried her meat, potatoes, eggs, gave her coffee and whisky whenever she wanted it. He had a closet with warm water inside, bought her clothes in Sioux Lookout. He never asked her to do anything except keep him warm at night. Vince was big and heavy. He had black hair, black eyes, skin whiter than hers, a pale Indian. He told her his father was white but his grandmother, Kills On One Side, was a Blood Indian from a reserve farther west. She was the daughter of Chief Standing In The Snow. Geraldine was pleased to know this, to know the baby Vince started inside her had the blood of two Chiefs.

Two months before Alexander was born, in March of the following year, Vince left in the truck and didn't come back. The road construction crew had moved on and he was following them. He said he'd already stayed with her longer than he planned. He gave her one hundred and fifty dollars and told her she could have his trailer, he didn't want it any more. He showed her where the hospital was in Sioux Lookout and told her to get there before the pains started — that was where women went to have a baby. Geraldine's mother had run through the bush when the pains started, until the women took her to a special teepee. Here there were no women and no teepee, so Geraldine did what Vince said.

By the time Geraldine had walked the three miles to the hospital, the baby was ready to be born. It was early morning. Soon after he came out, a black-haired baby, pale like his father, Geraldine was wheeled into a room with a big window in it. She looked out the window and saw a cloud coming toward her over the fir trees. It had a pinkish-yellow light from the rising sun around its edges. That was why she called her baby Peetana-quot, clouds rising. She didn't put this name on the piece of paper the nurse brought. There was beauty and promise in the name. It would be spoiled if she put it on the paper. Instead, she printed in large letters, ALEXANDER BEAR. Geraldine remembered Alexander from one of the stories the nuns at residential school had told her. The stories of Alexander the Great, Charlemagne, Joan of Arc, were the only things she had liked about school.

When she got Alexander settled back in the trailer, Geraldine returned to Sioux Lookout to buy baby clothes, a blanket, some food. She did this twice before Vince's money was gone. By then she'd become used to the insides of stores. She knew how to get baby sweaters, diapers and pants outside without paying money. Before she went to town, she fed Alexander and waited until he was asleep on the bed. Then she went out on the road and stuck up her thumb the way she'd seen other people do.

One day, a man with no hair on his head came by and asked if she wanted a ride. When Geraldine got inside the car, he told her he'd give her ten dollars if she'd do him a favour. Geraldine didn't know what he meant by this, but when he explained, she said yes. It looked like an easy way to get money. The man drove down a side road and parked in some bushes. They didn't even get out of the car but did it on the seat. Then the man drove her into town. Before she got out of the car, the man gave her ten dollars. Geraldine thought she was doing okay to get a ride *and* ten dollars, but the man said, "Listen, whatever-your-name-is, let me give you some advice. Don't do the favour until you get the money. Not every man's as honest as I am." Then he drove away.

When Geraldine worked the streets in Sioux Lookout, she followed the man's advice. She worked in town for over a year before the cops started hassling her. But she learned to disappear quick when the cop car came in her direction. She got enough money to buy Alexander a red snowsuit, a pair of shiny brown boots also.

Alexander was a good baby and didn't cry when she tied him in the bed before she left for town, fastening the bag she'd made for him around his middle so his arms were free and he wouldn't choke. His dark eyes watched her steadily as she tied the rope around a wall hook and a chair back, as if he understood she was doing this so he wouldn't hurt himself.

One afternoon, a man in a Texaco cap showed up at the door and said, "Our company bought this land. We're building a service station out here soon. We don't allow squatters. You'd better get a move on. If you're not gone in two weeks, we'll tow your trailer away."

After he left, Geraldine bundled Alexander into his red snowsuit and put him in a sled she'd made for him out of a cardboard box. She went down the road asking people if she could move the trailer onto their land. No one said yes. Two slammed the door in her face. One wouldn't come to the door but peered around the curtains at her.

At first Geraldine didn't recognize this reaction as fear. It was only later, in Winnipeg, after she'd seen one of those stupid cowboy shows with braves yelling and leaping off horses, dragging people into the woods and scalping them with knives, that Geraldine learned how afraid whites were of Indians.

When the Texaco man came back two weeks later, Geraldine told him she was selling the trailer and moving away. She got seven hundred dollars for it, enough to take Alexander and her as far as Winnipeg, where she got two rooms for them to stay in. With the rest of the money she bought a bed, a crib, a table, food and some white-children's toys she saw in the Bay store. Nothing was too good for Alexander Bear.

2: *February, 1953.* Geraldine Bear was leaning against the dirty window of the Chinaman's café, trying to keep the weight off her feet. She wasn't used to high heels, but she did better with them on. She was wearing a dress she got from the Salvation Army store. It was red like her beret. And she had a blue sweater also.

Geraldine thought about her money to keep herself warm. She had two hundred dollars under Alexander's mattress, fifty inside a sack of flour, seventy-five in her dresser drawer. She had sewn two fifty-dollar bills inside her beret. Most nights she did real good, two or three men sometimes, if it wasn't too cold. Tonight wasn't so good. There was a cold wind blowing. Geraldine shivered and pulled her sweater close. She kept a close eye out for cops. Cops everywhere in this city. Nosy people. Trouble-makers. Four times she and Alexander had to move on account of neighbours complaining about her bringing men back to her place. One woman threatened to report her to Children's Aid for leaving Alexander alone so much. But Alexander didn't mind. Most of the time he was busy drawing pictures.

The money Geraldine was saving was to take Alexander and

her back to the reserve. Alexander was five, almost ready for school. She didn't want him going to a white city school and get treated like a dog. Alexander was friendly. He'd get kicked around too easy.

Geraldine saw two hookers standing across the street in front of the theatre, the same theatre where she'd seen that stupid cowboy-Indian picture. The hookers were wearing fur coats, fake fur, not like the fur coat her mother made for her when she was small. But she'd take fake fur now, she's so cold. She shoved her hands inside her sweater sleeves and looked at the shiny green leaves in the window. It was a lemon tree with no lemons on it. There were pieces of folded paper on the tree. They reminded Geraldine of the birds she used to see in the bush. The Chinaman told her his little girl had made them. Geraldine looked at the birds instead of the hookers. She used to work in front of the theatre. That was her spot before those white bitches came along and started pushing and shoving her, saying it was their spot, if she didn't get out, they'd sick their boss on her. Geraldine moved across the street to the Chinaman's. No pimp was telling Geraldine Bear what to do.

People started coming out of the second show, stepping onto the yellow pavement in twos and threes, putting up hoods and collars against the wind, pushing up the sidewalk, heads down. The last one to come out of the theatre was a small man in a long blue coat and a hat pulled over his face. He walked fast, with small steps like a ptarmigan when someone chased it. He went past the hookers and came across the street. When he was on the sidewalk in front of her, he said, "You free?" He looked at his boots.

Geraldine could tell he wasn't used to it. Maybe this was the first time. She took him by the elbow and, wobbling along on her high heels, steered him to her place.

Her place was on the second floor. She held onto his arm in case he changed his mind. One man did that. She let go only long enough to get the key out of her dress pocket.

Inside, she kicked off her heels and stuck out her hand. "Pay first."

"How much?"

"Twenty dollars."

The man gave her the money, and Geraldine put it in the top drawer with the other money.

"Toilet's down the hall," she said.

The man left. Geraldine went into Alexander's room. He was asleep on the floor. Every night he took his blankets and slept on the floor in front of the window, his head on the rug she got for him. On the floor beside him was a box of crayons and a picture of a moose. Alexander was always drawing animals. He had drawing paper, paints, brushes, coloured chalk. Whatever she could steal, Alexander had. Quietly, Geraldine closed his door and turned the key.

The man came back, and Geraldine went down the hall and washed herself down there. She always did this for white men. Then she went back to the room and took off her sweater and dress. She did not take off her beret. She lay down on the bed and spread her legs. The man got on top of her. He didn't take off his glasses or his socks. It was over real quick. After he got dressed, he thanked her. White men were funny that way. When he was gone, Geraldine put on the dress and went down the hall. She was going to get warm in the bathtub. She ran hot water, got into the tub and looked at her body, sleek as a muskrat's. Then she closed her eyes. There was a loud banging on the door.

"Hey, you in there!" the voice said. "Get out! I need to piss."

The man in the room next to her. Pestering her again. Crabby old drunk.

Geraldine felt like running the water so she couldn't hear him, but he'd make more noise if she did, and the landlady had already warned her about noise. She pulled the plug, got out of the tub and slipped on her dress. Then she opened the door, shoving him out of the way as she passed. Nosy old bugger.

"Didn't clean the tub, I bet," he said. "Hoor."

He'll piss on the floor. Next time she's in there, she'll step on it.

She went down the hall, opened her door and closed it before she saw one of the hookers sitting on her bed smoking a cigarette. The bitch's legs were crossed; there was a red smear on her lips. She had grey-white hair that looked like dirty smoke coming from a train. And there was another hooker behind her. Geraldine swung around and saw a red-haired bitch with snake eyes leaning against the door.

"We come to tell you something," Snake Eyes said. She put her arm around Geraldine, but Geraldine pushed her away.

"We want you to move off the strip," she said. She stuck her face close to Geraldine's. "Got it?"

Geraldine stood there, feet astride, silent. *Alexander must not wake up.*

The bitch's hand came around her shoulder again, red nails digging into her flesh. Geraldine tried to shove her away, but the nails dug deeper.

Smoke Hair got up off the bed and shoved her knee into Geraldine's back. She put both hands on her shoulders and pushed her flat against the floor. Snake Eyes sat on Geraldine's belly. She slapped Geraldine's face on both sides. Back and forth, her head wobbled, back and forth. Geraldine tried to scratch out the snake's eyes, but Smoke Hair got hold of her hands and pinned them down. She was strong. Geraldine was strong but not strong enough. She tried arching herself up off the floor, but Snake Eyes wriggled off her stomach and sat on her crotch. She bounced on it. Then she slapped Geraldine's face again. Hard.

"You're pretty," she said softly, "real pretty. Some men like your type, but our boss ain't one of them. He's got a thing about squaws. He told us to get rid of you. You'd better go. You stick around the strip, he'll come after you. Beat you up. Leave you for dead in some alleyway. You won't be pretty any more. Got it?"

Geraldine stared at her, wild-eyed, mute.

"I figured you'd see it our way." She winked at Smoke Hair,

who let go of Geraldine's hands. Geraldine made a grab for the red hair, but Snake Eyes was too quick. She got up fast and kicked Geraldine in the leg. Then she went to the drawers, opened the top one and took out Geraldine's money.

"Thanks," she said and went out the door. Smoke Hair kissed the air as she followed Snake Eyes outside.

For a long time Geraldine lay on the floor holding herself, rocking. She began to moan.

She heard the bathroom door slam. She heard the old drunk stumble down the hallway, thumping against the wall as he went. There was no sound from Alexander's room. She got up from the floor, listened at his door. Nothing. He was still asleep.

Geraldine put her hands on her cheeks, which burned from the slaps. She felt the inside of her mouth. A side tooth was loose. She locked the door. She didn't look in the small mirror she kept on the top of the drawers, knowing the worst was someplace she couldn't see. She began to pull her hair, her voice keening tight as a bowstring inside her. She pulled and pulled, rocking and keening.

All that time those white bitches slapped her around, she never screamed or yelled. They kicked her, they slapped her, they took her money, and she lay on the floor and never said a word. She was Geraldine Bear, and she never opened her mouth.

3: "What happened to your face?" was the first thing Alexander asked her in the morning. She told him she fell down the stairs. Then she cooked him some eggs. During the night, she had decided to move them to another place, but first she was going to the Bay store to get Alexander a winter jacket. Sometimes Alexander came with her to the stores, but this time she was going alone. She told Alexander to stay inside and make a picture. Then she put on the raincoat a man had left behind. It was too big to work in, but good for hiding things under, which was why she sometimes wore it to the stores. She picked up her paper shopping bag, took two pins from the drawer and went outside. It was freezing, and her leg hurt where she'd been kicked, but she walked, coat held close, to the Bay store half a mile away. It was Saturday. The store would be crowded and busy, nobody would notice her. She already knew which jacket she wanted for Alexander. It was brown with a furred hood, gold buttons down the front, a gold deer stitched on the top pocket. When she got home, she would take Alexander for a walk in it, buy him a hotdog and pop, ice cream also.

Geraldine pushed her way through the crowd in the women's wear department, shoving shoppers aside as if they were overgrown bushes in her path. She slowed down only when she saw the brown jackets still on the rack in boys' wear. Geraldine stopped in her tracks and looked around.

The clerks were busy at the place where they took the money. There was a thin man in a grey suit not far away, but he wasn't looking in her direction. There was a woman on the other side of the rack looking at snowpants, taking her time. Geraldine glared at her, willing her to hurry up, but the woman went on pushing the hangers sideways one by one.

Geraldine turned around and looked through the pants stacked up on the counter behind her. She did this carelessly, messing up colours and sizes. Alexander didn't need pants yet. When she turned back, the woman had gone. Geraldine glanced at the grey-suited man, but he was still looking the other way. Quickly, Geraldine jerked a brown and gold jacket off the hanger and shoved it into the shopping bag. Then she sauntered past the counters, pretending to look at underwear, pyjamas and shirts. She drifted into girls' wear, cut across women's wear and headed for the toilets.

Once inside a cubicle, she ripped off the tags and flushed them down the toilet. Then she took off the raincoat, wrapped the jacket tightly around her waist so it wouldn't slip down the back, crossed the sleeves over each other and pinned them to the front of her dress. She put on the raincoat and buttoned it up. She shoved the hanger into the garbage bin and looked at herself in the mirror above the sink. She looked fat around the middle, as if she had Alexander inside her belly again.

Now for mitts. She picked up the shopping bag and went back into the crowd, threading her way through women's wear and girls' wear to boys' wear. She saw the mitts piled on the table. She began riffling through different colours. Gold was nice but got dirty fast. Green was pretty also, but the green mitts were too big. She picked up a pair of brown wool mitts. Before she slipped them into her shopping bag, she looked up and saw the grey-suited man staring at her. She put the mitts back and began sorting through the pile again, waiting him out. She tossed the mitts left and right. Two pairs fell to the floor. The man walked toward her, hands folded behind his back. When he came closer, Geraldine saw "Hudson's Bay Co." printed on a bar in gold letters pinned to his jacket pocket. The man picked up the mitts, put them back on the counter without looking at her. Quickly, Geraldine dropped the brown mitts into her shopping bag and walked away.

This time she went through infants' wear, where she spent a long time looking at carriages, strollers, toys, highchairs and bottle warmers, things Alexander had never had, before making for the stairs. She knew she should go into the toilet and flush away the tags from the mitts, but she wanted to get out of here fast. It was stuffy and her leg hurt. She couldn't be bothered going to all that trouble for a lousy pair of mitts. She went through the big doors, and two uniformed cops came for her, one on either side, moving in silent as wolves.

Tagged and numbered, Geraldine was dragged through the crowd to a small, bare room where the grey-suited man was waiting for her. Terror flip-flopped inside her chest, thrashed about in the red water, squirmed on a hook, then sank helplessly to the bottom, a dead weight.

She couldn't make them understand about Alexander, that he had no one but her to look after him. She wailed and keened, pleaded to be let go. She pulled her hair. She wept. It wasn't enough. She promised she'd never steal again. She offered herself to Grey Suit for free, right there on the floor — anything, as long as she could go back to Alexander. But Grey Suit wanted something else. One of the cops, a pale man with a blond mustache, asked Grey Suit if he wouldn't consider dropping the charges this one time, considering the boy. But Grey Suit said no, he was pressing charges. The Bay had been watching this woman for months, knowing she was stealing from them. Now that they'd caught her red-handed, they weren't about to let her go. It was obvious she was a criminal, the kind of thief who would continue to steal unless she was punished.

Geraldine went wild. What did Grey Suit know about her, this man who wore a shiny gold badge on his jacket? What did he know about where she came from, who she was, where she was going? What did he know about the son who'd grown inside her — the boy who was waiting for her in a room half a mile away? Geraldine Bear got up on her hind legs, opened her mouth and roared. She pawed Grey Suit, raked her claws across his face. She would have clawed out his eyeballs and swallowed them, but the cops pulled her out of the room and drove her to jail. The blond cop told her she was allowed one phone call. He advised her to phone Children's Aid; he had the telephone number in his desk drawer. They would send someone over to get her little boy. They'd make sure he'd go to people who would take good care of him while she was in jail.

When the Children's Aid woman came on the telephone, Geraldine shouted at her to take good care of Alexander, he was a good boy and wouldn't make trouble. She gave her the address, told her she'd find Alexander on the floor of his room drawing a picture. She was to walk in slowly so as not to scare him and tell him his mother had told her to come, that he was to go with this woman and wait for her, she must make sure to tell him Geraldine would be back for him.

After she'd been in jail a week, the blond cop showed up with a box of her things. The landlady had kept the beds, the drawers, the table and chairs, and all her money, to pay for back rent. In the box was her knife, which she was stupid not to take to the Bay store. The cops wouldn't let her keep the knife, only the sheath. There was one of Alexander's pictures. There was nothing else of his — they'd taken it all. The picture was of a big brown moose with wings coming out of its sides. This wasn't a picture Geraldine had seen before, so she knew it was the picture he'd been making while he was waiting for her to come back.

Geraldine curled up on the metal bunk and slept through the winter. She woke long enough to eat the food the guards brought — porridge, toast, soup, sausages — then she went back to sleep. Inside her, dreams lay dormant, flattened by the weight of the snow. She grew fat.

In the spring, after the snow had melted, the cops opened the cage and let her go. Geraldine took the picture off the wall, went outside and sniffed the air, the leaves on the trees. She took a fifty-dollar bill from her beret, went to a hardware store and bought a knife.

It didn't take her long to find the Children's Aid office, to roar at the woman sitting at the front desk that she had to talk with the woman who spoke to her on the phone the day the cops took her away. The woman at the desk lied. She said the woman wasn't working in the office any more. Geraldine roared at her again and was taken into an office where a man in a brown suit with pink hands and two chins sat in the big chair behind a desk. He told her Alexander had been placed in a suitable foster home where he was being well cared for. He said she should be pleased that they had found him a superior placement. Fuck the fancy words, Geraldine growled, she wanted her son back now. The man said that wasn't possible, the foster family didn't live in Winnipeg any more, they had moved away. Geraldine took out the knife. She wasn't stupid enough to cut him up. She remembered what the blond cop told her — that if she hadn't clawed Grey Suit, she would have been out of jail sooner. She only wanted to scare this man into telling the truth. She tested the knife tip with her fingers to show him how sharp it was.

"Put that thing away," Brown Suit said.

"Tell me where Alexander is."

"I'm not at liberty to tell you. You should realize this is for your son's good. We are thinking of his best interests, whether you realize it or not." Brown Suit folded his pink hands on the desk. "Now, if you don't put that knife away and leave peacefully, I'll call the police."

Geraldine began to track herself in circles, always coming up on her own tail. She tried six churches, three of them RC, but each time she was told to go back to Children's Aid. She began to haunt parks, hanging around swings and slides and wading pools. Once she saw a kid who looked a bit like Alexander, but only at first. The kid was a different kind of Indian, from a country called India. Soon the second fifty-dollar bill was gone, and she was back at work. Now she was free to work anytime, night or day. She didn't need a place to stay, but moved around, worked different streets. She began to think maybe what Brown Suit said about Alexander not being in Winnipeg any more was true.

She drifted to Kenora, Fort William, Sioux Lookout. With no kid to drag around, she could go anywhere she pleased, work or not work, it didn't matter. She hung around bars and cheap hotels until she picked up a trick or a drinking partner, sometimes one and the same. More often she drank alone, taking the bottle with her to park benches, under heating vents, inside culverts. If anyone bothered to ask — which was seldom — why she was slowly killing herself, she'd laugh scornfully and say, "Me, kill myself? Crapshit." She wasn't killing herself. She was having too good a time.

4: Sometimes Geraldine landed in the hospital. If business wasn't too good and it was cold outside, she'd fake a pain in her belly so she could go to the hospital where there was warm water, beds, and they brought you food on trays. One day Geraldine got a pain for real, a bad pain low in her belly, and was taken to the hospital. A man in a green dress lowered a mask over her face and told her to breathe in. Geraldine would have wrestled him, but he had her tied to the table with thongs. The mask came over her nose, and she could not push it away. Geraldine inhaled something so heavy and warm she thought thunderbirds were trying to suffocate her.

When she woke up, a nurse told her they had cut her belly open, taken out something rotten called an appendix and sewed up the wound. It took a long time for the cut to heal. Geraldine got bored inside the hospital and walked around the hallways. This is how she met Gerald Gull, who had had his belly cut open also and an appendix taken out. They got out of the hospital the same time. Gerald wanted to marry Geraldine and take her back with him to this place called Niska. Geraldine figured she had nothing to lose. It was winter, and she did not feel like being cold on the street. She married Gerald and moved to his reserve.

The next winter, Joan was born. Then Teresa. Annie. Later, the twins. The twins died before they could sit up, of bad coughs. The girls grew up and went away. Joan to Winnipeg, Teresa to Yellowknife, Annie to Big Trout, where she lived in a fancy house with a man named Louis Webique. Geraldine was stuck with Gerald and his old lady, who never spoke. Quit talking ever since Gerald showed up with Geraldine. Stupid Cree. Same as the others in Niska. They all turned up their noses when she came close, except Elizabeth Mack, who had nothing but empty space inside her head, and Nazarene Rose, who used to go over to the air base with Geraldine. That was years ago, before Nazarene Rose started working for the priests.

Gerald Gull liked his liquor. Used to be he'd drink with her. When they got a couple of bottles, they'd go into the bush, get drunk as skunks and pass out of this world. Sometimes Gerald would try to rough her up, but she'd belt him back and he'd quit.

The last time they got drunk, Gerald was set to beat her up. They hardly got started before he was walking around, swinging his fists. Geraldine was sitting on the rock holding the empty bottle when he came at her, both fists punching her face. She slid off the rock and onto the grass, pulling her knees up under her while he pounded her back. Geraldine saw blood on the ground. She spit out a tooth. There was more blood coming from her nose. She saw that she was still holding the bottle by its neck. She broke the bottle against the rock, swung around and shoved the top half of the bottle into Gerald's face. He quit pounding. Blood spurted out of his forehead and covered his eye. He swore, then sat on the rock and cried like a baby. Geraldine tied her sweater around his head, yanked him to his feet and dragged him back to Niska. She dragged him all the way to Xavier's door and told Xavier to get a doctor. Xavier took them to a doctor in Severn.

After she knew Gerald was fixed up, Geraldine didn't stick around long. Two days after the fight, she got a ride back to Niska with Johnny Mack, who'd been visiting his girlfriend in Severn. Geraldine didn't stick around Niska, either. After a week with the old lady, she faked a bad pain in her head. She groaned and carried on so they wouldn't send her to a rinky-dink nursing station but a hospital outside. They sent her to Sioux Lookout, where the doctors poked at her and asked questions about her broken nose and teeth. They told her they could do nothing for the pain, they would have to send her to a bigger hospital somewhere else. The game was up. Geraldine said the pain had gone away, and they let her go.

Geraldine went to the Friendship Centre to see about getting her government cheque. She wasn't going back to Niska. Maybe this time she'd never go back. While she was waiting for someone to talk to about her cheque, she wandered around the centre and into the room where they had a store. There were moccasins, mitts, mukluks made of caribou hide and trimmed with beadwork, purses, vests fringed with leather — stuff they had tried to get her to make in jail, but there was no way she would ever make that two-bit stuff — key chains, coasters, necklaces, earrings, belts.

On the walls were pictures in bright colours painted by an Indian named Copper Thunderbird; Geraldine could read the syllabics. Pleased that these pictures were done by an Ojibwa, Geraldine moved in for a closer look. There was a picture of a shaman with a thunderbird on his head and creatures with black beaks and claws inside his stomach. There was a picture of a man with snakes wrapped around him. Geraldine stayed away from that picture. But she kept walking around the gallery. There were pictures of men with big pricks, women with cow tits. There was a sacred medicine bear, loons, ducks, a picture of a Mishipashoo, the water god with the lynx head and the serpent tail. Her mother used to tell her stories about how the Mishipashoo lived in the deepest parts of rivers and lakes. She came to a big picture where thunderbirds were fighting underwater snakes. The thunderbirds looked angry, but the snakes with their evil eyes looked worse. Geraldine beat it out of there fast.

She went back to the office and sat on a chair. A young Indian who said he was Randy Moonias came into the room and sat behind the desk. He had long hair and beads around his neck. He spoke to her real soft and slow like she was one of the old ones. Geraldine put up with it because she wanted money. Randy told her it would take a month to get her government cheque, maybe she'd better find some work to keep her going. He knew a bakery where they needed someone to clean for a couple of hours early in the morning after the bakers had finished and had gone home to bed. It was mostly washing baking sheets and pans and mopping up the floor.

Geraldine took the job. A long time ago she had done some cleaning for a white woman in Kenora. The woman had a big house and spoiled kids who dirtied the floors as soon as she got them washed. All the time the woman was yammering at her to clean them over again. After three or four times, Geraldine quit. The bakery was different. There was no one to get on her back, she had the place to herself. Plus there was stuff to eat. The bakery owner had told her she could eat the culls — that was what he called the split loaves, broken cookies and flat cakes he couldn't sell.

The bakery job lasted six months, longer than any job she'd had except when she'd worked the streets. It was warm inside the store. There were the culls, and the owner never treated her like dirt. At night, before work, she went to the bar, but she never got plastered. She knew why the bar was called the Zoo. Geraldine wasn't acting like a stupid animal to give white people a laugh. Whenever she wanted to get blind drunk, she went into the woods behind the Texaco station out where Vince's trailer used to be. The rock floor of the cave where she'd once holed up was split in the middle; it was in this cleft that Geraldine hid her whisky.

The bakery owner paid her once a week. The day before she was fired, a soft Indian summer night, Geraldine took ten dollars from her knife sheath and went to the bar for beer. The Zoo was crowded and noisy, which is why she went. Sometimes all she wanted to do was sit there and let that noise run through her head like water, ice-cold water that numbed the inside of her head to a standstill landscape of snowdrifts, polar bears and ice. But no matter how much she drank or how long she sat there, the water inside Geraldine's head never froze. The river flowed through her head, dragging along mud, broken limbs, rocks; all that crap she could never be free of kept jamming her head like a log boom.

Geraldine positioned herself at the table closest to the side wall so she could entertain herself by seeing who was coming in the door. She knew them all by sight. It was the young men who got most of her attention. See the bulge on that one, she'd crow, looks like a coiled-up snake inside his pants! Wooeee! Or she'd make a remark about their hair. It was like a beauty contest, watching them. Two braids, one braid, long hair with headband, short and straight, long and scruffy as a dog's ass. One with both sides of his head shaved and a long pigtail down his back.

This night started the same way as the others. She watched the young men slouch into the bar, peaked caps pulled low over their eyes, girls hanging onto their arms, jeans tight over their asses like stretched caribou hide. The men sat down and tipped back their chairs, paying no attention to the waiter, who did not bother wiping up the beer that slopped onto the table when he slammed down the mugs.

About midnight she was getting around to leaving. She had a sleeping place staked out, an old car in the alleyway behind the bakery — if she got there too late, Harry Cutfoot would beat her to it. She drained the last of her beer and looked through the doorway. A young man was coming into the Zoo. He was tall and thin with hair to his shoulders, one side tucked behind his ear to keep it out of his eyes. He was wearing jeans, a T-shirt and was carrying a sheet of plastic under one arm. Geraldine squinted through the fog of cigarette smoke. The young man was pissed; she saw that, saw his arm go out to the wall to steady himself. Like a blind man he felt his way to the bar and sat on an empty stool, tenderly, as if he would hurt it by putting his weight on it. Then he took off the plastic and held up a picture. Slowly he turned himself around on the stool until he faced the others.

"Anyone want to buy a picture by Alexander Bear?" he yelled. People were hooting at each other across the room, making catcalls. No one heard what he said, including Geraldine.

"Alexander Bear is a great young artist," he shouted. "Got a wonderful future. That's what the critics say. His work is in big galleries all across the country. Private collections. Oil company offices. He's everywhere." He stood up and dangled the picture in front of the people sitting closest to him. Two girls looked up and giggled. He shoved the picture under their noses. "This is your chance to get a great painting at a bargain price. If you don't take it, you'll be sorry some day. After I'm famous."

"Shove off," one of the men said.

By this time Geraldine was on her feet, pushing past chairs and tables. She was too fat to squeeze through narrow openings between tables. If a sitter wouldn't move, she tipped his chair forward so that his body was pitched onto the table, knocking over beer glasses, jolting butts out of ashtrays. She paid no attention to the curses following her. The young man was given a shove. Geraldine caught him before he hit the floor. He grinned at her foolishly as if he was surprised to see someone coming to help him. Geraldine sat him on the stool and stood close so he wouldn't fall off.

"The picture," she barked. "How much you want for it?"

Whenever she thinks back on this moment, like now, Geraldine is certain she knew right away who he was. She knew as soon as he came in the door. She knew, though she had pushed him downriver, out of her mind, had tried to forget all that crap about a kid who drew pictures on the floor. Long ago she had burned the picture of the moose that had been on the wall of her jail cell.

"Whatever you can give me," he said. "This artist has pictures all over the world. People pay big money for his work. Buy this picture and you've got an investment for the future." His eyes followed the bartender as he talked.

Geraldine jerked his elbow off the counter.

"Show me the picture," she said.

He was about to lay the print on the counter when the bartender said, "Not here. The counter is for drinks."

So the print was held up for Geraldine to see. It was another flying animal, a large bull caribou with antlers spread like wings. Alexander was still drawing crazy animals that flew. As soon as she saw the signature at the bottom, Peetanaquot, there was a booming sound inside her head like river ice at break-up. She snatched the picture from Alexander.

"Careful," he whined, "you'll wreck it."

Geraldine took him roughly by the arm.

"Forget the picture, we're getting out of this dump." She could hardly breathe, and the smoke was so bad she couldn't see.

"Give me back my print or pay me," he said.

Just like a baby. She covered his stupid picture with the plastic sheet and shoved it at him.

"I want a drink," he said.

"You'll get a drink," she told him. She grabbed him by the arm.

He followed, half leaning on her. Just like Alexander. Always trusted people, stupid enough to follow anyone. She pulled him along so fast he stumbled into the passing waiter.

"Out, you two!" The waiter pointed to the door.

Geraldine gave him the finger. No chickenshit waiter was getting in *her* way.

On the street, Alexander became suspicious. He pulled away from her, swaying.

"Why should I come with you?" he said. "Who are you?"

Geraldine felt like telling him to stuff it, leaving him there to look after himself. Instead she gave his arm another jerk. "C'mon, there's lots of booze where we're going."

He stumbled with her along the streets and out onto the highway. She steered him to the left side of the road, facing oncoming traffic where cars could see them. Indians had been killed on this stretch, some by accident, some like Alexander, who looked like he'd lie down in the middle of the road if she'd let him. Except for the occasional pair of headlights swinging past, there wasn't much traffic. The sky was moonless, dark. Geraldine marched forward; she was afraid that if she stopped, if she looked around, she'd see all the streets and roadways she had ever walked on. She was afraid she might see Alexander behind her in his cardboard sled. There was no way she was turning around, there was no way she was pulling that goddamned sled again. She pushed them forward through the dark night, both of them blind as bats.

Alexander seemed too drunk for thinking, for knowing who she was. And she wasn't going to tell. Fat body, crooked nose, broken teeth, what would he want with a mother like her? And what did she want with a son who looked like he couldn't wipe his own ass? The girls, Joan, Teresa, Annie, they knew what was what, that in this stinking world it was no use counting after number one. So how come this one turns up like a bear cub that was sent up a tree and wouldn't come down, stayed up there bawling like a baby?

She should have left him in the Zoo. Left him alone with his stupid picture. Because now she's got a picture inside her head that wasn't there before, a picture that's stuck up there and won't come loose no matter how much she drinks. It's jammed up there so deep there's no way she can shake it loose.

There are two people sitting in the dark beneath an over-hanging rock. They are leaning against the cave back, passing a whisky bottle back and forth. They do this for a long time. Then the young man begins sucking on the bottle and blubbering about his mother, since he's been five years old he's been looking for her. Did she know anyone by the name of Geraldine Bear? After this, the picture gets fuzzy, like it's raining. Even though the cave is dry, it's raining inside the picture. On the other side of the rain Geraldine can make out two blurred figures, a man and a woman. They are sitting close together, rocking and laughing, rocking and laughing, holding each other in the deep, dark woods.

THREE

1: Looking out the plane window at the roadless map unrolling below, you see shadows of cloud moving across the river, spreading over the muskeg, staining it grey. The shadows look like the ghosts of giant animals drifting above the land. You see lakes that look as if they have been made by the paws of a giant Wapusk as he roams the land in search of food. You see the cold blueness of Hudson Bay, the horizon blocked with rotting pack ice.

Once you are on the ground, diminished by the divided emptiness of land and sky, you become Wapusk's quarry. You become a black speck on the horizon. There is only you and Wapusk, there is only the gun between you and Wapusk. You must never forget the gun. You must never forget that Wapusk sometimes comes off the ice and roams your shore. When you are picking over what's left of the dump at the goose camp or hunting ptarmigan on the islands, you must never forget Wapusk might be there, stalking you. Like a shadow of a cloud, he spreads across the land, staining it the grey-white of unbleached bones.

2: Willa looks at Rita Marie's painting, which is a huge bear with a human head. The bear is standing on its hind legs, its claws extended. Its face has a gaping hole for a mouth, fang teeth, hooked nose. Inside its body is a large, dripping heart. The legs and arms of the bear are hollow tubes filled with piles of white bones.

"What is that?" Willa asks.

"The wendigo," Rita Marie says. "It eats people."

Rita Marie is the last person Willa would have expected to create such a painting. Rita Marie, who is twelve going on eighteen, comes to class wearing tight jeans, earrings, eye shadow and lipstick. In the first class she drew girls with high-heeled shoes and curled eyelashes from pictures she had seen in magazines. She drew the same girls in the second and third classes, the fourth and fifth. Today Willa asked the class to paint their dreams. "Your worst nightmare," she told them.

Rosena Sutherland, a shy, pale girl who looks as if she has spent her childhood inside a convent, has painted a house going up in flames. There are three kids trapped inside, their mouths open, their arms raised above their heads. There are no parents in the picture.

Only two boys have shown up today: Josh Hunter and his cousin, Marcel. Originally there were six boys in this older class, but after the first day, Baptiste Bird, who is fifteen, didn't return. Mark Wabano, Rita Marie's older brother, didn't return, either. Today is the first time Danny Gull and Eustace Bird have missed.

Josh has painted a boy out in the bay, standing on an ice pan surrounded by floating ice. He is shouting for help, but no one on the shore hears him.

Marcel has painted geese. This is what he's been painting and drawing since classes began: geese taking off, geese in flight, landing, nesting, feeding, swimming. Today he's painted six black, white and grey geese flying against a bright blue sky.

"No nightmares?" Willa asks.

He shakes his head no.

None of the kids say much to Willa. Sometimes they make comments to each other in Cree. When Willa's explaining something, her hands dart through the air. She makes faces. The kids think she is hilarious. The girls giggle, the boys grin.

"What is the wendigo?" Willa asks Rita Marie. "A monster or a ghost?"

"A monster," Rita Marie says.

"A bear monster or a people monster?" Willa says.

Rita Marie shrugs. "Both."

"A ghost," Josh says, speaking with his father's quiet authority, "is what they have in England."

3: From Xavier's notebook:

This is the story of Sakchekapo.

In the old days, Sakchekapo used to camp with his family on the shore of the great bay. Every winter when it got cold and windy, Wapusk would walk across the ice. Sakchekapo would come out of the teepee and see Wapusk coming close, his head swinging this way and that. Sakchekapo would take his gun and kill Wapusk. His wife would cut up the meat and make a blanket from the fur. The kids grew healthy and strong.

One year, Wapusk did not come. The caribou did not come. It was a bad year for animals. Sakchekapo took his gun and went hunting far away, leaving his family behind. He was gone a long time. When he got back after break-up, his family was okay, except one of his kids was gone. The wendigo got him, his wife said. Wapusk came off the ice while they slept and dragged the smallest one away. That summer, Sakchekapo's wife had a new baby.

The next winter, the same thing happened again. No Wapusk, no caribou. Sakchekapo left his family and went away to hunt. When he came back after break-up, the smallest kid was gone. It was the wendigo, his wife told him. That summer his wife had a new baby.

The third year, the same thing happened, except this time Sakchekapo came back early. He saw his wife before she saw him. She had the polar bear skin pulled over her head, and she was outside chopping up the smallest kid with an axe. The others were hungry, she told Sakchekapo, so the wendigo killed the baby. After that, Sakchekapo moved his family to another place far from Wapusk, but the wendigo stalked them wherever they went.

4: None of the younger kids, eleven of them altogether, have missed a class. They rush into the schoolroom eagerly, spread paper on the floor, take out brushes and paint Willa has mixed in jars and tins the kids have brought from home, and begin painting. They paint huge suns and moons, sometimes with animals inside. They paint birds, fish, bears, moose, caribou, but no dogs. They paint islands with low shrubs, water, tundra, a cabin, a teepee, a solitary shape dwarfed by the landscape.

Their pictures are different from those the kids in Willa's Saturday morning classes in Ottawa painted. The city kids painted their families, pets, houses, planes, cars, boats, soldiers, spacemen, UFOs, sometimes fairy-tale characters: Sleeping Beauty, Jack climbing the beanstalk. The kids in Niska paint land, water, sky. Except for birds and animals and the occasional hunter and canoeist, the landscapes are empty. There is no attempt to fill them up. Willa thinks this is because in Niska, the kids' imaginations haven't been captured by a coloured screen. Not yet, anyway. Their imaginations occupy a place of loneliness and isolation. Willa hadn't expected to see this much difference between the kids' paintings here and those painted in the Ottawa School of Art. But there is a common denominator. All the kids Willa's taught have shown a raw confidence, a bold energy; left on their own, most kids paint with hopefulness and optimism.

Several years ago, when Willa was looking through a book of photographs, *Artifacts of the Holocaust*, in the public library in Ottawa, she came across a photograph of a crayoned picture a ten-year-old Jewish girl had drawn in Buchenwald. It was called "The Ladybug's Birthday Party." The ladybugs were dancing inside a pastel-striped tent. There were balloons, streamers, ice cream and cake. During her first class here, Angelina Loon painted a picture she called "The Feast of the Skunks." Willa has tacked the picture on the wall. In this painting, the skunks are having a picnic on the grass. They are sitting around a blanket

115

spread with cookies, cake, chocolate bars, potato chips and pop. All the skunks are smiling because there is enough food for everyone.

5: Willa's sitting on a kitchen chair parked on the edge of the gully. She's working on an easel made from three stakes tied together. The drawing board is a square of Masonite she found beneath the kitchen sink, where it was used to cover the crack in the wall. This is the third day in two weeks that the sun has shone in Niska, so she's making the most of it by wearing shorts in a futile attempt to acquire a tan. Her arms and legs have been rubbed with repellent. Runt is close by, snapping at deerflies. He has become Willa's dog. When it became apparent that he was going to hang around whether or not she fed him, Willa started giving him scraps. Now she's glad to have him around because he barks whenever anyone comes to her door.

Father Aulneau and George Kostiuk knock before they come inside, but the girls who visit her cabin every day never knock. Nor do they speak to her. Usually there are three of them: Rita Marie Wabano, Sarah Gull and Angelina Loon. Sometimes Rosena Sutherland comes, too. The girls file into the sitting-room, sit on the sofa and look through the magazines Willa has brought inside: *Time, Maclean's, Life, National Geographic*. At least once a day, sometimes twice, these magazines are thumbed through and giggled over, then put back on the shelf. The boys never come.

Though the weather's been overcast and coolish, Willa's spent most afternoons outside sketching. She has set herself the job of drawing the village from end to end. In addition to the graveyard, she's drawn the mission house, the church and school, her cabin and the shacks at this, the poorest end of the village. The larger cabins are at the other end of the boardwalk, near the Bay. Today, Willa is trying to draw Gerald Gull's boat.

The boat is large, about sixty feet long and thirty feet wide. There's so much lumber lying helter-skelter across the deck that it's been difficult to draw the cabin Gerald has built on top. Gerald has been working on the roof of the cabin since Willa started to draw. Though she's been sketching for two hours, Willa's yet to see Gerald use a measuring tape. She remembers that when her father added a garage to their house in Sussex, he was continually taking the tape measure out of his pocket. Gerald has a two-by-four he holds up here and there and marks on with a pencil. Willa hasn't seen Gerald use the electric saw. Perhaps Geraldine has it hidden somewhere. It isn't in the hardware section; Willa's checked.

The church bell clangs, a single note that spreads over the rooftops toward Willa. She imagines but cannot see Father Aulneau's small figure leaning into the bell handle. On the other side of the gully a dog wails mournfully. There's another clang followed by more wails, now coming from the middle of the village. By the third clang, the wails have reached the far end of the village. The sounds are off-key, punctuated by sporadic yips. Even after the last rings have faded over the bush, the dogs continue to wail. Willa has come to think of the chorus as a ritual exorcism, as if the dogs were possessed, haunted by the demons of hunger and despair. Every day these demons must be called up and exorcized. As she listens, the wails sink to low moans. Willa sees Gerald cross the plank from the gully and walk toward the church.

After a while, Willa picks up the easel and chair and carries them back to the cabin, Runt following. She's not finished the drawing. There's still the background to do, but she's hungry and she has two deerfly bites. She'll have to sketch the background from memory. She walks along the boardwalk, past the shacks and cabins, the church where the priest is conducting the mass.

I believe in one God, the Father Almighty, Creator of heaven and earth; and in Jesus Christ, His only Son, Our Lord; who was conceived by the Holy Ghost, born of the Virgin Mary, suffered under Pontius Pilate, was crucified, dead and buried. He descended into hell; the third day He arose again from the dead; He ascended into heaven, sitteth on the right hand of God, the Father Almighty; from thence he shall come to judge the living and the dead. I believe in the Holy Ghost, the Holy Catholic Church, the communion of saints, the forgiveness of sins, the resurrection of the body, and life everlasting.

The dogs are waiting by the porch steps. There are three of them, one the black and white mongrel with the rope around its neck. These dogs aren't from the larger packs at either end of the village but from the shifting middle ground. Willa's seen these dogs before, singly, when they've been scavenging in the swamp alongside the boardwalk. She's been careful not to carry too much food down the boardwalk at once. She puts the groceries in her backpack and carries it high on her shoulders. She has yet to carry fresh meat. George had hamburger in last week, but Willa didn't buy it, because she didn't want to carry it past the dogs.

When Willa comes up, the dogs slink away from the steps. The black and white one crawls beneath the cabin, its snout close to the bottom step, but the other two circle behind their quarry. Willa turns around, holds the chair in front of her, wooden legs toward the dogs, and backs up slowly. Runt whines, runs up the steps and leans against the door, so that Willa has to move him off the top step before she can open it. To do this, she has to put the chair down, turn sideways and manoeuvre him to the lower step with her boot. On the other side of the chair, she hears the two dogs snarl and growl. Willa gets Runt away from the door, but as he lands on the bottom step, the black and white dog lunges out from beneath the cabin, grabs hold of Runt's front leg and tries to yank him under the cabin. Runt yelps and tries to pull himself back, but the black and white dog is twice his size. Willa kicks the dog's snout, but it won't let go. Instead, it yanks harder. Runt yelps and yelps, the sound trickling from his mouth like water. Willa hits the dog's snout with the end of the easel and the dog lets go. She flings the door open and pushes Runt into the porch. She follows him inside, picks up four pieces of firewood and pitches them at the dogs. They run away, squealing and cringing. She looks under the cabin. The black and white one isn't there. It must have crawled out the other side.

Willa carries the chair and the easel inside, slips off her backpack, then kneels down beside Runt, who has limped to his spot beside the stove, leaving a trail of blood snaking across the floor. Willa looks at the leg. Above the paw there's a hole big enough to put her forefinger through. Runt is licking at this hole, but he can't keep up with the flow of blood. Willa grabs a dish cloth and ties it around the paw. She does this slowly, cautiously, unsure if Runt will let her touch the wound, but he does. No sooner does she get the dish cloth around the wound than it's spotted with blood. She'll need bandages and tape.

Willa keeps her dog stick inside the porch. She picks it up and goes outside, walking gingerly in case the dogs are still around. She doesn't see a dog all the way up the boardwalk.

"We don't need to go over to the store," George says. He's in the kitchen of his house, a drink in one hand, a fork in the other. He pokes a boiling potato to see if it's cooked. "I've got tape and bandages in the bathroom. Look in the medicine cabinet."

Willa's been in George's bathroom twice so far, using his shower. It's the only shower in the village. She opens the cabinet door and takes out a roll of bandages, tape, cotton and a bottle of Dettol.

In the kitchen, she holds up the Dettol. "Mind if I borrow this, too?"

"Keep it. Keep it," George says. "I can get another one from the store."

"No," Willa says firmly. George has already given her too much: dented tins, a box of broken crackers, a squashed loaf of bread, slightly mouldy cheese. "I'll replace this stuff tomorrow."

"Why don't you stay for supper," George says. "You look beat."

"I should get back. I don't want to leave Runt lying there bleeding."

"He'll lick the wound," George says. "Fifteen minutes won't make much difference. Everything's ready."

"I suppose you're right," Willa says. She would rather eat someone else's cooking than her own.

This will be the fourth time Willa's had supper with George and Ralph. While George puts the food on the table, Willa goes into the bathroom to wash her hands. When she returns to the kitchen and sits at the table, George says, "It's not a good idea, you keeping that runt." He passes her a bowl of boiled potatoes. Besides potatoes, George has cooked pork chops and heated up a tin of green beans. Before she leaves for the day, Lucy Bird peels the potatoes and sets the table so that all George needs to do is cook the food and put it on plates. The dirty dishes are left for Lucy. "It upsets the balance," George says, "the order of things. The other dogs will never leave that runt alone, and you won't be able to do a thing about it."

"They leave Xavier's dogs alone."

"Maybe they understand he's Chief." George laughs. His face is flushed from the heat of the stove and the whisky. "It's because he's got a gun and has used it on those marauders a few times. They've never forgotten it." George picks up his pork chop, intending to gnaw on it, then puts it down and picks up his knife. "How'd you get those dogs to back off without a gun?" he says.

"I held them off with a chair," Willa says. "The one under the cabin, I kicked. Then I poked it with my easel."

George looks under the table.

"You kicked him in bare legs?" he says.

"With my boots," Willa says.

"You're lucky he didn't bite you. One of Lucy Bird's daughters — Lorraine, I think it was, she's not here now — got herself bitten when she kicked a dog. She was wearing a skirt, and the dog bit right through it. You should've seen her leg after three weeks. It was every colour of the rainbow. Lucky for her, they got her out to the hospital in time or she'd have lost her leg. If I was you, I wouldn't wear shorts around these dogs." He winks at her. "They don't appreciate a nice pair of legs anyway."

Willa blushes. This blushing is a nuisance, an inconvenience. It makes her appear more embarrassed than she is.

"And don't kick any more dogs," George says.

"I'm not in the habit of kicking dogs," Willa says testily. "Besides, that one couldn't have bitten me unless it had crawled out from under the cabin."

Willa skips the dessert of canned plums.

"I'll drop by later," George says as she's going out the door.

Runt is lying on the floor where she left him, licking the wound. The bleeding has slowed down, but it hasn't stopped. Willa packs the hole with cotton, winds the bandage around the leg and secures it with tape. Then she picks up the water buckets and walks toward the river. She hears the sound of Gerald Gull's hammer. Mass is over. She looks at the river, which is bronzed from the sun. A flaming sun hangs above the islands to the west. Because of the flat terrain and the vast amount of sky, the sun looks enormous up here. The river, with its burnished skin, appears innocuous, benign. The current seems to slide rather than push, as if slowed by the warm sun.

Walking back to the cabin, a sloshing bucket in each hand, Willa sees the lace curtains in the mission office move imperceptibly. It can only be Father Aulneau; Nazarene Rose goes home every night, sometimes slipping away before mass. Willa's often seen her walking past the cabin window. Like everyone else in the village, Willa's become a silent watcher, telling time not by her watch, which remains unwound, but by the church bell, the arrival of planes, people's comings and goings. Every evening after mass, Father Aulneau comes for a cup of coffee. George comes about an hour later, soon after the priest leaves. Patrick Eagle comes to the school house around noon, near the end of each class. Sometimes he walks over to the cabin for a cup of coffee afterwards. The magazine girls show up in the early afternoon. The Chief has never been back. Except for passing them on the boardwalk or in the store, Willa has had no contact with other women. The closest she has come so far was the day she walked past the Wabanos' shack wearing red knee socks over her jeans. Denise Wabano was outside pegging wash onto the line. When she saw Willa's knee socks, she giggled and held a wet shirt over her mouth.

The men never look at Willa, exept to stare. Once, in the store, she turned quickly and saw Jeremiah and Xavier staring at her. More than once, she has seen Nattie Eagle watching with her ears. Nattie, Jeremiah, Xavier, Denise: these are the faces Willa would like to draw. How can she draw them if she can't get close enough to ask? She's already drawn the kids when they've been working in the class. She's drawn Father Aulneau and George Kostiuk. She has also drawn a village map, using small squares to show where each family lives. Both George and Patrick have helped her with this.

Willa's also picked up bits of information about the people here. The Crow boys are Métis. Evangeline's still married, but she may get a divorce. Patrick's single, no brothers or sisters. Marious is Xavier's brother. Josephine Loon is their sister. Mary and Lucy Bird are sisters. Agnes Sutherland and Betsy Bluecoat are also sisters from Severn. Simon Gull is Gerald's brother. Though Willa's isolated as the white art teacher, she's managed to find out who everyone is. If a visitor walked into the village right now, she could immediately identify him as a stranger.

6: Father Aulneau is sitting in the rocking chair beneath the picture of the Holy Mother and staring at the lace curtains in the window. He will have to speak with the art teacher, that is certain. It is his duty to speak with her. He must speak with her before the others see her bare legs. He cannot have a teacher who shows bare legs staying in the mission cabin. She is like the young people today. They call themselves modern, which means they do not think of anyone but themselves. Father Aulneau stares at the hands in his lap. He lifts them up and weaves the fingers together. Then he raises both forefingers and presses them together. *Here's the church. Here's the steeple.* He opens up his hands. *Open the door and here's the people.* This is what he sometimes does for the children in his catechism class to make a small joke. It is the children he is thinking of. The teacher must set an example. But he does not wish to give the teacher what Agnes calls her "walking papers", to tell her she can no longer live in his cabin. It is good to have the children drawing and painting. He will be gentle with her.

Father Aulneau rocks back and forth. The rocking is good for his arthritis. Back and forth he rocks, back and forth. He will make it a short visit. He will say what must be said, return quickly to the mission, say his rosary and retire to bed. It has been a bad day. The translation did not go well and Nazarene Rose made rice pudding for the third time this week. It was a mistake asking the teacher to make rice pudding. She did not make it like Agnes makes it. It was salty and stuck to his teeth. Nazarene Rose makes it better, but she makes too much. Every day now she feeds him rice pudding for supper. He sees a long line of bowls heaped with rice pudding stretching ahead into autumn and into winter.

Father Aulneau sighs and gets up from the rocker. He walks through the kitchen, past the table and past the cuckoo clock Agnes gave him. The ticking clock and the tap-tap of his shoes on the wooden floor are the only sounds in the house. He goes outside, crosses the grass and knocks on the door of the mission cabin.

"Mademoiselle," he says.

The door swings open and there she stands inside the porch with those long bare legs.

"Come in," she says. "I've got the water heating. I'll have a cup of coffee for you in five minutes."

"I will not have coffee this evening," Father Aulneau says. "I do not feel well. I am upset, ver-ee upset." He notices the dog lying beside the stove, one of its legs wrapped in a bandage. "What is this?" he walks to the opposite side of the room and sits on the woodbox. He does not like dogs, inside or out.

"Three dogs attacked him," Willa says. "One grabbed him by the leg."

"Mon Dieu," Father Aulneau says. He remembers hearing a dog fight during mass when he was trying to pray. "These dogs are savage. They are ver-ee dangerous. You make a mistake bringing this one inside."

Willa spoons instant coffee into a mug. "You're sure you won't change your mind?"

"Non, merci. I regret I must decline." Father Aulneau does not feel well. And his back hurts from the translation work. "Mademoiselle," he says again.

"Yes?" She turns.

He sees she is wearing the same kind of shirt he wears beneath his soutane. Except hers has a picture of four men on it. And she is not wearing a brassiere.

"Is something wrong?" she asks.

"C'est difficile pour moi de vous expliquer." Father Aulneau coughs, then says, "Mademoiselle, you must not show bare legs in the village." He looks at the legs. They are white, so ver-ee white. Except for the two pink bumps on the thighs.

She laughs.

This makes Father Aulneau angry. "It is not joke, mademoiselle. You do not live here. You do not know. You must think about the influence on les jeunes filles. It is bad for them to see your bare legs. They will do the same as you. It will make trouble with the boys. You are a teacher. C'est votre responsabilité de donner l'exemple, n'est-ce pas?"

He watches as she sits down, still holding the spoon. She has not thought of this before. She is une personne moderne who does whatever she wishes with no thought of God's will.

"Comprenez-vous?" he asks.

"Oui. Je comprends."

"Bien. I will go now." Father Aulneau gets up from the woodbox and opens the back door. "A bientôt, mademoiselle," he says, to show he has forgiven her.

7: George Kostiuk walks down the boardwalk toward the mission cabin, cradling a brown paper bag in the crook of an arm. He walks slowly, head down, watching for broken slats, though he's been down this boardwalk so many times he knows where every slat is. One of these days, someone's going to break a leg on this boardwalk. Then maybe the band council will get it fixed. Last time the boardwalk was repaired was when Brother Charlie did it. That was over three years ago. The boardwalk weathers so badly it needs to be fixed every year. The Indians won't fix it. They don't have the get-up-and-go. This is why he hasn't hired one of them as a helper in the store, though he knows it bothers the Chief. He needs someone like Ralph, who will go up the ladder and repair the roof and the eavestroughing. Someone who will paint the siding, clean the windows. Someone who will do it today, not next month or next year. George doesn't look at the cabins and shacks as he passes: the Eagles', the Crows', the Gulls'. Nattie Gull can't see him, of course, but someone will be watching him, maybe Saul or Marsha, Rebecca or Simon and at least two or three kids. They are watching a short, stocky, grey-haired man with thick shoulders and wide buttocks hustling down the boardwalk to visit a woman half his age.

Willa's twenty-six. He asked her age right out one day. George has found out quite a bit about her during the last two weeks. She has two older sisters, both of them married. She's been living with one of these sisters for the last three years, doing contract work for the government, which is how she heard about this job. She'd been out of a job for two months, drawing Unemployment Insurance when this job opened up. George had wondered about that, why someone like her would land up here. Just goes to show you what a mess this country's in when someone who can draw as good as her can't make a living. She's a good artist. Not that he's an authority. All he's got on his living room wall is a calendar. He moved the velvet painting he got in Tijuana into his bedroom before Willa came for a shower. He was nervous around her at first, after she told him she had a college degree. He was afraid of using bad grammar and all that, but he's over that now. She's from a small town, same as he is. She worked for what she got, doing waitress work, even working as a chambermaid to put herself through college. And she doesn't act superior, like some college people do. She's real easy to be with, low-key. Time zips by when he's with her. She's never been married. She went steady with a guy for a couple of years in college, but he broke off and married someone else. He must've been crazy to let her go. Not that George expects anything to come of Willa and him. Hell, she's young enough to be his daughter. She probably thinks he's an old man, and he's no cradle-robber, though that doesn't seem to bother the prime minister. He just likes being with Willa, is all. It helps pass the time. And it sure beats rereading *Cat Among the Pigeons* or *Elephants Can Remember*. George has forty-eight Agatha Christies, one for every week of the year — he doesn't read the four weeks he's outside. He usually spends his holiday staying with his sister in Edmonton, where he can see Bobby. Sometimes he drives down to Brooks to visit some of his cronies. He watches TV, sees the latest movies, or he follows the sun. Once he spent two weeks in Hawaii. He's been to Mexico three times.

George knocks on the porch door, opening it before Willa gets up from her chair. The inside door is open, and he sees Willa sitting at the table beside the stove, writing a letter. She's still wearing shorts. Runt, who is dozing beside the stove, growls softly, then goes back to sleep.

"Hi," she says, but she doesn't smile like she usually does when George comes.

"Thought you might be able to use this." George sets the paper bag on the table and sits down in the other chair.

Willa opens the bag and looks inside.

"A teapot!" she says. Still she doesn't smile.

"Yeah. The spout's chipped, but it should pour okay," he says. "I can't sell it like that."

"Couldn't you give it to someone else?" Willa says.

"Don't you want it?" George is disappointed she's not more pleased.

"Sure, but I'll only be here another four weeks. Maybe one of your regular customers would like to have it."

"You keep it," George says. "They wouldn't appreciate it anyways." When he was in Sandy Lake, he gave all kinds of stuff to the Indians, but no one appreciated it. When he was in Sachigo, he gave Marian lots of things, but she never appreciated any of it, either. Last year he gave Lucy Bird a parka that had a rip up the back, and she never even said thanks. It comes from being on the dole. People who get used to handouts aren't grateful. They bite the hand that feeds them. And not just Indians, either.

"Thank you," Willa says. Then she smiles. "I'll make us a pot of tea. That'll cheer me up." She takes the pot out of the bag. It's a shiny, dark brown colour with yellow daisies on one side. The chip is barely noticeable. She pours hot water from the kettle into the pot, slishes it around and dumps it down the drain, then adds two tea bags and more hot water. She sets the pot at the back of the stove to steep.

George waits until all this has been done before he says, "What do you mean, cheer you up?"

Willa bends over and stares at her legs.

"See these?" she says. "The priest had something to say about them when he came to see me a little while ago. He advised me not to show my bare legs in the village. He said it was a bad influence on the young girls."

George laughs. He can't help it. It's so damned funny. Who'd have thought the old bugger would even notice? "What'd you tell him, to go back to saying his beads?" George's family is Ukrainian Orthodox, but George has never had time for church. In his opinion that's where you go to find the biggest hypocrites.

"How could I?" Willa says. "Where would I go if he threw me out?"

"You could move in with me. There's a third bedroom. I specialize in fallen women." George grins at her.

"No, thanks," she says, too quickly, and gets red in the face.

George knows he went too far this time. He shouldn't have squeezed her arm last week, either. That time he had a couple of drinks in him and got carried away.

"What I mean is, that if you ever want a place to stay, you can bunk with Ralph and me. You wouldn't be stuck. That's what I meant."

"Thanks," she says. This time she smiles. "You've been extremely kind as it is, giving me stuff like this teapot, feeding me meals, letting me use your shower. You mustn't do any more for me."

George doesn't want her to feel beholden. If she turns gun-shy, he won't be seeing her much, and he's come to depend on seeing her every day.

"Too bad Father Vachon isn't here instead of Aulneau," he says. "He'd have told you to wear shorts more often. He was that kind of man. Everyone called him Pierre. There was none of this Father stuff. He was here when I got here. Altogether, he spent eighteen years in Niska. He was the one who made the converts. He was as different from this priest as day is from night. He was a good hunter and fisherman. He'd go out on the traplines in winter. Went goose hunting every fall. Gave away most of the stuff he brought back. Four years ago, when Johnny Mack was lost in a storm with three goose hunters and their canoe over-turned, Pierre was out there searching with the rest of us. Now, you wouldn't catch *this* priest out on a search. He'd get down on his knees and pray and let the poor buggers drown."

Willa pours two mugs of tea and sets them on the table. George adds a stream of Carnation milk to his mug and takes a swallow.

"Why is it tea tastes better when someone else makes it?" he says. Then he goes on, "That storm was really something. Worst one I've seen up here. Went on for days. High winds. Rain. Christ, it was awful. Those poor buggers were out in it all that time. Sorry. I did it again," George says. "I mean those poor goose hunters. You let your language go when you're not around women. I was out with Xavier. We searched all one night. I was carrying a twenty-five-pound lantern and Xavier was tracking. There's no one can track like Xavier. Or shoot, for that matter. He shoots forty-four shells, he comes back with forty-four geese. Anyway, we were searching on one of the islands, and he told me to shine the light on some mud that had a jumble of marks on it. "There were three men here," he said. "One had sock feet and two were in rubber boots." That's exactly what they had on their feet when we found them."

"What happened to the fourth?"

"He drowned."

"Was it Johnny Mack?"

"No. It was one of the hunters he was guiding. An Irishman. He couldn't hold onto the gas can, which is what they were using to stay afloat. Johnny Mack was in the best shape of the bunch, though they were all pretty far gone when we found them. Xavier and me were within fifteen feet of them, and they didn't call out. Another thing about Xavier. He got a fire going right away. The bushes were wet from all that rain, but he peeled willow branches and cut chips and got a blaze going."

"He sounds like an amazing man," Willa says.

"He is," George says. "Too bad there aren't more like him. He's one of the few people here who doesn't owe me anything. Him and Patrick Eagle. And Nattie, of course."

"Did the Chief go to church when Father Vachon was here?" Willa asks. "I notice it's mostly the women who go and only two or three men."

"A lot more people went to church when Pierre was here," George says, "men and women both."

"Nazarene Rose?"

George grins, then says slyly, "Of course. Father Vachon was a father in more ways than one."

"Francis?" Willa says.

"Francis."

"Is that why Pierre was sent outside?"

"Hell, no. The bishop didn't even know about Francis. Or maybe he did and ignored it because Pierre was such a good man to have up here. No, Pierre retired. He was nearly seventy when he left."

"So people here do accept white people," Willa says, "eventually."

"Well, it depends on what you mean by *accept*. When I first came North, anyone could walk onto a reserve and think nothing of it. The Indians didn't say much one way or the other. Now all that's changed," George says. "You can't do that any more. You need permission or an invitation. I'm not sure I'm accepted here, and I've been in Niska six years. I don't think about it much. If I did, it would interfere with my job."

George drains his mug. "Are you going to show me what you drew today?" He and Willa have got into this habit of her showing him her work. It's an excuse for his coming down here every night.

"I'm not finished," Willa says. She gets up and lights a lamp.

George notices she doesn't offer him another cup of tea. Maybe she wants to get back to the letter she's writing.

"I'm off," he says. He stands up. Better not wear out his welcome. He'd like to see what she drew today, cheer her up, tell her she's a good artist, but he feels clumsy all of a sudden. If they were in a city, he'd ask her to go to a movie. Of course, if they were in the city, she might not have anything to do with him. In the North, you make strange bedfellows. You meet up with people you wouldn't meet up with otherwise. Makes it interesting. Only thing is, it's too long between people. And there's no white women to speak of.

8: *July 13*

Dear Karen,

I've been in Niska over two weeks now and the surprises keep coming. Today it was the priest telling me not to wear shorts so as not to corrupt the young girls! Talk about the Dark Ages. I didn't think there were priests like that around any more, telling women not to use birth control or eat meat on Fridays. Tinpot tyrant. The women up here must be suffocating under his paternalism. Today's edict makes me wonder if the women up here wear cotton skirts because he told them they couldn't wear slacks. Even the girls wear skirts. The boys wear jeans. By the way, the kids' clothes are kept very clean, which must be hard on the mothers. They have to haul water from the river and heat it up. A lot of them don't even have a proper stove but use an oil drum with pipe sticking out of it. Or they rig up a tripod outside and hang the bucket over the fire. Some families don't have bedstands either but sleep on mattresses on the floor,

*four and five to a mattress. Compared with the shacks they live
in, this mission cabin is the lap of luxury.*

*That's really what bugs me about the priest's edict — living in
his cabin. Because it belongs to the church, I must be the dutiful
handmaiden, the obedient child. I feel like doing something
outrageous and defiant. (I'm beginning to get a glimmer of why
Geraldine burned the catechism books.) In some ways, this
place reminds me of a military camp, the priest-commandant
issuing orders from one end of the compound, the Bay issuing
rations and uniforms from the other.*

*George just came for his nightly visit. He says I should tell the
priest to go to hell and move in with him and Ralph. He has an
extra bedroom I can use. I said no. If I moved into his house, I'd
never have a minute to call my own. I don't think I've told you
much about George. He's fiftyish, divorced and lonely. Starved
for a woman's company. He's been very kind to me, kinder than
anyone, but I'll have to watch it. Lately he's become a bit too
friendly, a pat here, a squeeze there; you know, like Uncle
Jasper. Enough said. I'm whacked, so I'm off to bed.*

Will send this out on the next plane.

*Love,
Willa*

9: There's a bang on the porch door. Willa unhooks the
door. Patrick is standing on the step.

"You look surprised," he says.

"Well, yes. You never come visiting at night." She immediately regrets saying this. She doesn't want him to think that she
doesn't want him to come at night. It's just that he hasn't. She
thought maybe he spent evenings with a girlfriend, though
there aren't many women his age in the village.

"Yeah, well I came to tell you I'm going away tomorrow. I

won't be around to see how things are going at the school."

"Want some tea?"

"Sure."

Patrick follows Willa into the kitchen, where he straddles a chair, slumps forward over its back and watches as she adds a tea bag and hot water to the teapot.

"Are you going far?"

"Nope."

"Will you be gone long?"

"Two or three days maybe."

Willa pours the tea.

Patrick looks at Runt sleeping beside the stove, his bandaged paw stuck out straight.

"Looks like some dogs got him," he says.

"That's right. Right here on my doorstep."

"It's a mistake bringing him inside."

"I've already been told that."

There's an awkward silence.

Patrick stares at her.

Willa stares back. In the lamplight, Patrick's face looks bitten, eaten away. It reminds her of a rotting stump riddled with termite holes.

"Would you let me draw you?" she says. It's too dark to do a good job, but she needs to do something with her hands. Patrick's staring makes her fidgety.

He shrugs indifferently. "Sure. Why not?"

Willa lights the second lamp, opens her sketchbook and begins to draw. "It's just a quick study," she says. "I should do another one in daylight."

"I suppose I have to sit still," Patrick says. He takes off his glasses, pulls back his shoulder and lifts his chin.

"That's right. Now hold that pose."

"I have a cheque for you in my back pocket," he teases. "Too bad I can't get it out."

Willa blocks in the head, the shoulders.

Sitting still makes Patrick talkative. "I might see Geraldine if she's there," he says. "She's got a hide-out where I'm going."

"Are you going to ask her about the pictures she was telling me about, the ones by Alexander Bear?"

"I might."

Willa sketches in the eyes. This is the first time she's seen Patrick without his glasses. His eyes are large and widely spaced, the irises a luminous brown.

"That's not why I'm going. I've got something I want to do there before Treaty Day."

"When's Treaty Day?"

"Next Friday. That's when the Indian agent, what they call the district manager these days, comes inside and hands out the treaty money."

"Wouldn't it be simpler to mail it?"

"It's a ritual here," Patrick says. "People like it when he comes in and hands them their money — cash, four lousy bucks apiece. It gives people a chance to air their gripes. Some reserves don't bother with it much, but Niska keeps up the ritual. Unfortunately, things here don't change much."

Patrick's nose is slightly hooked. He has a wide mouth; the lower lip droops a little.

"This year we're going to make the meeting work for us. We're going to hit the district manager with our plan. See, we're thinking of moving this place, pulling everyone out."

"Where would you go?"

"A place twenty-five miles south of here that's on higher ground. Niska's been flooded out twice in spring break-ups. Washed houses into the bush. You know what this cabin is sitting on?" Patrick moves his head.

Willa stops sketching. "Wooden posts."

"I mean, under that. It's sitting on permafrost. That's why none of our homes have basements or sewers. It's because of the ground ice. That goes for some of the other Indian villages also. See, our ancestors got herded onto these bad sites. They camped here, but they never meant it to be permanent. As long as we stay here, we'll never improve our standard of living. Only way to change things is to move. You finished?"

"Not quite. Turn your head slightly to the left again. That's right." Willa sketches Patrick's hair. "When are you hoping to move?"

"That's a $64,000 question. We've been talking about it for years. Around spring break-up, people get worried and talk about moving. Then summer comes and the water goes down. Well, usually it goes down. This year it hasn't. Goose-hunting season comes. When that's finished, we go after caribou — what we can find, that is. After that, we go out on the trapline. People forget about moving. They stop talking about it until spring break-up comes again. This year I'm going to keep them talking about it." Patrick turns again. "Oops." He gives her his profile.

"It's okay," Willa says. "I'm finished."

Patrick puts out his hand for the sketchbook. He spends a long time looking at it, turning the book upside-down, sideways, making light of it. He seems pleased.

"Do you think it looks like you?" Willa says.

"Who knows?" Patrick reaches into the back pocket of his jeans and pulls out a cheque and puts it on the table.

"Thanks," Willa says.

"The kids like the art classes," Patrick says. "Interesting what comes out of them."

"By the way," Willa says, "is there any chance of having easels made? It would really make it easier for the kids to paint."

"When I get back, I'll see about that," Patrick says.

He tips back his chair and goes back to staring at her. He still hasn't put his glasses back on.

"Do you want more tea?"

"Sure."

As she stands to pour the tea, Willa feels Patrick's eyes on her bare legs. She sits down quickly and shoves her legs under the table. She doesn't mention the priest's visit. To do so would draw attention to her legs, and Patrick has already shown himself to be a bold starer. They drink tea in silence except for one or two remarks about the weather and this morning's class. After what seems an hour but is closer to twenty minutes, Patrick puts on his glasses and goes outside. He does this without saying a word. Willa thinks Patrick might have been waiting for her to make a move, to ask him to stay longer, maybe to spend the night. But she has no intention of becoming involved with Patrick Eagle, attractive as he is. She thinks this is something she must resist. The art classes are going well, she gets along with the kids, the women smile at her when they meet on the boardwalk, the men avoid her, so she must be following the rules, whatever they are. She intends to keep it that way.

FOUR

1: *July 12, 1978.* When you are about five miles from Niska, you notice that the land begins to rise as you move upstream through the massive plain of the Hudson Bay Lowlands. The prow pushes against the current, parting the water into smooth, shiny folds on either side of the canoe. You notice the river banks no longer merge with the tundra but slope upward, away from the water. Gradually the embankments become higher and rockier, so that you feel as if you might be entering a canyon. You begin to see trees far off to the west. The shoreline steepens into layers of conglomerate and shale. By the time you have gone twenty-five miles, there are treed cliffs rising over twenty feet on the western side. The cliffs on the east side of the river are somewhat lower. In one place, steps have been hacked out of the layered shale. These were made long ago by your father. To the right of these steps is a ladder down to the water, built last summer. You prefer the ladder. The rock steps are slippery when wet, which is why you built the ladder. The ladder has fifteen rungs. When you reach out to grab the fourth rung to hoist yourself from the canoe, you get a large splinter in your thumb. You curse: the first words you learned to speak in English were curses.

You reach the top of the ladder and step onto the clifftop. Already you have forgotten the splinter because after the sour, decaying stink of Niska, you are breathing fresh, clean air. In front of you are more trees than you could ever want. Spruce. Here and there are small clearings where trees have been felled. Between the stumps are bluebells, sheep laurel, anemones, arctic cotton. A small brook runs through this plateau and spills over the cliff into the river. You have followed this stream a mile east to its watershed, which is the lake. This is where you like to fish. Brook trout. Rainbows. If you keep walking across the plateau, you will see the ridge straight ahead. It is thickly wooded and curves around the plateau like a protective wing. Up there, in the feathery thickness, is Geraldine's hide-out, a teepee made of poles, plastic sheeting and brush. You found the hide-out last winter when you were up there setting traps. This end of the ridge is your trapline. At the bottom of the ridge, in the curve of the wing, is the log cabin you built last summer. The cabin is small, one large room, but it's warm and dry with an airtight wood stove against the south wall. Looking at all this, you know you have arrived at some place special.

You were born on this trapline. Nattie sent your father out of the winter teepee. She was alone when she pushed you out. She bit the birth cord, cleaned you with moss and packed you in a *tikinagan* before she allowed Joseph to come back inside. You are lucky you survived; you were born on your mother's change, her only child before she became an old woman. It wasn't only luck you survived. Your mother is strong and sinewy, never been sick a day in her life. She knows the old ways of healing. They have worked well, though they weren't enough to cure your mother's failing eyesight or your father's TB. You spent all of your first nine winters here. Your father died before you saw your tenth winter. He flew south the same month as the geese.

2: *September, 1955.* Patrick and his father were in a blind far out on the tundra, waiting for the geese. They'd been crouched in the blind since a giant red sun had risen, silhouetting the spruce islands against the horizon. The sun rose higher, spilled over the tundra in a river of red. Patrick and his father had made this blind from willow bushes dragged from the bush. They had stuck the taller branches upright in a circle and tucked the smaller ones in the spaces at the bottom. Then they peeled Y-sticks and shoved them into the ground. While they had been doing this, Pawley, the white boss, and his woman watched them, hopping from one foot to the other in the cold, their hands curled up their sleeves like paws. Pawley's woman was wearing mukluks with flowers on them that her husband paid Nattie to make. His woman had black hair, not shiny like Nattie's, but dull, curved up like a dog's tail. She never stopped talking. Patrick didn't speak English then, so he didn't know what she was saying. He thought Pawley's woman was stupid because she talked so much. She had a small black box which she kept pointing at everything.

Patrick liked the man better. Pawley was big and quiet. Instead of the blue uniform with gold on the shoulders and cuffs he usually wore, he had on a brown parka that Nattie had made also. Pawley was the boss at the air base. That was how he happened to have his wife there when none of the other men did. When Pawley asked his father if his wife could come on the goose hunt, his father didn't tell him that women didn't go on the hunt, that it was bad luck to bring a woman, same as it was bad luck if a woman skinned a bear if it was her time of the month. His father didn't tell Pawley to leave his woman behind, because he needed the job at the air base. His father drove one of the Caterpillars. With the money he earned, he'd bought a wood stove, a gun, traps, new boots, cloth for Nattie's dresses. Sometimes his father came back from camp coughing so bad he brought up blood, and Nattie made Patrick go outside until it was over.

It took longer than usual before the *niska* appeared. Eventually they came. They came so thick that morning, the sky was black with them, the air beating with the rush of their wings. His father waited until the flock was overhead and the leader honked and swerved, signalling the V to head southwest. They always flew southwest. His father began calling the geese. Crouched down in the blind, hands cupped over his mouth, he called *ka-ronk, ka-ronk* over and over. The leader veered to the left and began the slow downward spiral. Patrick's father kept calling, down on his knees, then up on his heels. *Ka-ronk, ka-ronk*. Then came the part Patrick liked best. The *niska* became a thin trail of black winding down to the bleeding tundra. His father called them in as if he had a fine thread from earth to sky and was pulling the geese down on it. Soon the geese were all around, honking and flapping, strutting and squawking. His father picked up his gun. Pawley picked up his. And right then, Pawley's woman stood up and pointed her black box at the geese.

"Get down, Sal," Pawley whispered. It was too late. The *niska* had seen the woman. There was a rush of wings, a loud honking, and they were off, flapping over the blind, lifting skyward on great beating wings. His father stood up and fired four shots. Four geese dropped like stones. His father picked up the dead geese and wrung their necks. Patrick helped him prop the geese up on the Y-sticks to make decoys. Then they crouched down. Again they waited. They waited all morning until to the tundra faded to brown, but the *niska* never came back. At last, his father told Pawley it was no use, no more geese would come because of the woman. Before they started back to the air base, Pawley said, "Joe, why don't you and your boy stand over there in front of the blind with the geese? We'd sure like a picture of you two to take back." So Joseph and Patrick stood in front of the blind, holding the four dead geese — they had never shot so few. They stood there feeling silent and ashamed, hanging their heads in the final humiliation of having their likenesses put into a black box.

When he and his father got back to the village, the coughing and spitting started. This time the blood wouldn't stop, and Xavier got Father Vachon to radio Moosonee. When the plane came, it landed on the river in front of the village. It was a yellow pontoon plane that was only used for emergencies and for government men. They carried his father aboard the plane. The plane took him away. When he came back, his father was inside a long, narrow box.

3: One of the reasons Patrick likes coming to the ridge is that it's dry. He's never had a drop here, only back in Niska. His father never touched liquor. Nattie's word for it is *pechiponapio*, poison. Patrick wasn't one of those babies born with poison in his veins because of a mother who boozed it up. He was born clean. Long as he stays here, he feels clean. Booze isn't part of this place — or of his people.

It's when he's back in Niska that he feels dirty, as if he's being sucked into the swamp by inches. Swallowed by muskeg. Before he came back inside two years ago, he'd made up his mind to try to get the village moved here. First he built this log cabin. Luke helped him. Gabriel gave him a hand for a couple of weeks when he was back last summer. The cabin's small. Patrick thinks of it as Nattie's. He plans to build a house for himself later on, over there, farther along the ridge, beyond that stand of spruce. He's not going to live with Nattie forever. It'll drive him crazy. His wife also, if he ever gets married. The rate he's going, it'll be a while before that happens. When he first came back inside, Nattie used to follow him around; it got on his nerves. She used to do that when he came home from residential school also. Once he asked Nina if Bernice followed her around. Nina said no, her mother was too busy with Luke, Josh and Rachel to keep track of her.

Patrick is proud of this cabin. He didn't put any windows on the north wall. On the inside of this wall, he put six inches of fibreglass and two layers of polyethylene. Over that he put up a wall of four-by-ones. Two beds are built against this wall. There's a four-foot-wide partition between for when Nattie's staying here. She stayed here a month last fall, berry picking, collecting plants and herbs. There are two windows, one on either side of the door, which faces the river. There's a table and benches beneath one window, shelves beneath the other. On the south wall is the airtight iron stove he had flown in, then rafted up from the airstrip. It's a beauty. Has this place warm in no time flat. When he gets his own place built, he'll put a bigger stove in the basement and use the old stove they've got in Niska upstairs. And of course, they can use diesel power for electricity, build roads and sewers.

One weekend last fall when Patrick was guiding at the goose camp, he met a young soils engineer, Dugald McKillop, fresh out of college. Patrick took him to Niska to look around, then brought him up here. Dugald said, "There isn't nearly the permafrost here as you have back in Niska. In Niska, the permafrost is anywhere from forty to one hundred feet thick. And there's no drainage back there because you're at sea level." Patrick already knew that. Most people in the village knew it, but Patrick wanted to make it official. He asked Dugald if he'd write a letter telling what he'd found.

After he went back outside, Dugald wrote a long letter, three typed pages, explaining the soil conditions here, comparing them to Niska's. Also, he went on about Niska being in a flood plain, gave reasons why this place would never flood. He put down a couple of paragraphs about how they could use the gravel here. How they could have heavy equipment flown in and start up their own gravel pit. Use the gravel for roads and as a base for paving an airstrip. Dugald had thought the whole thing out. He got so carried away that he told Patrick if they ever got this new place going, to give him a holler and he'd see if he could help. Maybe he could hire himself out to the government as construction manager or construction consultant. Patrick's got that letter filed away. He plans on reading it at the Treaty Day meeting next week.

This time Patrick's remembered to bring his Polaroid with him to the ridge.When the weather clears up, he plans on taking a few pictures and making a display of them on posterboard. Next best thing to a brochure. Everybody in Niska has been here. They know this place. The pictures are to show the various building sites so they can imagine a new village. The people have been talking about moving to the ridge for years. Patrick remembers his father talking about it. Xavier's for it, but as Chief he's caught in the middle sometimes. Jeremiah is for it. That's important. People won't go against the elders. Most people are for it, except maybe John and Amos Bird, whose traplines are closer to Niska than here. Most of the people are scared to move, leaving the store and the church. Because of the broken promises, they don't trust the government to help if they get in a tight squeeze. They're afraid of jumping from the pan into the fire. They've been stuck in the swamp so long they don't realize it can't get any worse. Niska's a godforsaken hole, but try to get them out of it. They talk and talk, but they do nothing. He's got a big job ahead of him on Treaty Day. The women will go on about sending the kids outside to school, about wanting to keep the kids inside until they're fifteen or sixteen instead of sending them out when they're ten or twelve. Patrick is all for this. He still thinks of his first years in residential school as a prison term, although he figures it was because of his time in residential school that he became a teacher.

4:   The year after his father died, when the plane came to take him outside to residential school, Patrick hid in the bush. Nattie came after him. In those days her sight was good; it was before the glaucoma started. She caught him and dragged him back to Father Vachon's canoe, which was taking them to the plane. Then she stood on the tarmac with the other women and watched as the plane lifted itself into the sky.

He had to sit beside a girl. Nina Hunter. She sat near the middle. Nina's older brother, Gabriel, was sitting in the back beside Louis Loon. After the plane took off, changing Patrick's mother into a small black dot on the ground, he began to notice Nina was quiet and scared also. He spoke to her. He told her she had a funny name. She said her father named her after a ship belonging to Christopher Columbus. Her father wasn't too happy with Christopher Columbus coming over here, but he liked the name he had given his ship. And the ship had given Mr. Columbus a big push in the world. Maybe it would give her a big push also. After a while, Patrick let Nina have his seat so she could look at the herd of caribou running across the tundra. He felt bold and proud doing this. Patrick has been over this plane ride many times since. He thinks giving Nina his seat was probably when he decided that when he grew up, he would marry her.

When they got to residential school, Patrick and Nina pretended the plane ride hadn't happened. They slept in separate dormitories; they ate at separate tables. They were together only in the classroom under the watchful eye of Sister Cecilia, a short, sharp-nosed witch who took away their clothes to burn and made them wear scratchy grey uniforms made by the other nuns. Sister Cecilia carried a stick which she used to crack across their knuckles if she heard them speaking Cree. The same stick was used to herd them along the corridors. They couldn't go anywhere without her lining them up in twos and getting them to march. *On the spot, get ready. Left. Right. Left,* she would screech, her pointed black toe keeping time, her stick tapping the floor. *Left. Right. Left. Set, go. Forward march! Left. Tap. Tap. Right. Left. Right. Left.* If anyone stumbled or was caught on the wrong foot, he got the stick across the legs.

After three months of this, Patrick and Gabriel Hunter ran away to the bush for a month, staying alive by snaring rabbits and squirrels. They didn't come back until it got too cold to stay in the bush. Sister Cecilia put them in a room by themselves and fed them bread and water for a week. Then she made them do the thing he hated her for most. She made Gabriel and him take their clothes off, except for their underpants, and run around the gym in front of the other boys. That was the worst shame of all, showing their bare bodies, white as plucked geese, bodies that were meant to be covered just as animals and birds were covered with fur and feathers.

The next fall, Patrick hid farther away in some bushes out on the tundra, but Nattie found him. That year was bad also, though he learned some ways of outfoxing Sister Cecilia: like hiding her glasses so she couldn't read the lesson and leaving his books in the broom closet so he could play dumb. The next year, Brother Francis came and things got better. Brother Francis wasn't a real priest but an ordinary guy who'd been a pilot, truck driver and a hockey player. He took the boys, leaving the girls to Sister Cecilia. He got a hockey team going. Patrick played defence. He was a good goal scorer. Nina used to watch the games and call out to him. That was when they started going around together. When they played basketball, Brother Francis never made the boys take off anything except their shoes. He built them a shack half a mile into the woods where they could go weekends to hunt and fish. Patrick and Nina used to sneak off there sometimes. Once, when they were running to the shack in the rain, Nina fell and cut her chin on a sharp rock. Had a scar there the shape of a new moon.

Brother Francis did a hell of a lot for them. It was mostly because of him that Patrick stuck it out after Gabriel and Louis quit. Soon as they turned eighteen, they went outside to look for work. After Patrick finished residential school, Brother Francis got him into Lakehead College to study teacher education so he could come back and teach on the reserve.

Nina came with him to Thunder Bay. She was going to take nurse's aid training. They got a room together, and everything went along real well for a while. Then Nina decided she didn't want to work in a hospital, she wanted to become a model, and the shit hit the fan.

Nina was tall, slim, with high cheekbones, big eyes and shiny black hair she could sit on. As long as she'd been in residential school where there were crucifixes on the walls, she didn't pay much attention to how she looked. But after a year in Thunder Bay with everyone making a fuss over her and white men asking her out, she changed into someone else.

One night after she went out with a white man, Patrick started drinking and smashed her mirrors — she had four of them by then. He threw her makeup into the garbage and tore up the pictures a photographer had taken of her. The next day, Nina went to Toronto with Linda Sasakeep. No good-bye, nothing. Patrick quit Lakehead and went after her. He learned from Linda's sister where they were staying. He found the place okay, but no way was Nina going to change her mind. She wouldn't even talk to him. For a year he hung around Toronto washing dishes, pushing a mop, waiting for her to come round. But the more Nina's face was on TV and in magazines, the less she'd have to do with him. One day he went to her apartment, and she was gone. After that, he hit the skids and didn't sober up until months later when he ran into Linda in the street.

She told him Nina had moved to Calgary, but she didn't know where she lived. The day after Linda told him that, Patrick started hitchhiking west. He got there just as the Stampede was starting. He hung around the Indian Village because it was the only place he felt halfway comfortable, and he thought maybe he'd see Nina there. That was how he met Jim Longfingers, who was earning money by dressing up in feathers and bells. He was from the Erminskin reserve up near Edmonton and knew how to do the chicken dance. Jim told Patrick he was studying to be a lawyer.

After the Stampede was over, Jim got a construction job and persuaded his boss to give Patrick a job running a jack hammer on an office building being put up downtown. Patrick moved into Jim's basement apartment. He and Jim did a lot of partying together. One night, they were out drinking and brought home two Sarcee girls, Nicole and Jackie. The landlady, Mrs. Smeltzer, who lived with her husband upstairs, stood behind the locked storm door and wouldn't let them inside. "Go away," she said, "and don't come back until you're sober."

Jim grinned at her. "Typical. Typical. C'mon, dollies. We'll find a better place to fuck."

Mrs. Smeltzer glared at them and slammed the inner door, but she wasn't fast enough. Patrick heard her say to someone inside, probably her husband who was a quiet, meek man, "Remind me never to feel sorry for Indians again."

Most weekends, if it wasn't too cold, Patrick and Jim would head up to Hobbema or out to the Sarcee reserve to see Nicole and Jackie. But at noon hours during the week, Patrick was back trying to track down Nina. He prowled through the Bay and Eaton's in his workboots and hard hat, looking for pictures of her. They had blowups of models, huge black and white photos, on the walls. He watched TV, leafed through magazines. She was never there. Then one morning, he picked up the newspaper Jim had left on the table, and there she was on the back page, a full spread. She was modelling a fur coat, and her hair was piled on top of her head. He was sitting there staring at her when Jim came back into the kitchen and pointed to the picture.

"I know that chick. Met her at a party a month ago. She's married to a guy who owns a car dealership out on McLeod Trail."

"Married!"

"Yeah. I think his name is Barkham. We went over to their place afterwards."

"He's white."

"Yeah. Lives in that big apartment building on Elbow Drive. Mayfair Place, I think it is. What a spread!"

The apartment building had an electronic door. Patrick bought himself a leather jacket and a briefcase and went during the day when her husband wouldn't be there. He told an old lady tenant he had left his key inside his apartment, and she let him in.

The apartment was on the fifth floor at the end of the hall. Patrick pushed the buzzer. When she opened the door, he stepped inside quick so she couldn't close it in his face. The first glance told him why she had married this white guy. The place looked like it was out of a magazine, same as Nina.

Nina went into the living room and sat down on a chesterfield behind the glass table as if she had to put something large between him and her real quick. Everything in the room was white: the mirrored walls, the carpet, the curtains. Nina was dressed in white slacks and a pink blouse. She had gold jewellery hanging from her ears and neck. Besides her wedding ring, she had six rings on her fingers. He counted them. The eyeshadow went all the way up to her brows. She pointed to a chair.

"Sit down."

He sat. She had so much goop on her face he couldn't see the scar on her chin.

"You don't have the scar," he said.

"The scar?"

"Your chin. The new moon scar. The day you tripped in the bush."

She didn't remember.

"Been inside lately?"

"Just after I got married I was. I'm going back next month for a few days. A few days is all I can stand."

"I'm going back to live permanent," he said, "after I get some money saved. I'm making good money now." He rubbed the leather sleeve, then felt foolish. Her husband had so much money, whatever Patrick earned wouldn't mean much to her.

"I'll never go back to live," she said.

"You can't go back anyway."

"I could if I wanted to."

Patrick stood up. "No, you couldn't. You gave up too much. You should've looked before you jumped. You might change your mind someday."

"I'll never change my mind."

"Those clothes don't make you white."

He knew he'd made her mad. It was the only power left him. He decided to make the most of it. He got up and strolled down the carpeted hall. He looked into the bedroom. Brown this time: brown drapes, brown carpet, brown pillows on the bed. Over the bed was a huge photograph of Nina, nude, curled sideways on an imitation fur rug, her head on a crooked arm. He looked at the photograph, then back to where she stood in the hall.

"See?" he said and pointed to her nude body. "There's your proof. You can't go back."

Whenever he replays this scene, Patrick sees two mistakes. Number One mistake was that he didn't dump Nina in Thunder Bay, that he didn't walk away first but waited for her to do it. Because after she got into the modelling stuff, he knew it wasn't going to work. He and Nina weren't after the same things, they weren't suited at all. Number Two mistake was leaving that briefcase in her apartment. Patrick cringes whenever he thinks of the briefcase. He can see Nina opening it and finding it empty except for the price tag.

5: Yesterday, before he left Niska for the ridge, Nattie made Patrick a big pot of stew: potatoes, turnips, onions, some of the goose meat she and Bernice Hunter bottle every fall. There's enough stew for six people. Patrick ate some last night, after he got settled in. Later on today, after he's finished taking pictures, he'll take the pot outside and heat it up on the firepit he rigged up for cooking. The smell of cooking food should bring Geraldine down quicker than anything. She's up there all right, though he hasn't seen any smoke. He saw the fresh mark of a rubber boot near the river yesterday when he went to get water. Just about everyone from Niska wears rubber boots, so it could've been someone else's. People often pass through here to fish at the lake or to cut wood farther south. But not many would go inside his cabin. First thing he noticed yesterday was wet mud on the floor inside the door. If Geraldine's up there in her hide-out, she'll have seen his smoke. She'll be watching his movements, will see him walking around, taking pictures. The rain's cleared up. The sun's trying to break through. He'd better get out there and take the photographs before it clouds over again. Patrick figures Geraldine's waiting to see if he's alone, to see if anyone else will show up. If she doesn't come down today, he'll go up to her hide-out to look for her. He doesn't think it's smart to do it that way. Better to wait it out. If Geraldine doesn't want to be found, she won't be found.

Patrick takes the Polaroid from his canvas bag, puts three packs of film into his jacket pocket and goes outside. He walks through the trees, heading for the clearing to the north, which is the area the houses will go. He takes a picture of a house site. It comes out fuzzy. He takes another. Times it right, counting out the seconds. It comes out fuzzy also. Same thing with the third photo. Must be bad film. Patrick sits on a stump, pulls out the film, puts it back into his pocket, takes out a second film and snaps it into the camera. This time the photo turns out. He takes one more picture, then walks toward the river.

Geraldine might be on his trail by now. He remembers Xavier telling him about one goose-hunting season when Geraldine took it into her head to stalk hunters. Nearly got herself killed when she jumped out at one hunter, a Yank. Surprised him so much his gun went off.

Patrick veers south until he comes to the area that will be the village centre: the store, school, church, band office and radio station, nursing station and meeting hall. By the time he's photographed each of these sites, his eight shots have been used up. He puts in new film and keeps walking south to where the sawmill will go. The selection of these sites has been made from walking through all this with Dugald, then walking through it again with Xavier. Nothing is carved in stone. There's a lot of flexibility depending on what the majority decides. These photographs are only to get them thinking about firming up plans.

The photograph of the sawmill site turns out fuzzy. So does the second. This film's gone bad, same as the first. Shit. That was the last Polaroid film in the store. George will give him a refund, send the film back to Polaroid, but that's not the point. The point is, the new film won't arrive back here on time for Treaty Day.

He should've taken these pictures last time he was here. He should've come up here last week instead of sticking around Niska. Of course he had to get Willa started on the classes, make sure they got going okay. And he didn't have his camera with him the last time.

Patrick tramps back to the cabin and throws the camera on Nattie's bed. Who should be lying on the other side of the partition but Geraldine, with her boots on, getting mud on his sleeping bag. She's wearing that torn blue parka she usually wears, a cotton skirt and red beret. She's lying on her back with her elbows behind her head. Her eyes are closed. Patrick grins. He knew she'd pulled a fast one with that hole in the canoe. He nearly said something to Xavier about it, to see what he thought about the hole, but he decided against it. Xavier might have sent the band police down here.

Patrick goes to the stove, gives the coals a poke, adds wood and closes the door. He shoves the pot of stew and the kettle onto the hottest part of the stove. Then he says, "So you fooled the cops."

Geraldine grins. Without opening her eyes, she says, "Why are you taking pictures of this place?" Her voice is low and thick, as if she's half asleep and doesn't care if he answers. But she doesn't fool Patrick. Geraldine's got more tricks up her sleeve than Houdini.

"For a new village," he says. He might as well tell her everything. Better to have her for the plan than against. "So I can show people on Treaty Day where everything goes. We're going to discuss it at the meeting."

"You better build a place for pictures," Geraldine says, still using that low, slurry voice like she's been drinking. But Geraldine's cold sober. He'd have smelled liquor on her by now.

"A gallery?" Patrick says.

That gets her. The boots slide off the bed and onto the floor. Geraldine sits up. "I got pictures to put in a gallery," she says, "pictures by Alexander Bear."

So Willa was right. Geraldine knew this artist named Bear.

"How'd you get this Bear's pictures?" Patrick says.

"He was my son."

"Gerald's son?"

"No." Geraldine scowls at him.

Patrick backs off. No point pushing. Geraldine never gives away more than she has to. Instead, he says, "Are you going to show me the pictures?"

"We eat first," she says.

Patrick dishes out the stew, sets out bowls, bannock, makes tea. Geraldine doesn't do a thing except move herself from the bed to the table, where she eats like a horse. Not only does she clean up the rest of the stew but she eats a big chunk of bannock and drinks three cups of tea. Then she gets up and walks around the room like she's sniffing for booze.

"There's none here," Patrick says. "I'm dry."

Once, he made the mistake of drinking with Geraldine from a bottle he'd found in a rabbit hole out in the bush behind Sutherlands'. He was out there setting snares when he found it. Geraldine came along just as he was getting started on the bottle.

"You know I quit," Patrick says.

"Ha!" Geraldine says. "Nobody quits."

"Some do," Patrick says.

Geraldine opens the door. "I'm going now," she says.

"What about showing me the pictures for the gallery?" Patrick says.

"You bring the artist woman here," Geraldine says. "The white teacher. She knows about pictures. You bring her here and I'll get out the pictures."

Patrick shrugs. It was worth a try. At least he knows the pictures are here.

"Okay, I'll ask her here," Patrick says. "But if she comes, you play straight with her. This new village is too important for you to mess it up."

Geraldine turns her back on him and goes outside, leaving the door wide open. Patrick gets up and closes it, then sits down to think. If he can get Willa here to see Bear's work, maybe he can get her to draw this place, make a plan to show where everything will go. They could use that instead of a handful of fuzzy photographs. Maybe she can draw the individual sites also. The people would go for that. Instead of trying to imagine a bare spot, they would see each building drawn out. It would be better than photographs. He could get her to draw a gallery for Bear's pictures. They could put the kids' work in it also. The parents would be big on that. The trick is to get the people serious about moving here without Geraldine horning in. That's another reason for bringing Willa here — to keep Geraldine away from the village. The more he thinks about bringing Willa here, the more he likes the idea. If he gets her away from the village, who knows what might happen? Not that he'd let himself get serious about a white woman. But he hasn't had a woman since he came back inside, and he likes Willa enough to try.

6: Behind the cabin door, there's a bookshelf Patrick made from wood left over from the beds. On the top shelf is a piece of weathered wood. It looks like driftwood, it's that colour grey, but this chunk of wood hasn't drifted from anywhere. It was part of an overturned tree root that was hacked off years ago then left on the narrow, shale beach. Patrick brought it here to use as a bookend. The root is wide at the bottom, tapered at the top. It's in the shape of a face, a spirit face that has risen from smoke. The eyes are two round holes. It's into one of these holes that Patrick has put Abe Goodstriker's marble. He feels self-conscious keeping this marble. He knows it's what you call sentimental. But he's not about to part with it. What the marble stands for isn't sentimental. He figures it belongs on the shelf with the books. That marble and Cardinal's books are all he salvaged from his two years in Calgary.

Patrick was lying in his usual spot beneath the Ninth Avenue bridge beside the Elbow River in Calgary. This was where he came after a night's drinking at the National. It was here that he was most likely to remember home, though by then Niska was so far out of his reach it seemed more like a hallucination than a real place. As he lay there on the hard stones, the occasional car rumbling overhead, he opened his eyes and saw two Canadas fly through the fuzzy grey dawn and land on the water at his feet. A drop of water from the wing tip splattered his face. Patrick watched the geese drift downstream to where the Elbow met the Bow, where on a broad, sloping field, an RCMP fort had been built. The idea was to monitor the whisky trade with the Indians while at the same time keeping them out. He tried focussing his eyes on the drifting geese, on the short-cropped grass stirring in the wind. He saw circles of arctic cotton so white he had to blink. And slowly, as if it was rising out of the water, he saw the back of the field lift higher and higher until it became a giant bird's wing where trees grew thick as feathers. The wing curved around a spruce plateau. The plateau ran between a river and a long, narrow lake that glittered like mica.

Patrick recognized the lake. He had caught trout there with his father. He drifted into that memory. He was in the canoe trawling a line across the clear water while his father paddled in silent, easy strokes, no sound except water drops plinking against the lake, the soft slap of rising fish.

Patrick must have gone back to sleep, because he didn't hear Goodstriker come up. Abel Goodstriker, forty-six-year-old Blood Indian, reformed alcoholic, who squatted patiently beside him, smoking, waiting for him to wake up. Abe gave him a pack of cigarettes, bought him coffee and, later, breakfast. Soft-spoken Abe, a skinny, short-haired man, small on the outside but big on the inside, had come along at the right time. Patrick had no money and no place to stay. Mrs. Smeltzer had kicked Jim and him out months before. Jim had left town, moving on to bigger things, like investing money for the Erminskin Indians.

Abe talked him into getting into his van. They drove to Prince's Island, where Abe found two more drunken Indians curled up on picnic tables. Abe gave them cigarettes and coffee. Before the day was out, he was driving the three of them south to St. Paul's Treatment Centre, only he didn't tell them that at first. He said he was taking them someplace where they could rest up. Patrick sat up front while the two drunks slept it off in the back. He and Abe talked most of the drive down. Well, Patrick did most of the talking. Abe wanted to know all about Niska. He'd never heard of the place. No surprise. Patrick never met anyone outside who'd heard of it. When they eventually drove up to a red brick building set in a field, Abe said, "This used to be a residential school. I went here to grade five. The day I left, I swore I'd never go back through those doors, but here I am."

"Why did you come back?" Patrick asked.

"I'm a counsellor. I work here."

Patrick shut up like a clam. He'd been tricked. There was no way he was being counselled. It was true he'd hit the bottle too hard lately, but he could go long periods without it. He wasn't like those two losers in the back seat. He was smart. He had finished school, a year of college. But he got out of the van and went inside. The red-brick building was in the middle of nowhere, so there wasn't much choice. Going inside meant having a bed and food. Abe didn't push. The only requirement, he told him, was keeping dry and attending the sweetgrass ceremony. Apart from that, he could do what he wanted.

Every morning after breakfast, Patrick joined the others in an old classroom that had been converted into a lounge. There was a picture of Crowfoot on the wall, a circle of wooden chairs and a battered coffee table in the centre. The ceremony started with Abe lighting a mound of sweetgrass he had piled in a bowl on the table. The sweetgrass caught in small flames. A trail of smoke spiralled up to the grey ceiling and a sweetish smell filled the room. Abe said this was Indian bread and wine. He asked people to join hands and pray to the Creator for strength. After the prayer, he carried the bowl around to each person. Patrick felt foolish, but he went along with it, cupping his hands over the bowl, breathing in the aroma. When he had completed the circle, Abe set the bowl on the table. While the others sat around in the room talking in low voices, Patrick went back upstairs to bed. He wasn't into all that confession stuff. It reminded him of Sister Cecilia marching them off to mass.

After he'd been at the treatment centre for a week, Patrick opened his eyes one morning during the sweetgrass ceremony when everyone else was praying. What he saw was nineteen people — twelve men, seven women — different ages, different sizes, different haircuts, some with glasses, some without, some had light skin, some had dark, but they all had their heads bowed and their hands joined. Just for a second, Patrick saw that except for being Indian, these people were as different in themselves as he was. Thoughts like that scared the shit out of him when he was sober. He closed his eyes and squeezed the hand of the girl next to him. She was fat with greasy hair. She squeezed back.

After that he began to attend the sessions — "workshops" Abe called them. What the hell, he told himself, he had nothing to lose, he might as well listen to what Abe had to say. It turned out not to be like mass at all.

"It's no wonder we're hooked on alcohol, the junk the whisky traders put into the booze to give it fire. Ink, tobacco, chili peppers, soap, everything but the kitchen sink." He went into all the ways white men had screwed them, how their dignity got taken away.

Patrick had to hand it to him. Abe had only a grade five

education, but he was smart and he had a smooth way of talking that was easy on the ears. By the end of the third week, he had turned the things he'd said earlier right around.

"There's no point bellyaching about all the wrong things been done to us. We did some wrong things ourselves. What you've got to realize about being an alcoholic is you always want to blame someone else for your troubles instead of doing something about it yourself. By going so heavy on the booze, we set ourselves up to blame others. It's a no-win situation."

And: "History helps us along with the blame. But we've got to remember, we're part of history also, we can change things around. If we're strong enough. Everyone in this room has got to find a way of keeping himself or herself strong."

Patrick was quick to see how Abe Goodstriker was keeping himself strong. He got his kicks out of helping people worse off than himself. Okay, but as far as he was concerned, that was like pissing in a puddle when they should be making bigger waves. Patrick Eagle was after something bigger. When Abe asked him if he'd like to stay on for another month and help out with the office work and the workshops, Patrick said, "Okay, why not?" Might as well stick around until he figured out what was next.

What was next turned up midway through the third month, when Abe got wind of a job in Calgary and Patrick went in to check it out. It was teaching at the Plains Indian Survival School. The job meant Patrick had to study up on the Plains Cree and the Blackfoot, but he liked doing that. He was thinking he might go back to the Lakehead someday and finish off his diploma, but so far it was just an idea. He got a hockey team going at the school and spent weekends out at Morley practising. His team won the tournament.

One afternoon in early spring, he was downtown in Calgary heading for the Friendship Centre when he saw a Hutterite family walking along Fifth Avenue. The father and son were in shiny black suits, black hats and shoes, the woman and daughter in long cotton skirts, black tops, their hair hidden beneath kerchiefs. They looked out of place with their odd clothes and scrubbed pink faces, but nobody on the street paid them any attention. They didn't look down their noses at them either, in the scornful, disrespectful way they looked at Indians. They were just part of the scene. Patrick figured this was because the Hutterites were sober, hard-working and made money. Jim Longfingers claimed the reason he liked working with money was because the only way Indians would get respect was to buy it back from the white man.

Patrick figured there was more to it than that. He thought the Hutterites were accepted because they kept to themselves. They had worked things out so they didn't need anyone else. It didn't matter if people understood them or liked them. They had their own ways of doing things and that was that. The only time they came into the city was when they needed something. The rest of the time they stayed out on their farms, their closed little islands surrounded by prairie, and went about their business. Patrick thought of the geese landing on the river, the rising field, the shining lake. That dream had been showing him the island he belonged on. It was telling him to get back to it.

The marble is the ordinary, clear glass kind with red and turquoise swirls, the kind of marble kids call an allie and throw against the side of the house to bounce in the mud.

"You've heard about losing your marbles," Abe said.

"Sure."

"You take a drink, you throw this marble away, or else you get nowhere." Abe looked so serious, Patrick had to laugh.

"Next thing you know, you'll be handing out screws," he said.

Then Abe gave him a copy of *The Unjust Society* by Harold Cardinal.

"Cardinal's writing another book," Abe said. "You look for it."

By the time *The Rebirth of Canada's Indians* came out, Patrick was already back in Niska. Abe sent him a copy. Patrick has read these books over and over. Maybe Cardinal wouldn't go along with this idea, but Patrick thinks of those two books as his Bible. There's sure a lot more in them for him than in the priest's Bible.

Before he cleans up the mess from supper, Patrick looks across the room at the bookend. "You cross-eyed bitch," he says, though the face could be either a woman's or a man's. "You won't suck me in again. There's no way I'm going through all that again just to give you a second glass eye."

FIVE

1: From Xavier's notebook:

People ask me, Where did you get your dogs' names? That's easy. Bippity, Boppity, Boo is a song I heard on the battery radio after Blackjack had a litter of pups. Blackjack's the oldest dog. She got her name from when I played poker with the white Chief over at the air base. She had six pups in that litter, but three got eaten up by strays before I got there. She had them in the bush behind our cabin. When the pups were three months old, I heard this song on the radio and it sounded like how the pups looked when the played, falling all over each other on the ground.

Teabag is the colour of wet tea bags. Fishbone looks like she has the backbone of a whitefish on her back. China's different from the other dogs. I got that name off the world map that's up on the wall above the table. It's been up there twenty years, ever since I asked Victor Shelby, a government man, to bring it inside for me. He was the one who used to come on Treaty Day, back when the air base was going. Whenever I met someone over at the base, I put a mark on the map. Same with the hunters who come to the goose camp. I got a lot of marks up there on the wall. I mark people by colour. Depends. On where they come from. France is yellow, England's pink, Scotland's red, Italy's blue, Russia's brown. The priest is on yellow, George is on brown, the nurse who comes here sometimes is on pink. Everyone here except us is from someplace else. That's how this country got taken. That's why the United States is a whole bunch of colours like Bernice's rag bag. One country I never met anyone from. That's China. It's a big orange country on the map. I've never seen an orange dog up here before, either. So I call the dog China.

2: "You get the pictures?" Xavier says. He moves sideways on the wooden step to give Patrick space to sit down.

"The film was jinxed," Patrick says. "Only eight pictures turned out."

"Too bad," Xavier says. He rolls two cigarettes, lights both and hands one to Patrick. He'd never use a camera himself. He's got good enough pictures inside his head.

Patrick takes the cigarette, breathes too deep and coughs.

"I'm going to try something else," Patrick says. "I'm going to use drawings instead."

Xavier rolls two more cigarettes and sticks one behind each ear.

"How're you going to do that?"

"I'm taking the art teacher to the ridge," Patrick says. "I asked her after class if she'd draw the new village for us, and she said sure."

"What about the drawing classes?" Xavier says.

"The teacher works fast. It shouldn't take her too long to draw the village. We leave today after class. Come back Sunday. We only miss Saturday."

"Might rain," Xavier says. "Take her longer if it does."

"Can't take longer," Patrick says. "I've got to get back. Something else I've been thinking is asking Dick Simpson to come up for Treaty Day. He's got a lot more clout than Oscar Hoffman. I guess we should've thought about that earlier. Probably too late for him to make it now."

"He can't come. I phoned him," Xavier says. "He's in the hospital. Broke his leg."

Patrick shoots Xavier a quick look, but Xavier keeps smoking, staring straight ahead.

Got the jump on him that time, Xavier thinks. You got to be quick to stay ahead of young people like Patrick. Young people think they got everything figured out way ahead of you. "I'm giving you the job of making out the agenda on Monday so I can show it to Simon and Saul," he says.

Simon Gull and Saul Crow are the band councillors.

"Okay."

"You got to cover the store, the school, the church." Xavier holds up three fingers. "People won't go anywhere without these three things." He squashes the cigarette butt beneath his rubber boot and rolls two more cigarettes. "You got to cover that territory."

"I got figures on a co-op from Dominic Yesno at Mink Falls. I got the school covered myself. That leaves the church."

Xavier lights two more cigarettes and hands one to Patrick. Patrick wants me to handle the church, he thinks. He's still sore at the RCs for what happened in residential school. Nina, Gabriel, the same.

Patrick butts the first cigarette and starts on the second. "What about the church?" he says.

"What about it?"

"You think the church would go along with a move?"

"Depends."

"On what?"

"On who we talk to."

"You think we should contact the bishop?"

"Nope."

"Who?"

"The man at the top. The one who lives in that big place in Italy and wears a white dress."

"The pope?" Patrick laughs.

"I figure it takes the same amount of earth to cover him as it does me," Xavier says. "I wrote him a letter. Sent it to him on the plane."

"When did you do that?"

"Last time you went upriver."

"It won't get there in time for him to answer before Treaty Day," Patrick says.

"Don't matter when it gets there," Xavier says. "I'll tell the people on Treaty Day that I wrote the pope a letter. The women will like that. They go for a good man in white clothes."

Patrick's grinning from ear to ear.

"I didn't use the typing machine," Xavier says. "When you're Chief, you can use the machine. You can get in some of those other fancy machines some bands got in their offices." Xavier knows Patrick's got his eye on being Chief. This is a good idea. If they get the village moved, they are going to need someone like Patrick who talks good, someone who can fly to Ottawa, Toronto, places like that and talk to government men, go to all these meetings and conferences. Xavier doesn't want to do these things. He wants to stay inside, look after the old ways of doing things, keep them safe for people like Patrick and for the kids — Luke and Josh and Rachel — who are coming after. It's important to keep on pushing for better ways, but they got to hold onto the old ways also. He knows how easy it is for Indians to get lost outside. His job is to make sure they got someplace good to come back to, to make them strong again.

"Who says I want to be Chief?" Patrick says.

"It takes a young man to go outside and speak for us," Xavier says. "We need that. Some big things going on outside."

"If I'd wanted to go outside, I'd have stayed outside," Patrick says. "I came back inside to stay."

"You were born too late for that," Xavier says.

He lets Patrick think about that for a while before he goes on. "Someday you won't turn your radio on without hearing what Indians are doing. You'll have to turn your radio off to get away from it. Someday I'll turn the radio on and Patrick Eagle will be talking at me, same as the man on the news." Xavier butts his cigarette and goes on. "When you come back with smelly feathers, I'll hold my nose and tell you the story of Mikkisseu so you won't get a big head."

"The story of Mikkisseu? That's one I missed," Patrick says. "You'd better fill me in on it."

"I'll tell you later," Xavier says. "You don't need it yet."

"Since you've got everything figured out, I'd better be shoving off." Patrick stands up and butts his cigarette. "Got to get my stuff together."

"One thing more," Xavier says.

"What's that?"

"This move might not work out. It might be too soon," Xavier says. "People might not be ready to go to the new place yet."

Xavier knows that like other young people Patrick wants the speed of light. Xavier heard about the speed of light on a school program he listens to. Light years were the words the man used. That means the light we saw yesterday is old today.

"It takes billions of years for the light to get from the stars to here. If the move don't work out this time round, a few more years living here won't matter so much."

"The way I look at it," Patrick says, "it's now or never."

"People don't move with the speed of light," Xavier says. "You better think about that."

"There's such a thing as running out of time," Patrick says.

"Never run out of light," Xavier says. "It's the same thing."

Later, he watches Patrick cross the swamp to his cabin. Patrick disappoints easy. Took Nina marrying that white man real hard. If this move don't work out, he'll take that hard also. Maybe he'll move back outside. Too many good people move outside and never come back. Xavier thinks this is the main reason for moving to the new place, to keep the young people inside, to give them something to work for.

3: The store's empty when Willa comes in after class. Ralph's at the front, behind the counter.

"Hi. George around?" Willa asks.

"In the office."

George is hunched over a ledger. He takes off his bifocals. "Look who's here," he says and grins.

Willa hands him her pay cheque. "Could you cash this? I'll take out fifty dollars and put the rest in the safe."

"Sure."

Willa goes to the shelves and picks out tins of spaghetti, sardines, Spam, corned beef, cheese and crackers. The Spam's for Runt. George doesn't carry dog food.

"Can you spare a big carton?" she asks Ralph.

"Sure." Ralph goes to the back of the store.

George comes to the front with fifty dollars and a deposit slip for the remainder of the cheque.

Willa tells him she's going away for the weekend.

"Where?"

"Some place upriver about twenty-five miles."

"The ridge," George says. "How come you're going there?"

"I've been asked to do some drawings."

George frowns. "How come?"

"Patrick Eagle wants them for Treaty Day. He says they're going to discuss moving the village upriver."

"Patrick Eagle," George says. "What the hell does he know about it?"

"Well, this *is* his village," Willa says. What's gotten into George? "He should know."

"His village, my foot. First four years I was here, he was inside once to visit his mother. He's only been back two years and he thinks he's some kind of big shot."

Ralph returns with a large carton. He holds it up. "This do?"

"Fine," Willa says.

Ralph puts the groceries into the box, and Willa hands him the fifty-dollar bill. She wants to get out of here. She doesn't want to be held up by a long discussion with George.

"Listen," George says. "Ever since I've been up here, people have been talking about moving out of this place. It comes up every spring. As soon as the weather warms up, people start talking about the river flooding and having to move. Mostly it's boredom. Something to jaw about."

"But the river *has* flooded," Willa says.

"It hasn't flooded for years. Certainly not since I've been here. I've got a friend in Severn who says they talk about the same thing up there. And they haven't moved, either."

Willa changes the subject. "By the way, I asked Rita Marie to drop by the cabin to check on Runt. I'm using this carton to fix up a bed on the porch. Rita Marie says she'll make sure he's got food and water. She'll take him outside a couple of times a day."

"You know what I think of that," George says.

"It's only until his leg heals," Willa says defensively. She picks up the carton and goes to the door. "I'll see you when I get back."

4:   George leans back, buttocks against the cash register, and crosses his arms over his chest.

"You mark my words," he says. "That woman is setting herself up for trouble."

Ralph says nothing.

George shakes his head.

"Patrick Eagle will use her to draw pictures," he says, "and she won't get one word of thanks." He glances at the counter. "She forgot her receipt." He looks sourly at Ralph as if he were responsible for this.

Ralph busies himself straightening tins of tooth powder, boxes of Aspirin and bandages. They keep drugstore supplies behind the counter.

"He'll use her," George says, "probably in more ways than one." He shakes his head. "I hate to see it."

Still Ralph says nothing.

"As for that little dog, she's killing it with kindness. After she leaves here for good, it'll never survive."

"Maybe she'll take it outside with her," Ralph says hopefully.

5: *Geraldine's walking beside a dark river. There's no moon, no stars. She can't see the water. She can't tell where land ends, where water begins. She stops walking, sticks out a boot, groping with her toe for the edge of the river. Nothing. The river has moved. The river is a big, silent snake sliding through the woods at night, everywhere and nowhere at once. If she's not careful, she'll step on it. The snake'll squeeze her hard. She can't swim. One step in the icy river and she's a goner. Water'll come up to her mouth, hurt her chest, push out the air. Even the Mishipashoo can't help her. She tries to stand still, but something pushes her forward. She takes a step, another, another, and she's caught — the snake has got her. It feels like a firehose is wrapped around her body, squeezing her legs, her chest, her neck. It's pulling her down under the ice-cold water, carrying her downstream toward the bay. She claws at tree roots, logs, anything she can get hold of, but the snake keeps rolling her over. It takes her down to the bottom of the river where it's cold and dark. When she comes up top, she has something in her hand. It's a tin can with something inside it. She tries to breathe, but the snake squeezes tighter and tighter, rolling her body over and over. Geraldine thrashes about on the spruce boughs, her body heaving, soaking with sweat.*

Ever since she came back inside with Alexander, Geraldine's had this dream. She knows what the dream is saying. It's saying, *Bury my ashes someplace else.* When she came back inside, she took the ashes to the priest. She asked him to put them in the graveyard with the twins. The priest asked a lot of questions about Alexander. When Geraldine told him what Alexander did to himself, the priest stuck up his nose in the air and said, "We cannot bury a suicide in the churchyard. It is sanctified ground. You will have to put him someplace else."

For a while, Geraldine put the ashes under a rock pile near the lake, but Alexander didn't like that. He sent her this dream. She took the ashes out of the rock pile, dug a hole in the field and put him there. She can see this field from her hide-out. It's on a hill that's not too close to the river. For a while, no dreams. Alexander liked it there. Now he's saying, "I don't like it here." Just like Alexander. Never stayed long in one place. After Children's Aid took him away from her, he lived with lots of different people, a new family every year. Maybe that's why he wanted to be put in a tin can — so he could move from place to place. Geraldine doesn't like Alexander being in a tin can. Tin cans are for spaghetti and soup, not for people. It is not the way Ojibwas get buried. They put their bones in the earth or inside a cave. Her grandfather, Moses Bear, was put inside a cave. She told Alexander that, but Alexander said, "I'm not like other Indians. After I die, I want to fly like a bird. I want to be cremated and my ashes flown up north. You do that for me."

Whenever Geraldine remembers the cops banging on the door of Alexander's place in Thunder Bay, waking her up to tell her what Alexander did to himself, she remembers what Alexander said, and she thinks maybe he planned to do it. That is why he told her what to do afterwards.

"You take my pictures away from here. Take good care of them like I showed you. You put them away until I get famous. Then you sell them. But don't sell them all. Build a gallery. You put the pictures you don't sell in the gallery."

Trouble was, Alexander didn't say where to put the gallery, where to put the ashes. He didn't say what pictures to keep, what pictures to sell.

The place Alexander worked in Thunder Bay was a big room over a record store. It was cluttered with tables, paints, tools, screens, paper, everything all mixed up together. Only thing Alexander took good care of was his pictures. He wouldn't put them on the wall but kept them inside pieces of stiff black cardboard with sheets of clean paper between. There was a bed piled with Alexander's clothes and a place for cooking. Alexander didn't sleep or eat much. At night he put on a fancy suit and shiny shoes and went out joyriding and drinking with his friends. Last time she saw him alive was when she went out with him. He was in his suit. He wouldn't stay at the table with her, but kept moving around the bar, going from table to table, blubbering crapshit about how he loved everyone, everyone was his friend, both Indian and white. He talked this way to bartenders, strangers, winos trying to get money off him. Geraldine got so mad she poured beer over his fancy suit before she walked out.

Two days later, she was at the police station where the cops took her so she could tell them whose body it was inside the cell. They were too stupid to know they'd arrested Alexander Bear. Afterwards she went back to Alexander's place, took $950 from the paint tin and bought the biggest suitcases she could find. She took Alexander's black folders and put them in one suitcase. She put the new pictures, the ones he had painted on canvas, in the second suitcase. She locked both suitcases.

Before she left Thunder Bay, she went to the place where they burnt Alexander's body and put the ashes inside a tin. She put the tin in the suitcase with the paintings. Then she flew north to Niska. It was Morris Mack who brought her upriver to the village. He was picking up Elizabeth at the airstrip. Geraldine didn't want to take the suitcases on the river, but she had no choice. Morris was sober, and the canoe didn't tip.

First she hid the suitcases with Gerald's lumber, under the canvas where it was dry. But the old lady kept poking around. Sometimes kids came poking around also. Geraldine didn't want anyone to know about the pictures until she had made some plans. She took the suitcases out of the lumber pile and carried them here. That time, she brought Elizabeth with her to help carry. Elizabeth was strong and never asked what was inside. She and Elizabeth stayed here all summer, only went to the village once to get food, tools and a lock from the Bay. Geraldine built the teepee and made a woodbox for the suitcases. She put the suitcases in the box and locked it tight.

Geraldine's getting tired of waiting for Patrick Eagle to bring the white teacher to see the pictures. Geraldine's been here alone since the cops came with the dogs. Not much to do except sleep and go into the woods for rabbits and grouse. Lots of animals around here, no trouble there. Lots of time to figure out a plan. As soon as she hears Patrick's canoe motor coming upriver, she'll take the suitcases down and put the pictures around. She's been inside his cabin before. Sometimes when she goes to the river for water, she lies down on his bed, but she doesn't stay long. She doesn't fall asleep. No way is someone going to surprise her again.

6: It's begun to rain again, a sudden shower that patters against Willa's yellow slicker, runs off her nose and chin. She lifts the backpack between her shoulders and climbs the ladder after Patrick. Patrick stands at the top, water dripping from the visor of his peaked cap, watching as Willa hoists her weight from the topmost rung onto the grass. She stands up and looks around. They are on a grassy escarpment about twenty feet above the river. Ahead of them are spruce woods. They walk toward them and huddle in the shelter of the largest spruce, waiting for the rain to stop. All around them, water slides off branches and thumps softly onto the brown-needled floor. Stooping, they walk beneath the branches until they come to a clearing. The air in front of them is bright and clear. Willa hears the suck and gurgle of a brook. She stops and looks across the clearing.

"So this is it," she says.

"Yup." Patrick turns and sees a big smile on her face.

"Well," she says.

"Well what?"

"It's so different from the village."

"Yup."

"It even feels different. More electric somehow."

"That's a good way of putting it."

They look across the brook and come to more woods. Beyond them is a second clearing. There's a small log cabin on the opposite side at the foot of a sweeping ridge.

"Is that yours?" Willa says.

"That's it."

"You built it yourself?"

"That's right. And I plan to build another one that's much bigger." Patrick points to where he plans to build his house.

They cross the meadow in silence.

Before he opens the cabin door, Patrick knows Geraldine's inside. He can feel it. He opens the door, steps inside. He expects to see Geraldine lying on his bed. Instead, there are pictures all over both beds, the table, the top of the bookshelf.

Willa comes up behind Patrick and sees the pictures.

"My God," she says, "it looks like a gallery in here."

She hasn't seen Geraldine yet. But then she turns and sees her sitting behind the door in her torn blue parka, the red beret on her head, her lips pulled back in a grin, showing stained and broken teeth. There's no mistaking the expression of pride on her battered face. The two suitcases sit on the floor beside her.

Even Patrick's surprised by the display of pictures. Coming upriver, he had told Willa that Bear was Geraldine's son, that Geraldine would probably be lying on his bed when they got here. But he never expected she'd spread Bear's pictures all over the place.

Willa begins to inspect the pictures, then realizing she's dripping water, she removes her rain gear, wipes her glasses and hair on a towel she digs out of her backpack. She goes over to one of the beds.

"You be careful," Geraldine warns. "Don't you mess them up. Alexander likes clean pictures."

"I'll be careful."

The pictures are prints. Alexander Bear was primarily a silk-screen artist. Each print is covered with a sheet of onionskin. One by one, Willa lifts each sheet. Beneath are the elegant designs Bear did so well: geese, swans, loons, their curved, lyrical shapes flying off the paper. There are birds in groups of two or three, often an adult bird with a smaller one following behind. There are airborne caribou, moose and deer, graceful winged creatures that soar and arc. Willa remembers Ursell's comment about Bear's work having its origins in Ojibwa picture writing, the language that so often took the shape of birds and animals. That may well be true. But there is a sophistication in Bear's work, a lifting of birds and animals from a particular time and place. Willa thinks no one except an Indian could put so much feeling into these shapes, could become the subject itself. It's this feeling that gives the work power, saves it from becoming mere stylization. Willa has seen about half these prints before, framed in galleries, but she has never seen the artist's proofs. There must be at least fifty of them spread around the room.

"How many do you have?" Willa asks.

"Fifty-eight," Geraldine says. Then she asks, "How much are they worth?"

"Each?" Willa shrugs. "I don't know, something between five hundred and eight hundred dollars is my guess."

"All the pictures together, how much?"

"Anywhere from thirty-five to forty-five thousand dollars," Willa says. "But you wouldn't get that much."

"Why not?" Patrick says.

"You'd need a dealer to act as your agent, someone who can look after mounting and framing for you, set the price, send them to galleries, sell them for you. But a dealer would have to be paid. They take a large cut. Forty-five per cent sometimes. Or you could sound out major collections. The National Archives or the Glenbow Museum might be interested in buying this work for their collections. If they can raise the money or find a sponsor, they might buy it for their permanent collections. Even then, you'd probably need an agent."

"Either way, you'd end up with half of forty-five thousand," Patrick says.

"That's right."

"I got more to show you," Geraldine says. She gets up and slowly puts the prints back into the suitcase. Unaccustomed to being methodical, her movements are awkward, stilted. Willa and Patrick watch as she picks up the other suitcase and heaves it onto the bed. "Now I'll show you different pictures," she says.

She props the canvases on top of the beds, against the wall. She puts the rest on the floor, against the beds. There are twenty-two altogether.

Willa's never seen these pictures, which are large, bold acrylics. There is nothing airborne or lyrical about these paintings. There are curved fetal shapes, smooth and cool as marble. There are circles within eggs, eggs within circles, suns and moons, seeds and seedpods, sacks and pouches. Each design is highly sculptural. It's as if Bear was painting the spaces surrounding his winged creatures, silhouetting the reverse of his earlier work. None of this work has been titled. There are six abstract bird shapes, black as ebony and so fluid they seem to have been poured onto the canvas. They are dated 1977. This was Bear's last work.

"How much?" Geraldine says. This time, she's been following Willa from picture to picture.

"I couldn't guess," Willa says. "A lot."

"More than the other pictures?"

"Original paintings sell for more money than original prints because there's only one of them," Willa explains. "I couldn't tell you what each of these would be worth. Something in the thousands. A dealer could tell you."

"You find out," Geraldine says. "You be my dealer."

"Me!" Willa laughs. "I'm an artist, not a dealer."

Geraldine scowls. "I want a dealer," she says. "You're it." She pokes Willa in the chest.

"It's a big job," Willa says. "You'd need someone who knows what she's doing."

"Learn," Geraldine says. She sticks her face so close Willa can smell her gamey breath. She gives Willa another jab in the chest. "Got it?"

Willa backs up. Her cheeks redden. You big lummox, she feels like saying, do you think you can bully me into this? Instead, she says, "Why should I? I have my own work to do."

The two women stand apart, glaring at each other.

"Geraldine, why don't you leave the pictures here and we'll talk about it some more," Patrick says. "Maybe we can figure out a plan."

"No!" Geraldine says. "I'll take my pictures away." She puts the canvases into the suitcase and snaps it shut. She picks up the suitcase and moves to get the other.

"It's raining," Willa says. "It's better if you leave them here where it's dry."

Geraldine says nothing. Still sulking, she reaches into her pocket, takes out two keys and locks both suitcases. Then she puts the keys into her jacket pocket and goes outside.

Willa closes the door.

"First she wants me to see this work. Then she won't trust me with it," Willa fumes. "It makes no sense."

"It's conditioning," Patrick says. "You get enough promises broken and you don't trust easy."

"Broken promises have nothing to do with me," Willa says. "I haven't made any promises."

"Haven't you ever been disappointed?"

"Of course." When Arnold Gates dropped her after two years with no warning so he could marry that dentist's daughter from Rothesay, Willa didn't think she'd ever get over it. She wasted a lot of time before she realized he'd done her a favour. "But I don't think my disappointment has anything to do with Geraldine Gull."

"Then it couldn't have been a very big disappointment," Patrick says.

"Listen," Willa says, her cheeks burning now, "everyone knows Indians have had a bad deal — unfair treaties, runarounds by government. But what makes you think the rest of us are responsible? Do you know what my father does to earn a living? He's a cabinetmaker. He builds kitchens, bookshelves, things like that. My mother's a nurse's aide. She empties bedpans."

"Hey," Patrick says.

It infuriates Willa that he's grinning at her. "Do you know how I paid for four years of college?" she says. "I worked as a waitress in a big hotel, carrying dinners to conventions of drunken men who were too soused to eat and who tried to feel me up, waving twenty-dollar tips at me while their wives sat there pretending not to notice. After two summers of that, I became a chambermaid. All I had to do then was change other people's dirty sheets and clean out their toilet bowls. Of course, neither job paid me enough, so I had to take out student loans, which I managed to pay off by living with my sister and her husband, babysitting their kid to pay for my board. Now I'm working to save enough money to support myself. In a modest way, of course. Maybe renting someone's drafty cabin when they aren't using it, so I can work at my job, which is drawing and painting. In other words, I've been extremely busy trying to be responsible for myself. That's why I haven't had time for major disappointments." Willa picks up her poncho off the floor, pulls on her boots. "I'm going for a walk," she says.

She's out the door before Patrick can think what to say. He straddles the chair and stares out the window at her receding figure. The rain on the roof has stopped, so she won't get too wet.

Patrick worked for a red-haired man in Toronto who had a temper like that. If you were ten minutes late, he'd fly off the handle, chew you out like you'd committed a crime. But he's got to admit Willa's got a point. There's no sense in dumping Indian disappointments on her. As Abe Goodstriker said, Indians have got to stop blaming everyone white for wrongs our people have suffered. It's stupid to tar everyone with the same brush. You have to pick your target, lay blame where it belongs, which is mostly on governments and bureaucrats.

Besides, Patrick didn't ask Willa here to pick a fight. That's the last thing he wants to do with her. He has something better in mind. Only trouble is finding out if she wants it also. He'd feel like two cents if she turned him down. He nearly made a move a few days ago when he went to see her that night she drew his picture, but she was so jumpy he figured she'd shy away from him. That was the other reason, besides drawing the new village, for bringing her here. He figured if he could get Willa away from the priest and George — especially George, who monopolizes her nights — they might get something going between them. There's a better chance of it happening here, if Geraldine doesn't keep butting in.

Patrick goes outside and sees Willa sitting on a stump on the other side of the clearing. He comes up behind her. This time she doesn't jump; she heard him coming.

"You okay?" he says.

She's taken off her glasses and is rubbing her eyes.

"You know, you're the first person to ask me that question since I left my sister," she says.

What's that supposed to mean, that she's not mad at him any more, or that she misses her sister?

"I don't want you feeling bad," he says. "Forget Geraldine. I'll take you around and show you where everything goes. Give you an idea of what the new village will be like."

They walk through the clearing, and he shows her where the houses will go, their fronts curving into each other, the backs flanking the north. The school, church, band office and radio station, the meeting hall, store, nursing station, will be built farther south, a U-shape on the other side of the brook.

"In the centre, we'll put a baseball field and playground. Good place for powwows," Patrick says. "See over there?" He points to where the brook makes a deep U in the clearing. "That's where we can dam up the brook and make a wading pool for kids. Put a bridge there. Make a park."

"The whole place is like a park," Willa says. She flashes him her perfect teeth. Patrick knew she'd like it here. "Who would think twenty-five miles would make such a difference?"

"C'mon. I'll show you the rest," he says.

They head south.

"We'll put a gravel road along here," Patrick says. "It'll run from the airstrip to the main part of the village. There'll be a detour to the sawmill. Someday that's where we'll have our factory."

"What kind of factory?"

"A fur factory. Why send all our pelts away to be made up? Why not start our own industry here? We can have a green-house also. Grow our own food."

Patrick points out the airstrip. "See that rise of ground beyond the airstrip?"

"With that white stuff on it?"

"Arctic cotton. That's where we can put the graveyard. Now I'll show you the lake."

They follow the brook half a mile back, passing the ridge on one side, the hill of arctic cotton on the other, until they come to the lake.

"It's not a big lake," Patrick says. "A mile long, half a mile wide, but it's full of trout. We can ice fish in winter, skate on it. Maybe get a hockey team going. Eventually we could put a sports arena here. Though people might prefer having it in the village centre."

As they are coming back to the cabin, Willa points to the

curve in the brook. "That would be a good place for a gallery," she says, "in the park."

Patrick's been having second thoughts about a gallery. If there's likely to be a big upset with Geraldine, he'd rather forget the gallery until after they get the village moved. He doesn't want Geraldine to sabotage their plans.

"What kind of buildings do you plan on having?" Willa asks.

"Log. At least the main buildings. The school, church and meeting hall. The houses will probably be a mixture of log and clapboard. The main thing is to make it look connected. Like it's —" He pauses.

"Integrated?"

"That's the word, integrated," Patrick says. "Come on. It's raining again. We'd better get inside."

After supper, just when Patrick notices Willa is beginning to relax with him, Geraldine turns up. He sees her pass in front of the window. Geraldine comes inside and stands behind Willa, feet astride.

"The spaghetti's gone," Patrick tells her. Shit. She would have to show up tonight.

Geraldine reaches across Willa's shoulder for the rest of the cheese and bannock, carries the food across the room, sits on Patrick's bed and begins to eat. She shoves the food into her mouth, hardly pausing to swallow.

"Geraldine," Willa says, "I've been thinking. There should be an inventory made of Alexander Bear's work. Each picture should be numbered and written down so you know exactly what you've got."

This is a surprise to Patrick. When they were walking around, Willa didn't say anything to him about changing her tune. He turns his chair around so he can watch Geraldine.

She wolfs down the last of the bannock and says, "I know what I got."

"Yes, but if you're going to sell some of the pictures, you

should have a record," Willa says. "I'll do that tonight, if you want."

"What about starting on the drawings?" Patrick says. That's what they came here to do.

"I'll need measurements first," Willa says. "The drawings won't be exactly to scale, but I'll need some sort of measurements to get the proportions right." she glances out the window. "With the cloud cover, there's only a couple of hours of daylight left anyway. I could do the inventory while you get the measurements."

Before Patrick can get a word in edgewise to say maybe she should come and hold the tape measure, Geraldine butts in.

"After you make the inventory, we pick pictures for the gallery," she says.

"Maybe," Willa says. "Before I do either one, I want to draw a picture of you."

"Why?"

"Because I'm interested in faces. That's what I like to draw." Willa stands up and pats the chair.

Geraldine sits down and crosses her arms over her chest. "Draw," she says.

Patrick's got to hand it to Willa. She's learning how to deal with Geraldine. That's all you can do with Geraldine, deal with her. You can't get along with her like you can with most people. You've got to bargain with her. If there's something she wants, she'll go along with you, maybe.

Patrick gets a measuring tape from the toolbox he keeps by the stove, gets paper and pencil and goes outside to measure the building sites. He should've thought of that himself. It's so obvious, he feels kind of sheepish Willa was the one to mention it. Maybe when he comes back Geraldine will be gone.

7: It isn't really possible to get someone's face down on paper. Even photography doesn't succeed completely. And Geraldine's face is particularly difficult to capture. When she's sitting still, as she is now, staring out the window, she looks like one of these early photographs of Indians taken at the turn of the century, the sort of photograph you often see in museums: the haughty, unsmiling face staring suspiciously at the camera. The face that looks as impenetrable as a mountain cliff. Only those faces belonged to men, Chiefs who were singled out as leaders, as spokesmen for their people.

The face Willa is trying to draw is a woman's face. It's smaller than you would expect, given the bulkiness of Geraldine's body. The chin is shorter than Patrick Eagle's. The nose might be shorter, too. It's difficult to say. Her nose is badly skewed because the broken bone was never properly set. The broken nose stamps her face with a sinister, malevolent expression. If it weren't for her nose and the perpetual scowl, you can see that Geraldine might have been considered beautiful once. Geraldine scowls with her eyes, which are large and hooded, set deep beneath her eyebrows, giving Willa the feeling that Geraldine's sitting inside a cave, watching her, that she has the advantage. Willa sketches the hair, the beret, the shoulders, before she abandons the sketch. Given her rusty hand with portraits and Geraldine's inaccessibility, it's the best she can do.

Geraldine gets up off the chair, takes the sketchbook from Willa's hands and makes a guttural sound that tells Willa nothing — it could mean approval or disapproval. But she notices a slight pushing out of Geraldine's chest, a straightening of the shoulders. Geraldine plunks the sketchbook on top of Patrick's spaghetti plate.

"We make that list now," she says.

We, she says, but of course she means *me*, Willa thinks. All Geraldine does is unlock a suitcase and take out the prints. Then she sits back and watches. Willa takes a notebook and pencil from her backpack and starts to work. She numbers each artist's proof on the back, then records the number, title and date in the notebook. While she works, she sees Geraldine walk over to the table, pick up the sketchbook and look at her portrait. She does this three times before lying down on one of the beds.

Willa returns the last of the prints to the suitcase.

"I'm finished," she says.

There's no reaction from Geraldine. Her eyes are closed. Willa opens the stove door and gives the fire a poke. She adds wood, then puts the kettle on to heat. Whatever possessed her to do this inventory? Was it Geraldine's bullying? No. It has nothing to do with Geraldine but with the work. By any standards, Bear's work is exceptional. The work of his lifetime is inside these two suitcases. A record of it should be made, that much is obvious. What is equally obvious is that the work can't stay here. What if it became lost or mistreated? What if Geraldine ended up in jail? With no record, people would not even know that some of this work had existed. Willa's amazed the prints are in such good shape, considering the fact they've been hauled around in a suitcase in wet weather. So far, there's no evidence of mould, but it will come if the work isn't moved to a safer place. This doesn't mean that Willa's decided to take on the job of finding a safe place. It only means she recognizes the fact that something has to be done, and soon. And even if she did ask around outside to see what could be done about selling Bear's pictures, she wouldn't be doing it for Geraldine. She'd be doing it for the work.

When the water's hot, Willa makes tea. As soon as she pours tinned milk into the mug, Geraldine's feet hit the floor. She takes a key out of her parka pocket and locks the first suitcase and opens the second. Willa lights the kerosene lamp, drinks her tea and gets back to work.

8: When he returns, Patrick's disappointed to see Geraldine is still there. In fact, she's lying on his bed. Does she plan to stay all night? Willa's sitting on Nattie's bed, pictures spread around her.

"Hi," she says. "I'm nearly finished. Did you get all the measurements?"

"Yup."

Patrick pours himself tea and picks up Willa's sketchbook. Not bad. No one would mistake the face for belonging to anyone but Geraldine. Somehow Willa's managed to catch that bold, arrogant look Geraldine has, the look that says she can take on the human race and win. But there's something else in the picture. The way Willa's drawn her, Geraldine doesn't look as ugly as usual. In a perverse way, she looks attractive.

Patrick puts the sketchbook on top of the bookshelf, sits down and waits for Willa to finish the inventory, knowing Geraldine will get up off his bed to put the pictures away. There's no way she's hogging his bed.

As soon as Willa's finished, Geraldine gets up and begins picking up the pictures. Patrick moves to his bed, takes off his boots, lies down, pulls the sleeping bag over his shoulder and turns toward the wall, hoping Geraldine will get the message and leave.

Patrick hears the lock on the suitcase click, followed by footsteps and a heavy thumping noise. He rolls over and sees Geraldine stretched out on the floor in front of the stove, his jacket bunched up under her head. He might have known she'd stay here the night. But he's too sleepy to fight it. Maybe tomorrow she'll leave them alone. Patrick hears Willa's boots fall onto the floor. He imagines her long white legs sliding out of the jeans and into the sleeping bag. He grins. Wouldn't his mother have a fit if she knew the white teacher was on her bed and Geraldine was sleeping on her floor. Patrick hears footsteps padding lightly across the floor. He looks over his shoulder and sees Willa bending over the lamp. The light from the lamp turns her red hair gold. She blows out the lamp and pads across the floor to Nattie's bed. Patrick rolls onto his back and closes his eyes. Far away a wolf howls.

9: The next day, the weather vacillates between sunshine and rain. Whenever there's a sunny patch, Willa dashes outside with her sketchbook to rough in another building. Soon she finds herself running back inside, sketchbook tucked under her poncho, to finish the drawing at the kitchen table. It's a frustrating way to work, especially since Geraldine hangs around the cabin all morning, eating everything in sight. Patrick intermittently gets up from the bed where he's been reading to peer at Willa's lack of progress.

In the afternoon, the sky clears, and Willa carries a chair outside, across the clearing to the village centre. The bugs are terrible, but she douses herself liberally with repellent. While she works, she hears a thrush singing. A deer walks through the woods in front of her. Later, she sees Patrick cross the meadow with his fishing gear. Soon after, Geraldine appears on his trail, following him to the lake. Willa finishes all the buildings in the village centre. Leaving the chair behind, she sketches the gallery, then the fur factory and the greenhouse. This leaves the houses. She only manages to get one house done before the sky clouds over and it begins to rain. This time the rain doesn't let up. She runs inside, gets into dry jeans and lights a fire. By the time the others show up, the cabin is warm and tea is waiting.

Patrick has caught ten rainbows. Six are three-pounders, the largest trout Willa has seen. They cook three for supper, one for each of them, which they eat with bread and margarine. Geraldine seems to have moved in with her suitcases, or perhaps, Willa thinks, it's the suitcases that have moved in with Geraldine. It it weren't for the suitcases, Geraldine wouldn't be here at all.

After they finish eating and are sitting around drinking tea, Geraldine starts bullying Willa about becoming her agent. Willa puts up with it for a while, then finally escapes by putting down her mug, taking off her boots and crawling into Nattie's sleeping bag. Within minutes, she's asleep. She doesn't hear the low murmur of voices, the rain beating on the roof, the fire spitting in the stove.

10: In the morning, Patrick is the first up. He goes outside and glances at the sky. It's still clouded over. The rain has stopped, but it looks as if there's more coming. As if they haven't had enough. They'd better get a move on, or they'll get caught in a downpour. Willa's finished the sketches. There's the master plan to do, but she can work on that back in Niska.

Patrick goes back inside. Willa's up, bending over the bucket, splashing water on her face. Geraldine's still on the floor beside the stove. He doesn't wake her up. He won't bother lighting the stove. The food's gone except for the remaining trout, which he's taking back to Nattie, and the sardines and crackers Willa brought. The sardine tins come with keys. Patrick fits the key into the tongue of the lid. As he rolls back the lid, his hand slips and he cuts his forefinger.

"Shit." This is all he needs.

Silently Willa digs Kleenex out of her backpack and hands it to him. He wads the Kleenex around his finger while Willa forks the sardines out of the tin and onto crackers. They eat standing up and wash the meal down with mugs of cold water. They finish the tin just as Geraldine wakes up. They leave the second tin and the rest of the crackers for Geraldine.

On the way to the river, Willa stops to pick a flower in the clearing. "For the priest," she says.

Geraldine follows them to the river. As the canoe's pulling away from the cliff, Patrick feels the first splatter of rain. Shit.

Nothing's going right this morning. It's too early, that's the problem. Plus he's feeling let down. It's true the drawings are done, but with Geraldine sticking as close as glue, there was no chance for anything to develop between Willa and him.

11: Geraldine stands above the river, watching Patrick and Willa until the canoe disappears around the bend. Then she goes back to the spot where the gallery will be. She walks around and around, sits on a stump and looks at the grass, the flowers, the brook. Listens to the birds. This is a good place for Alexander. It's like he's having a picnic here. He will like it. But it's too soon to bury the tin can. People might decide to move the gallery someplace else, and Alexander would be unhappy again. This time she's going to do it right, wait until she knows the gallery will go here for sure. For now, she will keep the tin can in the suitcase with the pictures.

She crosses the clearing and enters Patrick's cabin. She eats the sardines and crackers, then she lies down on Patrick's bed to think. When she was talking to Patrick yesterday while he was fishing at the lake, he told her he would speak to the people about the gallery on Treaty Day. He said he'd make a bargain. If she stayed here at the ridge, he'd push the gallery idea at the meeting. He said if she turned up, George might call the cops again and there'd be lots of trouble. If there was trouble, people might not want the gallery. They might vote against coming here. It was important they stick to the point, Patrick said, so they could come to a decision.

Geraldine's not sure about this. Patrick's not so bad, but he don't know everything. She can get back to Niska without George knowing. George doesn't go to Treaty Day meetings but sticks in the store waiting for the people to spend their money afterwards. *She* should speak to the people about Alexander, not Patrick Eagle. He doesn't know anything about Alexander. It is time to tell those sleepy Crees who Alexander was. And she's got that piece of paper to read also, the talk her grandfather, Moses Bear, read out to the Ojibwa people. Patrick can't read that. He's Swampy Cree, not Ojibwa. Maybe she will go to the meeting. She will decide what to do later, after she has a sleep.

Geraldine is running across the clearing, away from the river. Thunderbirds are in the sky. She can hear their wings beating against the air. She can see their giant shadows on the grass, moving across the ground like big grey clouds. Geraldine runs. She runs and runs. She's got to get away from the river. She's got to get away from the thunderbirds. She runs so fast she trips on a root and falls on the ground. She looks down and sees the root is changing into a snake, a grey slithering snake with its white belly turned up to the sky. Geraldine hears the thunderbirds rumble. They are mad because she tripped and rolled the snake belly-up. The thunderbirds don't like this. They rumble louder. The cloud shadows get darker and bigger. They spread over her like a grey jail blanket. Geraldine gets up off the ground and kicks at the snake, trying to roll it onto its belly, but the snake turns into a root and trips her again. This time she falls into water. The river has moved. It has slid in front of her and now she is in it. The river is wrapped around her shoulders, her neck, pulling her under. She calls to the Mishipashoo to help her, but there is nothing, nothing but water pulling her down, pulling her toward the ice-cold bay where Wapusk stalks his prey.

12: On the table between Patrick and his mother is a bowl of red willow bark soaking in water. Patrick's right hand is spread palm-up on the table while Nattie wraps bark pieces in a clean cloth and ties the cloth around Patrick's cut.

"Odoshee," Nattie says. "Soon the cut will heal."

Nattie's the only medicine woman in Niska. Her mother, Semolia Meekis, taught her the remedies before she died. As long as Patrick can remember, Nattie has cured people's ailments: cuts, sprains, high blood pressure, indigestion; she has a different remedy for each ailment. It's Labrador tea for headaches, boiled spruce cones for sore throats, black poplar buds for toothaches, wild ginger root for a bellyache. On the shelves behind her are jars filled with bark, herbs, crushed leaves, root cuttings. Hanging from nails are branches and bunches of dried plants. Patrick doesn't know what most of this stuff is used for. He only knows that for many ailments they work. Last year, for instance, Stanley Bluecoat had a scalp infection Nattie cleared up in a week. It amazes Patrick that Nattie can go into the bush and come back with whatever she needs. Nattie takes away the bowl of willow bark and sets out bannock on two plates, pours them tea.

The bannock has raisins in it. Even though Patrick's been sending Nattie money when he was outside, he's never become used to eating raisins in Niska. Nattie never used them when he was growing up, just as she never bought the tinned peaches or marshmallow cookies other kids used to eat. She never owed the Bay a cent, either. Nattie makes all her clothes, sews them by hand. She makes moccasins and rabbit-fur blankets which she sells at the goose camp. Xavier helps, gives her geese to can, caribou and moose.

"Bernadette's back," Nattie says.

"Bernadette who?" Patrick says to tease her. His mother mentions Bernadette every chance she gets.

Nattie sucks her lips inward, a sign of exasperation. Most of the time, she goes without her teeth, which gives her mouth a sunken, puckered look like a dried-up slough.

"Lucy and Elias's girl. The youngest," she says.

"The youngest? How young is that, twelve or thirteen?"

"Twenty," Nattie says. "Old enough for you."

"Oh, that one," Patrick says, though he remembers Bernadette, a shy, serious girl who wears horn-rimmed glasses.

"You should talk to her," Nattie says.

"Why should I talk to her?"

"A man who is twenty-seven needs a woman."

"True," Patrick says, "but there's not much to choose from in Niska." About the only woman his age around here is Evangeline Crow, who's still married to a white man. "Besides, I haven't had time."

"You have time for the white woman," Nattie says and sucks her lips in disapprovingly.

So that's it. She must know Willa was at the ridge. Probably Lucy Know-it-all Bird told her.

"That's business," Patrick says. "She's giving me a hand with the plans for the Treaty Day meeting."

"Bernadette can help you," Nattie says.

"Bernadette can't draw. I need someone who can draw. Don't worry, the white teacher's only here for another three weeks."

"Bernadette will be here another two weeks."

"I'm not going to get stuck with a white woman, kishay-ininiw," Patrick says. "If I'd wanted that, I wouldn't have come back inside."

At that Nattie smiles, showing bare gums.

Patrick looks at her, at the wrinkled brown skin, the braided hair, black, hardly any grey in it. He looks at the shiny, bluish-grey membrances over her eyes. He thinks how much Willa would like to get this face in her sketchbook.

13: George answers the door himself. Rain or no rain, Ralph has gone off with Luke and Francis to look for small game. George was snoozing on the sofa when the knock woke him up.

He pads to the door in sock feet. Opening it, he sees Willa standing on the top step. It's good to see her, but he has to admit she looks a mess, uncombed, greasy, wet hair, no lipstick like she had when she first came inside. She's upset, he sees that right away.

"Hi," he says. "Come on in."

She steps inside and stands there, huddled on the mat like an orphan.

George can smell her body odour.

"Come into the front room," he says. "I'll pour us a drink. You look like you could use one."

"No," she says. "I'll stay here. My boots are muddy."

She seems different somehow. Unfriendly. Maybe it's his imagination because of what happened.

"What happened to Runt?" she says, right to the point.

"I shot him."

"Why?"

"Because a pack was ripping him to shreds," George says. He doesn't want to go into the gory details. The poor dog was a mess. Two legs torn off by the time he got there. The squealing was something fierce. "I thought it was a dog fight at first," he goes on. "That's why I went for my gun. Every once in a while, there's a bad fight where the only way you can break it up is with a gun. When I reached your cabin, I saw it was something else. That happens here too, a pack will gang up on some dog and kill it."

This brings the tears. She would get attached to that runt. Go all sentimental over it. He tried to warn her, but of course it did no good.

"How did they get him outside?" she says.

"I don't know. Maybe the door to your porch was open and they went in and dragged him outside. I had to shoot him. No other way to put him out of his misery."

"What happened to him afterwards?"

Jesus, she's a killer for punishment. "What do you think?"

George says irritably. Surely she didn't expect him to bury the dog. There was no question of that. The pack would've dug him up again. The main reason they killed him, besides them being cowards and him being a runt, was because they were starving.

"They're jackals," he says to her. "They prey on carrion. That's how most of them stay alive. Are you sure you wouldn't like a drink?"

"No!" she says, so fiercely George feels like he's made an enemy.

"You got a letter," he says. "I put it in your kitchen."

"I saw it," she says. She opens the door and goes outside into the drizzling rain.

George gives the door an angry push. Hell, why is she pissed off at him? He was doing the dog a favour. She never even thanked him. Funny, he never took her for a bleeding heart. He thought she was more sensible than that. Of course, that's what happens to a lot of white people when they first come up here. They see the terrible conditions the Indians live in, and they bleed all over the place. Then there are those whites who carry around some strange ideas about Indians. They seem to think Indians are exotic, like those natives in the South Seas and places like that. Take that anthropologist, for instance, who was up here one summer three years ago studying Indians so he could get a degree. The questions he asked the people were a hoot: how many times a couple had sex, how many times they brushed their teeth. The Indians fed him all kinds of phony answers. He never seemed to figure out they were laughing at him behind his back. He went back outside the same way he came inside, with a lot of silly ideas in his head. Probably wrote some sentimental slop about Indians, the kind that makes you want to puke.

When he's been outside, George has read some magazine articles about Indians. Most of them were written by university types and church people who walk around with their tape recorders and notebooks trying to make instant heroes of these people, all that noble savage stuff. Most of them know bugger all about Indians. Most of them couldn't care less. What they're looking for is a way to shore up their jobs and their Christian consciences. You wouldn't catch them living inside on a reserve. The reason people can afford such high-falutin' ideas about Indians is because they can walk away from reserves. They aren't living with Indians, they aren't laying it on the line.

George goes into the kitchen and gets out a bottle of rye whisky. There's half a bottle left. He'll have to spin it out until Wednesday. He's got more coming in on Treaty Day. He'll have one stiff drink now and put the bottle away. George doesn't add water but carries the glass into the front room, sits on the sofa, puts his feet on a chair and picks up the book he was reading before he fell asleep. Another hour and he'll have finished *Lord Edgeware Dies* for the fifth time.

14: Willa starts the fire in the stove, hauls two buckets of water and puts them on to heat. Then she sits beside the stove to read the letter.

July 7

Dear Willa,

Your letter came this morning. It took a week to get here. I'm answering it right away while Danny has his nap so it can go out in this afternoon's mail. It won't be long, not an epic like yours. What a welcome you had! That Geraldine character sounds like someone out of a book. But you seem to have withstood it all right. If I had been slapped like that, I would have burst into tears.

I don't think I should send your letter to Mum and Dad. You know how Mum worries. I'll write them an abbreviated version and leave the Geraldine part out. The priest sounds like a

*character, too. I had the impression the church sent these politi-
cal activists up north nowadays. Maybe they don't have enough
of this kind to go around. Or maybe the village you're in is so
small it was sent an oddball. Makes you wonder if there are
many other villages up north like that.*

*You picked a good time to leave Ottawa. We're having a heat
wave. The fans run all night. Danny practically lives in his
wading pool. My ankles have swollen to the size of tree trunks.
The doctor told me to cut back on fluids and keep my feet up. I
suppose it'll be this way until the baby comes.*

*Bert finished the room downstairs, so it'll be ready for you
when you come back. All that's left to do is the wallpaper. Don't
worry. It's nothing splashy, some beige fibre stuff I got on sale.
We're going to repaper the upstairs room you were in with some
jungly paper I found: pink lions and blue elephants, just in case.
The doctor says it's a girl.*

*This letter is so much shorter than yours, but if I add any
more, I'll put you to sleep. The truth is, not much is happening.
We are leading a quiet life (leaving the excitement up to you).
But we like to read about it, so please write again. I'm glad
you're finding time for your own work. By the way, you were
right, you bake rice pudding, like custard.*

Love,
Karen

There's eleven months between Karen and Willa. Bev was
six years older than Karen, which explains, as much as anything
can, why the younger sisters have always been close friends.
They are not at all alike; in fact, all they have in common is their
sisterhood. Karen is the opposite of Willa: easygoing, dependent
and domesticated. She and Bert married soon after they gradu-
ated from high school. Karen worked for an insurance company
while Bert earned his education degree. As soon as he started
teaching, Karen quit her job and became pregnant. Her ambi-
tion is to stay home and look after kids. Willa isn't sure she ever

wants kids. She's not even sure she wants to get married. She figures she's had too close a call with Arnie. But marriage and kids suit Karen. Willa thinks the closeness between her sister and herself is based on an easy acceptance of each other, from the knowledge that whatever the other one does, she can depend on her sister's support.

Willa folds the letter, opens up a can of tomato soup, mixes it with tinned milk and puts it on to heat. She's out of crackers and bread, but she'd rather do without than ask George for food. She doesn't want to see George again today. She's still upset about Runt, that he suffered. And she's disappointed, though not with George. Now that she's thinking rationally, she realizes it isn't his fault the dog got out. She's disappointed with herself, knowing she should have taken the dog with her to the ridge. It occurred to her, but she didn't want to be bothered. George was right. She shouldn't have taken in the dog in the first place. All she did was prolong the inevitable. And he was probably right about the porch door being left open. Willa remembers what Father Aulneau told her when she took the flower to the mission. He said he'd been awakened from a nap yesterday by a dog fight followed by a gunshot. He looked out the window and saw George walking away with a gun. He saw the cabin door open. He came over himself, he said, and closed it.

The main reason Willa doesn't want to see George has nothing to do with Runt, but with Geraldine. Willa doesn't want to accept George's hospitality, knowing what she knows about Geraldine. If he knew Geraldine was at the ridge, he might phone the police again. Willa's not about to spill the beans, to risk trading the contents of two suitcases of Bear's work for a Black & Decker saw and a hundred-foot cord. It isn't that she's taken Geraldine's side. She has no illusions about that happening. All she and Geraldine have done is meet on an island named Peetanaquot.

After Willa finishes the soup, she hooks the porch door and closes the curtains. She lays clean clothes, towels and shampoo on a chair and pours warm water into the dishpan. She peels off her T-shirt, jeans and underwear. Sniffs her armpits. She stinks, she reeks of sweat and repellent. Did Patrick notice how much she stank? Well, so what if he noticed? She can't be expected to tramp around drawing village sites and stay clean and sweet-smelling. Anyway, it's ridiculous to be thinking about that. She's not up here to become involved that way with anyone, especially an Indian. She knows why Evangeline Crow lost her status. The Scottish fur traders and the occasional priest may have gotten away with it, but they lived here. Besides, they were men. When she first came here, Willa thought the men she passed on the boardwalk avoided looking at her out of shyness, out of politeness and deference. She doesn't think that way any more.

The fact that she's physically attracted to Patrick doesn't mean anything. Since she and Arnie broke up, this has happened at least twice a year. She went to bed a few times with Clive Hartwell, an artist who made collages out of junk mail and hawked them on the street before he decided Ottawa was too bourgeois for him and moved to Vancouver. For a while she was even infatuated by Dick Simpson with his handlebar mustache and balding head. Willa figures this sort of infatuation is one of the hazards of celibacy. In any case, it never got to be a problem with Dick. He was married, and she only saw him once a week. The problem here is that there's no way to avoid seeing Patrick, there's no place to go. She only has to get through the next couple of weeks and, as with the others, the infatuation with Patrick will pass.

SIX

1: *Treaty Day, July 21.* Gerald Gull's up early, sitting on the deck of the ark, wrestling with a hammer and a bent nail. He's back to salvaging nails out of old boards because he's run out again. He needs more nails to get the plastic on the roof. His brother Simon gave him a bag of nails two days ago, but he used them up to nail down the roof boards. His government cheque came. He spent it on three rolls of plastic, a bag of porridge, brown sugar and tinned milk. Geraldine's cheque hasn't showed up yet. His mother's hasn't showed up, either. It's happened before; the Lord doesn't have much clout with the post office.

What he needs is a staple gun. There's one in the store, but he was a few dollars short of the price, not counting the staples. He can't ask George to put it on credit. Last time he asked, George said no, not until he paid his bill down. It's up over six hundred somewhere. George took some money from his cheque to pay against it, which is why his cheque went so fast. Today he gets four dollars from the government man. He won't bother going to the meeting for that amount; Simon will bring back his four dollars.

Gerald forces the hammer claw around the nail head and works it sideways, trying to wrench it free. Goddamn thing won't budge. C'mon, you bugger, he says, get outta there. You don't want to be stuck in a board, bent over like my old mother. You wanna stand up straight, don'tcha? Do something useful? Gerald gives the nail a big wrench, and the head breaks off. Goddamned nail. More trouble than it's worth. He throws the board into the gully water. Get down there where you belong. Gerald looks at the jumble of boards beside him. He's got a long ways to go before he's got enough nails to finish nailing the plastic on the roof. At first, the work on the roof went fast. With the electric saw, he got the boards cut the same length. He did the work at Dave Wabano's. That's where he keeps the electric saw. Dave's got the generator, and he's got a chain saw that makes a big racket. Before Gerald turns on the electric saw,

Dave turns on his chain saw to cover up the whine so George can't hear.

There's still work to do before the ark is ready. There's out-houses to build: one for women, one for men, the kids will use both. There's a walkway to build for when the people come on board two by two, like the story says. There's stoves to get in. They'll need two for cooking and heating. Gerald looks at the sky, wondering how long the good weather will last, how long before the flood will come.

From the clearing he hears the familiar sound of stone hitting metal. Gerald knows what his mother wants. She wants the same thing she wants every morning — her porridge. If Geraldine would get her ass back here and do the cooking, things would move a lot faster. But she's lying low, holed up at the ridge. The cops are gone, she should come back. Gerald kneels down on the deck, pulls off his peaked cap and prays:

Dear Lord, hold off the rain for a while yet. I'm doing the best I can, but I need your co-operation. If you can manage it, send that goddamned Geraldine back. Put her to work. And while you're at it, Lord, calm her down. Baptize her with the Holy Ghost. Amen.

Another stone hits the pot.

Gerald gets up and goes to his mother.

Old Martha sits cross-legged on the packed mud in front of their dirty white tent, the place she sits all day, every day, a ring of stones in front of her, the pot dangling over the ashes by one wire tired to a wooden tripod. Beneath the tattered army blan-ket pulled over her head, two eyes stare piercingly at her son. Gerald never knows what his mother's thinking. Her eyes follow him everywhere. Sometimes it's the only thing about her that moves. She won't cook, won't wash, won't get water or split wood like the other women in Niska. The day he showed up with Geraldine, his mother quit doing these things. She stopped talking before Geraldine got here. Long ago, before his father was run over by a tractor at the air base, his mother used to jibber-jabber all the time. Soon as his father got killed, she shut up like a clam. Hasn't spoke a word since. Gerald carries the water buckets to the river. The river's just about over the top step. If the Lord wants him to win this race, He'd better keep the water down a while yet.

Gerald returns with the buckets. He pours water into the pot, lights the fire beneath. While the water heats, he goes behind the tent, falls on his knees, pulls off his cap and offers another prayer:

While you're at it, Lord, send the Holy Ghost down to this poor woman so she can speak. Loosen her tongue, Lord. Amen.

Gerald gets to his feet. He hears his mother cackling. She's making fun of him again, always she's making fun. Gerald throws a fistful of oatmeal into the pot. Maybe it's better that his mother don't speak. Maybe the Lord keeps his mother this way for a reason. Maybe He figures that with a wife like Geraldine, he needs a silent mother.

After they've finished their porridge, Gerald goes back to salvaging nails. He gets a run of good luck, twenty nails straight enough to finish nailing down the plastic so the wind won't blow it off and the rain leak through. Gerald mounts the ladder and begins nailing down the plastic. That's when he catches sight of Geraldine. Up here he can see clear over the bush to the tundra. He can see Geraldine walking along like she's got all the time in the world. One hand is holding a green plastic bag, the other is deep in her parka pocket. The way she walks with her head bent down reminds Gerald of the first time he saw her.

She was walking along the hall of the hospital in Sioux Lookout as if she was interested in the squares on the floor that a man pushed a machine over to make them shine. When Gerald came close to her, she lifted her head and looked straight at him with those eyes that looked like they'd burn you clear through. Back then, Geraldine was good-looking. Even wearing a hospital gown, he could tell what a good shape she had to her. She was different from the other girls he knew. There was something frozen-looking about her face. She never giggled the way most girls did. He used to try to make her smile. He made jokes, gave her chocolate bars the churchwomen brought around, but he couldn't get her to laugh. It was her eyes that did all the work. First time he saw Geraldine laugh was after she tripped a nurse who was carrying a tray and couldn't see Geraldine's foot. He liked that. He liked a woman with some spunk in her. Back then he didn't know that Geraldine had more spunk in her than he wanted. He married her before she showed her warrior side.

Geraldine walks softly through the bush, avoiding the main paths. The reason she stayed out there on that spruce island all night was so she could get into the village early in the morning before anyone got up. Gerald's up early same as always, but he don't count. It's the others she wants to avoid. Gerald better have some food. She ran out yesterday. Her last big feed was the sardines and crackers she ate in Patrick's cabin. She picked some crowberries on the way here, but they were green and sour, so she spat them out. After she eats, she's going to sleep on the mattress below deck. She's going to sleep all morning so she'll be ready for the big meeting this afternoon.

2: Willa's posted in the bedroom window of the mission cabin watching people straggle up the boardwalk to the schoolhouse. The women are in their sweaters and flowered skirts. Two of them, Betsy Bluecoat and Josephine Loon, have their babies strapped in *tikinagans*. The men wear the usual baggy green pants, plaid shirts and peaked caps. The kids run ahead, the girls with their brushed or neatly braided hair, flowered skirts and white socks, the boys in T-shirts and jeans. Nancy Hunter has a new pink dress with a lace collar. Richard and Stanley Bluecoat have new runners. Rita Marie has on what look like new jeans. Yesterday afternoon, Rita Marie, Josh, Rosena and Danny stayed behind class to help arrange the pictures around the schoolroom. Every available inch of wall space is covered with their paintings and drawings. Patrick came in as they were finishing up and taped the drawings of the new village on the front wall, over the blackboard. In addition to the sketch of the village layout, Willa's drawn a rough picture on the blackboard. Patrick asked her to draw today's meeting, to get down everyone present, being sure to write in each person's name. A historical record, he called it. Willa's waiting until the last minute before she goes over, so she can slip unobtrusively into the back of the schoolroom, where she's less likely to attract attention.

She sees a short, stocky man with close-cropped blond hair coming up the boardwalk. He's wearing grey flannels, an open-necked shirt and a tweed jacket with leather elbow patches. This can only be the district manager, who's come to hand out the treaty money. Willa sees him look around, glance from side to side as he walks up the boardwalk. He seems intent both on making a cursory inspection while at the same time being careful where he puts his feet. His walk has the air not of assurance but of cautious enthusiasm, as if he's an emissary walking into an enemy camp and is determined to keep the peace at any cost. He swings a brown briefcase out from his side as he walks. He looks first at the schoolhouse, then at Willa's window. Quickly, Willa lets go of the curtain and ducks down, out of sight.

Seconds later, she sticks her head up, lifts the curtain and looks out again. The man is still on the boardwalk, walking her way. He steps off the boardwalk into the swamp and looks up. Once again, Willa drops the curtain and ducks out of sight. She must hide. She doesn't want this man to see her. She's afraid of this stranger.

There's a knock at the door.

He's here!

Willa covers her ears.

She should've hooked the door. What if he comes inside? He might do that. This stranger might walk right into the bedroom and see her.

Willa scuttles under the bed and crawls into a rectangle of air. She flattens herself against the hard plywood floor, trying to make herself invisible. Dust tickles her nose. She hears the man again.

"Hello in there! It's Oscar Hoffman. I'd like to have a word with you."

What does he want? Why must he bang on her door like that? She puts her hands over her ears, blocking him out.

"I have a message for you!"

That's just a trick to get her to come out. *Go away,* she mouths into the dust, *Go away, go away.* She holds herself rigid against an opening door, the sound of footsteps. He tells her again he has a message for her, then he goes away. She can hear his footsteps receding across the grass. The stranger has gone.

For what seems a very long time, Willa lies there hearing nothing. Gradually she becomes aware of her own breathing. On the other side of the plywood wall there's a soft thudding sound as someone moves across the grass. Farther away, she hears footsteps on the boardwalk as people walk to the schoolhouse. Willa's muscles relax slightly. A dustball catches a nostril. She sneezes, then goes rigid again. *Someone has come in the porch door, is moving across the floor.*

She turns her head and sees two moccasined feet standing on the floor beside the bed. While she's staring at these feet, two brown hands come down on the floor, two blue-jeaned knees, two braids, a beaded headband. A face appears, pock-marked and serious. A familiar face wearing horn-rimmed glasses.

Face, knees, hair disappear. Willa wants to cry out, *Don't leave,* but she can't speak. She lies there and watches the moccasined feet. They move to the foot of the bed. The bed is on casters. It begins to slide. The walls of her rectangle fall away, and the box disappears. Willa shuts her eyes, covers her head, her face in the dust.

"You okay?" a low voice says.

Willa feels a hand on her back.

She hears a squeak. *Is that her voice?*

He takes his hand away.

Willa opens her eyes, blinks into the light.

She sees Patrick standing there, grinning at her. He puts out a hand. Willa takes it. He pulls her to her feet.

"You look like a mop," he says. He reaches out and picks dust out of her hair. Then he casually brushes dustballs from her sweater where they cling to the wool over her breasts.

Abruptly, Willa flings her arms around him and holds him as if her life depended on it.

"It's okay," he says, patting her shoulders. "It's okay."

He holds her so close she can feel his sex against her belly.

"Hey, you're one crazy lady," he says into her ear. "I've never met a woman as crazy as you."

Willa pulls away, fishes a Kleenex out of her pocket and blows her nose.

"I don't know what got into me," she says. She feels silly, embarrassed.

"You're spaced out. Bushed. Don't let it worry you," Patrick says. "Sometimes it happens to white people in the North."

"But for it to happen so soon — "

"It's when you first come in that you have to watch it the most. You're not used to the isolation. You become afraid of strangers. It's quite common." He's smiling at her. "You all set to go over to the school? The councillors gave permission for you to draw the meeting. I guess I told you that."

"You did."

"Yeah. I guess I'd better get back."

"I'll be over in a few minutes."

After he leaves, Willa walks around the cabin, trying to understand what happened. Whatever possessed her, hiding under the bed like that? When she and Karen were kids, they used to play a game in which they pretended to make themselves invisible, discovering the power of seeing, unseen. These were tantalizing, exhilarating transformations. Hiding under the bed wasn't like that. There was nothing magical or exhilarating about it. She felt instead a deep, primitive fear that came from the darkest places. The sight of a stranger made her feel like burrowing into the earth, camouflaging herself with leaves and twigs. She thinks that if Patrick hadn't come along when he did, she might have stayed under the bed indefinitely. She probably made a fool of herself grabbing hold of him like that. It was gratitude and relief that made her do it. Not that Patrick objected. But she doesn't want to give him the wrong idea. She doesn't want him to think she's one of these silly, helpless females. Of course, if she was silly and helpless, she wouldn't be here, would she? So, what's she worrying about? Willa picks up her sketchbook and pencils, goes outside and walks to the schoolhouse for the meeting.

3: From Xavier's notebook:

In 1929, after my father, Solomon Hunter, signed Treaty Number 9, he invited the commissioner to sit on the rush mat in front of our meekeepwap *and smoke together. When they were finished smoking, the commissioner, who was in a blue uniform trimmed with gold threads, said, "I speak from the heart. The white man loves his red brother." To this, my father replied, "The white man loves the ground the red man walks on."*

Later, my father spoke to me about this meeting. He said the government was wise to send a good man. If the government had sent a bad man, he wouldn't have signed, even though the people were starving. Sending a good man made it harder to say no.

4: The schoolroom is full. Women are jammed into desk seats, children nudge each other for desk tops and floor space, men lean against the walls. Xavier sits up front at the teacher's desk. At his feet is the cardboard office box. Beside him are three chairs, two occupied by the councillors, Simon Gull and Saul Crow. The third is for Patrick, who is fiddling with a tape recorder on the desk. Willa leans against the back wall, just inside the back door. Not the best place to sketch the meeting, but it will have to do. There's not a seat left anywhere. Willa looks around the room at the palette of bright kerchiefs, skirts, sweaters, the children's artwork on the walls, the women's craftwork on the desk: pouches, moccasins, mukluks, mitts, headbands. It's a festive, colourful occasion. She'll have to do a painting of it later on.

The district manager is sitting on Willa's left, close to the side wall. Willa ignores him. She draws a circle for each head and pencils in the name. Her hand moves quickly back and forth across the rectangle of paper. Mothers and children sit in family bunches, fathers nearby, against the wall. She fills in the names by families. Nazarene Rose and Francis Crow. Xavier Hunter's family, Bernice, Josh and Rachel, Luke. Marsha Crow. Sophie and Marious Hunter with Marcel, Edward and Nancy, Rebecca Gull with Jake, Sarah and Danny.

Morris Mack and Elizabeth. Betsy and Alphonse Bluecoat with Richard, Stanley and the baby. Henry and Agnes Sutherland with Rosena, Ernst and Tom. Jeremiah Crow, the only elder at the meeting. Lucy and Amos Bird with a young woman named Bernadette, who came inside last week. Mary and John Bird. Baptiste. Denise and Dave Wabano with Mark, Rita Marie, Amos and Aurora. Albert and Josephine Loon with Maurice, Angie and the baby. Aglace and Frances Loon. The only people who aren't here are Evangeline Crow and her boys, Nattie Eagle, Gerald Gull, his mother. And Geraldine Gull.

All around her, Willa hears small stirrings, coughs, whispers. Outside is the sound of Gerald Gull's hammer.

Xavier gets to his feet.

The tape recorder clicks on.

"This year we decided to have ayamihitowin on Treaty Day to decide something important," Xavier says. "We planned it this way so the district manager can hear what we got to say. He can take our words back to the other people in the government. Patrick Eagle speaks first."

Xavier sits down.

Willa sees the district manager shift awkwardly in his chair. Did he expect to speak first?

Patrick sits on the edge of the desk.

"When I was a kid here," he says, "I caught a fish in the river." He holds up a finger. "Only one. I felt proud because I was six years old, and I thought that was why I never caught any before."

He pauses.

"I didn't know it was the only fish in the river." Some of the women giggle.

"When I was nine years old, a caribou walked into the village. I ran home to get my father's gun, but when I was coming back with it, Monsignor Dupuis, who was visiting Niska that day, stopped me. 'You can't kill that animal,' he said. 'It's Sunday.' "

More nervous giggles.

"That was the only caribou I ever saw here," Patrick says solemnly.

The room erupts with laughter. Willa smiles. She's sure this is an exaggeration, but it's probably the right approach, leading the people into the meeting slowly, using humour to make a point. She watches him put his foot on a chair, lean forward, one elbow on his knee, braids hanging down.

"That wasn't why I left Niska. I left to get an education so I could understand what was going on with us, with you and me, all of us. What I found out was how badly we've been screwed."

The district manager fidgets with the lock on his briefcase.

"Now I've come back here to stay," Patrick continues. "I plan to build a house, make a life for myself. But when I look around, I see there's still no fish, no caribou, no timber. I say to myself, Why should I build a house here? Why should anyone build a house here?"

The room is still. In the distance is the rat-a-tat of Gerald's hammer.

"You know why we're here?" Patrick asks. "We're here because the Roman Catholic Church and the Hudson's Bay store wanted us here."

Willa sees the government man nod his head in agreement.

"The Bay wanted our furs. The Church wanted our souls. Trouble was, our bodies were starving. Wapusk was always stalking us, so we begged to be included in Treaty Number 9. Meanwhile, the Bay realized that, thanks to the government, we were a good credit risk. Being a good credit risk made us dependent on the system. All this time, the Church kept telling us to sit tight. If we could put up with living in this swamp, things would get better in heaven. One thing sure, they couldn't get much worse."

Several of the women wriggle uncomfortably.

Outside, in the porch, a door opens quietly.

"The fact is," Patrick continues, "we didn't have the choice. We still don't have much choice. That's because we don't have much. We can choose between life and death, but that's not what I call choice. That's no more than we were born with. Do you call that a choice?"

The Loon baby whimpers.

Footsteps cross the porch floor, walking softly.

"Well, I don't," Patrick says. "The fact is, though, we do have something."

He holds up a finger. "One choice. We can choose whether we stay here and rot in this swamp or whether we move someplace better. The great thing about this choice is that once we make it, all kinds of other opportunities are open to us. It's time for us to make a giant step forward."

Patrick pauses. "Most of you know that twenty-five miles from here there's a better place to live. Twenty-five miles. That isn't far to go, but it would put us millions of miles ahead. It's still reserve land. There's good fishing, lots of timber for houses. It's high enough above the river so we don't need to worry about being flooded out of our beds. I had some pictures drawn up to give you a better idea of what a new village could look like." Patrick points to Willa's drawings tacked above the blackboard, then he points to the blackboard itself. "Down here is a rough drawing to show where buildings could go."

There's a slight rustle inside the porch as a plastic bag is opened. No one turns around. They are staring at the sketches.

Patrick takes a pen out of his shirt pocket to use as a pointer.

"This area here," Patrick points to the centre of the blackboard, "is where the village centre would be — the store, the school, the church, band office and radio station, meeting hall, nursing station. These buildings would be arranged in a U, with the space in the middle being left for sports — ballgames, powwows, things like that. As you know, there's a stream over here in the field. If we could dam it up, we would have a wading pool for the kids, a park with benches for people to sit on. We could — "

"The gallery goes in the park!" Geraldine hollers from the porch. She shoves past the bodies blocking the aisle and pushes her way to the front, holding two of Alexander's pictures over her head.

There are gasps of astonishment, then silence. All eyes are on the wild Ojibwa woman as she marches across the front of the room. They stare at her, then look away, then back again, as if they are trying to decide whether or not they are being visited by a ghost. Their eyes say, *Maybe it's a trick.*

"These pictures were made by Alexander Bear," Geraldine says. "We'll put them in the gallery." She swaggers back and forth, holding the pictures close for people to see.

"My son, Alexander Bear, made these pictures. He was a

great artist. World-famous," she crows. "You take a good look. See how good they are."

After she shows them around, Geraldine puts the pictures on the blackboard ledge. She picks up a piece of chalk and makes a big X in the park. "This is where we build the gallery," she says. "We will have kids' pictures in it also, beside Alexander Bear's. I will get some money to make the gallery."

Geraldine goes to Patrick's chair and sits down. Patrick is standing behind the desk watching the people. The people begin to whisper and point, their eyes darting between Geraldine and the blackboard.

Xavier gets to his feet. Geraldine is *kesquakan*. He will ignore her.

"Patrick Eagle will finish talking now."

Patrick points his pencil at the extreme left of the blackboard. "Over here, we can put the airstrip, the sawmill, someday a fur factory and a greenhouse. A good place for a graveyard would be this place on the hill. We can build a gravel road from the airstrip, past this area to where people live. On the other side of the village centre, we can build houses. Not cabins or shacks — real houses with logs if we want. We can have basements and sewers because the ground is better than here. We have drawings of houses also, to give you an idea how they could look. The thing that's important to remember is that if we plan it right, we can build a model community second to none in the North. There's all kinds of people can help us get started — Health and Welfare, Ministry of Transport, the provincial government, DIAND." Patrick looks pointedly at the district manager. "We might be able to hire an engineer to help us plan and build things, show us how. There's lots of help out there. It's a question of going after it. But first . . ."

Patrick scans the room, his eyes sliding across the faces.

"First we got to realize that when the chips are down, it's our decision. We're the ones that have to decide."

He pauses, then goes on. "I'd like to ask the district manager what help the Department of Indian Affairs is prepared to give to this move."

Xavier stands up and looks at Mr. Hoffman. "You can speak now," he says.

The district manager picks his way through the squeeze of bodies. Nobody moves for him. Halfway there, he nearly trips and loses his balance. There are nervous titters, giggles, Geraldine's guffaw. When he finally makes it to the front, he unlocks his briefcase, sets it open on a corner of the desk.

He clears his throat and says, "If I may be permitted a few minutes of your time, I'd like to talk to you about a new project that I think would be of great help to you whether you stay here or not. For some time now, our department has been making inquiries into the feasibility of building windmills up here. With the amount of wind you people get off the bay — "

Xavier is on his feet. "No talk today," he says. "Just answer Patrick Eagle."

"Sorry. I just thought — " The district manager folds up his notes and shoves them inside his jacket pocket. "I just thought . . . well, never mind . . ." He turns to Xavier. "What was it you wanted me to say?"

Xavier gets up. "You answer Patrick Eagle," he says and sits down.

The district manager rubs the back of his neck.

Patrick Eagle ejects the tape, turns it over, snaps it on again.

Finally the district manager says, "What do you figure you'll need?"

Patrick holds up the fingers of both hands, then ticks off the items. "Tools, cement, windows, doors, airtight stoves, a sewer line, diesel generators, an airlift of food and temporary shelters like trailers to live in while we build our homes. But first, and most important, is transportation. We need some way of getting there."

"Ah, well," the government man hedges, "that's a pretty tall order. I'm not sure DIAND could offer much in the way of financial assistance. But Transport might be able to supply a plane for a short period of time. Maybe I could locate trailers somewhere. I don't know about getting the other items. I could work on it. Contact the other departments. See what I could come up with."

"Then we can count on your help," Patrick puts in quickly.

"Well, speaking personally, I'll do what I can, but I can't speak for the minister," the district manager says. "Exactly where were you thinking of moving?"

"The ridge."

"The ridge?"

"You know the place. Twenty-five miles south along the river, 114 feet above sea level."

"Now that's interesting," the district manager says. He gives a jokey half-laugh. "That's very interesting. Only last week, I received a memo from the minister about the ridge."

"And?"

"A certain oil company — I am not at liberty to say which one — has approached the Department of Energy and Mines about doing some exploratory work on that piece of land. As you know, there was some work done out in Hudson Bay, but it wasn't very promising. Apparently, geologists think the ridge would be a better place to look. But nothing's come of it until recently. I was going to bring this up later, but while we're on the subject, I should mention that it might be possible for the government to arrange a deal for you. Cash in hand. With interest rates what they are, you people could do very well for yourselves. But of course, you'd have to hold off on that move." The district manager almost drawls as he says this.

Xavier's on his feet. "I don't know about that. We have to think about that ourselves before we talk to you about it," he says. "If we decide to lease our land to this company you speak of, we can do it ourselves, not the government doing it for us. You better sit down now." He nods at Patrick, who has indicated he wants to speak.

Patrick stands up. "If we lease our land," he says, looking

directly at the district manager, "we invest the money ourselves. We don't want the same thing to happen to us as happened to the people on the Erminskin reserve, like the government investing the people's money, then forgetting about it, leaving it at four per cent for years and years, never bothering to roll it over to current interest rates. We don't need that kind of bureaucracy to botch up our affairs. Enough's gone wrong already."

"Wooeee!" Geraldine shouts.

"And we'd want to manage how it's spent," Patrick continues, "afterwards."

John Bird gets to his feet. "I got something to say."

Xavier gives him the nod.

"We can't move. We can't leave the airstrip," John says. "We've got no roads or trains like they've got outside. We depend on planes."

"We can build our own airstrip," Patrick says. He takes an envelope out of his back pocket and holds it up. "I got a letter here from Dugald McKillop, an engineer who was at the ridge last fall. In the letter, he says we got enough gravel at the ridge to build our own airstrip. He has a lot of other good ideas also."

Simon Crow gets to his feet. "At the ridge, we can build a better runway, one that is close by," he says, "not one over six miles of rough water."

"What about the Bay?" John says. "We can't leave the store. We need the grubstake they give us to go out on our traplines."

Patrick takes another envelope out of his pocket and holds it up. "This is a letter from Dominic Yesno at Mink Falls, where they started their own store. He sent me the information about how to start it up, how much it would cost and so on. If we have our own co-op, one we run ourselves, we cut nistum moosan, the birth-cord that ties us to the Bay. A birth-cord that's wrapped around out necks, choking us to death."

"We must eat," John says. "What do we do for food while we are building the airstrip?"

"We use float planes," Patrick says. "They can land on the river."

"Float planes cost more. Make food prices go up."

"True, but when we get our co-op built, we get some profits back. Eventually we can lower the prices. It should even out. We might get to the point where we could pay cash instead of being dependent on the store. The way it is now, the Bay owns us."

There are murmurings of disapproval. *The people don't like this. They know what Patrick says is true, but they do not want to think about that now. This is Treaty Day, a day to dress up and spend their treaty money.*

Geraldine claps loudly. "Get rid of the Bay!" she yells.

"You speak out of turn," Xavier says to her.

"What about the goose camp?" Amos Bird says. "We make good money off the hunters."

"We can still work there," Patrick says. "It only means travelling nineteen miles instead of six."

"What about the school?" Mary Bird asks. "We want our kids to stay past grade eight."

"I can teach the higher grades," Patrick says. "I can go back to the Lakehead for summer courses."

"You can't do everything yourself," Mary says.

"Maybe I'll get some help."

Denise Wabano speaks out. "What about the church? We need a church."

Xavier gets to his feet again. "I been thinking about the church. In this new place, we can build an Indian church. Make it of logs, build it into trees. Make it part of the woods. Maybe if we worked in more Indian ways of worshipping Kitche Manitou, more of us would go to church."

"The Little Father might not like that," Denise says.

"The priest's got nothing to say about that," Xavier says. "I wrote to his Chief, the one in Italy who wears a white dress."

"His Holiness," Denise says. "You wrote to him?"

"I did," Xavier says. "I wrote and explained the situation."

The women begin whispering to each other.

"There's a lot more to work out," Xavier says. "We've got

more talking to do. But first we got to show that this time we are serious about making a new village. The band council decided to start up a special fund to help us get going. We are asking you to put your treaty money into the fund. Patrick Eagle will collect the money in the moccasin pouch he's got. If you put your money into the pouch, you are saying let's go for a new village. I'm putting my Chief money in. Simon and Saul are putting their councillor money in. First we'll have the district manager pass out the money."

Xavier sits down.

The district manager gets to his feet. He takes from his brief-case an envelope containing new one-dollar bills, enough to give fifteen dollars to each councillor, twenty-five to the Chief. The one-dollar bills for everyone else are in a second envelope. He takes out this money and lays it on the desk.

Before he can pass out the money, Geraldine Gull is on her feet. "I want to talk!" she says. "I got something important to say."

"Sit down," Xavier says. "The district manager is passing out the treaty money."

Ignoring Xavier, Geraldine bends over, lifts her skirt, pulls her knife out of the sheath and stabs it into the desk.

Mr. Hoffman jerks backward.

Geraldine snickers, then scowls at him. "I'm the boss around here," she proclaims. She gives the government man a shove. "Got it?"

The district manager nods.

Xavier's on his feet again. "You leave now," he says.

Geraldine pays no attention. She smirks at the audience. "He got it," she says.

Geraldine reaches into her sheath and pulls out a yellowed wad of paper which she painstakingly unfolds. Then she holds the creased paper between thick fingers.

"My grandfather was Moses Bear, Chief of Osnaburgh," she boasts. "When the government man came to Osnaburgh with the treaty in 1905, Moses Bear made a big talk. I got the talk here, and I'm reading it to you."

Geraldine plants her feet astride and pulls the dirty red beret to the front of her head, positioning it above her forehead like an officer's hat. She begins to read, her voice booming through the small schoolroom.

Mr. Commissioner, it is true we live in a cold climate with poor hunting and poor food. It is true we are starving. It is true we need help. But we should not sign the treaty to get help. The treaty says we have to stay here on poor land without good hunting and fishing. The treaty draws lines across the land. Stay here, the lines say, do not go there. That is wrong. Kitche Manitou did not make land that way. He did not make animals to stay inside lines. He did not make people to stay inside lines. The land is not the white man's. It is Kitche Manitou's. Kitche Manitou makes good land and bad land. If we are on bad land, we move. The treaty says we don't move. That is wrong. If we want to move, we move. We should not sign this treaty. To sign this treaty is to make war between people and the land. That is what I have to say. Moses Bear.

The room is silent. Geraldine carefully refolds the tattered paper and puts it in her sheath with her knife and the rabbit snare, then she snaps a dirty hand under the district manager's nose.

"The money," she barks, shoving against the silence of the room.

The district manager counts out four one-dollar bills.

"All of it!" Geraldine roars.

"But — "

Geraldine pulls her knife.

He hands her the wad of bills.

Geraldine slams the money on top of the desk with the other money and skewers the pile with her knife. "There!" she says triumphantly. "We use this money for moving to the ridge. You heard what Patrick Eagle says. We should go. Get out of this stinking hole. This place is no good for us. It turns us into sleepy toads. We've got to wake up fast. Get out of here quick. We use this money to move. Go to the ridge where we can have a gallery for pictures." She points to Alexander's work, the kids' paintings on the walls. She looks around the room for approval. "We need a special place for pictures. We cannot have a special place here. It's too wet."

The people stare back, stony-eyed. Their eyes say, *You have taken our money and put holes in it; the money won't be good any more.*

"My old man's building a boat to take us to the ridge," Geraldine says expansively. "It's big, bigger than the school. Bigger than the store. It has room for everybody to go on it. You be my friend, you can go for free." Then she adds a joke. "Others got to buy tickets."

No one laughs.

Xavier goes to the desk, pulls the knife out of the wad of bills and returns it to Geraldine. "This is the people's money," he says quietly. "You go now."

Geraldine's eyes shift angrily. "No one tells Geraldine Gull what to do!" she roars, brandishing the knife. "I go when I want!" She turns to the people. "Who wants a ride in Gerald Gull's boat?" she bellows. "I'll take orders now."

No one says anything. *They do not like the knife. They do not like this wild Ojibwa woman who does not belong here. She should go away again and leave them alone.*

Geraldine puts the knife in the sheath. "It's a good boat," she says. "Big. Strong. Big enough for tables and beds. My old man's working on it now. . . . "

She stops. Waits.

Still they sit, watching, saying nothing.

"Gerald Gull's a shaman!" she yells. "He says more rain's coming. Soon. Lots of it like in the book the priest reads from. It's going to rain and rain. Look!"

Geraldine points toward the window, where an army of grey

clouds awaits her command. "See those clouds? Rain's going to come down. There'll be a big flood. Niska's going to wash away. You want to be saved, you got to get on Gerald Gull's boat."

Geraldine stops long enough to gulp in more air, then she begins again. "I make you a deal. You give me four dollars, and I'll give you a ticket to get on the boat!" She stretches out her hand, coaxing, wheedling for the money.

Patrick leaps to his feet. "That's enough," he says sharply. "Sit down."

Geraldine turns, grins at Patrick.

"You've gone too far with your sales pitch," he says. "Now that you've had your say, you'd better sit down and shut up."

Geraldine scowls at Patrick. "Stupid Cree," she says scathingly, "you're no better than the others."

She clomps to the back of the room, whacking bodies sitting in her way, kicking people who don't move fast enough.

Willa sees her coming and moves aside.

Geraldine ignores her. She pushes toward the porch. When she reaches it, she stops, turns, hawks up phlegm from deep inside her throat and spits through the doorway.

"Dogs!" she growls and slams the door.

Mr. Hoffman gets up, says something to Xavier. Willa can't hear what it is, but Xavier nods. The district manager looks at the silent faces. "Is there anyone here who can check off names?" he says. "I need someone to write down any new information for the Welfare Department."

Bernadette stands up and comes forward. Mr. Hoffman shows her what to do. She sits down at the desk, and the ceremony begins. Slowly, each woman gets up from the desk and, followed by her children, files to the front. Mr. Hoffman counts out four one-dollar bills into each hand while Bernadette marks them off. When the women are finished, the men peel themselves from the wall and go to the desk.

Patrick stands beside the door, holding the moccasin pouch, so people have to pass him on the way out. Willa watches to see who contributes to the fund: Bernice Hunter, Marious and Sophie Hunter. Nazarene Rose, Albert and Josephine Loon. Old Jeremiah, Aglace Loon. The others leave without so much as a glance at Patrick. He could be carved of wood.

Willa goes outside and walks slowly across the grass to her cabin. She wants to get out of the schoolhouse before Mr. Hoffman tries to speak to her again. And she can't stand it inside, she can't stand the wooden expression on Patrick's face. Fringed vest, beaded headband, long braids, he stands at the door holding a moccasin pouch, stands there like a cigar-store Indian, like the one in front of Dave's News back home.

5: Geraldine hurtles herself down the boardwalk toward the Bay. She's hungry. When she gets mad, she gets hungry. That's why she's fat. She's so mad and fat right now she feels like a Bear. Usually when she makes this joke, Geraldine laughs. Today she doesn't think it's funny. The people in this dump are stupid, all of them stupid toads. They need something big to wake them up, and she knows what it is. She told them about Gerald's boat. Maybe it won't float with all the nails in it, but she thought it would get people thinking about getting out of this dump. They didn't go for the shaman idea or buying tickets, either. They did not even care about Alexander's pictures. When she was showing the pictures, some of the toads were so stupid they couldn't crawl out of the mud to look at them. That's how sleepy they are.

The grey bitch slinks out of the swamp, udder swinging slack beneath her belly. She fawns against the back of Geraldine's leg. Geraldine swings around, gives the dog a vicious kick. The bitch rolls over into the wet muck, whimpering and yelping. Anything gets in Geraldine Gull's way, she gives it a good kick. Show who's boss around here. But her satisfaction is momentary. Only porridge this morning. Nothing to eat all day. The hunger returns, swoops down on her, talons clutching her stomach like an eagle tearing at raw flesh. Goddamn Eagle. Goddamn Patrick. She gave him an idea he's too stupid to think of himself, and he told her to shut up. What does he know? He's never been hungry like her. He's never walked out of the bush like her. His mother's been hungry. She's walked out of the bush, but she's like the other women in Niska, buried like toads in the mud. Bury yourself in the mud and nobody knows you're alive. Except for fucking, she's sorry she's a woman.

By the time Geraldine reaches the end of the boardwalk, her black mood has begun to lift. She steps off the boardwalk onto the grass, making her way toward the Bay. Today things are going to be different. No porridge and tea for her. Today she's going to eat big. Today's the day Geraldine Gull gave her big talk. She feels better, remembering how good her talk was. But when she steps inside the Bay, she realizes, under the stark glare of fluorescent lights, that she has no dollar bills. She left her treaty money in the school. She won't go back for it. She'd do without before she'd go back to that roomful of dogs. That would be saying she's sorry. And she's not sorry. She's never in her life said sorry, not to anyone. She's never said please or thank you or you're welcome. Those are white man's words, not Indian words. Please, she hears them say, please and thank you and you're welcome, like the priest saying stupid beads. Someone kick the white man in the ass, he'd say thank you.

Except for George, Ralph and the pilot who brought in the government man, the store's empty. Ralph is putting stuff on shelves same as always. George is sitting on a stool behind the counter with the pilot, waiting for the treaty money and drinking coffee. They know as soon as the meeting's over, everyone will come in here to spend their treaty money quick. Out of the corner of her eye, Geraldine sees George get to his feet and gape at her. For once he doesn't open his mouth. He's surprised she isn't dead. She don't care if he calls the cops. She'll be gone before they catch her.

Geraldine saunters toward the clothing bins, conscious of the eyes following her. To give these watchers something to worry about, Geraldine grabs hold of a green nylon parka, green this year, every jacket green. Last year jackets were blue. All the jackets in the store are the same colour, like the clothes they wear in jail.

"What do you want?"

Geraldine hears George's voice shoot at her like a bullet bouncing off her back. The prick won't take his eyes off her. But he won't get too close. He's afraid of her knife. And maybe he goes for that ghost idea also. She smirks at him. When he makes no move to throw her out, she strolls up to the counter.

"I want food," she says. "I forgot my treaty money. I'll get the money later. Gerald's also. The old lady's. First I'll pick what I want. Eggs. I want eggs."

Her eyes devour the fresh food that came in on the plane with the government man. George and the government man and the pilot must be in business together. Always on Treaty Day, there's lots of fresh food.

"Cheese also. Bananas. You put those there."

She taps a dirty forefinger against the counter where she wants the items to go while she hatches a plan inside her head.

"Bacon. You got bacon? I'll take some. Hamburg also. Bread. Oranges. Six. I'll take six."

She rattles off more items than she can carry just for the fun of it. She likes to see George hustle his fat ass to the shelves and back. Work for his money, the prick. When she has a stack of food big enough, she says, "I'll go get the money."

She goes out and turns to the right as if she's heading for the gully. She walks along the right side of the building, turns the corner and crosses the open space between the store and George's house. She gives the back door a shove. It opens easily. She steps in and closes the door. She's never been inside George's house before, only the store. This is the best time to go through his house. Everyone's at the meeting, she'll have the place to herself. Still, she walks softly, going from kitchen to living room, from bedroom to bathroom, her eyes missing nothing. She's surprised there's so little to see. The woman in Kenora had a better house than this.

She goes back to the kitchen and opens the cupboard door. The door sticks from the dampness. She gives the handle a jerk. The hinge squeals and the door scrapes open. Inside the cupboard are rows of packages: cake mixes, cereals, crackers, cookies, potato chips. She opens the next cupboard. Its shelves are jammed with canned goods: beans, peas, peaches, pears, coffee, spaghetti, tuna, sardines, ham, Spork. George never goes hungry. George never has a stomach that growls and roars.

On the floor inside the door are two boxes, one of them just off the plane. One contains a jumble of vegetables, fruit and cheese. The other, six rye whisky bottles, Seagram's, forty-ouncers.

Geraldine grins. This is her day. This is her day to eat big. Drink also. She looks around for a brown paper bag. She finds one behind the fridge where stupid Lucy Bird puts the mop and broom. Geraldine puts a package of cheese, two oranges, an apple, a banana, into the paper bag. She leaves the vegetables — she doesn't like vegetables. She adds a package of crackers, one of cookies, potato chips. She drops in four cans of sardines, the ones with keys in them. She leaves the other cans because she has no opener. She closes the cupboard doors and takes two whisky bottles out of the carton. She looks at the empty holes. George will see them for sure, soon as he looks in the box. She searches around for empty bottles. In the back room she finds three cartons of empty bottles. George is a big drinker, bigger than her. The bottles, Geraldine notices, still have tops. She takes two bottles into the kitchen, unscrews the tops, turns on the tap and holds first one, then the other under the water. George's lucky. He's got hot water coming from a tap. When the bottles are full, she screws the covers back on and wipes the bottles dry on her skirt. Then she puts them inside the empty slots in the carton. She puts the two bottles of whisky in the paper bag and carries the bag outside. She feels her belly hollowing out, getting ready for the food, but she's too smart to eat here. She'll go to the spruce island out on the tundra where no one will see her, where hungry dogs will leave her alone.

Geraldine closes the back door and steps onto the grass. She scoots across the swamp, head down, watching where she's going. When she gets to the boardwalk, she looks around. At the far end of the boardwalk, she sees kids spilling out of the school, people coming down the steps. The meeting's over. Quickly she darts into the bush. Once she's out of sight, Geraldine breaks into a half-walk, half-run, bobbing along the path, the bag under one arm.

She bobs through the stand of willows behind the village and crosses an open stretch of muskeg, water squishing beneath her rubber boots. She keeps going until she comes to the large island of spruce and lowbush cranberry. She crawls toward the centre and sits beneath the large, stunted spruce. She squats down and opens the bag, takes out an orange, peels off half the skin and sticks her nose and teeth into the orange, snuffling and sucking its sweet juiciness. Then she gulps down the whole package of cheese as if it was raw meat, not even slicing it with her knife. She opens a tin of sardines and scoops the fish into her mouth, mopping up the oil with crackers. The banana comes next. Only after she's eaten that does she uncap the whisky. This is different from what she usually does. Usually she drinks first, eats later. But Geraldine's decided she won't get drunk, not yet. Later she will, after she gets the work done, but for now she'll go part way into the bottle and quit. Because Geraldine Gull's got a plan. No chickenshit, two-bit plan. This time it's a big plan. A plan she thought of before, that she decided she'd try if the ticket and shaman idea didn't work. It's a plan that will change things around here. A plan that will show Patrick Eagle a thing or two, show the people here she won't be beaten down. Geraldine takes a swallow of whisky and wipes her mouth on her sleeve.

Patrick was too stupid to know she was selling tickets so people would get on the boat for sure like little kids with candy. She will do the same thing when they get the gallery built and they come to see Alexander's pictures. *First* they come to Geraldine Gull. That's the way it's going to be.

She leans back against a spruce tree, eyes narrowed. She takes another swallow of whisky. It slides down her throat, scalding pink flesh to red. She'll have two more swallows, two and no more. She's got to stay sober. There's only herself to do this job. When the people here find out what she's done, they'll feel lucky to be in the same place as her. They'll feel lucky to pay money to see Alexander's pictures. People'll come from every-where to see her. Patrick Eagle will never say shut up to her again. No one will say that to her. She'll save these Crees who are too stupid to save themselves. She'll save them because she wants a place to put the pictures. She wants Alexander to be famous in a nice place, not a stinkhole. Alexander could not do it himself, so she will do it for him. Geraldine remembers that two of Alexander's pictures are still in the schoolhouse. But it's dry and warm there, it's a good place for them to be. She will leave them there until she talks to the white teacher. Willa is part of her plan.

Geraldine takes two more swallows of whisky, then screws the cap back in place. Later she'll get drunk, after she's done the work. Now she's got to rest. She needs to be strong to do the work. And she's got to work out every step of her plan so she'll be ready to move after dark. One thing for sure. When Geraldine Gull takes over, these toads will know who's boss around here.

6: After everyone leaves the schoolhouse, Xavier, Patrick and the councillors stay behind for a meeting. They sit on the desk tops, their boots on the wooden seats.

"If it weren't for Geraldine Gull," Patrick says, "we might have gotten somewhere. As it turned out, we never had a chance. Jeremiah never even got a chance to speak because of Geraldine hogging the floor. It might have made a difference if he'd spoken."

"Nah," Simon says. "If the people want to move from here bad enough, one elder speaking won't make much difference. If they wanted to leave, they would've put their treaty money in the fund instead of running to the store to spend it quick."

"They're used to spending money on Treaty Day," Xavier says. "Maybe we made a mistake asking them to put it in a fund."

"Can't they see how insulting it is," Patrick says, "to be paid off with four lousy dollars?"

Xavier takes out tobacco and papers and begins rolling cigarettes.

"And that welfare roll," Patrick goes on. "It's like we're prisoners in our own land."

"The oil," Simon says. "The district manager mentioning oil didn't help. That did as much harm as Geraldine. People don't want to live in an oil field."

"It's good for us that the government sent a weak man — it made it easier to say no," Xavier says. "But the district manager did some harm. He put the oil idea into people's heads, and now they'll want the oil money bad enough to stay here."

"The oil is a red herring," Patrick says. "There's no oil. At least not enough to get excited about. If there was much of it here, they'd have been searching for it before now. They wouldn't be looking under the ocean for it. It was just another bureaucrat throwing his weight around. What does us the most harm isn't the government or Geraldine, it's apathy and indifference. That's what keeps us here. We forget how to fight."

Xavier passes around the cigarettes.

"How much money is in the fund?" Saul asks.

"Counting the councillor money, ninety-one dollars," Patrick says. "Twelve people, including us, put their money in."

"There were twelve disciples," Saul says quietly. "That is something to think about."

"That won't help us much," Patrick says bitterly.

"I think we better go home now," Xavier says. "We'll have another meeting soon. After people spend their money, maybe they'll listen better. Just because they want to spend their money on Treaty Day, doesn't mean they don't want to move."

"You know the white man's saying about putting your money where your mouth is," Patrick says.

"You got to have the money to put it somewhere," Xavier reminds him. He gets up from the desk. "No more talk today. We'll go home now and cool down."

"I think I'll stick around here for a while," Patrick says.

"You do that," Xavier says. "Me, I'm going for a piece of lemon pie. Bernice makes it with real lemons every Treaty Day." Before he follows the councillors outside, he says to Patrick, "You want a piece of pie, you come on over."

He closes the door, leaving Patrick alone.

7: For a long while after the band council has left, Patrick sits on one of the desks, staring at the blackboard, at Geraldine's large X. That frigging bitch, he thinks, barging in like she did, showing off, trying to get attention, trying to take over the most important meeting they've ever had up here. All she was think-ing of was herself and that artist son of hers. He should've known better than to have anything to do with her. Xavier was right. You can't get mixed up with Geraldine without it leading to trouble. It was the gallery idea that sucked him in. It seemed like a good way to bring some money into the community, to get people interested in the new building, to get to them through their kids. This is what people here live for, their kids.

Patrick gets up and wanders around the room, looking at the kids' pictures on the wall: pictures of geese and the goose hunt, people on the trapline, skunks having a birthday party, the wendigo, women skinning a polar bear. Rita Marie's painted the last two pictures. In the polar bear picture, she has the polar bear still alive while the women are going at it with their knives. Like the wendigo, it's a powerful picture. He's got to hand it to Willa. She must be a good teacher to have pulled this stuff out of the kids. The longer he looks at the kids' pictures, the more dispirited Patrick becomes. The kids are one of the big reasons for moving to the ridge, to make a better future for them. Why didn't more people see that? Maybe he should just move to the ridge himself and say to hell with them all. It'll take a miracle to get them out of this sewer.

Patrick sees the office box under the desk. Xavier left it behind. Patrick takes the money out of the moccasin pouch and roots through the box for an envelope to hold the money. Beneath the letters, government memos and notepads, he finds a package of envelopes. He also finds a bottle. He holds it up: Lamb's Dark Rum, a forty-ouncer, half full. Without a second's hesitation — he doesn't want to know whose bottle it is or how it got here; he doesn't want to give himself an opportunity to change his mind — Patrick puts the bottle inside his vest. Then he walks out of the schoolhouse and into the bush.

8: Willa's been alone in her cabin since she left the meeting. Not even the magazine girls have shown up. The makeshift easel is in front of the sitting-room window where the light is best. Ideally, she should be painting outside, but it's muggy and overcast, the worst weather for bugs, and there are occasional spittings of rain.

Willa's painting the meeting in watercolours, working from the sketches. She's done three watercolours so far, working quickly, dividing the schoolroom into sections so that when she puts them together, she's painted the entire meeting. The meeting should really be done on a large canvas using acrylics to get the vibrant colours: Geraldine's red beret and old blue parka, Nazarene Rose's emerald green sweater, Nancy Hunter's pink dress, the men's plaid shirts, the women's flowered skirts.

Willa paints Geraldine sitting up front, shoulders hunched, boots turned under the chair, beret askew, hands between her knees as she bends forward, sizing up her audience. Patrick stands behind the desk in a fringed vest and jeans, braids down to his chest, beaded headband across his forehead. He looks grave and serious. Xavier sits in front of the window, facing the meeting. The light falls on one side of his face, paling it, while the other side remains dark, austere. Beside him are Simon Gull with his full cheeks and heavy shoulders, and Saul Crow, who is so thin and straight he seems to have been carved out of a plank. Willa concentrates on body gestures, the overall design, turning half the figures in profile, arranging family groups.

As she's finished the fourth painting, Willa sees Father Aulneau pass in front of the window on his way to evening mass. That time already. He walks with the top half of his body bent forward, as if he's leaning into a stiff wind. His robe swings around his legs. He doesn't look sideways, up or down, but straight ahead at the church.

Soon the bell resonates through the village, one long note, imperious, resolute. The sound spreads outward, and the dog chorus begins, beginning as always with one mournful howl from the gully. This is answered by another howl from the store end of the village. The yips and bayings follow, moving along the boardwalk, until there is a melee of discordant sounds, all in minor key.

The small congregation straggles along the boardwalk: Saul and Marsha Crow, Betsy Bluecoat, Bernice and Sophie Hunter, Josephine and Frances Loon, Gerald Gull. Once they have assembled inside the church, Willa hears Father Aulneau leading his flock through the penitential prayer of the Eucharist:

I confess to Almighty God
and to you, my brothers and sisters,
that I have sinned through my own fault
in my thoughts and in my words
and in what I have done
and in what I have failed to do;

I ask the blessed Virgin
and the angels and saints
and you, my brothers and sisters,
to pray for me to the Lord our God.

Then the priest's high, droning chant:

Lord, we have sinned against you;
Lord, have mercy.

The congregation's singsong response:

Lord, have mercy upon us.

Willa goes into the kitchen and lights a fire in the stove. It's too humid for a fire, but she's having a cooked supper: bacon and eggs. As a treat, she'll make fresh coffee. Father Aulneau is bound to come by after mass for a cup of coffee. Perhaps Patrick will come. She hasn't seen him since she left the school. He wasn't in the store this afternoon. As soon as she heard the district manager's plane take off, Willa went down to the store for groceries. The place was packed. For the first time since coming inside, there was an impressive selection of food: fresh fruit and vegetables, doughnuts and cakes, eggs, pork chops, sausages, bacon.

When she's finished eating supper, Willa carries a mug of coffee into the sitting-room, lines up all four paintings on the floor and looks at them. From across the grass, she hears mass coming to an end.

May the mingling of the body
and the blood of our Lord Jesus Christ
bring eternal life to all who receive it.

She really should have painted Geraldine in the centre of the picture, dominating the meeting. When she does the painting on canvas, she'll paint Geraldine standing up, reading Moses Bear's speech.

Lamb of God, who takes away the sins of the world,
have mercy upon us, grant us peace.

There's a tap on the door.

"Mademoiselle?"

"Come in," Willa calls out.

Father Aulneau pokes his head around the kitchen door. "Where are you, mademoiselle?"

"In here," Willa calls. "I've been painting."

Father Aulneau comes in and looks at the paintings spread sideways on the floor. "Très bien. Watercolours. As you know, I am ver-ee fond of watercolours."

"I was trying to capture the meeting," Willa explains, "but I need a large canvas to do it justice."

"Oui, like 'The Last Supper,' " Father Aulneau says, then hastily adds, so she will not think him un blasphémateur, "your picture is long and narrow and you have many people sitting down." He peers more closely at the painting. "That woman in the red beret is the Gull woman, is she not?"

"Yes."

"I thought she drowned."

"No."

"Mon Dieu, she is back." Father Aulneau's white face becomes whiter still. "I am afraid she will do something bad."

"I perked some coffee," Willa says. "Would you like some?"

"Oui, s'il vous plaît."

Willa pours him coffee and brings it into the sitting-room.

"Did you know her son was an artist?"

"Vraiment, her son?"

"Yes. A fine one, too. He died last year. Suicide."

Father Aulneau looks into the mug. "That is why the Gull woman is angry at the Church," he says. "That is why she hates me. She wanted to put his ashes in the graveyard, but I could not permit it. What could I do?"

"You didn't go to the meeting," Willa says to change the subject. The Church's attitude toward suicide is as antiquated as its attitude toward birth control, but she doesn't want to wrangle with the priest about it.

"The Church does not belong at a meeting between an English monarch and the people," he says.

Willa laughs.

"It is no laughing matter," Father Aulneau says severely. "Do you remember your history? Au commencement, it was an English monarch who ordered these people onto the reserves and who took their land through treaties, but it was France who sent the holy fathers to help the people. They were the ones who went among the people, teaching them and learning their ways, giving them their alphabet and their Bible. The holy fathers sacrificed their lives for the salvation of the Indian people. Lalemont, Brébeuf burned at the stake, martyred for the glory of the Lord. Did government men sent by the English monarch become martyrs?"

"No."

"Bien. Now you understand why I do not attend Treaty Day." Father Aulneau looks over his glasses as if he is about to begin an inquisition. "The government man came to see me after the meeting. He came to give me a message for you. He said he came to your door, that you were here. He saw you in the window, but you would not answer the door."

"Is that what he said?"

"Oui. He said he saw you at the meeting, but you left before he could speak with you."

"Oh? Why did he want to speak to me?"

"He had a message for you from a Mr. Dick Simpson." Father Aulneau is still looking at her over the tops of his glasses, suspiciously, Willa thinks.

"And?"

"Mr. Simpson phoned him from the hospital."

"Patrick Eagle told me Dick had broken his leg. Chief Hunter told him."

"Mr. Simpson said to tell you he regrets he cannot send in — how you say it — le prospectus?"

"The brochure."

"Oui. Because of the leg, he did not get it from the printers on time. He said he was sorry to tell you because of the work you did." Father Aulneau pauses before asking what the brochure is about.

"The goose camp," Willa tells him. "It's promotional material intended for hunters."

"Vraiment?" he murmurs absently, standing up as he speaks, in the way he has of ending an audience. He drains his mug and puts it on one of the shelves. "I regret I must go now, mademoiselle."

Willa sees a small smile on the bloodless lips. Is he satisfied? Does he know she hid from the district manager?

"Have you painted the flower I brought you from the ridge?" she asks.

"The sheep laurel?"

"Is that what it's called?"

"Oui. It is also called lambkill, *Kalmia angustifolia*. It is a dangerous flower. It kills lambs and sheep who eat it when there is no other food. I am going to finish the painting now, while there is still light."

"A bientôt," Willa says. "Thanks for giving me the message." Then remembering Geraldine is back on the warpath, she adds mischievously, "Et bonne chance."

9: By evening, Patrick Eagle has:

(a) emptied Morris Mack's bottle

(b) fallen asleep

(c) been sick to his stomach

(d) gotten back on his feet.

10: It's nearly dark. Willa's hauling water from the river, walking quickly, a sloshing bucket in either hand. She puts the buckets on the ground, opens the cabin door, carries one bucket and then the other onto the porch and closes the door. She carries one of the buckets into the kitchen. Patrick is standing in the middle of the room.

"Hi," she says. In the darkening light, she cannot see his face, but it's clear that he's having difficulty standing up. She smells liquor. She puts the bucket beside the sink carefully, and waits.

"I came for a visit," Patrick says. "I thought maybe we could get better acquainted." His voice is slurred. "We could finish what we started . . ." his voice trails away, "this morning."

"Why don't you sit down?" Willa says.

"That's not what I had in mind." He takes a step forward.

Willa backs up.

"C'mon. I know you like me."

"I don't like you when you're drunk."

Patrick takes another step toward her. For a minute, he looks like he's going to fall.

"You must be one of those," he mumbles.

"One what?"

"A tight ass."

"Don't be a jerk." The flush creeps up Willa's neck.

"It's because I'm an Indian."

"Don't try that crap on me," Willa says. Why does she bother talking to someone this drunk? "Sit down and I'll give you a cup of coffee."

"Who says I want coffee?"

"You certainly need it."

"I need something else," Patrick says. He comes toward her.

Willa backs into the porch.

Patrick leans against the door frame. His chin drops to his chest.

If he comes any closer, she'll step outside. Not that Patrick looks dangerous. He can hardly stay on his feet. She wants to avoid an embarrassing tussle.

His head jerks up. "Shit," he says. He goes back into the kitchen.

Willa hears him bumping along the wall of the sitting-room. She hears the creak of iron springs as he flops onto her bed. Soon he begins to snore.

Willa goes back into the kitchen and stands in the middle of the room, uncertain what to do next. It's too early to go to bed. When she does, she'll have to sleep on the sofa, broken springs and all. It annoys her that she can't sleep in her own bed, that she has to listen to Patrick's snoring, but she's not as angry as she could be. What she feels isn't anger but fear. She's not afraid of Patrick, that he will try to hit her or knock her around. She's afraid of what she might do if he wakes up, what she might do when he becomes sober. Moving quietly, Willa stokes the fire, adds wood, sits by the stove and begins to write a letter.

11: *July 21*

Dear Karen,

I got your letter; it was waiting when I returned from the ridge. Thanks for writing back so soon. I mailed you a letter on Monday, one I wrote at the ridge. Since coming here, you're the only person I've managed to write. I had great plans to write Bev and Mum & Dad and my Mt. A. friends, but I never seem to have the time. It seems to melt away in all this space. Up here, you don't pay much attention to time, clock time, I mean. I never wind my watch. I rely on the light. The light up here is wonderful (when it isn't raining, that is). When the sky's clear, the light is almost too bright to work by. There's nothing to block it. Sometimes you get the feeling you're standing on the rim of the world, on a thin, curved line, a perfect, uncluttered point with nothing between you and "out there."

This morning I had the opposite experience. This will sound weird, but I hid, I actually hid under the bed! I was looking out the window and I saw the district manager coming down the boardwalk toward me. I knew he was coming to this cabin. Suddenly I was afraid of him, so I crawled under the bed and didn't answer the door. I feel stupid telling you about it; it's a kind of catharsis, I guess. Patrick Eagle told me that sort of reaction isn't uncommon in the North, that a lot of white people get "bushed" when they first come inside.

The Treaty Day meeting started off with a bang. Everybody was there, dressed up and in a party mood. It was held in the schoolhouse. There were kids' pictures on the walls, a lot of the women's crafts on display and the sketches I'd drawn for the new village, which I mentioned in my last letter. There were speeches. Even Geraldine made a speech. (By the way, she is very much alive! The hole in the canoe was a ruse to throw the police off her trail.) The meeting was going extremely well until the district manager started passing out the treaty money. Then everything fell apart. It was Geraldine's doing. She started bullying people to put their money into a fund set up to help move the village. She turned people off. Eventually she was thrown out, but it was too late. The meeting never got back on track.

12:   Geraldine pulls the metal handle on the mission door. The door opens easily. The artist woman has forgotten to use the hook. Geraldine crosses the porch floor. She sees Willa lying with her head on the table. She's asleep. Geraldine jabs Willa's shoulder.

Willa's head jerks up. A pen rolls to the floor.

Geraldine sits on the other chair. "I got to talk to you," she says. "We got to be quick. I got work to do."

Willa sits up. She grabs hold of her arms as if she were shivering, though it's like an oven in here. Geraldine can see orange coals inside the stove. She hears someone snoring on the other side of the wall.

"Who's that?" she says.

There's a look on Willa's face like a cow's when it chews and stares. Then she says, "Patrick Eagle. He's drunk."

"Ha!" Geraldine says scornfully. She knew he didn't quit. She pulls her chair close to Willa. "We talk low," she says. Geraldine doesn't want Patrick Eagle butting in on her plans. "I'm leaving this dump. I'm leaving soon."

"Where are you going?" Willa asks.

"Someplace," Geraldine says. "Not the ridge." She's going upriver, past the ridge. When the cops come after her this time, she'll lead them away from the ridge like a mother bird faking a broken wing. She don't want them finding Alexander's pictures in her hide-out. After the cops give up, she'll come back. "Before I go, I need a dealer to sell Alexander's pictures," she says. "You be it."

"I told you," Willa says, "I'm not a dealer. I'm an artist."

"If you sell Alexander's work, you can pick two pictures for yourself. I'm giving them to you," Geraldine says expansively. She doesn't want to give away Alexander's pictures, but she's up against it. She's got to get the pictures sold before something bad happens to them. She waits for Willa to say something, but all she does is sit and stare like she hasn't heard a word.

Finally, Geraldine says, "I got no one else to ask." She winces as she says this. She doesn't want any white person feeling sorry for her. People felt sorry for Alexander, and look what happened.

Willa stares at her with those pale eyes. Geraldine stares back, willing this woman with the paint-spattered face and kinky hair to say she'll sell Alexander's work. Geraldine watches while Willa picks up her glasses from the table and puts them on.

There's a big sigh, and then she says, "Okay, I'll try to sell them. But remember, that's all I'll do is try. It may take a long time to sell them all."

Geraldine grins. "Wooeee," she says.

On the other side of the wall, she hears the creak of bedsprings. The snoring stops. Both women wait, listening. The snoring begins again.

"Where are the pictures?" Willa says.

"At the ridge. You can use the pictures in the schoolhouse. You can use the list you made. After you get someone to buy them, you send me the money, and I send you the pictures."

"I'm not sure it'll work like that."

"It will work. We build a gallery in the new place."

"Maybe there won't be a new place," Willa says. "The people at the meeting didn't decide to go."

"They will go," Geraldine says darkly. "Soon this place will disappear. People will move. Niska will be gone forever."

"What makes you so sure?"

"I got plans," Geraldine says mysteriously. "Big plans. When I'm finished, the people will leave this place." She stands up. She can't stay here any more talking. She's got work to do.

Without another word, Geraldine goes through the porch, opens the door and steps into the black night.

13: *Hi again,*

Speak of the devil. Geraldine just came to see me. I had fallen asleep while writing this letter (the heat from the stove made me drowsy, I guess). The next thing I knew, someone was jabbing me on the shoulder. I opened my eyes and who should it be but Geraldine. I felt like telling her to get out, that she'd caused enough trouble for one day, but you don't talk that way to Geraldine, not if you value life and limb, so I sat there and listened.

She was very different tonight. Subdued, not chastised (never) but calm in a low-key, deadly sort of way. I can't explain it exactly. It was something I felt. Anyway, she started talking about her son's work. Alexander Bear's. This time, she asked, not told me if I'd act as her dealer. Like a fool, I said yes. (Maybe I am going crazy.) I said yes, and I don't even know where to begin. The whole effort will cost me months, years maybe and probably money I don't have, time and money I planned on spending on my own work. As you know, that's the reason I came up here in the first place. I feel badly when I think of my drawing instructor at Mt. A. Remember him? He was the slave driver who tore everything I did apart and wound up telling me I was the best student he'd had in ten years. He also told me that if I wanted to become a serious artist, I shouldn't get married or have kids, that I should put my work above everything else. And I've just turned around and done the opposite.

Yes, I know I need my head examined. But, Karen, imagine this: here's this big, ugly Indian who knows nothing about art except what's in her bones, an outcast who has given birth to a son who becomes a first-rate artist. He dies and she's left with a lifetime's work, significant stuff, and she hasn't a clue what to do with it. She told me she had no one else to ask but me, which is the first honest thing she's said to me. It's true. There is no one else. And I am the obvious one to do it.

When you see the poverty up here, the overcrowded, unsani-

*tary shacks people live in, when you think of the fact that except
for trapping and guiding, people here are unemployed, when
you see the scandalous prices they pay for food — well, you'd
have to be hard as nails not to want to help. Not that you can
help much, there's very little you can do on a personal level.
That's why I said yes. For that reason and for the work itself.
The art curators in this country would have a fit if they saw
where Bear's work is now. The sooner I can get that stuff out of
the suitcases, the better.*

*Must sign off and get some sleep. I feel like Goldilocks
tonight. That teacher I wrote you about, he's sleeping in my bed.
Alone, damn it. I'm stuck with the sofa.*

Love,
Willa

14: By midnight the clouds are as black and low as nuns'
skirts. As Geraldine pulls the toboggan loaded with groceries
alongside the boardwalk, she remembers the nuns in residential
school, how afraid she was of the black robes as they glided over
the pale floor at night between rows of beds, making sure everyone was asleep. Sometimes Geraldine held her breath so long
she thought Bony Spectre had got her for sure.

Geraldine gives the toboggan a tug to free it from the clump
of swamp grass on which it's snagged. It's an old toboggan with a
rough, splintered bottom, but it's okay to carry food from the
store to the schoolhouse. This is better than lugging the cartons
up to the schoolhouse one by one, which is what she was doing
after she broke the Bay window and opened the back door. She
realized it would take all night lugging the cartons out one at a
time. She remembered seeing a toboggan in the bush behind the
Wabanos' where kids left it from winter. Geraldine took a flashlight from the store and hunted around until she found the
toboggan. The toboggan would go faster on the boardwalk, but

it'd scrape against the wood and wake people up, so she's using the ground beside the boardwalk instead. She's got a track worn in the mud, she's been up and down it so many times tonight.

When Geraldine gets to the schoolhouse, she carries a carton up the stairs and into the schoolroom. She puts the carton on top of the others she's stacked against the side wall. The flashlight dangles on a length of string she's tied to her waist, making wobbling moons on the chairs, desks and floor. As she works, she snickers. Won't these stupid Crees be surprised when they see the stuff she's put here? Their eyes will pop out of their heads when they see this much food. They need an Ojibwa to figure things out for them. Geraldine's feeding them because she doesn't want a lot of broken-down people who are too sick to make a new place with a gallery. She's Joan of Arc leading the people. The people are blind toads, and she's got a toboggan instead of a horse, but she's leading them to battle anyway. When these toads wake up, they'll be happy she did this for them. They'll say, "Geraldine Gull's a great leader. We're happy we have a smart woman like her leading us." Trouble is, leading an army is hard work, especially when you do it alone. She didn't ask Elizabeth to help, because Elizabeth might make noise and wake people up. When she gets back to the store, she'll have a rest, something to eat. It's a good thing she doesn't have to haul this stuff to Gerald's boat. It's twice as far. Would take twice as long. And she's got to finish carrying out her plan before it gets light.

Geraldine shines the flashlight over the provisions stacked against the wall under the open window, the cartons of peas, corn, baked beans, tuna, ham, Spork, sardines, spaghetti, tomato soup, peaches and pears. She's pleased she's brought so much.

Geraldine goes outside, picks up the rope and pulls the toboggan back to the store. It's still dark outside, but soon it'll begin to turn grey. She'll make three more trips, and then she'll quit. From now on, she'll take light stuff: Sugar Smacks, marshmallow puffs, potato chips, crackers, tea. She left this stuff to the last because she knew she'd get tired hauling heavy cans. Because she's fat, she gets tired fast. The stupid nurse who came to see her once when Joan, Teresa and Annie were sick with fever and spots told her they were eating the wrong food, like bread and cookies. It was making them tired and sick, she said; they should be eating more fruit and vegetables. But she never told them how they could get fruit and vegetables.

By the time Geraldine's finished hauling groceries, the sky is the colour of a prison blanket. She stands back and proudly surveys the troops: the cartons of food stacked on the school-room floor, on the desks and chairs, like rows of soldiers standing at attention. There's enough food here to feed a small army. She goes to the blackboard, fumbles behind Alexander's picture for chalk. Patrick Eagle's drawing of the village is still on the blackboard. Holding the flashlight in one hand, the chalk in the other, she slowly prints her general's message on the map. These toads better get it. She's got the food; she's got the pictures — so they'd better do what she says.

Geraldine goes back to the store and takes the last of the oranges, cheese, more crackers, sardines, chocolate bars, cookies, potato chips. She puts these in a paper bag and carries them to the river, where she dumps them into George's boat. She's already stashed the booze under the seat. She unscrews the extra gas tank and sniffs. Pokes her finger in. It's full. She shines the flashlight on the boat bottom to make sure the paddles are there. She goes back inside the store, takes another bag, drops more food into it, soups and stew, a can opener, matches. She opens the freezer and takes out six packages of caribou meat. She does all this by flashlight. She can't risk turning on the lights. She goes to the clothing section, takes off her old blue parka and puts on a new green one, pulling the hood over her red beret. She takes a Hudson's Bay blanket also — she's always wanted one of those, but never got around to lifting one off George.

After she carries these to the boat, she goes back inside the

241

store, takes two-gallon tins of kerosene off the shelf, unscrews the tops and empties the kerosene onto the floor, the counter, shelves, the bedding, clothing, packaged food. She skirts around the broken window glass and steers clear of the red gasoline barrel just inside the back door. She doesn't want the barrel to catch fire and explode, to wake up George before the store's burned through. She pours kerosene on the floorboards inside the front door where she wants the fire to start, then dribbles a trail leading into the middle of the store, fanning it out to one side. She's got to gas it down good to get a big fire going because it's wet outside. She opens the front door, steps out, lights a match and drops it onto the floor. A river of red spills in from the doorway, then streaks toward the counter. Geraldine runs. She runs to the river and gets into the boat, picks up the paddle, leans over and unties the boat. The current is so strong it carries her downstream faster than she can steer.

She can't start the motor too soon or she'll wake up the people. She wants the fire to get going real good before she makes a noise. The current carries the boat diagonally across the river to the opposite island. Using a paddle, Geraldine manoeuvres the boat into the willow bushes. The river is so high the bushes float on top of the water. She unscrews the cap off a whisky bottle and takes a deep swallow, then another. She's got a good view from here, a front-row seat. Through the grey air, she can see smoke pouring out the front door. Shit, she made a mistake. She should've closed it. If George smells smoke, he'll come too soon before the store's gone. She smirks, imagining his face when he sees what she's done.

She feels the wind against her cheek. A north wind. Cold. It moves against the heavy clouds, unleashing rain. Geraldine feels wet drops on her nose and cheeks. *Go away, rain. Go away until the fire gets going good.* She sees flames on the roof of the store. The wind is helping it. The fire is moving fast. She's going to win this battle, rain or no rain. Geraldine grins. Being a leader feels good; no wonder men like it so much.

She takes another swallow of whisky. The whisky warms her throat. It circles round her stomach like a warm, furry animal looking for a place to curl up. It makes her feel sleepy and tired. So tired. Leaning forward in the boat, elbows on her knees, she holds the bottle loosely between her hands. Some of the whisky spills out. Geraldine curses, tilts the bottle upright, takes two more swallows before she recaps it. She jerks her head up and looks across at the village. The store is completely swallowed in smoke. Yellow-red flames reach up into the heavy grey sky. Fingers and tongues stroke and lick the air. Black smoke roils southward, toward the bush.

Geraldine's enthralled by the splendour of the fire; she has never seen anything so pretty. Even blood-red sunsets splattered across the ice at Osnaburgh weren't as pretty as this. And Geraldine Gull was the one who made it. The sleepy toads will wake up now. They'll crawl out of the mud and onto Gerald's boat. The boat will take them to the new place. They'll be mad at her at first for burning down the store, but soon they'll find the food she put in the schoolhouse, and they'll be happy they know Geraldine Gull. No one will tell her to shut up again. Geraldine gropes on the bottom for the paddle, her eyes still on the fire. She's got to go. She's got to get far away before the cops come with the helicopter and dogs.

15: Nattie Eagle wakens to the smell of smoke. She gets up, pushes aside the curtain enclosing her bed and goes to the stove. Holding her hand above it, she slowly lowers it onto the iron surface. Cold. She goes to Patrick's bed, pats the top blanket. Flat. She probes beneath the smooth pillow. Her fingers touch the wad of bills she put there last night so Patrick would know she is giving her treaty money to the new fund they are starting. Nattie has never gone to a Treaty Day meeting. She has never spent her treaty money. It is all here beneath the pillow.

Nattie sucks her lips inward with a disapproving smack. She knows where he is. Nattie takes the wad of bills and puts it back in the Maxwell House coffee tin. If Patrick takes up with a white woman, he cannot have her money. The smoke smell is stronger now. Nattie goes to the window and sniffs. It's coming from somewhere outside.

She takes the skirt from the bottom of the bed where she has folded it, pulling it on over scratchy beige stockings. She puts on her rubber boots, buttons on a heavy sweater and goes outside. She stands in the drizzle, sniffing. Smoke smell is coming from the west. The north wind is blowing smoke this way. Something at the west end of the village is on fire.

But Nattie doesn't go west; she goes east. She takes her stick from under the step and goes toward the boardwalk. But she doesn't use the boardwalk, because she's in a hurry. She knows where each broken slat is, but to find them she must go slow with her stick. It's faster to use the swamp, even though it has garbage in it. Holding the stick in front of her, she swings at the clumps of grass, tin cans and sleeping dogs. That is how they bite you. You step on a dog when it sleeps and it bites. Nattie goes as quickly as she can toward the mission, smoke following.

When she gets to the mission cabin, she hits the door with her stick. She will not go in. She has never been inside a white man's house, and she will not go in one now. She is angry at Patrick, but she will not shame him by going in. Patrick is a man. Men need it. Sometimes more than women. After Joseph died, she went into the bush with Matthew Gull only twice before she did not need it any more. It's worse for young men. When their women marry white men, like Nina Hunter did, something drives them to lie with white women. What is happening to her people, Indians and whites mixed up together? It's no good. Nattie sucks in her lips disapprovingly. Maybe it will be better when they get to the new place. She hits the door again.

16: Patrick opens his eyes. Pain shoots across his forehead. He closes his eyes. The knock comes again. He opens his eyes again. Sees weak morning light filtering through the yellow curtains, clothes hanging on the wall, an iron bedstead, a crucifix. Where is he? The knock comes again. Patrick sits up. Through the open door, he sees Willa's bushy head on the sofa. Holy Christ, he slept in her bed all night. The pain feels like an iron hand is squeezing the top of his head. He must have been polluted, that's how he got here. He doesn't remember anything. The knock comes again. Who in hell can it be? He goes through the sitting-room and kitchen to the porch and unhooks the door. His mother is standing on the doorstep.

"Smoke," she says. "Down there." She points with her stick.

Patrick runs outside onto the grass to look. "Holy Christ! It's the Bay. It's on fire!"

He grabs hold on Nattie's shoulders. "Wake up as many as you can. The Gulls, the Crows, the Wabanos, everyone," he says. "Tell them to bring buckets. I'll go wake George."

Patrick rushes through the porch to the sitting-room and shakes Willa awake. "The Bay's on fire!"

"What?" She sits up, looks at him stupidly.

"The Bay. It's on fire. Start waking up people. Tell them to get down there quick and to bring buckets."

Patrick slips on his moccasins, grabs his shirt and runs down the boardwalk. He feels a drizzle against his face. That should help. He sees smoke billowing in a funnel away from the store across the boardwalk, fanning out over the bush, blowing away from the house, which is probably why George can't smell it. As he comes closer, Patrick sees orange flames licking up from the top of the store. He hears the crackling roar. Hand over his nose, he makes a dash through the smoke to the other side of the Bay and looks up, smoke stinging his eyes. The roof at the front has burned right through to the timbers. Jesus, it's moving fast. Fortunately, the back and side walls are still standing. Flames roar across the top of the walls, racing with the wind. Patrick sees the store's too far gone to save, but if they hurry, maybe they can save the house. Unless the wind changes direction and the east wall gives way. George has got a firehose that runs off the generator. They'll have to get that going quick. Patrick avoids the side of the house. It's too close to the store for comfort. He goes round to the front door, which George seldom uses. He bangs on the door, yelling. He rattles the knob. Shit. The door's locked. He runs back to the side, opens the door and charges down the hall to George's bedroom.

Once George is on his feet, struggling into his clothes, Patrick gets the front door open and runs across the grass to the pump-house near the embankment. He's not sure how to get the pump going, but at least he can get the hose ready. He uncaps the pipe attached to the pump, screws on the coupling and unrolls the hose. While he works, Patrick hears a motor out on the water somewhere, but he doesn't even look toward the river.

17: Geraldine sees someone running toward George's pump-house. It's a man, she can tell that much, but not who he is. Her eyes aren't good like they used to be. Doesn't matter who he is anyway. He can't save the store now. Geraldine Gull's wiped it out. Using the paddle, Geraldine eases the boat away from the willows. She shifts her bulk so she can pull the cord on the motor. The first few jerks produce nothing, not even a cough. She feels the boat move beneath her as the current carries it along. The engine won't catch. Her arm feels heavy, leaden. She can hardly lift it to pull the cord. All the work she did makes her weak. The boat is now adrift, being carried backward toward the bay where there's nothing but Wapusk and ice. She doesn't want to go where Wapusk stalks his prey. Geraldine manages one massive tug on the cord, and the motor catches, splutters, roars to life. She grins, pleased to have won another round, relieved to have stopped herself from drifting into the bay. Wapusk won't get Geraldine Gull. She turns the lever to low, and the boat begins its slow journey up stream, fighting the current all the way.

18: George Kostiuk zippers up his windbreaker as he dashes outside and runs to the pump-house. He cranks up the generator and opens the valves, working jerkily, frantically.

"Give Patrick a hand with the hose!" he yells as Ralph, who is barefoot, dressed only in jeans, runs outside.

"I got it unrolled," Patrick yells back. "Turn on the pump!"

Patrick and Ralph haul the hose toward the burning building.

George snaps on the switch. The pump makes a deep gurgling sound as air is gulped into its neck where it's coupled to the hose. A small jet of water spurts out of the hose mouth.

"Wet the east wall so the house won't catch!" George hollers.

Patrick and Ralph already have the hose trained on the east wall. Water spews out. The drizzle has thickened to rain, which helps. They wet down the east wall.

"See if you can get water to the back," George bawls. "If the gas blows, there'll be a big explosion."

Patrick and Ralph shift the water toward the back of the store.

Xavier and Luke come running with buckets. Behind them are Simon and Saul. Alphonse Bluecoat, Henry Sutherland.

"You guys keep wetting the house," George yells, "the east side. Ralph, you help them."

The men head for the river, buckets clattering.

While Patrick keeps the hose on the gas tank, the men throw water on the east side of the house. The Wabanos have joined them. John Bird and Francis Crow. The men work in relays, sloshing buckets of water from the river and dashing it against the house. A crowd gathers at the edge of the river. Women holding babies, children rubbing their eyes as if they can't believe they're awake. Father Aulneau watches, his black slicker flapping in the wind like the wings of a storm-tossed crow. Gerald Gull has come to witness. He stands there, massive and unmoving as a wet boulder. He won't help put out the fire. Fire is part of the Lord's plan. Soon the people will be coming aboard his ark.

Willa has brought her water buckets. She runs in the relay of men, throwing the water against the side of George's house. Soon the rain becomes a torrent. More rain falls in a minute than she can run up from the river. She goes inside George's house.

Keeping the hose trained on the gas tank, Patrick closes in on the smouldering building. The flames are out. The blackened wood sizzles and spits. Dark smoke billows southward. Over his shoulder, Patrick sees George yell something at Ralph. He sees Ralph run into the pump-house and then to the river. Within seconds, Ralph is running back to George, shouting something. George runs to the river.

Patrick douses what remains of the inside walls. Then he floods the store bottom, which is a ruined tangle of burnt wood and merchandise. But the gas tank is okay. He can see some of its red paint through the black smudge.

He hears George yelling at him from the pump-house, his voice hoarse. "That's enough. We got it under control."

George disappears inside the pump-house.

The jet of hose water arcs downward to a slow dribble.

Slowly the watchers drift homeward.

The men put down their buckets.

"C'mon, you guys. Let's go inside and get some breakfast," George bawls.

Patrick, Xavier, Simon and Saul follow George inside; the others drift home.

The men file down the hallway to George's living room. In the kitchen, Willa has put the coffee on and has arranged slices of bread across the counter. Now she's looking inside the fridge for something to put between.

George comes into the kitchen. "What's this?" he says, water dripping off him in puddles.

"I thought I'd make sandwiches."

"That's not what I call breakfast. We'll have bacon and eggs," he says. "I've got fresh eggs that came in yesterday. You can use that bread for toast."

Willa stacks the bread beside the toaster, gets out eggs and bacon.

George goes into the living room. "Any of you guys want a shot of rye whisky?"

Xavier, Saul and Patrick shake their heads no. But Simon says he'll have a drink.

George digs a bottle of whisky out of the carton, unscrews the top, tips back his head and chug-a-lugs a belt. Soon he's bent spluttering over the sink.

"Water!" He spits out the word disparagingly.

He empties the bottle into the sink. Then he jerks the five remaining bottles out of the carton and lines them up on the counter. One other bottle has a broken seal. He unscrews the cap, sniffs and pours the water down the sink. Then he uncaps a third bottle and pours himself a double whisky. He drinks it neat. He pours himself another double, adds water. He takes down another glass, fills it a quarter full with whisky, adds water and carries it into the living room for Simon. Then he comes back into the kitchen and picks up the telephone receiver. He gives the number to the operator.

Willa hears the line crackle noisily.

A staccato voice comes through the receiver.

"George Kostiuk in Niska," George shouts. "I want to talk to Constable Kulyk. Oh, it's you. Didn't recognize your voice. What? . . . I know it's early. My store burnt down." There's a pause. "To the ground. A total write-off. Geraldine Gull set fire to it. . . . What? No, she's not dead. She pulled a fast one on you boys. I saw her yesterday. She was in the store."

Willa hears the staccato voice again.

She wipes up the egg she dropped on the floor.

"You kidding?" George yells. "Of course she's not here. This time she stole *my* boat. Plus two bottles of whisky. You guys better get up here quick." George shifts the receiver to the other ear.

Willa hears more crackling, the staccato voice.

"What's that?" There's more crackling. "Why can't you get up here?"

George takes a swallow of whisky and shouts, "Listen, I've seen a lot of bad Indians in my time, but this one is by far the worst. She's a dangerous criminal. And now that she's got two forty-ouncers with her, God knows what she'll do next. You guys know how crazy these Indians are when they get into the booze. You'd better get up here quick before she does something else."

While George talks, Willa sees Xavier, Patrick, Saul and Simon file quietly down the hallway and out into the rain. None of them look into the kitchen, not even Patrick. Willa begins to shiver from being in wet clothes.

"Soon as the storm lifts," George says, "I expect you fellas to get up here and track her down. Bring up the dogs again, and this time keep on her tail until you find her. I want her behind bars for a long stretch. I'm warning you, if you don't deliver the goods this time, I'll go to the top with this." He slams down the receiver.

George goes into the living room and then comes back to the kitchen. "They left," he says, mystified. "What in hell got into them?"

Willa looks out the window. Through the blur of rain, she sees Patrick walk toward the blackened shell of the store.

"They were probably offended about the way you talked on the phone," she says.

"Holy Christ. How was I supposed to talk? That bitch just burnt down my store, stole my boat *and* my whisky. Do they expect me to be feeling pally-wally after that?"

"That crack you made about how crazy Indians get when they drink," she says.

"It's true," George says. "You haven't been up here long enough to know the truth about Indians."

"I know that's what some people think about Indians and liquor," Willa says, "and some of it's true. But they don't all go crazy when they drink. Besides, it doesn't mean you should ride roughshod over their feelings."

"What's your problem?" George says. "Have you become some kind of an Indian lover?"

"Probably," Willa says.

Without a word, George pours more whisky into his glass and carries it into the living room.

Willa puts on her poncho, goes outside and walks up the boardwalk to her cabin. She'll light a fire, get into dry clothes, make breakfast. Afterwards, she'll work on her sketches, write Karen about the fire. Maybe she'll make tea biscuits and wash the floor. All this is pretense. She's tired of kidding herself. She knows perfectly well that what she'll be doing is waiting for Patrick Eagle.

SEVEN

1: *In time, even the high hills were submerged and the world was drowned. When at length the water seemed to rest, Wesakaychak began to consider what to do. One by one he sent Otter, Beaver and Muskrat to bring up some mud from the bottom of the world. Otter and Beaver both failed, but after a long time, Muskrat emerged from the water, to all appearances dead. Wesakaychak breathed on him and brought him back to life. Then he blew on the little bit of mud Muskrat had brought up with him. The mud grew and grew until it became land. This is how, out of the flood, land was reclaimed and Life multiplied again.*

From the Cree Trickster Tales

2: *And it came to pass after seven days, that the waters of the flood were upon the earth.*

And the waters prevailed, and were increased greatly upon the earth; and the ark went upon the face of the waters.

ᐁᐧᑯᕀ ᐱ ᐃᙱᐱᐧ ᐅᐸᑯᐧᑊ ᑲ ᐃᒑᙢ ᐱᕒᑊᑊ ᐊᓄᒫ ᐁ ᐃᐣᐳᐁᑊ
ᐱ ᐊᕀᐤ ᐅᒡ ᐊᐣᐱᑊ
ᐁᐧᑯᕀ ᐊᓄᐃ ᓂᐱᕀ ᐸᕁᑐᐧᒫᐸᐊ• ᒣᐊ ᐊᑊᐱᐠ ᐱ ᒥᐧᓬᑊᕒᐧ
ᐊᐣᑊᑊ ᐁᐧᑯᕀ ᐊᐧᐣᐱᑎᙢ ᐱ ᐊᕀᐤ ᐊᓄᒫ ᐱᐧᕁ ᐊᙢᑊᐧ •

Genesis 7:10,18

3: *Noah was a big, clean-living man. He didn't drink or keep bad ways like many of the people. One day the Lord spoke to Noah. He told him to build a large boat called an ark. He was to make the ark big enough to get his people on board. It took a long time for Noah to finish the ark. When it was done, the Lord told Noah to get the people on the ark, two by two, to make sure there was male and female so they could procreate. When the ark was finished, the Lord sent the rains. The waters rose and there was a big flood. The ark was lifted up and taken away to a better place.*

Father Aulneau's Bible story

4: From Xavier's notebook:

The flood of '66 was a bad one, worse than the flood in '55. It hit us early in the morning. I was asleep when I heard a big boom. A short while later there was a bump against the side of the cabin. Then I heard another bump above my head. I got up and looked out the window and saw that two big chunks of ice had landed against the cabin. There was water everywhere. Bernice woke the kids and got them dressed and fed. I put on my hip-waders and jacket and went outside to get the canoe. The step was covered with water. None of the canoes were on the river bank. They had floated away. Mine was out back, snagged on a willow bush. I brought it back and tied it to the stove, which was the only thing in the cabin heavy enough not to move. Then we piled the kids in the canoe with the food, blankets and my gun. Besides Bernice, there was Ruth, Luke and Josh in the canoe. Nina and Gabriel were in residential school and Rachel wasn't born yet. By the time we got everything in the canoe there wasn't room for anyone else. I told Bernice to paddle toward the bush, to get there before the cabins started moving. Then I went after the Eagles' canoe. By the time I found it, water was up past my knees. I took the canoe back and got Nattie out of her cabin. That was after Joe died, and Patrick was away with Nina and Gabriel. I just got her out before her cabin started moving. They were all moving by then except for the mission house and the Bay. It was bad. People were scared. Kids were crying. Women screaming. Dogs whining. I had to let my dogs

*go free. Only got four back, Blackjack, Bippity, Boppity and
Boo, the rest stayed in the bush. The strays had already run off. I
found Morris Mack's canoe and took it over to him. Then I gave
the Wabanos and Sutherlands a hand. Pierre Vachon was out
doing the same thing, trying to get people to quiet down and get
in their canoes. It took all morning before everyone got out.
Then we had to clear out quick because some of the cabins were
moving so fast they'd knock you down. I was in Pierre's canoe. I
didn't find Bernice and the kids until late in the afternoon. They
were about two miles south of here with the Bluecoats and the
Loons. I was sure happy to see they were okay. We spent the
night out there. By morning the water had gone down, and we
came back to the village. You never saw such a mess. All our
cabins had moved into the bush. Some, like mine, were tipped
over. Saul Crow's was flat on its side. The outhouses were gone.
There were chunks of ice and garbage everywhere. I counted
eighteen dead dogs, bitches with litters that couldn't swim or
run fast enough. It took a long time to get the place cleaned up.*

5: The flooding in the Hudson Bay Lowlands usually
occurs in mid-May or early June. This is break-up time, which
means that far upstream the ice cracks and separates, then
begins to move swiftly downstream to the river mouth, where it
meets spring tides from the bay. Water spills over the lip of the
embankment and into the swamp. Sometimes the ice build-up is
heavier than in other years. Sometimes it breaks cataclysmi-
cally, the result of a quick thaw. You can hear the terrible,
wrenching crack for miles around.

This year there is no warning sound. All spring, mild rains
have been falling on the ice, rotting it slowly, silently. The rains
have been falling three hundred miles south of Niska, lifting the
water in the river's drainage basin, sweeping away beaver
dams, loosening log jams from streams and tributaries. The

water level rose steadily, first by inches, then by feet. Except for brief, intermittent periods, the rain did not stop. So much rain has fallen that the ground above the permafrost is saturated. Now in the third week in July, the boardwalk bobs up and down when you walk on it. The gully has become a small narrow lake. All of the wooden steps built down the embankment are underwater. There are scattered pans of ice on the river, none of them large enough to be dangerous. The river looks calm, innocuous. Except for logs, branches and debris swirling past the village, the current appears to move slowly, even sluggishly. Rain spatters the surface of the water. The lightness of the drops seems to impede the relentless, forward push of the river. This is an illusion.

6: Xavier Hunter pushes wearily through the rain, pushes through thoughts he'd rather put off but which are knocking against the inside of his head, demanding attention. One at a time, he tells them, you come one at a time. First, it's too bad about the store burning yesterday. The people are in big trouble with no store where they can buy things. Next, the store's been here a long time, longer than George. George should have remembered that. He should have spoken to him about who started the fire before he phoned the police. He's Chief around here, not George. It shows how mixed up white people are: they tell Indians to help themselves, then do it for them instead. George gives them credit, takes moose and caribou for payment, cashes government cheques, smiles when he gives you cash for it, but like Luke says, when the chips are down, the smile goes away. George's got no respect for the people, that's his big problem. The rest of him's not so bad.

Next, he never knew anything about the Bay boat being gone until George spoke about it on the phone. Same with the whisky. He can't telephone the OPP if he doesn't know about these things being stolen. He can't get Luke and Francis working on it if he's not told what went on.

Next, George says Geraldine started the fire. Maybe she did. Or maybe it started itself like fires do sometimes up here. Depends. Geraldine's a wild one. She does crazy things. If she did it, she's not thinking of the people. Because with the store gone, what are they going to eat? They don't have food in their cupboards like George has. Bernice's got six bottles of goose left from fall, a bag of oatmeal, a bag of flour, tea, coffee, milk powder, a few cans this, a few cans that. That's it. Most of the people in Niska got less. One thing sure. The councillors are going to have a meeting quick. Decide what to do.

Xavier keeps his head low, his parka hood up over his peaked cap. The boardwalk bounces beneath his weight. Much more water falls and the boardwalk will float. The signs don't look good. Most of the ice has gone, but there is too much water for this time of year.

As he passes the schoolhouse, Xavier looks up out of habit, to see if everything's okay. The schoolhouse door is half open. Patrick Eagle was the last one out on Treaty Day. He must have forgotten to close it, same as he forgot to take the office box home. Xavier climbs the rickety steps and goes into the schoolhouse to get the box. He stops in his tracks. In front of him, lined up against the far wall beneath the windows, are cases of food, there must be forty of them, labels on the sides. Peas, corn, beans, soup, tuna, ham, peaches, pears, cookies, corn flakes, Sugar Smacks, potato chips — the boxes are piled up everywhere. How did they get here? Xavier scratches his forehead, trying to figure out who has played this trick on him. Whoever did it put them in here last night, because the boxes sure weren't here yesterday when they had the meeting.

Xavier sees crude letters scrawled on the village drawing. He goes closer to the blackboard. Maybe the letters will help him understand.

I GOT FOOD FOR YOU. YOU PUT IT ON THE
BOAT AND GO TO NEW PLACE. BILD GALRY
FOR PEETANAQUOT. GERALDINE

Xavier rereads the message. He looks at the pictures on the
chalk ledge, the pictures Geraldine's son painted. So Geraldine
set the fire. She set the fire and stole this food. People here don't
steal, except maybe booze. Geraldine does things his people
don't do. Most of the time he doesn't like the bad things she does,
but maybe the Ojibwa *kesquakan* has done them a favour for a
change. Because now, with no store to tie them down, people
will go for a move. With their bellies full of this food, they will
say, "We need to build a new store. We should build it in a better
place and not in this swamp."

Again, Xavier forgets the office box. He locks the schoolhouse door, puts the key in his pocket and steps outside.
Through the rain, he sees the outline of Patrick Eagle coming
across the boardwalk toward him. Looks like he has been in the
mission cabin. Xavier meant to speak to Patrick about how
much time he spends with the white teacher, but he can't be
thinking about that now. There are more important matters to
think about.

"We are having a councillor meeting. You better come also,"
Xavier says. "First you get Saul. I'll get Simon. We'll meet here
quick as we can."

When the four men assemble outside the schoolhouse,
Xavier takes the key out of his pocket and unlocks the door.
They step inside and look around.

The councillors walk between the desks, shaking their heads
at the cartons of food piled up against the wall.

Finally Patrick says, "Geraldine. I had her wrong. I found the
empty kerosene tins in the store, so I knew she set the fire, but I
never thought she'd go to all this trouble."

"Must've taken her all night," Simon says.

"Look at the village plan," Xavier says.

The men study the message printed on the blackboard.

"Now we've got to move," Xavier says, "the quicker, the better. Before the Bay gets the jump on us and talks about building another store."

The men stare out the window and then at each other.

Finally Saul says, "We've got to see Gerald Gull about that ark he's made."

"Do you seriously think we can make it to the ridge on that barge?" Patrick says.

"It's better to get on the boat than stay in our canoes and watch our homes get carried into the bush," Simon says reprovingly.

"Looks like we're mostly for it," Xavier says. "We'll talk to Gerald. Then we'll decide."

7: Gerald Gull spent his four dollars buying enough nails to cover the windows with plastic. Last night after mass, Simon showed up with a bag of spikes and a bag of three-inch nails. That was enough to build a walkway so the people can cross the gulley to the ark. He still has enough nails to build the outhouses. First, he's building the women's. So far he's got the walls up. That leaves the roof and the shithole. The shithole will be square because he hasn't got a drill to make it round. Gerald is building the outhouse seat inside the cabin where it's dry. His mother has already moved into the cabin. She sits on a lumpy mattress at the far end of the room, mending a large rip in their grey tent. Gerald hears water lapping against the side of the ark. He's working fast because the Lord's decided the time has come.

Gerald hears footsteps outside on the deck. He sees four men walking past the plastic window. He's been expecting them. He doesn't put down his hammer until the men have come inside.

"At last you got here," he says.

"Took us a while," Xavier says. "Saul showed us."

"Wasn't me," Saul says. "It was Geraldine. The school's full of food she moved out of the Bay before she burned it down. It's for the ark."

"The Lord heard my prayers," Gerald says. "He put Geraldine to work again."

"Geraldine took off in George's boat," Patrick says. "She's probably headed for the ridge."

"Where we're going," Gerald says.

"The police also," Xavier says. "George called them."

Gerald looks toward the water. "She's out there on the river," he says. "Wants to be first. As usual. Soon the Lord sends the flood. The ark will rise up out of the gully and into the river."

"The quicker we can get to the ridge, the better," Xavier says.

"Hey," Patrick says, "if the river floods, this will be declared a disaster area. We'll be eligible for relief funds."

"Better spend them at the ridge than here," Simon says.

"Flood comes tonight," Gerald says ominously. "Wind'll turn after dark. Niskipewin tonight for sure."

"Means we haven't much time," Xavier says. "Lots of work to do. Got to get the food out of the schoolhouse. I'll use my dogs."

"Better do that after dark," Patrick says, "so George won't get wind of it."

"We'll need gas," Simon says. "Going to take four canoes, four motors. And rope. Lots of strong rope to tow the ark."

Patrick remembers seeing the smudged gas barrel that survived the fire. "There's gas in the Bay," he says.

"If we tie everybody's clotheslines together," Simon says, "it should be enough rope."

"How long do you figure it'll take to get this boat up river?" Xavier asks. He refuses to call it an ark.

"A day. Two days," Gerald says. "It's up to the Lord."

"We got enough food for a couple of weeks," Xavier says.

"We should take the mission saws with us," Patrick says. "Get the sawmill going as soon as we can."

"I'll talk to the Little Father," Gerald says. "I'll ask him for the keys to the sawmill. We'll need stoves also. Two should do it."

"I'll bring ours," Xavier says. "It's got a big oven on it."

"I can bring ours also," Patrick says. "It's still in pretty good shape."

Xavier looks at the councillors. "Seems like it's decided."

Saul and Simon nod their heads.

"That's it. We're going," Xavier says. "Simon, you and Saul round up the canoes and motors. Don't forget the rope. Patrick, you get the gas. I'll get the message out to the people. I'll tell them they better get moved onto the boat quick or they'll get left behind. I'll phone the district manager our plans so he can line up some help. After it gets dark, we'll all pitch in and move that food out of the schoolhouse. That's it."

8: 2 tins tomato soup
$\frac{1}{2}$ box corn flakes
1 square margarine
10 tea bags
1 cup flour
baking soda & salt

This is what remains in Willa's kitchen cupboard. She and Patrick used the last of the bread for toast this morning. Since he left, Willa's built up the fire and made a double batch of tea biscuits.

While she waits for the second batch of biscuits to bake, Willa peers out the kitchen window at the rain. She cannot see the river. She cannot see anything on the other side of the glass but the large, blurred square of the mission house. But she'll have to go out — the water buckets are empty.

Willa puts on her poncho, picks up the buckets and goes to the river, splashing through several puddles on the way. The edge of the river bank is difficult to locate. Rain has lifted the water table so high the grass seems not to be growing through water but floating on it. Willa fills the buckets and carries them back to the cabin. Then she returns with the dishpan and two pots. If the river moves into the main part of the swamp where people throw their garbage, the water will be unfit to drink. From now on, she should start to boil her drinking water.

The tea biscuits have burned on the bottom and are as hard as rocks, but they're food, which at this point is all that matters. Willa puts the biscuits in a plastic bag, then goes outside and crosses the boardwalk to the school. She forgot to ask Patrick if there would be art classes today. With the upset of the fire, no one is likely to show up, but she'll check to make sure.

Willa tries the door. It's locked. Odd. It's never been locked before. The locked door gives Willa an unpleasant jolt like an electric shock or a slap. She should have been told about this. She looks through the window nearest the door. She sees cartons stacked up against the opposite wall. There are more cartons on the desks. Dozens of them. They seem to be all over the place. Willa can't see the blackboard clearly, but she can see two white rectangles on the chalkboard. Alexander's prints. She'll have to get inside and rescue them. They shouldn't be left there. Willa goes down the steps and walks up the boardwalk toward the Eagles' cabin. She passes Marious and Sophie Hunter, who are carrying a wooden box between them. Nancy, their youngest, comes behind, holding a green plastic bag.

"Wachiyi," Willa says, but they do not reply, not even Nancy, who is usually quick to giggle.

Farther along, Willa sees Betsy Bluecoat hurry past, carrying two bulging plastic bags. She doesn't smile or look at Willa, either. What is going on here?

Willa knocks on the Eagles' door. She can hear her heart thumping inside her chest, pumping away faster than usual.

But it's Patrick's mother who answers the door.

"Is Patrick here?" Willa asks.

"No."

"Would you tell him I want to see him?" Willa says. She speaks slowly. Patrick has told her Nattie doesn't speak much English. "It's about the school."

"You come in," Nattie says.

Through the open doorway, Willa sees a wooden chest and cartons on the floor.

"Come in," Nattie says again. A command.

Willa steps inside and Nattie closes the door.

9: Nattie points to the chair by the window. She hears the white teacher sit down. Nattie goes to the open chest and, sorting quickly through the moccasins, mukluks, mitts and headbands, lifts out a pair of beaded moccasins. She carries them across the room and puts them on the table in front of the other woman.

"For you," she says and sits in the opposite chair.

"For me?" she hears the white teacher say.

"For you."

"They're lovely. Thank you."

"Caribou skin," Nattie says. "Muskrat fur."

There is a long pause before the white teacher says, "How much do they cost?"

"No!" Nattie says. "No money. I give. You keep."

Nattie hears the white teacher thank her again. Behind her sightless eyes, Nattie is thinking hard. Long ago, Joseph taught her English words, but she has forgotten most of them. Now she must drag up the words and put them in their places. She must do this quick before Patrick comes back. He thinks she is packing up their things while he is working on Gerald Gull's boat. Patrick would not like her doing this. But since the first night Patrick did not sleep in his bed, Nattie has known she must talk to the white teacher. When the news of the flood came today,

Nattie thought she would not have to speak to the teacher, that they would leave her behind with the other white people. But now that she has come chasing after Patrick, Nattie will have to speak.

"Caribou comes from Xavier Hunter," Nattie says.

"Oh."

"Xavier Hunter Chief," Nattie says.

"He's a good Chief," the white teacher says.

"He's old now," Nattie says loudly, "like me. In the new place, we need a young Chief. A Chief who flies in planes. Talks to government people. We need that now."

"Are you going to the new place?"

"We go soon. We get on the big canoe tonight and go to the new place," Nattie says. "Tonight the river floods." She lifts a gnarled finger. "You leave. Go back where you come from. Patrick will marry Indian woman, not you." Nattie drops her finger and waits.

When the white teacher does not speak, Nattie leans across the table and pushes the moccasins toward her guest. Then she sits back in her chair, waiting.

The white teacher does not say anything. After a while, Nattie hears the chair scrape on the floor. The white teacher stands up. Nattie hears her cross the floor toward the door. She is wearing men's boots. The door opens, closes. Nattie reaches across the table. The moccasins are still there. Nattie sucks in her lips disapprovingly. The white teacher has not learned much. She has not learned that it is not the Indian way to refuse a gift. What bad manners white people have.

10: Gerald Gull sits on a hard chair in the mission kitchen, a cup of tea balanced on one knee and a plate of toast thick with raspberry jam on the other.

Father Aulneau has had to make the toast himself. When

Nazarene Rose heard Xavier Hunter speak about the flood and the boat, she stopped what she was doing, which was washing the breakfast dishes, and left, saying she and Francis were moving to the ridge. The dishes are still in the dishpan. After he and Gerald finish their tea, Father Aulneau will add hot water and wash all the dishes together. He is not used to doing women's work, but he will not be doing it for long.

This morning after Nazarene Rose left, Father Aulneau telephoned Bishop Bonhomme in Fort Albany. He told him about the store burning and the flood coming and asked for instructions. "I am so glad you phoned me, Father Paul," the bishop said. "You have been much in my thoughts." That was what he said. The line was poor, but even with the disturbances, Father Aulneau heard those words clearly. Before he knew what he was saying, Father Aulneau told the bishop everything. He had not intended to, but he couldn't help himself. It was the strain of these last weeks. He told him about Geraldine Gull burning the catechism books, about Nazarene Rose leaving, about the people moving to a new place — all of it came out of him in a torrent. The bishop's deep voice came booming quickly over the line. "I am sorry that my brother in the faith has been so distressed." To this, Father Aulneau humbly replied, "There is no need for you to be sorry. It is my own weakness which has caused my distress." The bishop replied, "No, no. I must bear some responsibility."

He had intended to visit Niska sooner, the bishop had gone on, but he had been busy in Fort Albany with the new hospital. For some time now, he had been thinking Father Paul would be better suited to a teaching mission, one that would make better use of his gifts. Perhaps he could arrange a post at the seminary at Richelieu. It was his responsibility, the bishop said, to see that the gifts of his brothers were used for the glory of God and for Mary Immaculate, Mother of us all. He had been derelict in his duty.

"Non! Non!" Father Aulneau had shouted into the phone. "I

am the derelict." Out of gratitude and relief, he would consent to any confession, any mortification. He was a drowning man in need of rescue.

And now, exactly an hour later, when the cuckoo on the wall tells him that if the fire had not consumed the store, if the flood were not coming, if he were not leaving this place, he would be working on his translations, Father Aulneau feels as light as a twig floating on the river. He picks up the teapot and pours more tea into Gerald's cup. A drop of tea splashes Gerald's knee, but he doesn't flinch. He chews steadily on his toast.

"Good jam," he says.

"My sister, Agnes, made it," Father Aulneau says. "She lives in Bathurst, New Brunswick. She is a good cook." He has never told Gerald about his sister or her cooking, but he cannot help himself from showing happiness.

"River floods tonight," Gerald announces.

"Tonight! Mon Dieu. So soon!"

Father Aulneau hoped the flood would not come until after he was gone. As a child he was thought to be too delicate for swimming lessons.

"Last time we had a big flood, water came up to here." Gerald holds his hand to the level of the chair.

"So much?" Father Aulneau is sobered by this thought. It occurs to him that he is abandoning a sinking ship. He has been so overjoyed to leave, he has not been thinking of his children. The priest begins to have warm thoughts toward Gerald. Gerald Gull is a good man. Even with the Pentecostal foolishness, he is a good man.

"You be okay," Gerald says. "This house is built on cement like the church. It won't wash away. Move upstairs and you'll be dry." Gerald helps himself to another piece of toast before he says, "We take the holy things from the church: the tabernacle, the statue of the Virgin, the Bible, the sacred cup. We put these things on the ark and tow them upstream like that box they carried across the desert."

"But what will the bishop say?" Father Aulneau cries.

"You ask him," Gerald says. He licks jam from his fingers. "I built an ark like the story says, like the story you told us in our language."

"My translation?" Father Aulneau says wonderingly. "You used my translation? C'est une révélation."

"I have a confession to make also," Gerald says. "I used wood from the sawmill that was left by Brother Charlie. I walked up to the shed and I took it."

Gerald braces himself for a reprimand.

Father Aulneau claps his hands. "But that is perfect," he says. "You have used the church's wood to build the ark that I told you about. C'est merveilleux! Bishop Bonhomme will be pleased."

Father Aulneau pauses, managing a sorrowful visage. "Unfortunately, I will not be going with the people," he says. "A short while ago, the bishop telephoned me to say that I am to leave. He is sending in a plane tomorrow."

The priest spreads his slender hands. "You see, I am not suited to this mission," he says apologetically. "I do not build houses like Brother Charles. I do not plant potatoes and show movies like Father Bilodeau. I do not understand politics like Father Arseneau. I do not hunt and fish like Father Vachon. I am too frail, too much a scholar. The bishop did not intend for me to stay here so long. Perhaps in the new place he will send you a priest who knows about building, carpentry, someone like that. This is what your people need."

This is Gerald's opinion also. This is a good time to ask for keys.

"We move the saws to the new place," he says. "We need them there. To help us build houses." Then he adds, "And a new church."

"The keys are in my desk," Father Aulneau says obligingly. He has no objection to giving the saws to the people. He is sure the bishop would give permission, since they are not abandoning the church but relocating it. He sets down his teacup and goes into the office for the keys.

When he returns, Gerald is already standing at the door, ready to go.

"Are all the people going to the new place?" Father Aulneau asks.

"When the flood comes, they all go." Gerald grins. "Can't swim."

Father Aulneau is feeling so good, he goes to the cupboard, takes the last four jars of Agnes's jam and gives them to Gerald.

"You take them," he says. "Where I am going, there will be much food." He can see it spread on his sister's table: tarte au sucre, soupe aux pois, tortière. He can taste the food already. "Tell the others there will be a church service soon, before you take away the holy things," he goes on. "We will pray for your move to the new place."

After Gerald leaves, Father Aulneau adds hot water to the dishpan and begins washing the plates and cups. As soon as he's finished, he'll empty out his desk drawers. He will give the rest of the candies to the women who come to church to distribute among the children. Except for one or two peppermints, which are his favourite.

11: Willa's back in her cabin slamming things around. Washing dishes, putting them away. Hauling more wood from beneath the cabin, muttering to herself as she works.

So the village is moving to the ridge. The people are getting on that crazy boat Gerald Gull's been building. Everyone is packing up and moving out, and Patrick hasn't bothered to tell me. That explains the boxes and the chest in the Eagles' cabin, the people I saw on the boardwalk, the people who looked through me as if I didn't exist. I existed when I was useful, teaching their kids to draw and paint. Oh yes, I existed then. I existed when I went to the ridge and made those sketches. I existed when I was sketching the Treaty Day meeting, when Patrick and I were making love. Oh yes, I existed then, all right. Now I'm invisible, expendable. Nattie Eagle's just explained it to me. It's because I'm white.

Well, it's time for this white person to think of herself. I'll have to figure out how to get out of here. George. I'll ask George. With the store gone, he's probably taking the first plane outside. I'll ask George, and then I'll pack. After that, I'll try to find Patrick. I've still got two weeks' pay coming to me, and I'm not leaving here without it. I also have to get the prints from the school.

Willa stands on George's doorstep, hesitating before she lifts her hand to knock. She doesn't feel good about this, running to George with her tail between her legs, but it has to be done.

George answers the door looking as if he has a hangover. The whites of his eyes are bloodshot and the eyelids are puffy.

"Oh, it's you," he says. "I figured you'd show up."

"I came to ask when you're leaving," Willa says. "I heard the river's going to flood and the people here are pulling out."

"You mean you're not going with them?" George says. There's no mistaking the sarcasm in his voice.

"No."

"How come?" George says. "I thought you'd be right in there."

"I wasn't asked," Willa says. She looks down at the step. "Listen, can I come in?"

"Sure." George steps aside to let her pass.

Willa stands in the hallway.

"Take off your rain gear and come into the front room," George says.

Willa hangs her poncho behind the door and follows George down the hallway to the living room. They sit on the chester-field.

"Where's Ralph?" she says.

"He went to drain off the gas from the barrel in the store — correction, what *was* the store. I told Patrick Eagle they could have it for their canoe motors. He seems to think they can tow that barge twenty-five miles upriver. Well, good luck to them, I say. They're going to need it."

"If the village floods," Willa says, "they have nothing to lose."

"True enough." George looks at her. "So you found out you're not an Indian."

"You could say that."

This admission seems to make George feel better. He springs to his feet. "You want a cup of coffee? I've got a potful in the kitchen."

"Sure."

George comes back with two steaming mugs and sets them on the coffee table. Then he perches on the edge of the opposite chair, leaning forward, arms resting on his knees, head down, staring at his sock feet. "Many people think it's only white people who are racist," he says, "but Indians can be racist too." He stares at the hole above his big toe and says, "Sometimes I think it's unavoidable. I mean, these people wouldn't survive as Indians if they didn't dig in their heels." George takes a swallow of coffee, looks at Willa and adds kindly, "I know you got attached to the people here, but if they shut you out, you don't want to take it personally."

"Haven't you ever taken it personally?"

"I used to. When I first came north. Not any more. Like I told you, I don't think about it much."

"Where will you go from here, George?"

George picks up his mug and leans back. "Hard to say. I doubt they'll send me to another post. The Bay's phasing out a lot of these smaller places because they hardly break even. I was in the red most of last year. Maybe the management will pension me off early. That's what I'm hoping, anyway."

"So when are you leaving?" Willa says.

"As soon as a plane can get in. Which won't be until tomorrow at the earliest. There's a storm warning out. After the storm, nothing will get in here except a float plane. With the river this high, a storm will put the airstrip under water. Flights will be cancelled. That's why I called Pickle Lake about sending in a float plane. I'm waiting to hear back."

"Will there be space aboard for me?" Willa says.

"I don't see why not. The Cessna that's landed out here before holds four besides the pilot. I'll ask them when they call back. I got a call from the priest. He's coming, too. If I were you, I'd bring my stuff down here tonight. You can use that spare bed I mentioned. Come for supper. If the water gets higher overnight, you wouldn't want to be stuck in that flimsy cabin. Only three places would be safe up here if there's a flood. The mission house, the church and this place. Take your pick."

"I'll take this."

"Good."

"Thanks, George."

"You're welcome. I'd do the same for anyone," George says. "Except Geraldine Gull."

12: By mid-afternoon, Willa's packed. Her suitcase and backpack are on the bed, her sleeping bag rolled up inside a plastic bag. While she's been working, people have been hurrying down the boardwalk carrying bundles, bags and boxes to the gully, taking advantage of the lull in the rain. Willa keeps glancing out the window, but there's no sign of Patrick. She sweeps the floor, wipes the kitchen table, the cupboards, the shelves. Why am I doing this? she wonders. If the flood carries this cabin into the bush, who will care if it's dirty or clean?

Willa sees three dark heads pass by the kitchen window. The porch door opens, and Rita Marie comes in with Angelina Loon and Rosena Sutherland. They file into the sitting-room and pick up the magazines Willa's left on the bookshelf. Willa nods a brief acknowledgement, then continues emptying the kitchen cupboards, knowing her visitors have come not only to look at the pictures in the magazines but to watch her over the tops of the pages. During the past month, these three girls have probably gone back to their families and faithfully reported every detail about what she does and how she does it, so that they end up knowing more about her than she does about them. As usual, the girls stay about fifteen minutes. As they file into the porch, Willa says, "You can keep the magazines." They dart back into the sitting-room, snatch the magazines off the shelf and run outside. Before the porch door slams shut, Rita Marie runs back inside, shoves a square of folded paper into Willa's hand and bolts away. Willa unfolds the paper. It is a bold crayoned drawing of a large canoe filled with men, women and children. Their heads are back, their mouths open as if they are shouting at the sky. Beneath the canoe, in the water, is a jumble of animals: fish, serpents, strange creatures with large mouths and forked tails. The picture is untitled, but it is obviously the flood. Willa puts the picture in her sketchbook with her own. Then she slips on her poncho, goes outside and walks down the boardwalk.

When she reaches the gully, she stands in the bushes away from the main path and looks across the gap at Gerald Gull's boat. During the past few days, water has entered the gully from the river and lifted the boat. Gerald's boat is floating. It's actually floating despite the fact that it's shaped more like a barge than a boat and has a keel made from uneven and mismatched boards that look as if they couldn't possibly keep water out. The cabin roof is covered with plastic sheeting.

Simon Gull is straddling one end of this roof, shoving a stovepipe through a hole. There's an old grey tent on the deck, in the V of the prow, and in one of the back corners, an outhouse. Gerald Gull is hanging a door on this outhouse. Francis Crow is carrying wood aboard from a toboggan that's been hauled onto the deck. Bernice Hunter has taken the polar bear skin off the frame and is carrying it across the walkway. Henry and Agnes Sutherland are wrestling a table aboard, Ernst and Tom following with chairs. Willa's never seen so much activity in Niska. It's as if everyone's awakened suddenly from a long sleep and is making up for lost time. Wherever she looks, people are busy building or carrying. She sees a canoe piled with boxes and bags enter the gully from the river. In the bow is Nattie Eagle. Patrick's in the stern. When the canoe is opposite Willa, Patrick looks toward her, then away. There's no sign of recognition, even though he's wearing his glasses and must see her standing there in her yellow poncho, not thirty feet away.

Xavier Hunter sees the art teacher coming up the boardwalk toward him. Oops. They have forgotten about her. They hired her to do a job she can't finish. Now what do they do? He will have to tell Patrick to speak to her about that. But as Chief, it is his job to see she won't be stuck behind in the flood. He waits until she comes close before he gives the harness a jerk and Blackjack and Wolf Eyes stop hauling the sled he has loaded with firewood.

"We're leaving this place," he says. "We're going to the new place you drew in the pictures."

"So I've been told," she says.

Xavier notices she doesn't look too happy to hear this. "Maybe you go there someday and draw pictures. After we get the new place built," he says. "Put them together with the others. Make a before-and-after book." Xavier has seen these pictures in magazines, pictures of fat people who get thin, women with white hair that gets brown.

"Maybe it's better if Rita Marie does it instead," she says. Then she smiles.

"You better pack soon," Xavier says. "Get to a telephone. Call about a plane coming to pick you up. Looks like the river will flood tonight."

"I'm going out with George when the float plane comes to pick him up," she says. "I'm already packed,"

"Maybe I better come by and stake your cabin," Xavier says. He did not bother staking his place, but if the teacher's not leaving until tomorrow, he'd better stake the corners of her cabin so it won't move off the cement blocks so quick.

"I'm staying at the Bay house tonight," she says. Then she adds, "But I want to see Patrick Eagle first. He owes me some money."

"I'll tell him," Xavier says. He waits politely to see if there is anything else. That is when she does it. She sticks out her hand for him to shake as white men do. It's okay for a man, but this is the first time a woman has done it. He cannot ignore it. The hand hangs there in front of him like a limp fish. Quickly he squeezes the cold white fingers and drops the hand.

"Wachiyi," she says.

"Wachiyi," Xavier says. He has no trouble with that.

The church bell rings, one long clang, the circle of sound echoing through the village. There's no answer from the dogs. A second clang, spreading out, following the first. There's a feeble yip from the gully, then a wail. A third clang. The lone wail rises to a howl, then sinks to a single low moan. Where is the dog chorus?

Willa lowers the sketchbook. The dogs have gone. She remembers Sandra Jellicoe, another fine arts student at Mt. A., telling her about being in Mexico when an earthquake hit Zihuatanejo. Sandra said that the day before the earthquake, birds stopped singing, and spiders and iguanas scuttled into the hotel where she was staying. The dogs must have sensed the flood was coming and run into the bush.

People appear on the boardwalk and enter the church. The service begins.

There's a light pattering on the roof. It's begun to rain again.

Damn. She should have carried her stuff down to George's while there was a break in the weather instead of waiting here for Patrick. The porch door bangs: the wind's picking up. Willa gets up and hooks it. Then she returns to the sitting-room and continues drawing, trying to sketch Gerald's boat from memory. But the light's bad and her mind's not on it.

Holy, Holy, Holy, though the darkness hide Thee,
Though the eye of sinful man Thy glory may not see.

Willa hears a tap on the door. She goes into the porch and unhooks the door.

Patrick is on the step. He must have taken the canoe back to his cabin. Willa was looking for him out the window, expecting him to come from the gully. He steps inside, shakes the rain off his windbreaker and peaked cap and follows Willa into the sitting-room. He sits on the sofa. Willa sits in front of the easel.

"Still at it, I see," he says.

"Of course."

"I got a cheque for you," he says. He reaches inside his windbreaker for the cheque and gives it to her.

"Thanks." Willa looks at the amount. Patrick has paid her until the middle of August.

"I added the extra pay because I've got a favour to ask."

"Naturally."

"Hey, you're not sore, are you?"

"You leave this morning after — well, after last night — and you don't show up until now. In the meantime, I find out there's going to be a flood and the village is clearing out, which means my job has been abruptly terminated. Why would I be sore?"

"Yeah, well this is a big thing for us, so naturally I got caught up in it. You know how important this move is to me, how hard I worked for it. After the meeting, I didn't think it would happen." Patrick leans forward, talking earnestly. "I never thought we would be getting on Gerald Gull's boat. I didn't take it seriously. I guess I couldn't see the woods for the trees. Now I can see that it could work."

"So what's the favour?" Willa says.

"That extra money. If I don't use it up on this project, I have to return it. I don't believe in returning money to the government." Patrick grins. "I figure a good way to use it up would be to buy art supplies. If you could buy some supplies outside and send them back, I can put the expense in the budget plus what you charge for your time."

"What address would I use?"

"Address it Niska, same as now. Until we get our own airstrip, we'll pick up mail and supplies over at the goose camp."

"I guess that's how I'll reach Geraldine."

"You still going to try to sell those pictures?"

"Of course. As a matter of fact, I tried to get into the school earlier to get those two prints of Bear's and to check if any kids showed up for class, though I didn't think it was likely. The door was locked. I thought you said it was never locked."

"Yeah. We locked it."

"Well, I want to get those prints out. And you should take the kids' pictures with you. They'll want them back."

"Yeah. Maybe we'll keep them for a gallery later on."

"By the way, I saw a lot of cartons inside the schoolhouse. What were they? Or shouldn't I ask?" Willa says.

"You can ask," Patrick hesitates. "It's food Geraldine took from the store. Stuff we plan on moving onto the boat after dark. We don't want George getting wind of it."

"I doubt if George would care now that the store's gone," Willa says.

"He'd do his job," Patrick says, "the same as the priest." He stands up. "You want to go over now and get the pictures?"

Willa gets a green garbage bag and slips it over her portfolio. She'll put Bear's pictures with her own. Then she puts on her poncho and follows Patrick to the schoolhouse. As they cross the boardwalk, Willa hears a familiar litany coming from the church. She hears Gerald's voice rising above the others.

Thy will be done
On earth as it is in heaven.
Give us this day our daily bread.
And lead us not into temptation,
But deliver us from evil:
For thine is the kingdom, and the power and the glory,
World without end.

They step inside the schoolhouse, and Patrick relocks the door.

"Don't you trust the others not to tell?" Willa says.

"No point in taking chances."

"You trust me," Willa says. She wants to hear an affirmation of this; she wants to take away more than a book of sketches from Niska, more than a mandate to sell Bear's work. She thinks she's earned some words of praise or acknowledgement, but all Patrick does is shrug.

Willa walks between the rows of desks. There are cartons of food everywhere, on tops of desks and seats, piled against the back wall.

"It's incredible," she says. "How did she move all this? Did she have help?"

"Nope. There were only her footprints. She used the Wabanos' toboggan. Must've taken her all night . . . while we were doing . . . well, something else."

Willa cannot get over the fact that Geraldine pulled this off, that she would show such foresight, that she would even care if the people here lived or starved. She's surprised that what she feels toward the woman who slapped her is admiration. Geraldine is a bully and a thief, not the sort of person Willa wants to admire. But she can't help it. The thought of this outcast working all night and alone, doing what, even for someone as big and strong as Geraldine, must have been brute work, overwhelms her. Willa stands in front of the blackboard, smiling and reading Geraldine's message.

"She really had a plan," she says.

278

"Yup," Patrick says. "The elders approve, Nattie and Jeremiah. Even Old Martha Gull, who's the oldest one in the village, got so excited she even spoke this morning."

"What did she say?"

"Manitou oskihtaw, which means the Creator makes it new," Patrick says. "That was important. We don't like doing something big unless all the elders go along with it."

"There aren't many elders here, are there?" Willa says.

"There's Jeremiah, Nattie Eagle, Old Martha. There's Toby Hunter, Xavier's older brother, but he lives down by the Sagamu River. We had two more, but last year they moved to Severn," Patrick says. He starts taking down the kids' pictures.

Willa gets cardboard and tape from the cupboard and makes a folder. Patrick puts the pictures inside. Willa puts Bear's prints inside her portfolio and wraps the plastic bag tightly around it.

"That's it," Patrick says. He looks out the window. "I got to be going. There's still a pile of work to do before it gets dark." He looks at Willa. "Next time I see you will be at the ridge. You'll have to come back there to see Geraldine and to get the pictures."

They go into the porch.

"Be careful crossing the streets," Patrick says. "Those traffic lights can get to you when you first go outside."

He reaches out and pushes up Willa's glasses, which have slipped down her nose. "I suppose you'll get your glasses fixed."

"I suppose."

"Wachiyi kamininwasisit," he says and kisses her hair.

He opens the door and they step outside, into the rain.

The church service is over. As Willa rounds the corner of her cabin, she sees Father Aulneau returning to the mission house, the wind whipping his cassock around his ankles. Willa puts the portfolio inside the porch, then follows the priest into the mission to tell him she's moving out of the cabin. Willa has never seen Father Aulneau so cheerful.

"Oui, mademoiselle, I am leaving Niska. The bishop is sending me to another place. I have been talking to Mr. Kostiuk, who has told me that it is possible for me to leave on the pontoon plane. I do not mind staying in the mission alone. I am sure it will withstand the flood. 'And I say also unto thee, That thou art Peter, and upon this rock I will build my church; and the gates of hell shall not prevail against it.' Matthew 16, verse 18. There is so much to be done. I must pack my books, my few possessions. I must pray to God for His guidance so He will guide them safely through the flood. And there is one last flower I must paint. The common milkweed. *Asclepias incarnata.* I found it growing beside the church door. Every day I go to the church, and I do not see it until today. Even in the rain I see it. Les miracles sont partout, n'est-ce pas? When I see the bishop, I will give him my book of watercolours as a gift to the Church. I will give him my translations. I will tell him how the translations have helped the people. He will be pleased. . . . Non, mademoiselle, no biscuits, s'il vous plaît, I beg you, no food, no food. I am still eating rice pudding. A bientôt, mademoiselle, à bientôt."

13: *July 22*

Dear Karen,

This will be my last letter from Niska. After tomorrow, Niska will be no more. Like my job, it's about to be terminated. Last night Geraldine set fire to the Bay and it burned to the ground. Tonight the river's expected to flood. Everyone here is getting on a big boat that Geraldine's husband built. Father Aulneau, George, Ralph and I are leaving tomorrow on a pontoon plane. I'm all packed and in a few minutes will be moving down to the Bay manager's house. I'm told the flood will move this cabin into the bush.

I feel absurdly reluctant to leave this pokey little cabin with its smelly toilet and thin plywood walls. I suppose it's because it's the first time I've had a place completely to myself.

Karen, I've decided not to come back to Ottawa. I appreciate the offer, but I'd like to stay closer to the North. I'm going to head for Thunder Bay and find myself a room or a small apartment. When I get settled, I'll write you the address. Now that I've had this time alone, I want more of it. (Don't worry, I won't get bushed.) I also have to sort out what to do with the promise I made Geraldine about selling her son's work. God knows, when the police catch her this time (after this fire, they'll probably try harder), she'll end up in jail for a long stint. If that happens, I'll have to come back inside for the rest of Bear's work.

The wind's picking up. I'd better end this and get down to George's. Will mail this somewhere along the way.

Keep your feet up!

Love,
Willa

P.S. I got quite a bit of work done. One way and another, I sketched all of the old village. This isn't much of a letter. Will fill you in on the details next time.

The stovepipe rattles, the cabin walls shake. The storm is moving in fast. Willa shrugs on her backpack and picks up her gear and the small bag of leftover food. She gives the bag to the first person she sees, Rachel Hunter. As she walks down the boardwalk, she hears the porch door bang.

In the distance, thunder rumbles like pain.

14: Geraldine Gull is three miles past the ridge. She's been on the river since yesterday, and she's only got this far. The strong current and high water have been keeping her back. Last night she wedged the boat between two rocks, pulled the Hudson's Bay blanket over her head and waited out the rain. She couldn't go ashore, because she knew that if she lifted her weight out of the boat, the river would sweep it out from under her. The river is bad, the worst she's seen it, but the boat's been putting up a good fight against the current. She didn't sleep, but she had a long rest and some of George's whisky and a package of cookies. Now she's got to get going again. She's got a long way to go before she can go ashore.

Using the paddle, Geraldine eases the bow from between the rocks, then before the current can grab hold of the boat, she leans over and pulls the cord. The motor chokes to life. She puts her hand on the tiller and steers the boat upstream.

She hears thunder rolling behind the clouds. Those are the thunderbirds who live in the sky. When Geraldine was little, her mother told her thunderbirds got mad if they saw a snake belly-up to the sky. Geraldine remembers the snakes she saw in her dream, the snakes that are in the river, their bellies white when lightning flashes. She half believes the thunderbirds see the snakes, the way she half believes her mother's story, half believes it like she half believes she had a mother a long time ago who told her this. The way she half believes she had children herself, six who came out of her whole. Six who died or went away. But that was a long time ago, that was far away in another place when she was someone else.

Geraldine's finished the first bottle of whisky. The inside of her head is fuzzy. Now she can't remember too good. She tries to remember the last time she saw her kids. The last time she saw Teresa was in jail. Geraldine had beat up on a cop in the Sioux, so they put her in the clink for a year. Teresa was in there the same time, wearing that stupid green dress they make women wear. She was sweeping the floor. They kept her in there until she was cured of clap. Geraldine didn't have it that time because by then no man wanted her, except Gerald, and he was clean. She was happy to see Teresa. Maybe that was the same time Joan came to see her with her kids. Maybe it was another time. Geraldine can't remember. All she knows is that the last time she saw Joan was when she came to see Geraldine in jail with her kids. After that, Joan moved to Winnipeg. Last time Geraldine saw Annie was in Big Trout, where Geraldine went to see her and her old man. Annie wouldn't let her inside that fancy house of hers. She locked the door and hid. Geraldine smashed the window, she was so mad.

Geraldine won't think of the last time she saw Alexander. She has thought of that too many times already. She's mad at him for doing what he did to himself. Stupid boy. He never learned to look after number one. All his blubbering about his mother. She's mad at him for believing all that crapshit, for waiting all that time for her to turn up.

"You stupid boy!" she yells at the clouds.

There's a sharp crack of thunder. Geraldine cowers. Maybe the thunderbirds don't like her yelling at Alexander. Geraldine leans over, gropes around the boat bottom for the second bottle of whisky. When she finds it, she jams it between her knees, bends over and loosens the cap with her teeth. She spits the cap over the side of the boat, watching it swirl around and disappear into a whirlpool. There's snakes down there, long and cold, sliding through the dark water. Snakes that would wrap around you, squeeze you hard, pull you under. Geraldine knows that as long as thunderbirds are up in the clouds, the snakes won't stick their heads up, but they see everything with their evil eyes. She swallows more whisky. The boat swerves, prow scraping against a rock. Shit. Goddamn rocks stick up from the bottom like teeth. She's got to be careful. Lots of people drown in the river. Snakes pull them down. River swallows them. River's always hungry. The Mishipashoo can't save people from the hungry river. Geraldine hasn't seen the Mishipashoo yet. Maybe there's too many snakes for them down there, maybe they are someplace else.

Geraldine scowls at the river, at the flat, grey surface swirling with whirlpools. For a moment she forgets the Mishipashoo and the snakes, the river's relentless hunger. The river becomes a road, all those roads she's been on going everywhere and nowhere, cars going past her, blinding her with white light. She thinks of the road she travelled with Alexander, pulling him behind her in his cardboard sled. Then she sees a picture of a thin body dangling from the jail bars, white shirt around his neck. Geraldine squeezes her eyes shut, and the bottle slides from her hand. She reaches up and grabs a fistful of hair, pulling hard, keening, *Peetanaquot, Peetanaquot.* Abruptly she lets go of her hair and yells at the clouds, *Go away! Go away!* Alexander will never leave her alone.

Thunder rolls over her shoulder. Lightning flickers. Beneath it, the river flashes belly-white. This time, Geraldine straightens. There are no thunderbirds up here, that's just a story her mother told her to make her be good. She's too smart to believe that stupid story. But she grabs hold of the knife sheath strapped to her leg and hunches down in the boat beneath the blanket. She pulls the red beret low over her ears. Still she's cold and wet. That's why she drinks whisky. It makes her eyes blurry, but it keeps her warm. She's got to hold on longer until she can get ashore. She's tired. She's tired from hauling all those boxes. She's so tired she can hardly keep her hand on the tiller to steer. As the boat moves slowly upstream, the grey water spreads and swells around her. When she makes ten more miles, she'll go ashore for a sleep. She should have a sleep before they come with the helicopters and dogs. Before they hunt her the way she once saw white men hunting Wapusk, shooting guns from the sky, until the white fur was splashed with red.

Geraldine thinks of the food she left in the schoolhouse. That will wake up those sleepy toads. They'll be happy she's at the ridge. They'll know she's a smart Ojibwa woman, a great leader who brought the people to victory. Geraldine Gull sure gave Joan of Arc a run for her money. Geraldine thinks about Gerald. He's smarter than she thought. His boat is going to come in handy with this rain. River's flooding. The boat'll save the toads, bring them to the ridge. Someday this place'll be famous. Alexander Bear will make it famous. People will come to look at Alexander's pictures in the gallery. They'll make TV pictures, movie shows. The whole world will know about Alexander Bear.

There's a rumble overhead. Geraldine crouches down, hand on her knife, ready to spring. *Go away!* she bellows to the thunderbirds. Still she crouches. Bony Spectre's up there. Geraldine hears his white bones rattling against the water drum. There's a loud, hollow bong as if bone is hitting skin stretched tight across a drum. Geraldine's hand jerks up. It lets go of the tiller, and the boat smashes into a rock. Geraldine is thrown forward. A large branch snags her beret. She reaches backward, trying to grab the tiller, but it's too late. The boat's pushed over by the force of the water hitting its side.

Geraldine's in the dark water, the Hudson's Bay blanket over her head weighing her down. She should fight, she knows, but she's so tired. Her arms are too heavy to lift. Her legs also. She can't reach for the knife or Moses Bear's letter, because the water turns her hands and feet into ice. No more trickling water. The dark river is carrying her, carrying her with broken trees and dead leaves, carrying her downstream toward the bay, where it is cold and white and frozen. She can feel the snakes wrap around her, squeezing her hard. They are pulling her down. They are pulling her so hard she can't move. Her mouth is open. She is swallowing the river. Her lungs burn, not with whisky but with water. The water locks the inside of her head into a standstill landscape of polar bears, snow and ice.

A Mishipashoo swims past. It flicks it's serpent tail against her head. She's slammed against a rock. Geraldine Gull becomes part of the river, the great northern river, the endless river flowing into the sea.

15: *July 24, 1978.* Willa Coyle is up in a Cessna, a small float plane. Besides the pilot and herself, there's George, Ralph and Father Aulneau. The plane circles Niska. Willa looks down at the drowned village, at the water shining in the sunlight. It looks like a tight membrane has been stretched over the swamp, sealing it shut. At one end of the village, the church tower pierces the membrane; at the other end, the blackened shell of the store pokes through. Scattered randomly in the bush behind the village are twenty-nine shacks and cabins. Far out in the bay, ice pans drift, breaking, shifting, regrouping.

Three miles upstream the plane comes upon the ark moving slowly against the current, being towed through the water by four motorized canoes. The pilot circles so his passengers can have a better look. Willa sees Xavier's dog team harnessed on the deck beside a pair of skidoos. The deck is crowded with so many bodies there is hardly space for people to move. Everyone seems to be waving at the plane. Three men in the canoes — Patrick Eagle, Dave Wabano, Simon Gull — take off their peaked caps and wave them at the plane.

The pilot flies upriver. Willa scans the flooded shoreline, the submerged willows, the debris floating on the water. On either side of the river, shallow lakes extend for a half mile or more across the tundra. When the plane comes within five miles of the ridge, Willa spots an overturned boat jammed between two rocks. It's the same boat that brought her to Niska. She nudges George and points.

"Look," she says.

He stares out the window. "That's my boat, all right," he says.

With a sinking feeling, Willa sees an uprooted tree snagged in the same cleft. On one of its branches is a tiny scrap of red. It bobs up and down as the current hits the branch. She points to the branch.

"C'est rouge comme une goutte de sang," Father Aulneau says.

From this height, the scrap of red is barely distinguishable from the jumble of debris and flotsam littering the shoreline. Unless you were in a small plane, flying low over the water and looking closely, you probably wouldn't see it. But Willa has been looking, and what she sees isn't a dirty, torn beret but a bright red banner, a brave and tattered flag.

EPILOGUE

During the summer of '78, the people of Oskotenaw lived in tents and trailers while they worked on their new houses. Dugald McKillop took a leave of absence from a consulting job in London, Ontario, to live in Oskotenaw, where he supervised the building of these homes, which have full basements and double walls on the north sides, as well as airtight wood stoves. "I was warned before I came up here that as soon as the goose-hunting season came, the Indians would drop everything and disappear for up to six weeks," Dugald told people afterwards. "They never did. They worked straight through the fall season. Long, eighteen-hour days. By late November, most families had moved into their houses. I'm going back there next year to help with phase three. Now that the sewers are in, they're planning to build a laundromat. They're also going to build an art gallery."

Willa went to Oskotenaw in the fall of '79 to pick up Alexander Bear's pictures, which Patrick Eagle had moved out of Geraldine's hide-out and into his mother's cabin. By that time, Willa had managed to sell only sixteen of the prints. The big break came four years later, when the National Exhibition Centre and Centre of Indian Art in Thunder Bay bought the bulk of Bear's work for an undisclosed sum. His work is now part of their permanent collection. In 1984, this gallery scheduled a show of Willa Coyle's work entitled "Sketches from Niska." That same year, Patrick Eagle became Chief of the Oskotenaw band. By that time, he had married Laura Fiddler, a Cree-Ojibwa education student whom he met while he was attending summer school at the Lakehead, and had two children. Jeremiah Crow was the first person to be buried in the new graveyard in Oskotenaw. He died in 1986. So far, he has the place to himself. Alexander Bear's ashes are buried beneath the new gallery.